By the Same Author:

HOUSE OF GUILT

. . .

An Avram Cohen Mystery

ROBERT ROSENBERG

SCRIBNER

SCRIBNER
1230 Avenue of the Americas
New York, NY 10020

Set in Stempel Garamond

DESIGNED BY ERICH HOBBING

Manufactured in the United States of America

1   3   5   7   9   10   8   6   4   2

Library of Congress Cataloging-in-Publication Data

Rosenberg, Robert
House of guilt: an Avram Cohen mystery/Robert Rosenberg.
p.   cm.
I. Title.
PS3568.O7878H6   1996
813'.54—dc20   96–30216
                                CIP

ISBN 0-684-82654-2

To my real heroes—
Silvia, Amber
and all the friends
who forgive me.

Tel Aviv, 1996

INTRODUCTION

House of Guilt was written between the Hebron massacre[1] and Yitzhak Rabin's assassination.[2] So although this book is a work of fiction, its roots are in the reality of life in Israel during that period. Therefore, it is also about the gap between Jerusalem and Tel Aviv.

Barely forty miles separate the two places. Yet the narrow physical distance between the two cities belies a profound rift between those who look to the past for the raison d'être of the state and society and others who look to the future.

When I wrote House of Guilt I was trying to tell a story that would take the reader from the gates of a Tel Aviv discotheque to the gates of Kiryat Arba, showing that neither, of course, is a shining heavenly gate.

[1]On Purim morning in 1994, an American-born doctor living in Kiryat Arba left the morning Jewish prayers at the Tomb of the Patriarchs in Hebron and, carrying an M-16 submachine gun, entered the Moslem chapel at the holy site. According to a Judicial Commission of Inquiry established after the events that morning, Baruch Goldstein mowed down twenty-seven praying Moslems before the survivors attacked and killed him. His grave in Kiryat Arba quickly became a pilgrimage site for the most radical Jewish fundamentalists, who regard the Israel-Arab conflict as essentially a religious war. According to Goldstein's supporters, he acted in order to halt the then-developing dialogue between Israel and the Palestine Liberation Organization. The attack came barely five months after then-premier Yitzhak Rabin and PLO Chairman Yasser Arafat shook hands on the White House lawn, beginning the long journey of putting an end to the hundred-year war over the tiny corner of the eastern Mediterranean known as the Holy Land, and proving that even the most deadly of enemies can work together for a better world. The Hebron massacre did not end the journey, though it added many obstacles to the travelers on that long and difficult road. A few months later that same year, Rabin and Jordan's King Hussein signed a peace treaty in public, putting an end to more than forty years of official enmity between Israel and its eastern neighbor.

[2]On November 4, 1995, Yitzhak Rabin appeared at what the police called the largest demonstration ever held in downtown Tel Aviv's City Hall Plaza, to support the Rabin-Peres peace government. Rabin was shot dead by a twenty-seven-year-old yeshiva student named Yigal Amir, who had stalked the prime minister for almost a year and told the court at his arraignment that his intention in shooting Rabin was to stop the government from dividing the Land of Israel.

Religiosity does not insure innocence, just as liberation does not guarantee wisdom. Nonetheless, the mere fact that I could only write about Cohen after leaving Jerusalem, shows that I made my choice.

Avram Cohen stayed in Jerusalem. Like many of the hardworking policemen I knew at the time, Cohen carries equal scorn for politicians across the political spectrum. He would much rather stick to real issues: a crime, its suspects, and the difficulty in discovering the truth.

Yet he survived Dachau, and became a cop in Jerusalem at the end of the twentieth century, when the pace of history is challenging Jerusalem's role in the imagination of the Jews, if not the world. So, if he's uninterested in politics, he cares deeply about its consequences. Cohen knows well that history, destiny, and all those words that he would rather ignore are part of the crime in such places, indeed are the fuses that can light the most dangerous of all crimes—those that are aimed at innocent bystanders. He knows well that the same faith in the truth that carried him from the concentration camp to his sun-drenched garden in Jerusalem can turn like a snake and become the suspect, the key witness, or the crime itself.

He stayed in Jerusalem because his heart is in that city with the strange light and stranger people who, like the biblical prophecy, believe they can lay personal claim to a city that has defied ownership throughout its history. I respect him for sticking it out in that city, even while tempted by Tel Aviv. I admire his constant struggle with his own conscience.

That struggle is Israel's own inner conflict, one that seems to stretch around the world—between those who look to the past for their inspiration, and insist they have an absolute knowledge, and those who can see that if indeed this is a messianic age, it is a result of the confluence of knowledge, the recognition of information as the only inexhaustible resource human beings possess on this planet.

This book was not prescient enough to be about the assassination of the prime minister, only about the circumstances that would lead to it. Unfortunately, as of early 1996, the danger has not yet passed in Jerusalem, even while, more than ever before, the future looks bright in Tel Aviv.

—ROBERT ROSENBERG
Tel Aviv
March 1996

GLOSSARY OF HEBREW TERMS AND VERNACULAR

abba: Father

Ahad Ha'Am Street: the Wall Street of Israel

ahlan usahalan: Traditional Arab greeting

ambah: Oriental chutney from India and Arabia

Anglo-saxim: Anglo-Saxon immigrants to Israel

Baruch: a Hebrew name meaning "Blessed"

Davar: formerly a Labor Party–owned newspaper

dos: religious; plural, *dossim*

Gare Tzedek: literal: righteous non-Jew; figurative: convert

goyim: non-Jewish peoples

gveret: a lady, sometimes Mrs.

haredi: ultra-orthodox Jews; literally, "fearful of God"; plural, *haredim*

Hebron massacre: Hebron is a Biblical town considered holy by religious Jews; home of the Tomb of the Patriarchs, where Biblical Abraham, Isaac, and Jacob are buried. On Purim morning in 1994, Dr. Baruch Goldstein (see key characters) entered the Moslem chapel in the Tomb of the Patriarchs and, using an army-issued automatic rifle, killed twenty-seven Moslems at prayer. He also was killed by the angry survivors.

intifada: the Palestinian civil uprising against Israel's military occupation of Gaza and the West Bank

Jerusalem syndrome: a diagnosed condition affecting severe neurotics who visit Jerusalem and confuse their identities with those of biblical characters or believe they receive messages from God.

kibbutzim: collective farms

kippa: skullcap; also known as a *yarmulke*

Kiryat Arba: the original name for the town of Hebron; nowadays

9

an apartment-block community of Jewish settlers overlooking the Arab town.

Knesset: Israel's parliament

kodkod: commander

kotel: the Western Wall

kova tembel: a sailor cap–style hat

Land of Israel: an ambiguous geographic term referring to the biblical lands, as distinct from the State of Israel, which refers to the country as defined by the borders before the Six Day War

LeHitraot: au revoir

Levites: the tribe of Israel responsible for maintaining the Temple

mador: elite plainclothes detective squads in the major cities

maniakim: informants

Merhav: Regional District Police Command

meurav: a mixed-grill sandwich, usually in a pita

misken: an unfortunate person

nokmim: the avengers, secret cells of Jews and anti-Nazis who conducted an assassination campaign against Nazis during the fall of Germany in the war and immediately afterward

payot: side curls worn by ultra-orthodox Jews

Purim: a winter holiday celebrating the failure of Haman, the vizier of Persia, to conduct an extermination campaign against the Jews.

rav: rabbi

Rebbe: an especially beloved rabbi. Often used in reference to the late Lubavitcher Rebbe, Menachem Schneerson, some of whose followers regard him as the messiah.

rebbetzin: a rabbi's wife

rehov: street

sabra: a cactus fruit, soft and sweet on the inside, prickly on the outside; popular (and old-fashioned) term used to describe native Israelis

s'hug: spicy pepper sauce

Sayeret Matkal: an elite unit in the Israeli army

Shabak: Acronym for Sherut Bitahon Klali, General Security Services; also known as Shin Bet

shaharith: the morning prayers

shahor: literal: black; in slang, refers to *dos*, as in ultra-orthodox, or *haredi sharav:* seasonal heat waves in the spring and fall that cross Israel from Africa and Asia

shmokim: from the Yiddish, plural for *shmuck*

shuk: market

Survivor: Holocaust survivor

tallit: the prayer shawl worn by Jews at prayer

tefillin: the phylacteries

tiul: a trip

Torah: the Five Books of Moses

tzitziyot: a small *tallit,* worn by ultra-orthodox Jews as undershirts.

vilde haya: Yiddish; literal: a wild animal; used idiomatically for uncontrollable children

Yahrzeit: the anniversary of a death

Yalla: Arabic exhortation

Yekke: a pedantic person usually of German ancestry

yeshiva: house of study

zedaka: charity

KEY CHARACTERS:

(in no particular order)

Avram Cohen, retired former chief of The Criminal Investigations Department of the Jerusalem Police

Yitzhaki, Cohen's neighborhood grocer

Judge Ahuva Meyerson, Cohen's longtime girlfriend

Meshulam Yaffe, police liaison to the police minister

Police Minister David Nahmani, a war hero turned politician

Raphael Levi-Tsur, chairman, House of Levi-Tsur

Emmanuel Levi-Tsur, Raphael's younger brother

Gabriel Levi-Tsur, Raphael's youngest brother

Simon Levi-Tsur, Raphael's grandson

Caroline Jones, Raphael's personal assistant

Ephraim Laskoff, Cohen's personal banker

Vicki-Bracha, Tel Aviv call girl

Uri Dromi, Tel Aviv celebrity

Eli Bookspan, Jewish settlement movement leader

Jeremiah Ben-Alon, American-born Jewish settler and activist

Baruch Goldstein, real-life American-born doctor; infamous as perpetrator of the Hebron massacre

Rabbi Menachem Levine, head of Yeshivat Ohaeli Levi'im; devoted to reconstruction of the Jewish temple of Jerusalem

Baruch, Jewish underground activist

Yoram Marciano, Jerusalem cop

Haim Reshef, Jerusalem Chief of Police

Camara, African guest worker in Israel

Avner "Avi" Bitusi, former Jerusalem cat burglar turned religious

Miriam "Miri" Bitusi, Avner Bitusi's wife

Victor, Cohen's former boss in the Tel Aviv police in the early 1960s

Nissim Levy, Cohen's former assistant

Hagit Levy, Nissim Levy's wife

HOUSE
OF
GUILT

■ ■ ■

· 1 ·

Cohen sighed. The smell of death never lasted long in the desert, but meanwhile it was somewhere in the garden.

He hissed, hoping it would bring out Suspect the cat, a tom he had adopted years before. In his old age, Suspect still caught prey that crossed the jasmine and vine borders of the yard. But the cat had long since ceased making his tours of the neighborhood, choosing graceful retirement over the need to hunt down his opponents.

The old long-hair crept into view at the east end of the garden, a bundle of gray against the glistening green and deep brown of the freshly watered garden that Cohen had nurtured over the years.

A swallow jumped down from a tree branch to the clothesline and from there to the little asphalt patio beneath three of Cohen's white shirts billowing like sails in the soft breeze.

Snake or rat, Cohen figured about the hidden corpse. Suspect dropped into his jungle cat pose, a hunting crouch that turned into three quick paces toward the bird. It had been years since Suspect could catch a bird, unless it strayed by accident into Cohen's apartment and Suspect got its claws into it before it found the window. But still the cat tried, making Cohen envious of the cat's eternal optimism.

Like the cat, Cohen picked his way softly and slowly along the flagstone paths he had put in around the beds of geranium, chrysanthemum, and tall Madonna lilies, up to the thick tangle of jasmine creating the natural wall between Cohen's garden and his neighbor's.

The cat was in front of him and downwind, concentrated on the prey. Cohen took three steps forward. Neither the bird, pecking at the berry seeds that fell from the tree shading that part of the garden, nor the cat noticed him. He crouched like an Arab, forearms on his knees, the hunting scene framed in his view. He wondered if he'd let the cat catch the bird.

17

But it wasn't Cohen's choice to make. "Mister Cohen," came a voice behind him. "Are you all right?"

The bird took flight. The cat washed furiously. Cohen rose wearily.

Yitzhaki the greengrocer was standing beside the wooden stairs that led up a closed pergola of wood, iron, and glass to Cohen's apartment on the second floor. He had lived there for almost twenty years on a side street off Emek Refa'im, the Valley of Ghosts in Jerusalem's German Colony.

"Something wrong, Yitzhaki?" Cohen asked, not rudely, but with a measure of annoyance at being disturbed.

"No, no problem," the grocer said. "Where do you want me to put this?" He shifted the cardboard box on his shoulder.

Usually Yusuf, the helper from the Dahaishe Palestinian refugee camp outside Hebron, made the weekly delivery of Cohen's standard order—the fresh fruits and vegetables for the Shabbat dinner he prepared every Friday evening for Ahuva, his lover. On the first of the month, Cohen would go to Yitzhaki's fruit and vegetable shop around the corner to pay his bill.

Now, in the garden, Cohen assumed the Baghdad-born grocer made the delivery because he was pressed for cash. His patted his hip pocket and realized his wallet was upstairs. "You shouldn't be embarrassed to ask me to pay my bill before the end of the month," Cohen said, starting for the stairs.

It was an apology, not a reprimand, but it made Yitzhaki sigh. "It's not that," the grocer said.

Cohen paused, guessing the problem. "Abu-Yusuf's under curfew?" Yitzhaki sighed.

"His sister has cancer. He went to visit her, got caught in the curfew right after the massacre. I wanted to go down there, talk to someone in the army, something, to get him out of there. For his sake. Not just mine."

The burly Iraqi Jew's deep-set eyes couldn't hide the embarrassment, with a shadow of sadness beneath them. He lowered the crate to the first step. "But Shula wouldn't let me go," he said, adding his confession. "And she wants me to fire him when he comes back." He was blaming his wife for the fear as much as he blamed the Arabs.

"She can't take it anymore," Yitzhaki added. "The worrying.

Every day, someone else gets it. From an Arab they know, someone who worked with them, someone they trusted. And now this business in Hebron. They'll take revenge. Everyone is waiting for it. I trusted him. But Mr. Cohen, maybe she's right. Today he's my loyal worker. Tomorrow he could stick a knife in my back. Or a customer. For him, we're Jews, the enemy."

"He's been with you since he was a boy," Cohen said softly. "You know him well. Do you really think . . ."

There was no judgment in his voice, but Yitzhaki could hear the reproach. "Shula says . . ."

"Are you afraid?" Cohen asked, emphasizing that it was Yitzhaki's decision.

Yitzhaki shook his head. "I don't know. I don't know anymore. It's so complicated. A Jew doing that. Killing praying people. And we all thought there was going to be peace."

"It will take time," said Cohen, trying to sound confident. He, too, had been hopeful when the prime minister of Israel and the chairman of the PLO met on the White House lawn to shake hands.

Cohen wasn't naive. He knew how deep ran the passions that ignited the violence, knew well that opponents of the new peace process would try to stop it. The handshake was only over a framework for building trust. It couldn't end hatred overnight. So, meanwhile, the terror continued. Molotov cocktails and tear gas, stones and gunshots in the night—and those, like Cohen, who tried warning of even worse, were ignored. When it came even the chief of staff had to say, "It was a thunderbolt out of the blue."

On Purim morning that year, at the peak of winter's brief but bitter breath over the Land, less than five months after the handshake, a Jew, born in America (where he had trained as a doctor), slipped out of the early morning prayers in the Jewish chapel at Hebron's Tomb of the Patriarchs—the burial ground, say the Jews and Moslems, of the biblical Abraham, Isaac, and Jacob.

The doctor walked through an arched doorway, down a short corridor, and into another windowless hall deep in the huge walled tomb. There, Moslems were kneeling to pray. More than fifty died that day—with twenty-seven dead from bullets fired from the submachine gun carried by Dr. Baruch Goldstein, until that morning one of the leading personalities in Kiryat Arba, the first of the Jewish settlements built in the occupied territories after the 1967 Six Day War. The others were Palestinians shot dead when they tried storming Israeli troops in the area.

Much hope—including Cohen's—was dispersed in the hail of bullets, rocks, tear gas and molotov cocktails that flailed across the entire West Bank that day. Now, three months later, tensions in Hebron remained high enough to keep it and its neighborng villages and refugee camps under curfew. Even the few hundred Jews of Hebron and Kiryat Arba, among whom Goldstein was famous for his selfless devotion to the Jewish cause in the territories, chafed under strict orders from the Israeli army to stay off the streets of the biblical town.

And Cohen, whose own last case as Criminal Investigation Department chief in Jerusalem before a retirement he didn't want was precisely about a warning for such a thing, was left with his civilian impotence, the bitter taste of self-reciminatory guilt, and the useless feeling of knowing he could say "I told you so" but having nobody to whom to complain.

"Yusuf's a good man," Cohen tried. "He needs the job. And you need his help." He knew Yusuf and he knew Yitzhaki. They were together too long for Yitzhaki to be so worried.

"It's Shula you should talk to," Yitzhaki said. "I tried to be logical. But her third cousin on her mother's side, she goes to that grocer, the one in Netanya. You probably saw his picture in the paper. Knife in the back. The shirt all red." Yitzhaki shivered. "His worker did that to him."

"I saw the picture," Cohen said.

"He never stole from me," Yitzhaki went on, the confession pouring from him. "Fifteen years, he never stole. At the beginning, I tested him. Left a tenner on the counter. When a tenner was really worth something. He brought it to me, asked what to do with it. But now? People are afraid."

"If I can help . . ." Cohen suggested again. Suspect crept a few steps away from the grocer, then crouched in wait for Yitzhaki to leave so that he could investigate the cardboard box on the stair.

"Maybe," the grocer said, taking a step away. The cat took its own two strides. "I'll think about it," he added almost hopefully, and then squinted toward the sun falling westward behind the weeping willow on the western edge of Cohen's garden. "I've got to get going. You want me to take this upstairs? It's heavy."

Cohen said no, then watched the grocer leave the same way he had come in, behind the tin-walled, one-car garage shaded by the willow. The shortcut behind Cohen's garden led to an alley where Yitzhaki kept a storage shed for his Emek Refa'im shop. But instead of taking the crate up the stairs himself, he sat down in the wicker chair in the shade of a wild vine that long ago stopped producing grapes but all summer guaranteed him a shady corner of the garden.

Two summers ago, Cohen painted the chair. Now, it felt better than ever under him. Just last week he mentioned to Ahuva that he was planning to paint it again.

She mocked him, saying, "You have more than enough money to buy a whole house, let alone a new set of garden furniture. You aren't a civil servant anymore," she declared. "And you certainly are no pensioner living off national insurance or your police pension." It was true. He was a wealthy man now, wealthier than he felt he had any right to be.

It was just after he finally told her exactly how much money he had inherited from an old friend. "You could finally buy a proper apartment," she said. "A villa, perhaps. On Caspi Street with one of those beautiful views down to the Dead Sea."

Cohen wasn't interested in moving, though he did have an idea about a change in his living conditions. He had been paying rent for more than twenty years through an estate lawyer for the extended family that owned the two-story German Colony house built in the last decade of the nineteenth century.

Lately he had begun discussing with the lawyer the possibility of buying the entire property. The problem now wasn't Cohen's ability to pay. The problem was getting a vote of all the shares of the twenty-nine heirs. Two of them owned 10 percent apiece. The rest owned variously sized shares, depending on the distance between them and the original patriarch, who had made the family fortune from his plan, conceived already in his native Russia, to build an industrial bakery in Jerusalem.

Ottoman troops in Jerusalem were among his first institutional customers. Then came the British. The visionary founder of the bakery didn't live long enough to see the Israeli army become the family's single largest customer. The first-floor apartment had been empty for years, for within the context of the family fortune the property on the little side street off Emek Refa'im, the Valley of Ghosts in the German Colony, was inconsequential, almost forgotten amid their myriad holdings.

For Cohen, it was suddenly an easy acquisition begging to be made—if the lawyer could arrange it. He had not yet mentioned the idea to Ahuva. Until everything was set, he didn't want her to know what he was planning. He wasn't even sure about what he would do with such a large house. But he knew he should buy it.

Meanwhile, he preferred talking about anything other than the money he had inherited from an old friend with whom he had survived Dachau, and whom Cohen had since always thought of as a somewhat estranged brother—even when they didn't speak for a decade at a time. The money embarrassed Cohen, made him feel guilty for taking something he didn't deserve, didn't need, didn't want.

"I like my chair," he insisted, just as he protested that he liked the flat in the German Colony and saw no need to move, even if it was to a penthouse with a clear view of the Old City, the Judean desert, and the northern tip of the Dead Sea far below in the Jordan Valley.

"That's not the point," Ahuva charged. "I'm not telling you to go out and spend it all. I'm not telling you to give it all away. And I'm not saying you should go cut fire lanes in the forests with work crews. But you have to be active. Involved with something."

"When the time comes," Cohen interrupted her, "I'll know what to do."

Meanwhile he was learning how to use a personal computer. He spent hours in front of the machine, manuals on his lap as his fingers learned to go from hunt and peck to finding the letters as he thought them.

He was amused by the random coincidence of phonetics and etymology that made the acronym for Disk Operating System into a bilingual pun, *dos* being Hebrew street slang for the ultra religious, and more specifically the *haredim*, the ultra-orthodox Jews who dressed in the style of sixteenth-century Polish aristocrats and tried to live according to the laws of Torah as rabbis over the millenia interpreted them.

There were no computer terminals on any of the desks when Cohen worked for the police. Now, Cohen hoped one day to know enough about the machine to connect to the Internet, which he read about in the newspapers. Meanwhile, he struggled with the logic of the machine's simplest language, the hand-eye coordination of using the mouse, and learning how to type.

Ahuva knew about the computer, of course. It sat on its own desk-trolley but, lacking a separate room for a study, he kept it in the living room. Sometimes he rolled it into the bedroom where he sat in bed with the keyboard on his lap, the manuals scattered around him on the bed, straining his neck peering at the large color screen he had bought.

When he showed off its ability to play compact disks, she was impressed with his newfound hobby for a few minutes. But then she curled up to him and whispered that he knew damn well she preferred her music live and missed the old vinyl records. "I can't explain why, but they had more feeling to the way they played back the sound," she said.

Not that Cohen was absolutely sure what he was going to do with the computer. He used a spreadsheet application to build catalogues of his record collection and cookbooks. Now that he finished the catalogues, he was thinking of writing something of his own. He even spoke with David Hefetz, commander of the police academy at Shfaram, about the need for a history of the force.

Hefetz was enthusiastic about the idea but cautious when Cohen suggested that he could undertake the job. "Don't misunderstand me, Avram," Hefetz said, trying not to identify himself with Cohen's old political adversaries on the fifth floor of national police headquarters.

Cohen didn't misunderstand. The new guard of university graduates, technocrats all, looked down on all the autodidacts of the old guard. The old guard of veterans mostly regarded Cohen with suspicion, for his methods were always unorthodox by their standards. In the toss-up between the two, Cohen preferred the technocrats, who at least expressed an interest in learning something new, even if it was old. The veterans mostly claimed to be Cohen loyalists, but he knew that behind his back they had not all shed tears when he finally left the force. Hefetz—one of the technocrats—and Cohen finished their lunch, exchanging gossip that interested neither of them.

Ahuva suggested teaching. "Moshe would love to have you lecture in his department," she kept telling him. Moshe was chairman of the criminology department at the university, a widower to whom Ahuva sometimes turned when needing a companion for the kind of social occasions that she so enjoyed and Cohen so despised. Cohen felt no need for jealousy. He knew of Moshe's occasional visits to Jerusalem's Independence Park in the old days when it was the meeting ground of the holy city's homosexuals from both the Jewish and Arab sides of the city. Not that Cohen's relationship with Ahuva would have allowed him the privilege of jealousy—they bound it carefully in a tight web of trust and independence.

So Cohen growled back at her, "I am not a scientist," remembering the occasional guest lectures he had given in the past, and how despite all the respect the students gave him, he could not shake the feeling that since his own formal schooling had come to an abrupt end after six years, he had little to offer.

He knew that learning was always the key to his survival, but the last thing he wanted was to be like the academics he met—barely able to talk about anything except their field, or so certain of their own brilliance that they couldn't notice anyone else's ideas.

"I am not a lawyer," he pointed out to her. "And I am not a forensic scientist. What am I going to do? Tell those kids stories about the old days? And," he summed up bitterly, "how long do you think they'd let me teach if I talked about the syndrome?"

It was the sore in his heart that refused to heal, the madness justified by the religions and encouraged by politicians. None condoned a madman's arson or murder. But politicians did little to dampen the fervor, and once the fever broke out it was difficult to cool down.

Cohen's last case had proved—at least to him—that the syndrome was spreading, becoming more dangerous as apocalypse and salvation became the chosen terms of reference for the mystics who wanted to be fingers of God.

That's what happened in his last case, and that's what happened in Hebron, when Goldstein—whose friends claimed he saw one too many victims of the uncivil war in the territories—tried to stop the peace process, tried to hasten the messiah's arrival, tried to . . .

"Well," Cohen said to himself, waking to the radio news that cold and foggy morning, "who knows what a man massacring people at prayer is hoping to accomplish."

One thing was certain. Now that it had happened once it could happen again, in Hebron or Jerusalem or any of the hundreds of places around the Holy Land where more than one religion placed its faith in the stones of ancient sites. Terrorists and freedom fighters and saints and martyrs mixed unholy messages into their prayers for possession of these holy cities. And, meanwhile, Moslems would seek their revenge.

Cohen—and others—called it "the syndrome." And exposing its original sin had made him into a pariah, an angry prophet whose warnings angered the powers that be. The last thing the politicians needed were religious leaders in jail for inciting thoughtless followers into foolish crimes, nor too much publicity about a psychiatric disease that seemed to strike as many as a hundred visitors to Jerusalem every year.

Yet the massacre brought it all back into the limelight—everything that Cohen tried to say in those final months on that final case, and now, with the madness under the bright lights of the Judicial Inquiry into the Hebron massacre, he felt more lonely than ever in the city. He did not believe the inquiry would go to the heart of the matter. He knew—without asking—that they wouldn't call him to testify, not wanting him to say what he'd been saying for years: You can't have the cake and eat it, too.

Not that he didn't have friends and loyalists still inside the system. Former junior officers who kept riding the rank escalator, they invited him to their weddings and their children's bar mitzvas. But they were like Hefetz, the police academy commander: eager to hear Cohen's view, afraid to sanction it.

Ahuva was the only warmth in his life, except for the music, books, and cooking. Cohen found his peace in his garden, the quiet that sealed him from the craziness stalking the streets of the city and about which he could now do nothing.

For a while, he was bothered by local gossips, both from the neighborhood and from the media, intrigued by his newfound fortune. He was glad when the gossips finally agreed, in all three local papers one weekend, that the deputy commander had never been considered a society item before he was rich, so why should he suddenly become so now. But they all said he deserved the money. From Yitzhaki the grocer to the society columnists in the national press, they all agreed: Cohen had done much for Jerusalem, for the country, for the people. He deserved a well-padded retirement. Even Ahuva said he deserved the money. What nobody understood, not even Ahuva, is that Cohen didn't want to be retired.

She wanted him to get a new wardrobe. But the strain for him was in the choosing, even before the fashionable cut made him feel uncomfortable. Yet with her he could laugh about it, and in turn make her laugh, which always gave him pleasure. He finally promised her that he would acquire a new wardrobe and would be wearing some new clothes when she next came to visit.

That Friday night, when she arrived as usual at nine, he greeted her at the door. She stared for a second and then burst out laughing. He had bought a complete new set of what he always wore: gray twill-cotton trousers, a long-sleeved white shirt rolled up past his elbows, and a new pair of tennis sneakers.

Still, the money had changed him, even if Yitzhaki, as well as the press, couldn't see it. He rubbed at the dry red rash on his forearm, the psychosomatic thermometer that reddened and paled over the tattooed number from the concentration camp. The rash had disappeared for awhile after he left the force, but by the time the money reached his bank accounts, and he had found Ephraim Laskoff, a Tel Aviv investment banker, to handle it all, the rash was back. Cohen had no doubt it was his effort not to think about the money that brought the anxiety to the surface. He rubbed at the dry skin, then cursed himself for his lack of self-discipline and stopped.

The cat, finally realizing that there was no raw meat amid the fruits and vegetables, interpreted the gesture as an invitation and jumped onto Cohen's lap. "Yes, money changes people," he told Suspect.

The phone began ringing in his living room overlooking the garden. He checked his watch, making the cat leap off and away to the wooden stairwell at the rear entrance to the building. Such a back entrance was a rarity in Jerusalem, and one of the reasons Cohen decided to buy the flat when he first found it so many years ago. Suspect disappeared up the stairs, as if the cat knew who was calling.

Ahuva would hang up after four rings if Cohen didn't answer. Her personal routines were as judicious as her professional rulings. In court—and in bed with Cohen—she believed in relying on precedent, but in stretching the interpretation. And the original precedent in their relationship was their weekly ritual, Friday night dinner together—except, during the long years Cohen served on the force, when he was called into the streets by his vocation.

The animal corpse in the garden that Suspect was hunting would have to wait. He hefted the heavy grocery box into his arms and took the stairs two at a time, dropped the carton on the floor, and caught the phone in the middle of the fourth ring.

"Mr. Cohen?"

It was a woman, but not Ahuva. "Yes," he said, disappointed. He eyed the box of groceries, planning an onion soup in his mind.

"Commander Avram Cohen?" It was a pleasant voice, but one with a slightly desperate ring. Her English was British, and it sounded to Cohen's ear like mashed potatoes, lacking consonants, full of words wrapped around themselves.

"Deputy Commander," Cohen corrected her. He didn't feel like adding retired, but it's what sprang to mind.

"Thank goodness," the woman exhaled. "You certainly are not easy to track down. Did you know that there are nearly thirty A. Cohens in Jerusalem?"

She was calling from a cellular phone, Cohen decided, hearing in the pause before he answered the voice of a man on the same cellular network, saying, "Please, Mama, please understand."

"Are you a reporter?" Cohen asked, though he doubted it. There was something too polite in her manner from the start.

"Oh no, dear me, no," she said, almost giggling at the supposition. "My name is Caroline Jones," she said. "I'm calling on behalf of Mr. Raphael Levi-Tsur." Her voice rose as she stated the fact in the tone of a question, seeming to test Cohen's familiarity with the name.

"Never heard of him," Cohen said.

She was not surprised. "Mr. Levi-Tsur is chairman of a private investment bank. He would like to make an appointment to see you," she said, adding, "in Jerusalem and at your earliest possible convenience." There was a pause, and then she emphasized again, "as soon as possible."

"These aren't banker's hours," Cohen said, holding the phone away from his ear and looking at the mouthpiece as if blaming the machine itself for what he regarded as a folly. "And I have a banker. So, you can tell your . . ."

"Oh dear, no," she interrupted. He could hear a slight laugh in her voice at the misunderstanding, and then she dropped her voice slightly, a signal of something much more serious than money. "It is not a banking matter. Oh no, of course not. It is a personal matter, in which he believes your expertise would be helpful, indeed indispensable."

"Why me?" he asked, pulling the celery out of the box. He slid a finger down the stalk, breaking one off and putting it under the faucet. The water ran as the woman answered with her own question.

"You are the Avram Cohen? The police commander? The detective?"

The crunch of celery should have told her what he thought of the question. He repeated his correction—"deputy commander"—this time adding "retired," still uncomfortable with the way it didn't roll off his tongue with ease. "And I have a banker, thank you. Now, if you please . . ."

"Mr. Levi-Tsur would greatly appreciate your help."

"Why me?" Cohen demanded again.

"He knows you are honest and discreet." She waited for him to say something in response to the flattery. He didn't. "This is a most delicate matter," she finally added.

"Are you going to tell me what it is?" Cohen asked, "or do you want me to guess?" Friday afternoon was the most sacred part of the week for him, as the Sabbath descended tangibly over the city for a few hours of peace and quiet while he prepared dinner for Ahuva.

"It involves a missing person," she said gingerly, leaving a pause that gave Cohen the feeling she was waiting for his expletive. He gave her silence instead, and she filled it. "Mr. Levi-Tsur's grandson is missing."

Cohen shook his head, sighing. "I am not a private investigator. If the boy is missing in Israel, he can go to the police here. If they cannot help him, then there are private investigators. That is all I can do for your Mr. Levi-Tsur. Now, if you'll excuse me, I have some of my own personal matters to attend to." He added "good-bye" without waiting for her response and hung up. A moment later the phone rang again.

"Ahuva?" he assumed.

"Caroline Jones here again," the sprightly voice began. "Please, commander. At least you could meet with . . ."

"Not interested," Cohen said, hanging up. The nerve, he thought to himself as he finished washing the celery. The phone rang a third time. He answered angrily. "I am not interested in a private investigation of any sort, and would appreciate it if you told that to your Mr. Levi-Tsur."

"Who's Levi-Tsur?" Ahuva asked calmly in her judge's even tone, seeking clarification of a prosecutor's point.

Cohen laughed. It came from his chest and was barely a grunt when it came out, but Ahuva recognized it. "I'm sorry," he said, ending his laugh with a sigh. "I didn't mean to shout."

"So, who's Levi-Tsur?" she asked again.

"I don't know," Cohen said, reporting back to Ahuva the contents of the surprising phone call. "She said he's a banker, that his grandson's missing. I assume she wanted me to find the boy."

"You mean *he* wanted you to find the boy," Ahuva corrected him. "You've never heard of him?" she asked.

"No," he admitted. "Have you?"

"There's a Levi-Tsur lecture hall at the university," she mused aloud. "Maybe . . . Why don't you do it?" she asked. "Look into it?"

Her question shocked him. "You heard what I said. I'm not interested in a private investigation of any sort."

"You're scared," she ruled.

He bit at the celery, thinking. There was a slight flicker in the line, the call-waiting signal. Cohen scowled. "I'm not scared," he finally said. "I'm uninterested. And I certainly don't need the work."

"That's what you think," she snapped at him, the only person who ever spoke to him that way. "But there's no need to discuss it now," she added lightly. "I'll be over at nine," she said. "We can talk about it then." She hung up. The call waiting immediately kicked in. Cohen unplugged the phone from the wall and then began chopping the celery for the strawberry gelatin mold he planned for dessert. It was one of Ahuva's favorites and easier to think about than her opinions on what he should do with the rest of his life.

· 2 ·

Cohen hated shopping. The economy had grown, the monopolies were gone, choices had to be made. A black basketball player imported from America to a Tel Aviv club became a celebrity spokesman for a new paint company, which was challenging a monopoly that had lasted for more years than Cohen was in the country.

"There must be some difference between them," he complained when the storekeeper put the two half-liter cans of paint on the counter. "The chemicals that they're made from, something?"

The storekeeper shrugged. "The price, that's all," he said. "This one's cheaper," he added shoving the new paint company's product on the counter toward Cohen. He took the cheaper paint and walked home down Emek Refa'im Street to go back to work in his backyard.

It was Sunday morning. On Friday night, Ahuva had tried to convince him that he should at least have listened to Levi-Tsur's problem. He ticked off the reasons for ignoring the request. "I don't need the money, I don't know Levi-Tsur. I don't care about his missing kid."

"You're scared," she challenged him.

"Of what?"

"Of getting involved in something. Anything."

"I'm involved with you."

"You know what I mean." She wasn't scolding or even attacking him. She was trying to make him see. But he preferred the quiet of the garden, found solace in his days of silence. If he was afraid of something it was of telling her about his plan to write. She'd be after him to see something on paper. And he wouldn't want to show her anything until he knew what he was doing.

"Do you remember that recording of Bernstein conducting the Ninth with the New York Philharmonic? They put it on disk," he suddenly said, rising from the table and going to his collection. He kept old long-playing records that he never used anymore, savoring them like bottles of unopened wine that would never be drunk. He collected tapes, both bought and lifted off the radio, and he savored his rapidly growing collection of compact disks. He selected the CD, grinned at her, and went to the computer. It was running a screen saver, but a moment later the computer's CD-ROM was playing through the stereo's speakers. He had decided to change the course of the conversation. There was nothing she could do.

She topped off both their glasses, emptying the Golan Chardonnay she had brought straight from the refrigerator in her apartment across town at the Wolfson Towers overlooking the Knesset and the Valley of the Cross. She brought him his glass, then coiled an arm around his barrel chest and laid her head on his broad back.

"Let's not argue," he whispered, turning to face her.

"I just want you to be happy," she said, raising her glass to his.

"I am," he insisted. But he could see doubt in her green eyes.

The next morning, while Cohen gardened, Ahuva sat on the stoop, reading newspapers, careful to stay in the shade lest the sun burn her pale complexion. She wore a two-piece bathing suit, her thick red hair up in a bun under a straw hat, and occasionally sipped from a glass of white wine, which she kept cold in its bottle in a silver ice bucket she had given Cohen early in their relationship.

The smell of the animal corpse was gone. A field rat. Cohen found it and wrapped it in newspaper and dumped it in the trash before she came downstairs.

She insisted on reading out loud from her favorite weekend commentator, who was complaining that the government didn't need a commission of inquiry to find out why Jews praying in the Tomb of the Patriarchs needed to carry guns.

" 'We all know the handwriting was on the wall,' " she quoted.

"He should speak for himself," Cohen mumbled, turning on the faucet for the hose and starting to water the new bed of petunias he had planted that morning.

" 'The big question now is whether the commission will investigate the root causes, conduct a review of the Occupation's rules of behavior for Jew and Arab, the presence of four hundred zealous Jews claiming that they own the town and that the forty thousand Moslems around them are interlopers, the unholy alliance between the...'"

Cohen finally couldn't take it anymore—journalists had the easy work and never had to do something to change anything. He flashed a spray of water at her and the newspaper.

She spluttered and threw down the paper, started laughing, then turned her face to the water, letting it cool her face. He suddenly turned the hose on his own face—he was bare-chested and in shorts made from cutting off the legs from an old pair of trousers. She got up and ran the few strides toward him, reaching for the hose. It was between them and in the embrace, the water chilled their skin against skin, but did nothing to cool the ardor. A few minutes later they were back in bed.

As usual, she left late on Saturday afternoon, with the weekly ritual offering that he join her at the Jerusalem Theater for that night's concert. As usual, he turned her down. It was no longer the secrecy of the relationship that needed to be protected. But he did want to protect her from the danger that he might lose his own self-control, embarrassing her in public by deliberately pointing out to some of the more rich and powerful of the city secrets that they would rather not have mentioned in public. He spent Saturday night at the computer. Just before going to sleep he remembered to plug in the phone. But nobody called all night.

Now, on Sunday, he carried down a toolbox from his apartment to the yard and carefully picked a large screwdriver with which to pry open the paint can's lid. The bamboo chaise, slightly ragged from the years of exposure to the elements, yet pliable under his hands, quickly absorbed coats of paint as he worked steadily under the sun, crouched on the balls of his feet, going from head to foot and back again. The sun was hot enough to dry one end as he reached the other.

He was so concentrated on the rhythm that he didn't notice the slam of car doors in the street outside the house, nor the footsteps up the walkway to the green iron gate at the entrance to the garden.

"Mr. Deputy Commander?"

It was the same voice he had heard on the phone on Friday afternoon. "Caroline Jones," the woman said. There were a few more strokes of paint left on the brush. He decided she could wait as he ran the brush over the armrest of the chaise, not even turning on the balls of his feet to look at her. Maybe if he ignored her she would go away.

"Mr. Cohen?" came his name. This time it was a man's voice, softly spoken but firm. Cohen turned in his crouch, aware of the open toolbox beside him, wondering if he would need a weapon. He was at home, but knew he had enemies—ex-cons with plans for revenge, sometimes the children of criminals he had sent to jail. They had come to see him, sometimes at night, sometimes in broad daylight. His Beretta was upstairs, but a screwdriver could be effective if he needed it. The thoughts ran through his mind as if blown by a gust of wind. Cohen put up a hand like a visor above his eyes to block the sun's glare.

The moment of decision passed as quickly as it came. The stranger—Mr. Levi-Tsur—was old, wearing an elegant gray suit with a blue-and-white-striped tie. His skin had an Arabian darkness, a mocha emphasized by short fuzzy white hair, crowned by a small white silk *kippa*. The old man's hands clutched the wrought-iron gate, giving the banker the pose of a man behind bars, clutching them in the hope that they'd suddenly give way. He was so short that his hands on the top of the gate were at the level of his chest. It was obvious he expected Cohen to invite them in.

Caroline Jones stood behind her boss. He wasn't surprised to see that she was taller than Levi-Tsur. She was wearing a pair of black sunglasses under a large red hat that shaded her face. Her business suit was also red—for power.

Cohen guessed she was in her thirties. He looked at the paintbrush and considered standing, but the rheumatic joints of his knees were already comfortable in the position he had assumed when he started the paint job, and it would take a decision to unbend them. He really wasn't interested in the old man's personal problems, he decided. He resumed his painting.

"I read about you in the newspapers," the man said. "Asked about you," he added. "I need your help." It didn't sound like it was an easy decision for the banker.

"Why?" Cohen asked.

"My grandson is missing," said the banker.

"Where are his parents?"

The woman answered for the old man. "They are dead. Simon was raised by his grandfather."

"I'm sorry," Cohen said, not insincerely. "But I am no longer with the police. You should go to them, if you think something has happened to him."

The banker shook his head vigorously. "No, no, I cannot do that."

Anger made Cohen ignore the pain in his knees, as he stood up. Behind the man and his secretary was a seven-seat Mercedes limousine standing in the tiny, one-way street. It was parked under the huge eucalyptus trees that shaded half the block. Cohen could see a mustachioed driver carefully folding a chamois and then using it to wipe at the hood of the car engine. There was no insignia of the Tourism Ministry on the side of the car, nor a taxi number on the roof.

Now a few steps closer, but still several strides from the gate, and without the sun in Cohen's eyes, Levi-Tsur appeared to be much older than Cohen had first thought. Perhaps as much as twenty years older than Cohen himself. And there was something in the man's eyes that gave Cohen the feeling that the man wore the white skullcap only while in Jerusalem. The woman took off her sunglasses and scrutinized him like an exhibit in a gallery.

"I do not conduct private investigations," Cohen said from his side of the gate. "If that is what you are asking for. And," he added, "if you cannot trust the police, it makes me wonder if I can trust you." He spoke carefully, with a deliberate quiet.

"I beg your pardon," the woman said, offended on behalf of her boss.

But Cohen ignored her, waiting for the old man's defense. They locked stares for a long moment until the banker finally spoke. "Some of the world's most powerful people trust me, Mr. Cohen," the old man said.

It was the wrong answer as far as Cohen was concerned. He shook his head and turned his back on the old man and the young woman, and went back into the garden, turning the corner around the edge of the building, disappearing from their view.

The banker's secretary tried calling out to him one more time, but then there was a long pause until Cohen heard the car doors close, the car engine start, and then the neighborhood's natural quiet returned, disturbed only by some cooing pigeons and a distant siren racing across the city somewhere far beyond Cohen's reach.

A few minutes later, Cohen was calling Ephraim Laskoff, his banker in Tel Aviv.

It had been Laskoff who explained to Cohen the full significance of the inheritance. "You can spend a hundred thousand a year and still have more at the end of the year than the beginning," the slightly hunchbacked Laskoff had said in his Hungarian-accented Hebrew, after leafing quickly through the stack of documents Cohen had brought him. Discreetly, Laskoff reached for an ebony cigarette filter leaning against the ashtray on the desk, instead of watching for Cohen's reaction; then, striking a match, the silver-haired banker added, "after taxes."

"Shekels?" Cohen asked, wondering what he would do with so much money.

Laskoff smiled, puffed at the flame lighting his cigarette, and then finally looked at Cohen. "Dollars."

Cohen told Laskoff to take care of the accounts and, ever since, once a month, they met in Tel Aviv at Laskoff's favorite restaurant. Their conversations about the money were as ritualistic as Cohen's weekly assignations with Ahuva. Laskoff would comment on how little Cohen spent, Cohen would say not to worry. Laskoff would sniff slightly and sigh, wishing for more clients like Cohen, who didn't care if he had one million more or less. Then they'd spend the rest of the long lunch at the Golden Apple sampling the new sauces and desserts Aharoni, the owner, invented out of French recipes and Israeli agritechnology's best products, drinking at least a bottle apiece. Laskoff always insisted on paying, but Cohen knew the money came from his account. He didn't care.

Ephraim Laskoff's secretary put Cohen's call through immediately.

"Avram?"

"Yes."

"What's the matter? It's not the end of the month already, is it?"

"No," Cohen. "But I need your help."

"It cannot wait until next week?"

"Have you ever heard of a banker named Levi-Tsur?"

There was a silence at the end of the line.

"Ephraim?"

"Yes, yes, I'm here."

"So?"

"Levi-Tsur you said?"

"Is he a banker?" Cohen asked.

"That's like asking if you are a detective."

"I'm not," Cohen snapped back. "At least not anymore."

"If you insist," Laskoff conceded, unconvinced. "But yes, they are bankers, and very good ones."

"They?"

"There are three brothers. The House of Levi-Tsur. Their father started the bank."

"Tsur, as in Lebanon?" Cohen asked. Tsur was the Hebrew word for Tyre, the ancient Phoenician port on the Lebanese coast north of the Land of Israel.

"Yes," Laskoff confirmed.

"I never heard of them," Cohen snapped.

"I'm not surprised. Very discreet. But professionally? Internationally? Very well known in very small circles around the globe. The father copied the Rothschilds—spread trustworthy relatives around the world, and make the globe the *shuk.*"

Cohen looked at the business card he had found in his mailbox after the banker and his assistant left. "Raphael Levi-Tsur" was all it said, in a cursive, raised type on a thick but nearly translucent paper. On the back a telephone number was written in green ink and a feminine hand.

"Raphael Levi-Tsur is one of the three brothers?" Cohen asked.

"Raphael is the oldest," Laskoff said. "Their chairman."

"And?" Cohen prodded.

"He lends money to governments," Laskoff said.

Cohen found it difficult to imagine the man at the gate to his house as someone who could wield so much power. Despite everything, the old man seemed frail, almost lost, bewildered by his situation.

"Avram?"

"I'm here."

"You want to know more?"

"Where is this bank?"

"That's a difficult question," Laskoff said.

"Ephraim . . ." Cohen sighed.

"This really isn't for a phone call," Ephraim said.

"I thought you were using Udi Hason?" Cohen said. He had recommended Udi, a lucky family man who left the police before it made him mad and worked for very select customers. Udi would never place a bug. But he could find them faster than anyone Cohen ever saw.

"I am, I am, but, still . . ." Laskoff stammered his apologies.

"When was he last there?" Cohen asked.

"He is very punctual. Once a month."

"If you're nervous about listeners, get him in more often," Cohen suggested. "Now, tell me about the Levi-Tsurs."

"Gabriel is in the East. Based in Sydney, Australia, but with an emphasis on the Asian tigers. Emmanuel takes care of the Americas, based in New York. And Raphael moves around a lot between them, but mostly works out of Europe."

"A tribe?" Cohen asked.

"Smaller. The three had ten children among them. Most work for the bank. The rest are doctors, academics, and the like. Actually, Avram, you might have heard of one of them. Annabella. She's one of Gabriel's daughters. But she grew up in Emmanuel's house," Laskoff added, turning it into a riddle.

"Annabella Levi-Tsur Cohen," Cohen whistled. The cellist. It seemed like only a few weeks ago when he was a young fan who spent a week hoping a case would take him to the King David, where Annabella stayed for her concert week in the city. Cohen even managed to get a ticket for her last performance, a rare outing for him.

In the lobby, between the ticket taker and the girl selling programs, his beeper went off. In those days there were very few of them around; indeed, Cohen's number was only three digits and reachable only through a complicated police switching network. It had to be an emergency. He had given strict orders that he wasn't to be disturbed unless absolutely necessary. The dispatcher told him that a Beduin Member of Knesset was found murdered in the parking lot of a Jerusalem hotel.

"Do they have offices in Israel?" Cohen finally asked, all the memories flowing through him until it took him back to the job at hand.

Laskoff's laugh was like a spaniel's bark, a huffing thrill over some expected food. "They only operate here for *zedaka*," said the banker. "Israel is for charity. But they put together consortia and conduct transactions involving tens of billions of dollars. There's no business here for them. Not yet. Maybe, if one day there's really peace . . ."

"They don't have any family here?" Cohen interrupted.

"Not that I know of," Laskoff admitted. "At least not people operating a banking operation. The brothers—each one comes in turn, about once a year, in cycles. One year Emmanuel, one year Gabriel, one year Raphael. To make a contribution to something. I'll send you up some material. But Avram, whatever your reasons, keep in mind that they are very well connected here, all the way up to the highest windows."

Barely an hour later, Cohen found out just how high, when, with the paint job done, and Cohen working at the computer, hunting and pecking for the keys, the phone rang.

"Remember me?" the voice began after Cohen's hello.

Six months passed since Cohen last heard Meshulam Yaffe's voice, but he did not forget its unctuous whine. Yaffe had been head of the unit responsible for liaison between the police and the diplomatically immune in Jerusalem, a perfect job for a gossip. A new government meant a new police minister, who needed a new liaison officer by his side. Yaffe fit the bill perfectly—a politician's politician is what Cohen always called the vain little man with the perfect haircut, his fingernails always manicured and his uniforms always well-fit.

"I have to talk with you," Yaffe jabbered, down the line. "It's urgent."

Cohen laughed at the fool, and then added, "I'm out of it. You, of all people, should know that."

"That's why we need to talk. I suppose you know I'm working at the ministry now . . ." He said it as if he'd be offended if Cohen didn't know.

"Shit floats," Cohen muttered to himself, not caring whether Yaffe heard. But the elections surprised almost everyone. "A politician's politician," Cohen said. "It's perfect for you, Meshulam." He added a "mazal tov," in a tone that made no effort to hide its sarcasm.

"Very funny," Yaffe whined. "I'm serious. He wants to meet you."

"Who?" Cohen asked, knowing the answer but enjoying the tease.

"The minister," Yaffe said, exasperated.

"What about?"

"It's not for the phone. I could be at your place in fifteen minutes . . . To explain."

"No." The last thing Cohen wanted was Yaffe visiting him at home.

"It's important, Avram. The minister asked for you. Personally. By name."

"Why?"

"I told you, it's not for the phone. It's a very delicate matter. It's best we meet."

"I'm not interested. He's got a whole force. He doesn't need me."

"He's asking for you," Yaffe pleaded. "Personally."

Cohen fell silent, listening to Yaffe's breathing on the line. Ahuva predicted they'd call him back into the force after the government changed. It was only a matter of time, she said. It was a prediction Cohen didn't want to believe, fearing it would paralyze him, fearing the disappointment when it didn't come true. "You're not too old for them," she had said. "I saw in the paper that a seventy-year-old policeman recently retired." She ran her finger through the gray of his chest, until she was touching his face, her breast tickling his rib cage, her face profiled by moonlight through the open window. "You've got at least ten years more, and" she added, "if they asked me," her mouth approaching his, "I'd say twenty."

Cohen wasn't so sure. But he tired easier than he used to, and sometimes he felt it was willpower, not his body, that kept him going.

"Avram?" Yaffe was waiting for an answer.

Fifty-fifty, Cohen was guessing. Either they're calling me back or it's Levi-Tsur. "I'll listen," Cohen finally decided. "I won't make any promises. But I'll listen."

Yaffe sighed with relief. "I'll call you back with a where and when."

"Not today," Cohen decided, just to make things difficult for the politician's politician.

Half an hour later, Yaffe was back on the line. "Tomorrow. But in Tel Aviv."

"Forget it," Cohen said.

"Please," Yaffe whined.

"Why should I go all the way to Tel Aviv for him?" Cohen asked. It was only forty minutes away, but a world apart from Jerusalem.

"For God's sake, Avram," Yaffe said. "He's the minister. I don't care what you think of him or of politicians. At least give some respect to an institution of the state. You're the one who didn't want to meet today. It's urgent, and he has to be in Tel Aviv tomorrow. Unless you want us to come to your place. Tonight . . ." He made the last offer as if it were a gesture of respect for Cohen.

But the last thing Cohen wanted was the minister paying a house call on him. The idea of any politician in his house made him nervous. "All right. Tel Aviv. Where and when?" he asked Yaffe.

"The Dan. Two o'clock. And please, Avram, be on time. We have a tight schedule tomorrow."

Hanging up on the politician's politician made Cohen smile. It was just like the old days.

· 3 ·

Cohen was fifteen minutes early. From his seat at the dark bar in the downstairs lobby, he could oversee three entrances to the underground salon: the elevator, the steps, and the entrance to the kitchen. It was habit.

Yaffe was fifteen minutes late. "You're looking well, Avram," he said, approaching Cohen's corner position overlooking the broad lounge.

"You're late," Cohen said. He looked over Yaffe's shoulder. The lobby was full of tourists in Israel for the Passover *seder*. Yaffe was wearing gray trousers, a navy blue jacket over a pale blue shirt, and a red tie. Yaffe always prided himself on being the best-dressed cop in Jerusalem. Now he had moved on to greater vistas, Cohen smirked as Yaffe raised a finger to the bartender at the end of the bar, and pointed at the espresso machine, holding up thumb and forefinger to indicate a short coffee.

"Where's your minister?" Cohen asked.

Yaffe pulled out a cigarette, shrugging as he puffed from the flame of his gold-plated lighter. "The schedule's a little late. That's all." He looked at his watch. "Don't worry," he added. "He wants you."

"For what?"

"I don't know exactly," Yaffe admitted. "You know how it is with ministers . . ."

"Does he want me back on the force?" Cohen demanded.

Yaffe could only make a tense face of wanting to answer but not knowing what to say. Just like the old days, Cohen thought. When he told Ahuva about Yaffe's call, she decided that it had something to do with the inquiry into the massacre. "He knows he'll have to issue new orders to the police," she said, "no matter what level the commission concludes is to blame. He knows you were warning it would happen. They didn't call him to testify, so he's clean. And so are you, my darling," she added. She was a judge, she believed in the system. So, believing Cohen was being called back, she was pleased for him. Cohen was not so sure.

Yaffe finally answered. "You haven't changed a bit, Avram," he said, his eyes scanning Cohen's figure at the bar, landing on the glass of cognac. "Still an early drinker."

"Haven't you heard? So is our prime minister," Cohen snapped back, draining his second of the day. Yaffe never found evidence that Cohen's judgment was ever impaired by alcohol, though Yaffe hadn't done anything to stop one of the many rumors that swept through the force after Cohen left, mostly from people who didn't know Cohen but heard of him, that he left the force because of drinking.

"Speak to me, Meshulam," Cohen demanded. "What am I doing here?"

Yaffe checked his watch. "I said two. It's now two-twenty. You know what they say at the university?"

"No, what?"

"A student waits half an hour for the professor."

"Do I look like a student to you?" Cohen snapped back, raising his hand to the bartender at the espresso machine at the end of the bar. But the tall young man glanced in the other direction just as Cohen made the signal.

"Just a few more minutes. Please, Avram." Yaffe worried. "Goodness, you haven't changed at all."

"Neither have you," Cohen said, not meaning it as a compliment. Yaffe pressed his tie as if to smooth out a wrinkle that wasn't there. In the darkness, a manicured fingernail caught a tiny reflection of the lights over the sofas in the lounge spread out before them. Cohen glanced toward the bartender. He was steaming milk at the espresso machine.

"So, the newspapers say you're a rich man now," he tried, using a small-talk tone to ask about what everyone in Jerusalem wanted to know.

Cohen turned on the bar stool and slid off the chair.

"Wait. Stop. Relax, Avram, relax," Yaffe was begging.

Staring down at the gossip he whispered threateningly, "Speak to me, Meshulam."

Yaffe checked his watch. "This has to be very discreet," he said. "I need your promise you will be discreet."

Cohen's eyes narrowed. Yaffe patted at his snow-white hair cut as perfectly as a movie star's. Yaffe was the last person on earth who could make demands for discretion. "Sorry, sorry," Yaffe quickly conceded, "you know what I mean." He checked his watch again. "Five more minutes." He smiled blandly at Cohen. The bartender finally arrived with the double espresso, steamed milk, and a rack of sugar packets. Yaffe opened one packet of sugar and poured it into the coffee, and dumped the other into the milk. He stirred first one, then the other. Then he poured the milk into the coffee.

Cohen reached into his wallet, pulling out a hundred shekel note. Yaffe, cup in midair to his mouth, froze. The phone rang behind the bar and the bartender went to it. "Avram, you're not going yet, please," Yaffe pleaded, putting the cup back onto the bar.

"It's for you, Mr. Yaffe," the bartender said, passing the phone onto the bar counter.

Cohen held onto the hundred shekel note as he watched the politician's eyes shift back and forth. "He's here. We're just having a coffee..." There was a brief pause. "Of course," Yaffe said. His eyes went to his espresso.

"He's ready?" Cohen asked as Yaffe hung up.

"Yes," Yaffe said. "Avi," he called out to the bartender. "Put it all on the bill, including the gentleman's."

Cohen deliberated for a second if he should pay for himself.

Yaffe noticed. "It's on me, Avram, not the office. Really."

Cohen relented, though he didn't believe Yaffe. They walked across the lobby, up the stairs, past reception, to the elevators. As they approached the elevator doors, Yaffe noted a pair of young women admiring the jewelry in the shop window beside the elevators. "There's a modeling agency in the hotel," Yaffe said to Cohen, pointing to the agency's logo, embossed on a small brass plaque hanging on the wall with an arrow pointing down the corridor toward the office. The girls were teenagers. There was something tired in their eyes that made him sad. The elevator doors opened. Cohen stepped in. Yaffe was still staring at the girls.

"Meshulam," Cohen ordered. Yaffe smiled and, trying to catch the girls' attention with an exaggerated sprightliness, stepped into the elevator and pressed the button for the top floor. The girls ignored the effort.

They were alone in the elevator cabin. "What's it all about?" Cohen demanded as it rode up the four flights.

"I don't know," Yaffe insisted, whining with the embarrassment of his ignorance. "But it's important. Yesterday afternoon he came back to the office from some lunch and was crazy. He needed to talk to you. Only you. I had your number. He told me to call. And here we are." Yaffe looked at his watch, relief spreading across his face. The elevator doors opened. Yaffe led Cohen to the right and then the left and then down a long corridor. Cohen studied the tiny flecks of dandruff in the little man's shiny white hair as he followed Yaffe to the last door at the very end of the corridor.

But just as Yaffe was about to knock, he paused, and with a worried look in his eye stole a glance at Cohen's impassive face. In Yaffe's frightened eyes Cohen could see the certain knowledge that the next few minutes could yet be very painful for the politician's politician who had been plying his trade with Cohen's pride.

He blinked in the brightness after the somberly lit corridor. The minister was sitting in an armchair turned to face the picture window looking down on the beach. He sat in the shadows of the curtain sheltering him from the sun but not denying him the view. His back was to Cohen and Yaffe.

For a moment, it flashed through Cohen's mind that David Nahmani, known to friends and foes alike as Dudu, had taken up a sniper's view of some target on the beach. The minister didn't turn away from the window as Yaffe and Cohen stepped into the sun-scorched hotel suite. Air-conditioning tried to match the sun's intensity, but the room's broad window seemed to magnify the white sun hanging above the sea. The glass glistened with condensation.

From where he was standing, Cohen could not see Nahmani's trademark—the empty right sleeve pinned to the shoulder. The missing arm was a symbol of his authority, a visual slogan for his rhetoric, proof he knew what he was talking about when he preached his politics. The arm was lost on the Golan Heights in the Yom Kippur War and, as such, became the ultimate justification for the minister's personal position against the prime minister's readiness to trade the Golan for peace with Syria.

Instead of turning, or even standing, the minister merely beckoned with his good hand over his shoulder, inviting them to join him at a single matching armchair at his side. Unlike Nahmani's chair, which enjoyed an angle of shadow, the empty seat beside him sat full-faced to the sun blaring through the window.

Yaffe stepped forward presumptuously, pointing to the desk chair for Cohen. "Meshulam," Nahmani said, just before Yaffe settled into the seat. "Didn't you have that Austrian to see?"

For a moment Yaffe looked like he was going to cry and then, as if remembering what had worried him only a moment before, he said, "No problem," and backed out of the room with a final pleading glance at Cohen.

"We've met, haven't we?" was Nahmani's first question after they heard the door close behind Yaffe, leaving Cohen standing in the middle of the room. "I can call you Avram? Can't I?" Nahmani added, finally turning in his chair away from the view out the window to face Cohen. The small golden pin glistened in the sunlight where it held the empty blue sleeve to the shoulder.

"In seventy-four," Cohen finally answered. "Your first year in Knesset. Your subcommittee wanted to know about the Mafia. I wrote the section on Jerusalem."

He knew the public legends about Nahmani, a wheeler-dealer who had spent the first year of his life in an old dairy crate that his parents had made into a crib for their youngest child in the tent camp when they arrived from Morocco, and how he had used the free university tuition offered to all students who had served during the Yom Kippur War to get degrees in both law and business administration. He had gone on to become wealthy enough as a contract maker to afford full-time politics, in which, he said, he found more satisfaction making deals that benefited all the people instead of just a few. He became one of the youngest ministers ever in the forty-seven-year-old history of the state. The public all knew Nahmani's rags to riches story.

Cohen knew another story about Nahmani. In his first year in the Knesset the politician's car tires were slashed one night. The assumption was that the criminal underworld that he was so vigorously pursuing was sending a message to the new member of parliament. As chief of Jerusalem CID, Cohen was under pressure from the inspector general, himself under pressure from the minister at the time, to catch someone. Instead of drug dealers and racketeers, Cohen's detectives found a frustrated, cuckolded husband seeking revenge.

Charges were never brought. Cohen doubted whether Nahmani knew that it was Cohen who suggested to the inspector general that some discreet conversations were probably the best way to help all three people involved—the politician, the Jerusalem socialite, and her temporarily crazed banker husband—save their lives. The inspector general brought it to the minister, who handled the arrangements. The banker and wife resumed their marriage. The society pages never knew what really happened, while Nahmani simply stopped blaming the Mafia for vandalizing his car. When asked about his previous accusations by inquiring reporters he used the politician's standard tactic and gave an answer to a completely different question.

It might have been his reputation as a legislative crime fighter that won him the police ministry, but as far as Cohen could tell, there was more reputation than action in the six months since Nahmani became minister.

Nahmani beamed at Cohen, slapping his thigh with his hand. "I thought so, I thought it might be you."

"I thought you were exaggerating the problem," Cohen said.

"Come, sit down," Nahmani said, ignoring the comment and pointing to to the chair beside him. "If you'd like, there are drinks in the refrigerator."

"I'd rather wait until I know why you asked to see me," Cohen said.

Nahmani turned his eyes on the families and tourists on the beach below. "Actually, it's a little embarrassing for us," he said. "The force, I mean. That we have to call upon you."

Cohen let a small smile creep onto his face. Nahmani kept his eyes on the beach. Cohen didn't want to sit directly in the sun's path. Nahmani gave him no choice. "I told Yaffe," Cohen said. "I'll listen. But I won't make any promises." He still didn't step into the bright sunlight falling into the room.

It was Nahmani's turn to smile, a slight twitch that gave a sudden cupid's form to otherwise thin lips. The dimple in his left cheek remained long enough for Nahmani to point to the chair, then it disappeared, and with it any more attempts at charming Cohen with a toothpaste-ad smile.

"I'm waiting to hear why I am here," Cohen said.

Nahmani sighed. "Someone very important has asked for you," he began. "Someone important to the state. A Jew. He is always ready with his support for us. Now he needs help. And he's asked for you." Nahmani paused, waiting for Cohen's response.

"Levi-Tsur," Cohen finally said.

Except for the spot Nahmani cleared, the condensation on the window made the view to the beach, sea, and horizon a pointillist blur of color, except for the cloudless sky, which instead of blue was almost white from the glaring sun.

Nahmani bit his lower lip. "That's why it is so embarrassing. He doesn't trust the force. Because of the leaks. He says he trusts you. He said you turned him down when he came to you. So he came to me, asking if there was anything I could do—without getting the force involved directly."

"Why?" asked Cohen, still standing.

"He says he wants only you, because he knows you can be discreet," Nahmani answered.

If Nahmani had asked him about the commission of inquiry, mentioned a job opening up where Cohen's experience would be useful, or asked for Cohen's advice on the syndrome—for any and all of that, Cohen would have gladly sat down. Instead, he growled, "Why not put Beno on it?" Beno was Beno Hasdai. Nahmani already made it clear he wanted to replace the inspector general he inherited from the last government, and Hasdai, a much decorated war hero who went from commander of the antiterror squad to commander of the Southern District, was the minister's clear choice. Beno Hasdai was one of the cleanest cops near the top of the pyramid, a kibbutznik who spoke of all the right values. But Cohen thought Hasdai was more expert at public relations than investigation, and as ex-army, more likely to use brawn than brain.

"I wanted to put Beno on it," Nahmani admitted, almost whining his complaint to Cohen. "But Levi-Tsur doesn't want publicity. And

47

he knows, just like everyone else, how leaky things are on the fifth floor. He asked for you. Besides," Nahmani added, trying his dimpled charm again, "you're a much better detective than Beno."

Cohen shook his head with disgust. "Too bad," he decided, getting up from the chair. "It's your problem. Not mine. I'm not interested."

Nahmani wiped at the window again, then turned to face Cohen, who was about to turn to the door.

"Have you heard from your friend Nissim Levy lately?" the minister suddenly asked.

Cohen put his foot down carefully. The memory of how the political problems resulting from his last case had soured Levy's career was much harder to take than the squeaking glass under the linen Nahmani was using to wipe clear the view to the beach.

"I understand that he's doing fine in Yeroham," the minister went on. "What was it you wrote about him in that personnel report? 'His know-how justifies his ambition . . .'"

Nahmani was quoting accurately. "Of course, a young man with so much intelligence should be closer to the real action, at the center. Don't you agree?"

If he were to cooperate with Nahmani and handle the Levi-Tsur case, Levy's career could be set right. "I really hoped it wouldn't come to this," the minister said softly. Then he drove in the knife. "But I'll tell you what we can do," he said, suddenly brighter, as if he was looking for a way to ease Cohen's burden. "You could call Levy. Ask him what you should do." The minister pointed toward the telephone on the table.

It was like cutting open a deep, dark vein of Cohen's guilt. The last time they were together was at Nissim's wedding, one of the rare social occasions Cohen had attended since his return to Jerusalem from Los Angeles. It wasn't a large wedding, which somehow made it even sadder for Cohen.

Hagit was wonderful, Cohen thought when Nissim brought her to the German Colony flat. Smart, sassy, and sure of herself. But Cohen worried whether she understood what it meant to marry an ambitious policeman. He could see how Nissim, looking to him, decided against loneliness, choosing marriage.

Cohen wanted to warn Nissim but knew he shouldn't. Who was

he to be explaining love to anyone? Even with Ahuva, he was careful about love, passing it back and forth with her as if it were a crucial piece of evidence in a chain of possession that could not be lost, lest the whole case collapse. Discreetly, almost embarrassed, Cohen had asked Levy if he needed any help. "You mean financial?" Levy answered, implying in his tone that he didn't. "No, of course not," he added, just to make sure Cohen understood. "Hagit's family is paying for the wedding."

Cohen sat in the corner throughout the ceremony, dinner, and the beginning of the dancing. Already then, he could sense there was danger ahead for Nissim in the force. Several of Cohen's old colleagues showed up, as well as many of his subordinates. They all came by his table to shake his hand, congratulating him on the sudden wealth, carefully avoiding the reason Cohen was no longer in the force. Some gossiped at the fifth floor level, about Beno's chances of replacing the former air force commander who parachuted into the inspector general's job as a new broom but spent less time sweeping clean the force than promoting his own political career. The air-force-commander-turned-police-inspector-general was eventually replaced by the current inspector general, picked from the ranks. But he was caught in the throes of a scandal, and his days looked numbered. That's why Beno was becoming so popular.

A wedding party in the force is open to anyone in the force. Cohen left when the dancing began. The honeymoon was a week in Italy. A week after their return, Levy was transferred to Yeroham. Not that he didn't sound enthusiastic as he told Cohen about trying to help the junkies and drunkards of the tiny Negev town.

But Cohen knew that no matter how much social work Nissim might be able to accomplish as a cop in the middle of the desert, he was sent into exile because he had been Cohen's protégé, and Cohen, rich, was still to be punished for showing the syndrome's face.

Cohen closed his eyes to the bright sun blasting through the window. The air-conditioning had a cold bite that made him long for the heat outside. He knew he didn't have much choice. "I'll listen to the old man," he finally agreed. "I don't make promises," he repeated.

Nahmani smiled. "I knew you'd be reasonable," he said. "He's in the presidential suite, the other end of the hall."

· 4 ·

David Levi-Tsur was the apple of Raphael's eye, born soon after the Second World War and raised as the natural heir to Raphael's senior position in the House of Levi-Tsur. He married a little later than his father wanted, but it was to the perfect catch, the grand-daughter of Max Wolfson, who took over a scrap iron business in Europe right after the war and turned it into an international corporation with holdings ranging from mines and forests to manufacturing plants producing the kind of consumer items that were ubiquitous in any household in the West by the end of the sixties. David and his wife, Miriam, who married the same year her grandfather was made a Lord for all his charity work in England, seemed to live a charmed life.

"Maybe too charmed," Raphael mourned, explaining to Cohen how Simon came to live with him.

"When the boy was nine months old, they left him at home with his nanny for the first time and flew to Switzerland in David's plane. I always hated that plane." A storm rose as suddenly as the plane. It crashed into one of the Alps. Baby Simon became Raphael's ward when the plane went down.

And by the time Simon was seventeen, Raphael realized something was very wrong with his youngest grandson. "I wanted him to become a banker. But he is a gambler," the old man wept to Cohen, who was also right about another thing concerning the aged banker—the *kippa* was only for Jerusalem.

They sat in a suite the mirror image of the minister's. Unlike Nahmani, Raphael Levi-Tsur preferred the curtains drawn and the lights dim, except for a single bright light aimed at the desk surface, beside which he sat in an executive's chair obviously brought into the suite for his stay.

But instead of a business suit like the gray one he had worn on

Sunday when he showed up in Jerusalem, Raphael was cloaked in a burgundy robe when he opened the door to Cohen. It was almost Arab in its length, nearly brushing the floor. He wore soft leather slippers and Cohen could see the cuffs of crimson pajamas.

"I don't know what has happened to him. His last trust fund check cleared the bank two months ago. Sometimes he travels, but he never goes more than five weeks without contacting the bank. To make sure he gets his money. It is not like him, not to use the money."

"How much does he get?"

"Ten thousand dollars a month."

Cohen didn't know whether to be disgusted or furious. He swallowed back the bitter taste rising in his gorge, deciding that when the job was done, he'd up the ante for Nissim's career.

"It sits there, unmoving," Levi-Tsur was trying to explain about the money. He shrugged in self-defense. "He is my dependent, no?"

"And his banker," Cohen grumbled, "able to look into his accounts."

"I have told nobody about this," Levi-Tsur protested, trying to preserve his pride. "You, me, and Caroline, of course, know. But nobody else. Nobody else should know."

"Nahmani," Cohen added.

The banker smiled weakly and then blew his nose. "Yes, and Nahmani."

"Does the boy know Hebrew?"

"Yes, of course. And all the Romance languages. An excellent student. When he studies, of course. Like anyone. But better than most, sometimes brilliant."

"You say you want me because you don't want any publicity. But you go to a politician for help."

"Yes, I admit, it is a delicate matter," Levi-Tsur said, holding one brown hand in the other. He smiled. "But his type is not a stranger to me. Nor are you. My grandson. It seems he is."

"Why so much secrecy?" Cohen said. It was a commiseration as much as a legitimate question.

Levi-Tsur sighed. "Our business, like yours, depends on discretion. The boy turns twenty-one next month. There are some documents requiring his signature. You must understand. He is the youngest of his generation of heirs to his shares in the bank." The banker's voice cracked, and he took a sip from a glass of water on the table beside him. He offered nothing to drink to Cohen, which only added to Cohen's distaste for the old man's methods. "There are very substantial amounts of money involved."

"I thought he's not in the banking business."

"It is a technical matter, involving investments made in his name when he was born. Nothing for you to worry about. But if it becomes known his signature is in question, there could be severe repercussions. For the bank."

"What is more important to you? Your grandson or the bank?" Cohen asked, even though he knew the answer. He wanted to see how the old man would tell it.

"I care for my grandson more than my own life," the old man answered, displaying no astonishment at the question. "But the bank is more important than any of us. It is our trust. As a family. My brothers, their children, their grandchildren—and their grand-children . . . The House must continue."

"If Simon didn't want to be a banker, what did interest him?"

"I never insisted on him being a banker. He can be whatever he wants," the old man said softly. "All I want is for him to find what he is seeking and settle down. He is a very smart boy. Very smart. It is a terrible waste for him not to be with us. In the bank, I mean. I hope." The banker didn't seem to see the contradiction between the start of his statement and its end.

"What if I find him and he doesn't want to return to the family?" Cohen asked. He had seen plenty of runaways, local poor and foreign rich. It was part of the cop's job in the Holy Land in the twentieth century. He wasn't sure yet if he believed that was a possibility, but he couldn't disregard it. He had seen it in the past: the children wanting to take charge of their lives. But at twenty, he didn't think the kid should be treated as a kid any longer.

"You would tell me where to find him. I would go to him," Raphael said. For a moment, Cohen could see the steel in the old man's eyes, a metallic certainty that made clear the power behind the seemingly frail persona.

"I don't suppose you know any of his friends?"

The old man shook his head.

"Your secretary? Perhaps she does?"

"She has never met Simon," Levi-Tsur said. "My last secretary, Rose, came to me after my wife died. Rose was with me for almost thirty years, and knew much about Simon. She went three months ago. God rest both their souls," he added. But then he changed his tone. "Caroline is new to her job. But she is very smart, in many ways that are helpful to me. Computers, for instance," he said, smiling abashedly. "I have not managed to learn them. But it is not really a difficult job anymore. I am not retired, but my commitments are my choices, not those of others. Mostly she administers my travel arrangements and appointments. She handles correspondence, and yes," he finally added the final justification, "she serves as a companion for certain social obligations. For me she is perfect. She is extremely professional, in every aspect of her work." Levi-Tsur seemed prouder of her than of his grandson.

"And you obviously trust her," Cohen said. "Where is she now?" he tried.

"I preferred to have this conversation alone. But she'll be checking in quite soon," he added, checking his watch, "to remind me about my five o'clock appointment."

"The boy's address?"

Raphael turned in his chair at the desk, taking an envelope from it. "He told me it was a good investment. I should have known better," the banker said. "When he said he wanted to go to Israel, I thought, why not. I tried everything else. He tried everything else. Schools, tutors, psychiatrists. Everything. I expressed my fear of the army, and raised an eyebrow when he said kibbutz. When he said university, how could I object?" He handed the envelope over to Cohen.

The whole thing was like one of those dismal soap operas Cohen saw on the cable television he allowed to be installed in his house. He didn't enjoy much of what he saw among the forty-something channels, except the fact that the pictures and sounds were coming from all over the world. "Did you spend much time with him?"

"I saw him as often as I could," said Levi-Tsur, not really understanding the question, but proving with his answer what was so obvious.

Cohen opened the envelope. A key fell out, as well as a Polaroid photograph and a sheet of heavy stationary with some typed telephone numbers. "The picture was taken last year," the old man said, watching mournfully as Cohen studied the photo.

The boy obviously inherited his genes from the grandfather's line. They had the same square jaw, hawk nose, and high forehead. But while the grandfather's mouth fell into a natural sobriety of moderate pessimism, the boy was an extremist, with the cynical charm of a desperado's smile. Already at nineteen, his hairline was receding into the same patterns as his grandfather's. But while the elderly banker cropped his hair close, Simon grew his long, slicked back into a black helmet.

In the picture, he was standing between his grandfather and an elderly woman. The boy was grinning at his grandfather, one arm over Raphael Levi-Tsur's shoulder, with a glass of champagne in his hand. The other arm was around the elderly woman's waist. Raphael and Simon were in tuxedos. The woman was in a long green gown, looking lovingly at Raphael. In the background Cohen could see a glass case, containing small objects, as if the photo was taken in an art gallery of some kind.

"Who's the woman?" Cohen asked.

"Rose, God rest her soul," the old man sighed. "It was taken last year. We gather every year." He brightened slightly.

"Who?"

"The entire family."

"Your secretary as well?"

"She was like family."

"Is Caroline Jones?"

"Is she what?"

"Like family?"

Levi-Tsur hesitated before answering. "No, not yet." There was something in the tone that made it clear he believed he wouldn't live long enough for the woman to become family.

"Do you have any family here where he might have gone? Any cousins, relatives of any kind?"

There was a knock at the door. "That's her," Levi-Tsur said, checking his gold watch. "It's open," he called out.

"Family?" Cohen asked again.

"No," Levi-Tsur said firmly. "No, no family." He waved his hand at the suggestion as if to belittle the idea. He was watching the door with more interest. It opened. Cohen kept his gaze on Levi-Tsur for a second longer, wondering how much of the truth he was hearing about the banker's family, watching the old man's expression change as Caroline Jones came into the room.

Cohen turned away from the closed curtain hiding the sea to face the banker at the desk. She showed no surprise to see Cohen sitting in the armchair near the window and barely acknowledged Cohen's nod.

"You mustn't forget your five o'clock," she said curtly to the banker, "and the dinner has been arranged. For eight-thirty."

Without sunglasses, she had bright blue eyes. Without a hat, she had auburn hair. Cohen tried not to think of what she'd be like without her pink business suit. In Raphael's eyes, he saw more than an employer's look. It was a hint of pleasure created by possession.

Cohen concentrated on getting the picture back into the envelope, then stood up. "How long are you staying?" he asked the banker, who looked to the secretary for an answer.

"Richard says the plane can be ready to go by tomorrow morning," the woman said. "Or, we could leave tonight after dinner by commercial airliner and he could bring the plane tomorrow."

"I'll decide later," Levi-Tsur said. "I must be in Brussels tomorrow at noon," he apologized. "But meanwhile, you have a telephone number where we can be contacted twenty-four hours a day."

The woman took a step into the room. Cohen was about to leave, when the old man stood up and grabbed his hand. Levi-Tsur's hand was delicate, and the skin had a dry cool touch. "Please, do your best. Find him." His voice was low and hoarse. "I am afraid for him."

Cohen nodded.

"And we of course have your number," the woman said. Cohen raised a slight eyebrow as he moved past her, deciding that the fragrance she carried into the room was a perfume and not a soap, realizing she was in her late thirties, not early.

"Miss Jones?" Cohen asked in English, pausing as he was almost at the door. "In the course of your work, did you ever speak with Simon?"

Her eyes flickered toward the old banker. "I usually contacted him directly," Levi-Tsur intervened, as if to prove that he was trying to keep the matter as private as possible. "Of course, sometimes, if he called, Caroline would answer the phone and pass it to me."

"And when was the last time you took one of his calls?" Cohen asked Caroline Jones.

"Mid-March," the woman answered. "More than three months ago. I can get you the exact date, if you want."

Cohen pushed on in the direction that interested him. "Did you get the call?" Cohen asked the banker.

"Mr. Levi-Tsur was at a lunch," the woman interrupted. "I told the boy, and he asked to leave the message that he called. Nothing else." Her clipped English added a forcefulness to her tone that emphasized she had nothing to do with Simon Levi-Tsur, or his disappearance. "To tell you the truth, he was very cold toward me on those few occasions when we spoke."

"Now, Caroline," the old man said. "He's just a boy."

"Did you pass on the message?" Cohen asked.

"Of course I did."

"Did you call him back?" Cohen asked the banker.

"I tried two days later," Levi-Tsur confessed sadly. His face brightened with hope for an acceptable excuse. "I assumed it wasn't terribly urgent, or he would have called back."

"But he didn't," Cohen pointed out.

"No, he didn't call back."

"And that's when you became suspicious?"

There was a long pause. "No," the banker admitted. "It had happened before. But this time it's different. I can feel it."

"When did you realize this?" Cohen pressed.

"Does it matter when he realized it?" the secretary asked. "What matters is finding him. You can see how upset Mr. Levi-Tsur is about this."

Cohen turned to the banker. "What happened to make you realize something was wrong?"

Levi-Tsur's face twisted, almost with pain, as he tried to place the feeling in his body. He tapped his stomach under the bathrobe, and then tapped his nose. "It was a feeling. The last week, it became very strong. I tried calling him several times. There was no answer. Until finally, at the end of the week, I came to see for myself."

The banker covered his eyes and shook his head, helpless in the face of his misunderstanding of his grandson. Cohen wondered if there was as much cunning as coyness in the sentimentalism the old man was displaying.

"Are you sure you don't have any distant relatives here that the boy might have gone to?" Cohen pressed again.

Levi-Tsur's eyes were still covered, his head bowed in privacy. His head shook from side to side, sadly. Suddenly he looked up, a wry understanding on his face and tears in his eyes. "Next Year in Jerusalem," he said. "The prayer, no? At the seder. My father was a capitalist. Not a Zionist. We help our fellow Jews. It is our responsibility. But to live here? No. If he is here, in Israel, it is not with family." He turned to the desk, searching for something. It was a handkerchief. He blew his nose with a large honk.

"You've been to his apartment?" Cohen asked.

"I went," the secretary said.

Cohen turned to her. "And?"

She shrugged. "I didn't know where to begin."

"It's down the street from here," the banker said, as if to make up for her failing.

Cohen had nothing more to ask. But he did have something to say. "Keep in mind that at most I can find the boy," he said, standing at the doorway. "I can't guarantee that he'll be ready to see you, or sign any documents, no matter how important they might be." The old man looked at him with hope. Cohen wasn't sure what he saw in the Englishwoman's cool eyes.

· 5 ·

The last time he spent more than twenty-four hours in Tel Aviv was nearly thirty years before, assigned to the *mador*, the plainclothes and undercover flying squad that roamed the city gathering intelligence on the hottest files pressing down on the local CID desk. The corruption he witnessed inside the Tel Aviv force depressed him so much that he had been on the verge of resignation.

Menachem Mizrahi had talked him out of leaving the force. Mizrahi was one of the veterans, on the job since the British mandate to keep law and order in the Holy Land. "There are always going to be *maniakim*," the aging Mizrahi told Cohen, using a slang that the underworld would eventually adopt to mean an informant. But Mizrahi used it to mean those who joined the police because it gave them a power to wield for their own pleasure. "Half a good cop's job is to prove that not all of us are *maniakim*."

"And the other half?" Cohen asked, as they sat in a sun-drenched café on Ben Yehuda street, two blocks behind the Dizengoff station where the *mador* kept offices. Mizrahi had asked for the meeting, wanting to keep Cohen in the force.

The old man smiled under his white mustache, which he stroked with gnarled brown fingers twisted by an arthritis that gradually made the hand useless, whether to fill out forms or wield a weapon. But he could still think. "The other half?" he murmured back at Cohen. "That's simple. Getting to the truth."

Stepping into the heat of the city, Cohen wondered what the truth would turn out to be when he found Simon Levi-Tsur. He was lucky about one thing, he thought, turning right and heading south on Hayarkon Street. The radio that morning warned of a *sharav* approaching. It was the hot wind out of the Sahara and Egypt, and it was due in Israel in the coming hours, possibly as early as late afternoon. The humidity in the seaside city wasn't yet in the nineties, but the temperature was already in the thirties centigrade, the eighties farenheit.

Cohen never hated Tel Aviv. But like many Jerusalemites, once at home up on the mountain, he came to regard the city on the Mediterranean coast as a distant place, far closer to America than Jerusalem ever could be. He never missed Tel Aviv once he was gone. But sometimes he missed Mizrahi, who had talked Cohen out of resigning just before the Six Day War, and had died seven years later, right after the Yom Kippur War.

The walk down Hayarkon was bringing back memories, except everything was different. He saw a fleabag hotel he had known as a rendevous point for illicit lovers and bagmen for the underworld in his years in Tel Aviv. Now it was remodeled, gentrified in a pastel yellow with white trim. It still had a front patio, where Cohen had once waited, playing a young drunk thrown out by an unhappy new bride, watching for a Russian spy.

Cohen paused on the corner in front of the hotel to check the information on the piece of paper against the number on the street sign at the corner. He was still several blocks away from the address just off Hayarkon Street, past the end of Allenby and the beach south of Mograbi.

"Avram!" the voice came at him from a patio chest-high to Cohen above the sidewalk. "Cohen!"

He looked around, bewildered. It was Yaffe, sitting alone at a table on the Aviv patio, a glass of beer in front of him. "Come," he said, waving a friendly hand.

Cohen didn't want to snub Yaffe, because it would only make the gossip more suspicious. He still wanted to know how much the politician's politician knew about the case. Sighing, he climbed the four stairs to the patio and went to Yaffe's table. Yaffe waved to a waitress as Cohen settled into the chair, making sure to turn it to face the sidewalk and sea beyond, instead of Yaffe's too familiar face.

"A beer?" Yaffe asked. "Isn't this great?" he went on, waving a hand at the view of the intersection, where two teenage girls in bikinis were on their way across the street to the park and the beach below. "The world's getting younger every day," Yaffe summed up, patting his stomach with an unconscious motion, while trying to share a lewd grin with Cohen. "But we haven't changed, have we? We aren't getting any older. Just wiser, eh?"

"Drinking on the job, Meshulam?" Cohen asked sarcastically. "That's a change for you. Isn't that what you used to say I did?"

"Come on, Avram. You know it's never personal with me," Yaffe defended himself. "Besides, I had a meeting with someone from the Austrian embassy. And you know how pedantic those *yekkes* can be. He had a beer, I had to have a beer. He paid for the first, I paid for the second. Two beers. That's all."

"I'm sure it has no effect on you, Meshulam."

"So," Yaffe suddenly changed tone, almost pleading, but lowering his voice to make sure the couple at the next table, an arm's reach away, couldn't hear the question. "What happened?" He leaned forward across the table. "He didn't ask you to come back, did he?"

There was something worried in Yaffe's tone, as if he didn't know how to respond to whatever Cohen would answer. Cohen gently rubbed the scaly patch of forearm, then leaned back in his chair, watching the pretty young waitress approaching. "A cognac, please," he ordered when she arrived. "And a glass of cold water. With ice. Please."

"Any particular cognac?" she wanted to know. For thirty years he had drunk Extra Fine, the medicinal brandy available only to Jerusalem. Here's another way the money has changed me, he thought as she rattled off the names of the cognacs available, adding grappa, at the end, as an afterthought. "Martell, please." He watched her cross the patio and guessed she wanted to be a dancer.

"Nu?" Yaffe whined, "tell me. If it's not a job, then what?"

Cohen shook his head, not to say he wouldn't tell Yaffe anything—which he wouldn't—as to remark on Yaffe's obtuse manners.

"Oh my God," Yaffe said, suddenly guessing his worst fear. "He wants you to race the commission of inquiry. Oh my God." It was Yaffe's worst nightmare.

Cohen stared back at the white-haired man. Yaffe took the silence as confirmation of his guess. Cohen felt sick. "He had some questions about an old case," he finally said. "Just some details he wanted cleared up. He thought I could help."

"Which case?"

"A missing person's file," Cohen said, using the tone of his voice to bend the truth into a different shape, without losing it completely. When telling a lie, it was best to stick to the truth. "Something personal," he added, as if it was truly a matter that only Cohen could have handled.

The drinks arrived. Cohen scowled as he lifted the small balloon to the sun, halfway down the sky toward the horizon. There was barely a full swallow in it. The colors shifted between gold and amber as he swirled the liquid in the glass. "To your minister," he said, sincerely appreciating the irony of the politician's distrust of his own officer. "A politician's politician's politician," Cohen toasted bitterly. He took the entire swallow into his mouth and then let it float down his throat.

"That's a relief," Yaffe said. "For a moment, I was worried he wanted you to come back. To put you on the fifth floor." He smiled, determined to get Cohen to respond, and was lucky that Cohen concentrated on his drink, not the attempt at a joke.

The burning in his throat and the warmth in his stomach faded. He thought about the task at hand. The Levi-Tsur boy's apartment was a few streets away. He'd find something, he was sure, that would lead him to someone who would know where to find the missing heir.

He had followed leads for thirty years or more, in one way or another. This time should be no different, he decided. It was a case to wrap up in a night, though he was disturbed by something he couldn't quite name in the Levi-Tsur story. He wasn't sure if it was a familiar feeling or a memory, or perhaps his suspicion of anyone powerful admitting to helplessness, or most of all the ease in which the guilt was spotted in the mix of the old man's explanation. But he felt confident, certain he'd find an answer.

The cognac reached his head, and he realized the last thing he wanted was Yaffe following him to the Levi-Tsur boy's apartment. "I'm surprised you're here," Cohen said.

"Excuse me?"

"After I left Nahmani, I saw a friend in the lobby. Then, as he was leaving the hotel, I saw your minister. He was on his way out to his car."

"What!" Yaffe jumped from his seat as if he suddenly spilled his beer all over his new suit. "Why didn't you say anything? My God,

Avram," he continued, "you haven't changed." Yaffe threw down a crumpled ten shekel note on the table so abruptly that Cohen needed to catch his glass of cold water teetering from Yaffe's jarring of the table.

Cohen was still laughing quietly to himself as the waitress came by, a worried look in her eyes that her customer had just run out without paying.

"Is everything all right? Your friend?"

"He's in fine form," Cohen said, adding a grin to his own twenty shekel note to pay for his drink.

The sun hung halfway to the horizon of the sea in the west, glaring down at the city. With a little luck, he thought, checking his watch, he'd have something to go with by sunset.

· 6 ·

The architect had combined portholes and skylights in the lobby, and there was something vaguely boatlike to the entire curve of the brand-new building on the corner just south of Allenby's intersection with the beach boardwalk. There was something angry about the postmodernism, as if the contractor couldn't decide whether he wanted his building in the Middle East or on the Mediterranean, but knew he saw something like it in Milan, or maybe Miami. Its color scheme was supposed to be azure and gold, but it came out a blue at constant odds with the sky, and an orange that looked like the kind of lipstick worn by a streetwalker trying to be coy.

According to the mailboxes, half the apartments were empty. Cohen guessed each floor was worth a million dollars because of its position overlooking the beach. But he doubted there was much added value in the construction.

S. Levi-Tsur, it said, on a mailbox at the end of the row. Utilities bills, some junk mail, but nothing personal. Cohen tore open the phone bills. The kid didn't have his calls itemized. And the bills were paid like Cohen's, with a standing order at the bank. The same was true for the electricity bill and a city water bill.

Apartment fourteen, the piece of paper said. Top floor. From outside, Cohen thought he counted nine stories, but the lift's buttons only went to eight. The elevator had the same color scheme as the building's exterior.

Cohen studied his face in the mirror on the elevator wall. His hair was much more white than black, the lines of his face ran deeply from the corners of his eyes down to the corners of his mouth. There were a few broken corpuscles on his nose, that he imagined only he could spot in his tan. He rubbed a hand over his face, drawing it from his brow to his chin. His hand came away sticky from the sheen of sweat, despite the whirring of the fan in the ceiling and the air-conditioning of the elevator cabin.

The elevator stopped, and Cohen turned. There were two doors. One directly in front of him, the other at the end of a short hall. Both were blue. He remembered the layout of the lobby, and realized the door in front of him was the entrance to the apartment, while the other led to the service stairwell and fire escape. Cohen palmed the flat, wide Multi-Lock key into the palm of his hand.

The apartment door swung open. Cohen immediately understood why Caroline Jones hadn't known where to begin.

Thin-slatted venetian blinds over sliding-glass windows stretched around the room, creating lines and shadows in the huge room. It stank of dirty laundry and dried sweat, of still air permeated by the decay of rotting food. A cockroach ran across the stone tiled floor in front of him.

Every piece of furniture held either a dirty piece of clothing, an old magazine, an empty compact disk box, a paperback book, or a pizza box lying across it. There were empty cans of beers, sodas, and juices, empty and half empty bottles of wine and liquor.

A dartboard dangled beside his head, hanging from a hook hammered into one of the wooden stairs of a circular staircase leading to a second floor. He brushed aside the dartboard and stepped into the room, wanting a cigarette. Instead, he strode straight across the room quickly, but careful not to step on anything, heading to the far sliding-glass doors that opened onto a patio that seemed to run around the entire apartment.

The sun dazzled him momentarily as he raised the blind. He slid the glass door open to sky and sea. The first winds of the *sharav* had arrived during the short walk down Hayarkon Street between the buildings that overlooked the beach and the rest of the city. The hot wind carried even more dust into the room along with the sounds of the city.

He turned to face the room again. It was at least ten strides long; and perhaps fifteen wide, he estimated, larger than an average family's in the country. To his left was a living area, with three long sofas forming a large U around a metal rack holding a black-screen TV, stereo, and shelves of videocassettes, CDs, and cassette tapes.

Below the huge windows that lined two walls was a bookshelf that went from the floor to Cohen's waist, topped by a counter. Books were piled on top of the counter and stacked inside the shelves, both in a library manner and as in a warehouse, one on top of the other. They were in four languages—English, French, Spanish (or was it Portuguese—Cohen wasn't sure), and Hebrew. The subjects ranged from philosophy and psychology to literature, history, and finance. But no subject had more than half a dozen books in its field.

Past the seating arrangement was the largest pool table Cohen ever saw. It was at least ten feet long, Cohen reckoned, with five carved wooden legs on each side supporting the length plus two more to balance the ends. A memory flooded him. It was in his father's large study in their house in Berlin, with its book-lined walls and huge shiny desk at one end and the billiard table at the other. Not that Cohen had often been allowed to play, and then only with his father in those few years of childhood between the time he was tall enough to reach the table wielding a cue to just a few nights before that day when Cohen watched in hiding as the Nazis took his parents away.

Until now, in Simon Levi-Tsur's apartment, he had never seen a pool table inside a private residence, except for that table in the house where he was born. He walked over to the table. Light from the half-blinded window fell in sharp straight lines over the dull green of the dust-covered felt. He blew at the dust on a cluster of balls, and for a second they seemed to sparkle with their colors. He picked up a green ball and raced it across the table to a side pocket. It made a sound that ended with a bump and then rolled again briefly until it made a click. Cohen smiled.

It was neither winning nor losing that he enjoyed but the competition against himself, finding something fateful in his hits and misses. Luck wasn't behind success as much as the control of patience at lining up the shot, considering the amount of force to throw past the ball down the stick. There were at least thirty balls on the table, Cohen guessed, half were red. He preferred pool.

Across the room was a twelve-chair dining table, and beyond it a kitchen open to the entire room. The counters were covered with the leftovers of meals both delivered and made. Four copper pots sat on the stove burners. All four pots were burnt. Cohen cast an envious eye over some of the abused kitchen equipment, and felt himself getting even angrier at the spoiled boy.

He stuck his head outdoors onto the patio, made note of potted plants gone wild, then dead, and looked up. He could see the roof of the room upstairs, and it drew him back into the wasteful anarchy of the boy's loft, to the circular stairs.

The heat was saunalike in the much smaller room, which was about half the size of the loft a floor below. Scattered about the floor were five mattresses and dozens of pillows. Stacks of sheets and towels were piled on a seat-width ledge that went around the entire room, except for a half-bath in the northeast corner of the room, just like one behind the kitchen area downstairs, where the toilets were hidden. The shower was not in a stall on the second floor. It was made of a showerhead hanging from the ceiling above a circle of white tiles that tilted in a slight concave way to a drain in the floor to collect the running water.

He walked across the room to the sliding doors that were like those a floor below. They opened onto a smaller patio than the one beneath him, but in the center of this terrace was a standing wooden tub large enough for at least six people.

He went out to the patio and looked down on the people on the beach below. They were small bits of color moving across the rippled field of white sand tracked by footsteps and the random wavy pattern of the tide's deposit at the edge of the damp sand all the way to the white curves of the surf. The water in the tub was green, sickly still, and smelling of decay.

Simon Levi-Tsur and his grandfather. Yaffe and his minister. Cohen swallowed back the sour taste rising from his stomach, which had only seen coffee and cognac that day, then began his search for a clue to the boy's whereabouts.

He started with the dirty clothes, searching every pocket for scraps of information, tossing them all into a pile in the middle of the area defined by the three sofas. A wad of cash turned up in the pockets of a pair of faded jeans. Two matchbooks turned up in two shirt pockets. He pocketed it all, continuing the search, gradually creating the semblance of order in the room. He didn't wash the pots, pans, or dishes, nor empty ashtrays—though he did sort through one with a pencil, found some dead hashish cigarettes and then noticed an instant porridge can on the dining room table. It was full of tobacco mixed with hashish.

The dining table served as a desk for the boy. There was a spilled stack of receipts beside a PC at one end of the glass table. He noticed it was cabled to the telephone. He smiled as he turned on the machine. It opened in Windows, right to the games window. Two dozen icons colored the screen. Cohen closed the games windows and went back to the program manager, and from it into the file manager. No directory was called Letters or Personal. But there was one called Fax. He learned enough about the computer not to be afraid to try out a program. Cohen opened the directory and went to the executable file, clicking to make the program run.

There was something called Log in one of the fax program's dropdown menus. Cohen clicked. A window opened with a list of nine faxes sent and received through the machine. Eight had gone out within two hours in the last week of December. Cohen clicked on one of those and the screen opened to a picture of the word Testing, typed in various typefaces made in the Write program in Windows. The ninth fax was the only one that was actually a correspondence, rather than merely testing the machine. It went to Raphael Levi-Tsur, and was sent on the last day of the past year. A short note, it wished his grandfather well for the new year, expressed rather formal condolences for the death of Rose, and apologies for missing the funeral. The fax was only four sentences long, including a postscript asking if it would be possible for the January deposit to be available for Simon's withdrawal on the thirtieth, and not the thirty-first of the month.

He used the file manager to search for the date of the last changed file in the computer, trying to find when Simon last used the machine. It was early March. Cohen clicked on the file. It turned out to be the most recent statistics for a blackjack game, showing Simon had won seven thousand dollars against the machine.

Cohen looked up from the computer screen, sighing. The sun was a gold platter standing on its rim at the edge of the sea. It was too easy to say that Raphael gave the boy everything but love. There was an illness at work in the cold formality of the condolence note about the death of someone the boy had known all his life. Cohen shivered slightly, but it wasn't because of the heat. Simon Levi-Tsur was a very lonely person.

The darkness outside crept around in the room until it enveloped him sitting at the computer staring at the lit screen. Finally, he moved, using his remote control to check his answering machine at home from Levi-Tsur's phone in Tel Aviv. Ahuva left him a message on his machine, saying she was attending a dinner party that night for a visiting law professor from an American university and that she had called to find out how the meeting with the minister went.

There were no other messages. He put down the phone, thinking. Then he punched a number on the phone pad. When he reached the fifth digit, he halted, cursed himself, and then pulled out his personal telephone directory from his wallet. The slim plastic-covered booklet was dog-eared, with many of the names and numbers written in a faded pencil mark. Those were the numbers he knew by heart. The new number he was seeking was written in blue ink in Cohen's neat, clear handwriting.

"Nissim?" he asked to the hello that answered the number.

"What a surprise," Levy answered, immediately recognizing the voice, and pleased.

"Just calling to see how you and Hagit are doing," Cohen said.

"They should have listened to you," Levy said, ignoring the personal question. "Are you going to testify?"

"They didn't ask," Cohen said. "And they won't."

"You could have asked them to let you speak."

"Their mandate was for the incident. Not for the history behind it. At most they'll make recommendations for the future."

Levy knew Cohen well enough to recognize the gruffness in Cohen's voice that said he didn't want to discuss it further. "We're fine," Levy said. "Hagit's teaching at the elementary school here."

"I thought she was a high-school teacher."

"No openings. They needed me down here pretty quickly, after Ravid was dumped." Ravid was fired from the force after a Justice Ministry squad investigating police corruption fingered the patrol commander for the Yeroham area as a police leak to a gang specializing in stolen cars in southern Israel.

"So Hagit had to take what was available," Levy was saying. "It's okay. We'll manage. Maybe next year she'll get a high school class."

"If you need anything," said Cohen. "Money. I have plenty now." There was a pause at the end of the line.

"I couldn't ask you," Levy finally said, quickly adding, "even if I needed. Which I don't," he ended with finality.

"Well, if you do, just let me know. I don't want you to have money worries."

Levy laughed.

"What?" Cohen asked, surprised.

"I worked five years for you, and you kept me worried twenty-four hours a day. About cases. Now you can't worry me about cases, so you want me to worry about money."

"Just promise me that if you need any help, anything, you'll let me know."

"Is everything all right, Avram?" Levy asked, suddenly realizing that Cohen was the one who was worried, using Cohen's first name in a rare display of emotion.

"Yes, fine, fine," Cohen said. "You take care of yourself. And your wife."

"That's just what I'm doing," Levy said carefully. "And you, too."

There was something more than caution in the turn the conversation took.

"Good," said Cohen. "So, I'll hear from you."

"Of course. The only reason I haven't called since we've been down here is that . . ."

Cohen interrupted. "No need for explanations. I understand. Learning the new job."

"Right," said Levy, picking up on Cohen's hint. "I've been terrifically busy. We rented a house right on the edge of town. Our backyard is the desert. I've got some pictures. I thought of sending you one. But I know you. Getting you down here would be impossible. Unless . . ."

"We'll see," Cohen said, interrupting again, and then adding a good-bye. He knew what Levy was planning to say—"Unless a case brought you down."

Hanging up, he lined up his findings on the table. The photo, key, and the piece of paper with the contact numbers he received from the old banker, the matchbooks, and, from under the last clean towel in the freestanding cabinet near the huge tub, a plastic-capped bottle of prescription drugs.

It was empty. The prescription was from London. The drug was lithium carbonate. He knew—but only vaguely—that it was used for certain kinds of mental illness, and he cursed himself for not catching that thread in Raphael Levi-Tsur's discomforting explanation of his grandson. Then he decided that Levi-Tsur probably wouldn't have admitted the boy was on a drug treatment.

If he knew more, Cohen would have started with the boy's doctor, one Harvey Lang of London listed on the sticker. Raphael or Caroline Jones should give him the phone number. He punched at the phone again. The number they gave him in Tel Aviv was an answering machine. Cohen expected a human voice. Getting an electronic mailbox made him growl at her that he had called. He checked his watch and added the time to his message before hanging up without saying good-bye.

He looked at his watch. The night enveloped the sea beyond the windows. The wind picked up, making the venetian blinds rattle. Before heading out into the city, he'd start with the neighbors.

He harbored no illusions they would be able to help. First there were only a few, as the mailboxes downstairs in the lobby proved. Second, he doubted whether Simon Levi-Tsur was the kind of tenant who made it his business to know his neighbors. But Cohen needed to try. Canvassing was the habit and custom and drill, the essential work of the policeman, and like the systematic roundup of all the waste and unwashed clothes upstairs in Simon's flat, the very familiarity of the process as something he knew how to do gave Cohen a good feeling.

He used the service stairs down the building, stopping at each floor to knock on doors, hoping for a neighbor who recognized the young man in the picture. But he wasn't very lucky. Most of the apartments were empty. Two doors opened to residents. One said he was a guest of the owner, who was out of the country, and knew nothing of the other residents. The other was an airline stewardess, who said she had rented the flat only a few weeks before and had yet to meet her neighbors. As Cohen backed away from the door, she asked him if he knew someone who was looking to share an apartment in the city.

On the fourth floor, he waited for the roar of a vacuum cleaner to come to an end before the bell or his knocking could be heard. An African opened the door. There were hundreds, maybe even thousands of them in Tel Aviv, earning day wages from which they saved monthly packets of money to send home. Most were from Ghana, many from Sierra Leone.

He was tall and thin and wore a three-button jersey and new jeans. Small beads of sweat were gathered on his forehead. Around his neck he wore a small gold cross on a slender chain. His face wore a natural smile created by a pair of dominating buck teeth. Behind him, Cohen could see a lavish living room of Persian carpets and carved wood furniture.

"Mister Goldberg is not home," said the African in a heavily accented English that carried a foreign melody to Cohen's ear. Instead of the gutturals that Europeans brought to the language, an African mother tongue made the consonants ring.

"Maybe you can help me," Cohen tried in English.

"Mr. Goldberg is not home," the African repeated, starting to close the door.

Cohen took a step forward, his foot preventing the door from closing completely. He pointed his forefinger up the stairs. "Not Goldberg. Levi-Tsur. Mr. Levi-Tsur, from upstairs." He patted his hip pocket where he had slipped the square envelope with the Polaroid.

The African took a step backward, afraid, trying to close the door. Cohen's foot was still in it, the door's edge digging into the sneaker. He managed to get the envelope out of his pocket. "Relax," he said, showing the African the square blue envelope with the hotel insignia in its upper corner. The black man eased his pressure on the door. Cohen plucked out the picture, and showed it to the African, but was unable to decipher the man's expression as the African studied the picture.

"The young man from upstairs. Mr. Levi-Tsur," he said. "Did you ever see him?"

"Upstairs?" the African repeated, raising furrows on his brow.

"Yes," said Cohen, relieved.

"Not here. Upstairs."

Cohen wanted to explode. He smiled. "I know. What's your name?"

"I have papers. Proper visa," the African answered nervously. Most of the Africans were long overdue on their visas, which were usually granted for a three-month study period at one of the agricultural training institutes. Most of the students returned to their home countries. Some stayed. Those who did found work that Israelis

71

wouldn't do themselves and preferred not to have Arabs perform. House cleaning for the upper middle class was at the top of the list.

"My name is Cohen," the Jerusalemite tried. He put on his friendliest smile.

"You are police?" the African asked, suspiciously.

"No. I'm not from the police," Cohen sighed, feeling as sorry for the African's fear as he did for himself. He smiled again. "What's your name?"

"Camara," the African said. He lowered his eyes as he shook Cohen's offered hand.

"Where are you from, Camara?"

"Sierra Leone," the man said.

"I'm from Jerusalem."

"Ah," the African responded, as if it explained everything.

"Do you recognize this young man?" Cohen tried.

"Yes. From upstairs. He's not here."

"I know," said Cohen. "I'm trying to find him."

"Ah," the African said again, as if everything was now clear. "I don't know," he shrugged.

"When was the last time you saw him?"

The African's posture changed as he thought, from holding the door, to hand on hip. He was thinking. "He made a big party. What is the holiday with the masks?"

"A party?" Cohen asked, surprised.

"Yes.

"Purim," Cohen said.

"Yes. Purim. A big party. I cleaned his place after this party."

The holiday fell late that February. "It doesn't look like anyone cleaned his house lately," Cohen pointed out.

"Yes," the African sighed. "Mr. Goldberg doesn't like him," he added, to explain his sorrow.

He backed out of the entrance, and his eyes flickered to the name on the doorbell of the apartment next to the doorway in the corridor. "Mr. Goldberg didn't want you working for Levi-Tsur?" Cohen asked.

"No, no. Mr. Goldberg does not like that wild boy." The African pointed up, toward the penthouse apartment and shook his head. "Mr. Goldberg calls him *vilde haya.*"

"But you did clean up? After the Purim party? And then Gold-berg said you couldn't work for him anymore?"

"Yes."

"Was it a big party?"

"Oh yes," the African said. "Two days to clean up."

"I believe it," Cohen said. He was still stymied. "Did he pay you for your work?"

"He paid. And asked me to clean again."

"But Goldberg said you couldn't."

"Yes. I tell him Mr. Goldberg said no. He got very mad. Lucky, Mr. Goldberg wasn't here. That boy is very wild."

"And that was the last time you saw him?"

Camara nodded.

"After Purim?"

Camara nodded again, then added, "He owes you money?"

Cohen shook his head. "No, it is a personal matter."

"Ah," said Camara. "Religious?"

The question shocked Cohen. "Why do you say religious?"

"Because one came, also looking for him."

Cohen was stunned, and couldn't help but start with the question of how the African knew the visitor was religious.

"Black pants. White shirt. Beard. And on his head . . ." He placed his palm on his head to imitate a *kippa*. "A yellow one," he added.

"Yellow?" Cohen asked, just to be sure, not doubting the African's description but the color's significance. The settlement movement made the knitted *kippa* as its fashion, while the non-Zionist *haredim* preferred black, with the respectable wearing hats.

"Yellow," the African said. He made a circle by touching the tips of his thumbs and the tips of his forefingers. "Smaller," he said.

"When was this?"

"Last week."

"What day?"

"Tuesday."

"How do you know he was looking for Levi-Tsur?"

"He asked me."

"Did he say why he was looking for Levi-Tsur?"

The African pursed his lips. "No. Just if Levi-Tsur lived here. I was taking down garbage."

"Has anyone else been here?" Cohen asked.

The African frowned and shook his head no.

Cohen thanked Camara, and then asked for Goldberg's telephone number. The African was nervous about giving it away. "It's all right. I work for the boy's grandfather," Cohen said. The mention of a grandfather seemed to make an impression on the African. He gave Cohen the number, and then said he still had much work to do getting ready for Mr. Goldberg.

To Cohen's eyes, the apartment beyond the doorway seemed spic and span. But Goldberg's standards were obviously higher than either Cohen's or Simon Levi-Tsur's.

· 7 ·

The wind was an evil yellow as Cohen came into the night. The *sharav* from the North African desert to the southwest was finally full-blown. The temperature was rising into the night and the yellow dust under the lights of the city gave everything a fake golden glow. He was facing south as he came out of the building on the quiet street between the beach and Allenby. To his right, a block away, the cars beside the beach boardwalk made a traffic jam that shimmered against the black of the sea at night.

He needed a pharmacist to tell him about the drugs, and he had the matchbooks to follow—one was white with an elegant typeface for an address on Allenby Street. The other matchbook was orange, with a nonsense name, Mazezuma, barely readable in a green handwritten scrawl of Hebrew imprinted as a logo. No address.

He had not eaten, but a meal would weigh him down in the heat and he didn't want to get tired. He wondered if he should take a hotel room, to form a base of operations. His car was still in the public parking lot in the northern shadow of the hotel where he had met Nahmani. But he didn't want to drive in the city if he could avoid it. Worse comes to worst, he decided, he'd hire a taxi.

He took a deep breath, tasting dust in the air. Only the young, desperate, and lonely would be out on such a night. Half a block up the street toward the *shuk* a Pepsi sign flickered above a fluorescent-lit sandwich shop's entrance. He entered the little shop, immediately aware he had interrupted something between the man behind the counter and a hipless woman in a miniskirt almost the same orange as her colored hair, and a head taller than Cohen. He asked for a bottle of water.

The sandwich maker seemed too eager to handle Cohen's request, while the streetwalker glared at him unhappily. Cohen

75

winced a smile at her as he reached into his pocket for coins, bringing out the matchbooks, as well as a few shekels. She scowled back and turned away to study her reflection in the mirror.

Cohen picked out four of the little squat coins and slapped them on the counter. Then he laid out the two matchbooks on the counter beside the coins. "Another half a shekel," said the sandwich man. He was balding, with shiny black hair that he kept combed carefully backward into dark strands on his head.

Cohen didn't like greed but controlled his temper as he reached into his pocket for the extra fifty agorot. "You recognize either of these?" he asked, pointing to the matchbooks, the half shekel still in his hand.

The counterman put down the bottle, and reached for the matchbooks. Cohen opened the bottle and poured cold water down his dry throat. As he tilted his head back looking over the bottle, he scanned the shelf behind the counter looking for a bottle of cognac, from which he could add some taste to the water. There were a few Arak bottles, no cognac. But he wasn't in the mood for the licorice. The counterman was studying a matchbook in one hand, using a finger from the other to carefully scratch in one of the greasy furrows of hair combed straight backward across his head.

"Shosh?" the counterman called to the streetwalker, who had turned away from both men and was preening herself in the mirror. "Ever hear of a place, Mazeh something." Cohen glanced toward the streetwalker and realized the preening had been an act while she watched his reflection in the mirror.

The counterman's question made the streetwalker turn, give up on her preening, and go to the counter. Cohen's eyes went to her hands when she picked up the matchbook. They were large.

"Shmokim," she said, disgusted. Her voice was as low as her absurdly cut dress, which displayed a shallow cleavage.

"What's there?" Cohen asked.

"That stupid game with the stupid stick and stupid balls," she snarled back. The counterman laughed. Cohen looked at her with expectation.

"What?" Shosh demanded, cocking a hip at him.

"Where is it?" he asked.

"Not far. I can show you," Shosh promised, sidling up to him.

Cohen grinned back. "All I need is the address."

Shosh shrugged, realizing he wasn't a potential customer, then tossed him "it's your loss," before adding "somewhere next to Dizengoff Center."

"The street?" Cohen asked.

Shosh pouted, trying to play coquette, and then gave up, hands angrily on hips and said, "What do I look like? A cab driver?" Cohen laughed, which surprised her long enough for him to leave the sandwich shop, making sure to take the two matchbooks as well as the water bottle. As he stepped onto the sidewalk he heard Shosh call him "another one of the *shmokim.*"

He continued up Allenby toward his destination. The number 56 was painted on the wall above a padlocked yellow steel door at the corner of the building.

Cohen stepped back onto the sidewalk. There had been a movie theater on this block of Allenby, near the *shuk,* he remembered from thirty years before. On the second floor, someone had painted the windows black. On the third floor, a dim light illuminated a single window. To his right, a restaurant bar with broad windows closed to keep the air conditioning inside was packed with more kids just out of the army. In between was an alley lit with a few faux gas lamps, leading down into a deeper darkness of the back ways of the *shuk* at night.

A girl was shaking long, light hair loose after pulling off a motorcycle helmet. She was dressed totally in black, from shiny plastic pants to the jacket over a tight halter shirt that exposed a narrow waist with a pierced navel, when she pulled off the leather and zipper jacket. Her motorcycle was Japanese, full of red plastic molding for an aerodynamic shape. She tossed her hair backward and then raised her arms overhead, displaying an hourglass figure as she pulled back her long hair and tied it into a knot. Then she unzipped one of the pockets on her jacket. She pulled out a packet of cigarettes and, with a toss of her wrist, flicked up a cigarette. She caught one, then noticed that a second fell out.

Cohen also noticed. It was hand rolled. Just then, another motorcycle pulled up onto the sidewalk, blocking his view as it rolled into place between him and the woman just as she bent over to pick up the joint. It was none of his business, he was reminding himself, when he heard a Motorola radio's static from behind him on the sidewalk. He turned, intuitively responding to the sound so familiar from years of police work.

A taxi was stopped at the curb, letting out a well-dressed couple. Cohen vaguely remembered the man's chubby bald face. Someone connected to the music business, Cohen decided from the archive of his mind. For a second, their eyes locked. Cohen couldn't quite decipher the man's expression, but it either recognized Cohen for who he was or as a dirty old man too interested in the affairs of the young.

The female motorcyclist distracted the round-faced man by embracing his date, a zaftig brunette in a half-open blouse that revealed the embroidery of a half-cup brassiere beneath. Cohen watched as the three walked arm in arm to the restaurant entrance. Like a music box turning on and off with the opening and closing of its lid, loud music poured from the restaurant, as the doorman in sneakers, jeans, and a T-shirt pulled open the glass door. Then the music from the restaurant bar was gone as the door closed.

Cohen finished the bottle of mineral water he was still carrying, tilting his head back to drain all the water, while he scanned the sidewalk in the other direction.

A dark curtain billowed slightly out of a shop entrance a little way up the block. Cohen went through the curtain, finding himself in an empty video parlor except for a skinny man sitting at a desk, reading a newspaper. Two neat piles of five shekel coins were stacked on the table in front of him. Cohen coughed, clearing some dust from his lungs. The man looked up. "Is this Allenby 56?" Cohen asked.

"Why?" the man answered.

Cohen sighed, wishing for a cigarette. Since the heart attack in California, he was trying to keep to a strict diet when it came to tobacco. He wouldn't give up the pleasure, but he'd try to control the addiction with dignity. He dug into his pocket and pulled out the matchbooks, holding up the one that said Allenby 56.

"That's from next door," the man said.

"What is it?" Cohen asked.

The man looked down again at his newspaper.

"Bar. Dancing. For kids."

Cohen looked around at the video parlor. A large screen on a race car simulator was showing scenes from a tropical country, where the cars raced beside the beach. "This place is for kids, too, isn't it?" Cohen commented.

"Not the same kind," the skinny man said.

"They open tonight?" Cohen asked.

The man shrugged.

"Doesn't look very busy for you here tonight," said Cohen.

The man shrugged again. "I get paid if they come or they don't," he added, looking over the newspaper at Cohen. The inside headline was quoting a rabbi who called the peace treaty with the Palestinians a declaration of war. The sub-headline said the rabbi's speech was made at the gravesite of Baruch Goldstein, the religious doctor who had massacred the Moslems at prayer in Hebron.

"I guess it's early," Cohen tried, checking his watch. It was barely ten o'clock at night. The newspaper had been out since just after dawn that day.

"They open at midnight," the skinny man admitted. "But don't expect the chickies in there to pay any attention to an old man like you. Unless you have really big money to spread around."

Cohen backed out of the dimly lit parlor onto the sidewalk. More kids on motorcycles arrived at the restaurant across the alley. Across the street a man in short yellow pants and a faded green T-shirt was at the automated teller machine of a bank. The lit shop windows at street level blinked and glimmered, the upper floors of the smog-stained buildings were mostly dark. Shosh the street-walker had said somewhere near Dizengoff Center. It was about a mile away on foot through the narrow streets until he reached little Gan Meir park, which he'd cut through on his way. Once at Dizen-goff Center, he figured, it would be easy to find the pool hall.

Meanwhile, he felt good, despite the annoyance of his mission's circumstances. There was something pleasing in the familiarity of his efforts. The map of Tel Aviv in his mind was beginning to come back to him as he crossed Allenby, heading north on little Bialik Street toward the ugly round tower of apartments above Dizengoff Center.

The table at Simon's apartment and the matchbook that Shosh had identified as coming from a pool hall were two early pieces that came together. He had no idea how they connected elsewhere in the puzzle of the Levi-Tsur problem. But he was certain he would find out.

· 8 ·

There was a man dying on a bus bench on Bograshov Street. The man was wearing an old raincoat, and lying on the bench he looked like a mound of old clothes hiding a suspicious object that the bomb squad would neutralize with a shotgun wielded by a robot.

Blue, yellow, and red lights filled the street. An ambulance and a police car blocked the traffic heading toward the beach. An elderly woman in a cream-colored bathrobe, whom Cohen guessed had called the police about the unmoving man, stood beside the ambulance with a worried look on her face.

She was talking to a patrol cop making notes on his clipboard as Cohen walked by. "I think he's Russian," the woman was saying, pointing to an empty bottle of vodka lying under the bench. Cohen paused, instinctively glancing at her evidence. He caught the young cop's eye for a second, but then realized he had nothing to say, nor was there anything he could do.

The ugly round tower of the apartment complex towering high above Dizengoff Center ahead was brown and white against the night sky. Lights on in the upper floor apartments gave off a fake glow of warmth as they peered down haughtily on the city. He offered his own moment of silence to the mortality of the homeless man and pressed on, lucky that day for a second time.

Turning off Bograshov he saw the sign Mazezuma. He waited for a bus to cross the street and hustled across, down the street and up the four stairs to the pool hall door. He pulled it open. A blast of freezing air blew into his face.

One table was occupied by a kid with an arm in a cast, whom Cohen guessed was probably a soldier on R&R from some accident or incident. The youngster was trying to teach his date how to line up a shot, leaning over her body as he held his hands on the cue over hers.

At a second table, three Thai guest workers were conducting a serious game. One of them was about to stroke as Cohen walked into his view down the cue. The little man had a wreath of dragons coiled up his arms in colorful tattoos, and he paused, waiting for Cohen to move. Cohen looked to his right.

A bearded man with deep-set eyes and a pair of gold chains around his neck sat behind a counter, looking bored. The Thai resumed his shot. Cohen reached into his hip pocket for the envelope with the photo as he approached the bearded man.

"Shalom," Cohen began.

"Ten shekels for half an hour," the man said. Behind him was a refrigerator. He turned on the swivel chair and opened the door. Goldstar beer bottles and Coca-Cola cans were stacked inside. The man pulled out a beer and used a bottle opener with a nude female as its handle to open the bottle.

Cohen laid the picture on the counter. The pool hall owner ignored it, studying Cohen's face with a suspicious curiosity. "I know you, don't I?" the man finally said.

"Maybe," Cohen said. "Look at the picture," he added, pointing a stubby finger at the boy in the middle.

The pool hall owner was still convinced he knew Cohen. Almost reluctantly, he looked away from the detective to glance again at the picture. "Okay. I looked," he said, refusing to take responsibility for what he saw, and more interested in why Cohen appeared familiar.

"Recognize him?" Cohen demanded, his voice a rough gravelly rumble.

The man looked down again. Cohen watched his face for a clue. But the pool hall owner's expression didn't change as he looked back at Cohen. The air-conditioning was freezing. The soldier on leave at the corner table with his girlfriend was leaning over her body lasciviously. One of the Thais was preparing to break. His friends were staring at the girl's exposed cleavage. The pool hall owner tilted the beer bottle back and sucked at it, looking first at the ceiling and then back to Cohen, who pulled out a cigarette and studied the dry tobacco at its end, rolling it back and forth between his thumb and forefinger.

"The rich kid," the pool hall man finally said, giving in to Cohen's patience. "All right. What about him?"

"His name?" the detective asked, testing his informant.

"Shlomo something, or maybe Samson. I can't remember."

"Does he come in here often?"

"For a while, every day. Then he stopped."

"When?"

"I dunno. Weeks ago. Months ago. Who knows? Time flies," the man said, and then slapped his hand on the table. "I don't even know why I'm telling you this. I certainly don't care."

"About what?"

"About what happens to him. Maniac. Crazy *Anglo-saxim*." He shook his head. There were streaks of premature white in the unkempt beard, which was as uncombed as an absent-minded rabbi's. "You're Cohen? Aren't you?" he suddenly said.

Cohen ignored the question. "Did he speak Hebrew?" he asked.

"Yeah, but with an accent, you know. Funny Rs and Ls." The pool hall man's accent was North African. "Yeah. You're Cohen. We never met. You wouldn't remember me. I mean, not personally, if you know what I mean. But I remember you. I'm from Musrara," he said, saying it as proudly as if he still lived in the West Jerusalem neighborhood overlooking Damascus Gate in the Old City's wall.

"And afterwards, Ramle?" Cohen added with a smile, naming the prison.

The bearded man grinned, exposing yellow teeth. "I wasn't that old. They sent me to Tel Monde," he added. "But they held me a few days in the Russian Compound. I would see you there. And some of the older guys talked about you. You were a lot younger then, too," he pointed out.

"Who took you down?" Cohen asked.

"Sa'adia Biton," said the pool hall owner. "I'm Dado." He stuck his hand out to shake Cohen's.

"He was from Musrara, too," Cohen said, holding onto Dado's hand a moment longer, forcing the explanation from him.

"I was a teenager. I stole cars. It was a long time ago." They were facts listed in order.

Cohen let go of the handshake and looked around at the pool hall. He didn't have to ask the question, knowing the answer would come.

"Don't get me wrong," the man said. "I'm clean. It straightened me out. A bit, at least. I've been clean for years. I pay my taxes. And," he added, lowering his voice, as low a grumble as Cohen's, "sometimes I help out your buddies if they ask me."

"Why a pool hall?" asked Cohen.

"Why not? Remember that movie, Paul Newman, Tom Cruise?" He pointed to the far wall of the room. A poster for the movie hung on the wall. "It brought in the kids. Good business," Dado said.

Cohen only went to the cinema at Ahuva's insistence, but surfed the media looking for answers to the questions the kids asked. Kids made trouble. Sometimes it was for a good cause, sometimes for a bad. Sometimes it was for no cause at all except the fun of the thing. Trouble wasn't bad as long as it didn't redouble on itself and hurt someone. When he got cable, the first thing Cohen looked at after CNN was MTV. Sometimes he didn't see much difference. Covering the media was a preventive measure against nasty surprises, as far as Cohen was concerned.

"I saw my chance," the pool hall owner was saying. He knocked the table. "Thanks god," he added, "it's worked out. Ten years I been here. And no trouble. My kid's gonna finish school." Over Cohen's shoulder the Thais were quarreling. "Hey!!" Dado shouted. The chatter died down into whispers.

"Tell me about this kid," Cohen asked, picking up the picture.

"Asshole. All money this way and that. Didn't know how to lose without going crazy."

"Money games?"

"Yeah, but nobody off the street could keep up with him. And none of the real players wanted anything to do with him. Too young, too loud."

"What about private? Games at his place?"

"Yeah, came in one day, bragged his table arrived. 'Won't need this dump anymore,' he said. Kicked the bad leg on that table," the man said, pointing toward the table beyond the kid in the cast and his tigress. "He knew it would fuck it up. Didn't care. Tossed down enough cash to buy a new one, and walked out."

"And never came back?"

"He's a shmuck," Dado said. "Of course he came back."

"When was that?"

"Few weeks later. Came in."

"When?"

"Few weeks ago."

"Alone?"

"No. He usually came with a nice piece hanging on his wallet arm."

"And?" Cohen pressed.

"What?"

"Did he stay? Play?"

"Yeah, they played. Until I threw him out."

"Why?"

"He got weird. This rabbi comes around. You know, some kind of religious type. Completely crazy, wanted to know if anyone put on *tefillin* that day. Crazy, right? It was the week of the demonstrations after the massacre. First for the commission, then against. Remember? There were a lot of 'em in town that day. And that night, this one shows up. Very strange. And this one," he said, stabbing with a finger at the picture, "goes absolutely nuts. He starts shouting at the rabbi for talking, for making his Vicki miss her shot. That's what pissed me off. You know, the guy's a rabbi, right? Where's the kid's respect?"

"Just because someone looks like a rabbi doesn't make him one," Cohen pointed out. He wasn't defending the kid, but Cohen didn't believe in coincidence. One religious man was one thing. Two, another.

"Okay, let's say he was super religious," Dado said. "A Jew working at being Jewish. Maybe there is something to that. Not for me, mind you. That's why I'm here, not up there. In Jerusalem."

"What did the rabbi look like?" Cohen asked.

"A *dos*," said the bearded man, using the Jerusalem slang. "Big white *kippa*, sneakers, jeans, *tzitziyot* hanging out from under his shirt."

"Wait a second," Cohen interrupted. "This rabbi? He wasn't *shahor*?" Cohen asked, using the Hebrew word for black, referring to the man's clothing, and meaning a *haredi* dressed like a Polish nobleman in the sixteenth century, or in their more modern version, in simple black suits and white shirts, usually with no tie.

Dado thought for a moment. "You're right. He wasn't *shahor*. But definitely religious. And a beard as crazy as mine." His smile made a yellow cave of stained teeth in the midst of his thick beard as he pulled at the hair and grinned at Cohen. "Like a settler," added Dado.

Something was wrong, Cohen thought. The African described working-class *dos*—black trousers, white shirt, black *kippa*. Dado was describing one of the more radical of the mystic nationalists from the settlements.

Coincidences were for the innocent, Cohen always said. Nothing he had learned so far about Levi-Tsur showed innocence, except perhaps the old man's desire to believe in his grandson's innocence.

"You know the rabbi's name?" Cohen asked Dado.

The pool hall owner shook his head.

"Was he Sephardi? Ashkenazi?" Cohen tried.

Dado scratched at his beard.

"American? Russian? New immigrant?"

Dado thought for a moment. "American," he decided, surprising Cohen.

"Was he alone?"

"He came in alone. But there was a buddy of his with him, on the sidewalk, waiting for him."

"How old was he?"

"Hard to tell. Forty? Fifty? His beard was grayer than mine. But who knows."

"I don't understand," Cohen pressed. "What was he doing here?"

"I told you it was strange. I thought he was a little, well, stoned. Maybe he was drunk. I don't know. They were probably at the demonstration that night. Against the treaty with the terrorists. He said he was in mourning and looking for psalm readers."

"In a pool hall?"

"That's what I told him. But he said that there must be one righteous man in Sodom."

"Sodom?" Cohen checked.

"Sodom and Gemorrah. That's what he called the city. At least that's what I understood he was saying. That Tel Aviv was like Sodom."

"Did he say 'in a city like' Tel Aviv or did he say it was Sodom?" Cohen asked.

But Dado the pool hall owner didn't understand the difference, while Cohen, knowing all too well the difference between those who believed in God and those who claim to know what God believes, wondered if his path on the search for Simon Levi-Tsur would yet cross that of the strange religious supplicant seeking mourners in the pool halls of Sodom.

· 9 ·

Cohen was lucky a third time that day. Dado gave him a graphic description of Vicki, the girl on Levi-Tsur's arm that night in the pool hall. "Tall, long legs, lots of blonde hair, and amazing eyes," said the pool hall owner. He did not display any envy of Levi-Tsur's money. But he couldn't hide his envy of Levi-Tsur's proprietorship over the girl.

Cohen arrived back at the yellow steel door on Allenby a little after midnight. This time it wasn't bolted with a padlock, but manned by a doorman conducting a selection process outside, picking and choosing from a crowd at the door, deciding who would be allowed inside to pay an entrance fee. Cohen brushed up into the first ring of onlookers pressed against the invisible space at the entrance formed by the bouncer's projection of his biceps. Most of the people lined up to get in were dressed in black. The young men around Cohen eyed him suspiciously, the young women either ignored him or eyed him with unabashed curiosity.

Beyond the bouncer, who was a squat, ex-footballer at least ten years older than most of the people trying to get into the club, Cohen could see a wooden table, with a black-haired woman sitting behind it, taking cash from those lucky enough to be allowed inside. The walls behind her were painted a bright red.

"Coming through, coming through," someone was saying behind Cohen. He turned. The shaven-head, round-faced man he saw earlier getting out of the cab was coming from the restaurant next door, flanked by two women, the blonde from the red bike and the busty brunette. The man walked with a slight tilt, as if on the deck of a yawing boat. Cohen stepped aside, and the three swept past him.

But just before they were swallowed up into the darkness of the red anteroom, the round-faced man paused, looked back, and then deliberately pointed at Cohen while whispering something into the ear of the blonde.

Cohen stared back. The girls eyes widened, then narrowed as she leaned over to recite into the other woman's ear what she just had heard from the man with the shaved head. "No!" the busty girl shrieked, and then quickly covered her mouth, glancing around the crowd as if she had let loose a terrific secret, embarrassed by her lapse, not its reason.

She giggled and ducked inside, dragging the blonde woman by the hand, leaving the round-faced man on the doorstep with the bouncer, whose attention was now drawn angrily to Cohen.

"All right, uncle. You've seen enough," the bouncer said, taking a step down off the sill of the door. "It's time for you to . . ."

"Uzi," the bald man said, grabbing the bouncer's arm. "I'd be careful if I were you. He's a cop." The bouncer froze. "It's okay. He's okay," the man added, stepping ahead of the ex-footballer and sticking out a hand for Cohen to take. "I was wondering if it was you when I got here, but wasn't sure. Now I am," he added when Cohen unhappily accepted the handshake. "I don't expect you'll remember me," the round-faced man said.

The voice, in addition to the tilted walk, jogged it all into place in Cohen's memory. It was not on the gossip page where Cohen first had noticed the man. It was during a raid on the army radio station's studio in the capital a few years before. The cops on the case had promised Cohen the raid would turn up cocaine. It turned out to be a little less than an ounce of Lebanese hash and a batch of soap powder, creating an embarrassment for Cohen as well as the army.

All seven staffers of the overnight shift at the Jerusalem studio were fired. Searches by the military police at their homes sent three technicians to trial, dropped down the tubes of military justice when the army needed a scapegoat.

The celebrity voices from the radio fared better. The round-faced soldier disappeared from the air after his trial but reappeared for his final year in the army as the hottest dj on Army Radio. It went to his head and he moved on to the state-owned station that caters to the teenage crowd. From there he was hired away as a talent spotter for a record company. Very quickly he rose to become a managing director. Cohen remembered that from the newspapers. But it was the entire memory of that unhappy night that passed through Cohen's mind when, for a second, he held the handshake. Only then did he remember the name. "Benny Dromi," he said, letting the disk jockey's limp hand drop away from his.

"Deputy Commander Cohen," smiled Dromi. "And what brings you down to Tel Aviv? And to such a place?" Dromi's smile was like an oval gash in his round balding face, and his tone was equally artificial, an actor's voice projected from an invented personality. There was something inherently snide in all of Dromi's radio personalities. That was something else Cohen remembered. He figured Dromi must be in his mid-thirties, older than most of the people Cohen saw go through the yellow door into the club.

"I'm on a search," Cohen admitted frankly.

"For the truth, I hope," said Dromi, thinking he was being clever.

"Are you going to take it inside, or leave it out?" Uzi the doorman asked.

"Come in, be my guest," the celebrity asked Cohen, obviously wanting to add the aged man to the two women already decorating his entourage's entrée to the nightclub.

"Too loud," Cohen guessed. "But give me a few minutes of your time," he went on, smiling as the music executive stepped aside while leering at a pair of slender kids in black heading through the yellow door into the lobby. "Just a few minutes," Cohen repeated. Dromi's eyes changed from amused to curious.

With the door open, the music from inside was a loud, insidious thump of electronic heartbeat. "It's too loud," Cohen protested again when Dromi made a gesture inviting Cohen into the nightclub. The standoff was making the bouncer nervous. A raven-haired woman, taller than both Cohen and Dromi, broke into the scene.

"Dahlia!" Dromi squawked enthusiastically, holding out his hands past Cohen to greet her. "Benny!" she squealed back, grabbing both his hands. They pecked at the air around each other's faces.

"Dromi," Cohen snapped. The music executive's eyes jerked back to Cohen. Dahlia looked down at Cohen haughtily. Dromi sadly turned to the young woman.

"I'll be right in," he promised the girl. She was flabbergasted that

Dromi preferred Cohen's company to hers. "Get in there and warm up the floor for me," Dromi added, waving her away as he followed Cohen into the alley beside the entrance. Cohen went a step past a pool of street-lamp light, turned his back on the *shuk* to face Allenby Street, then pulled the envelope from his hip pocket, removing the Polaroid carefully. It was already beginning to crease from handling.

"Recognize him?" Cohen asked, handing the picture of Simon Levi-Tsur with his grandfather and secretary to Dromi, who held it by the corner and out to the light to study it. "The kid," Cohen prompted. Dromi shook his head. Cohen believed him. "You come here often?" Cohen tried.

Dromi's head wobbled with ambiguity. "Not every night. At least once a week."

"Know the owner?" Cohen demanded.

"Sure. What's this all about?" Dromi tried.

"What's his name?" Cohen asked.

"Why?" Dromi insisted. The reflection of yellow light from the street lamp glistened off his shaven head.

"Maybe he knows the kid," Cohen said.

"Who is he?"

"If you don't know, you don't need to know," Cohen said. "What's the owner's name?"

"Danny."

"Good," Cohen said patiently. "Progress."

"Why should I help you? You aren't even a cop anymore, from what I hear."

Cohen put a hand up, like a traffic cop stopping a car, and then dropped it gently into a fingertip touching Dromi's sternum, with just enough pressure to let the man know it wasn't a game. "Let's just say I remember when you still had hair," Cohen said softly. Before he could ask his next question, a girl's voice interrupted them from behind.

"Benny?"

Cohen waited for Benny's eyes to turn, and followed them to see the young woman. She came from around the building. "Dahlia said you were out here," she said to Dromi. Up close, Cohen realized the blonde was really honey colored. Cohen looked into her eyes but she nervously avoided his, stepping into the light of the street lamp and taking Dromi's arm. But the glance was enough to notice what Dado meant by amazing eyes: an extraordinary cool green, like a mountain forest after a brisk rain, when the sun is trying to burn away the last of the clouds.

Cohen followed his instinct. "Your name is Vicki? Yes?" he asked her.

"Benny?" she asked, completely surprised. "Who is this man? Now I don't know what to believe. I thought you were kidding, you said, telling Dorit that he's a policeman. But then Dahlia came in and said . . ." She turned to Cohen. "And how do you know my name?"

"Shut up, Vicki," Dromi said, his eyes wondering if Cohen would hold him to blame for not volunteering what he didn't know that he knew.

Cohen showed Vicki the picture. "You know him?" he asked. She scowled, disliking quizzes. But it only took a single glance from her at the picture to get the response he was after. "Oh my God. Don't ask. What a nightmare. Don't ask."

"You shouldn't have said that, Vicki," Dromi moaned, grinning at her as she handed the photo back to Cohen as if it was contaminated.

Cohen smiled at her, holding out his arm for her to take but ready to take hers. "*Gveret* Vicki," Cohen said, using the Hebrew word for lady, as well as missus. The gesture confused her. She looked at Dromi. He shrugged.

"Vicki, this is Deputy Commander Cohen," and added a slight shove of his own, pushing her toward him. Cohen smiled modestly at her. "But don't worry, darling," the music executive added. "He's perfect for you. A real millionaire. Just your style."

Cohen didn't use any strength, just a gentle touch, but it led her down the alley beside the dance hall toward the darkness of the *shuk* at night. He broke the silence once the rhythm of her boots was louder than the rumble of action behind them.

"Have you eaten today?" he asked.

"No," she admitted. She threw one backward glance over her shoulder at Dromi standing under the streetlight laughing at them both, and then asked Cohen, "Are you really a millionaire?"

Cohen nodded. "I know a place," he added.

"And a detective?" she asked him.

"This way," he said, pointing to the left, away from the last reflection of night-lights from the strip of action on Allenby, into a short block that connected to the central avenue of the open market's locked stands and steel, iron, and aluminum doors shut against the empty *shuk* at night. He let go of her arm. It was a mistake.

"You parked in the *shuk*?" she asked.

"No," he admitted, "But we're almost there."

"Oh, God, no," she said, pausing in the middle of the street. "You're taking me to Nahlat Binyamin. To Rotem's. I can't stand that place. Nobody'll admit that the food's lousy, the music's too loud, the . . ."

"I do not know Rotem's," Cohen said, reaching for her arm. She relaxed slightly. "We are going to another place. Come. It's good food. Just through there." He pointed down a narrow alley that had not changed in thirty years.

Neither had the restaurant. Two burly old men, sitting at two separate tables with their backs to each other, both looked up from their silent meals as Cohen and Vicki came in. The two old men glared at each other, and then ducked their heads back to their solitary meals. In that moment, entering the neon-lit room, which served a few good salads, bean soup, humus, tehina, and ful, and seeing the hawk-faced man behind the counter, he forgot that old Zevik was dead.

But the man behind the counter only looked just like the dead man, a well-respected underworld judge in the days when the struggle for turf in the *shuk* included protection rackets and matters of family honor between warring tribes. The same photograph of Zevik's father, who walked from Bukhara all the way down through southern Turkey when he heard Jews were going back to the Land of Israel, hung on the wall under a flickering electric red eternal lamp.

Cohen figured the man behind the counter was one of Zevik's grandchildren. The family long ago stopped earning its living from the secrets of the *shuk*, but it kept the secrets of their family kitchen—and out of respect for their traditions, made the little restaurant in the *shuk* a way station of work for everyone in the family. Zevik's children all went to university. But they kept the little restaurant going. In his day, Zevik was as fair as most of the judges Cohen knew on the bench, and did much to keep the streets of Tel Aviv safe. Cohen had gone to Zevik's funeral. But he wasn't in the restaurant to relive his personal history.

"Two regulars," he said to Zevik's grandson. "And a couple of water bottles."

He took Vicki's arm again, pulling her away from the gallery of generals, right- and left-wing politicians, various football players as well as stage performers, all hanging in photographs showing them at the tiny tables of the restaurant. In all of them, Zevik, short and dark, grinned back at the camera.

"You know, I was wondering when you'd show up," she said as he led her to the table in the far corner from the counter.

"Me?"

"Well, you know, the cops, someone looking for him. People don't disappear like that."

"So you know he disappeared."

"Are you kidding? I was there."

"Where?"

"Maybe I should start at the beginning," she said.

"That's always a good idea," Cohen agreed.

So she began. It started, she said, when Simon appeared one night in the winter at the Allenby club, walked across the dance floor without bumping into anyone, and asked her to join him for dinner. "I knew he was rich, of course. Very Anglo-Sexy, if you know what I mean. And Benny's right," she smiled at Cohen. "I'm only interested in very rich men." Cohen bowed his head to her, in an exaggerated gesture that carried enough irony to make her laugh, first at him, and then herself.

Their first night together began at the opening of a new Japanese restaurant in Herziliya, and continued to a high-stakes poker game in a Tiberias hotel where she sat bored in the corner for two hours while Simon won and lost, won and lost, while dance raged in the nightclub and the TV in the suite he took showed German skin flicks.

"I finally got him out of there," she told Cohen.

"How?"

She leaned forward, crooking a finger for Cohen to do the same.

She kept her eyes on his and brushed away the thick rope of hair that fell from the knot where she kept it tied in the back. She licked her lower lip slowly and then leaned even further across the table until Cohen could hear her breathing in his ear. "Like this," she whispered, the single Hebrew word two open-mouth breaths that turned into a warm, wet feeling in his ear. Even steeled for it, he was stirred, and just as suddenly she stopped, sitting back and smiling at Cohen like one of his detectives proving he had made the case.

Her expression changed as she tried to decipher Cohen's. He finally raised an eyebrow.

"He was young. It worked on him." She laughed. One of the burly old men raised his head. The other finished his soup and began admiring her animated figure.

"How did you get to Tiberias?" Cohen asked.

"He drove. A rented car. Fancy jeep. Later I found out he owned a very hot Alfa of his own. But he lost it."

"How?"

"In a poker game."

"In lieu of cash?"

"No, it was for the car itself. It was a very hot car. Only available through personal import, if you know what I mean."

Cohen grinned slightly, a twitch of his upper lip. "That night at the pool hall . . ." he searched for the name in his mind.

"Mazezuma," she offered. "Yeah, he took me a few times. Then that table showed up in his flat, so he played at home."

"Except that one time, when the rabbi showed up."

She nodded.

"Who did he play with?"

"People," she said.

"What people?"

"People he bought," she explained.

"Bought?" Cohen asked.

"He didn't really have any friends. I realized that afterward. I mean nobody really cared when I told them what happened."

"Afterward? After the rabbi?" Cohen asked.

"Sort of, but later. I mean the rabbi thing was weird, of course. At the pool hall. What the hell was he doing there in the first place? He asked me if I was Rahab."

"The prostitute from Jericho?" Cohen asked. "Who helped Joshua?"

"Yeah. Weird, no? Especially because of me being religious. I mean originally. From a *haredi* family."

"Did Simon know that?"

"Sure," she said, proud of how she went from one extreme to the other in her rejection of religion.

"Please," Cohen tried again. "Maybe you should start at the beginning again."

"He was so screwed up. It's just that he was so, so . . ."

"Rich," Cohen suggested.

"He's very smart," she answered for herself. "Very educated. There was a lot I thought I could learn from him."

"And rich," Cohen added again, testing her cynicism. But Zevik's grandson interrupted before she could answer. Hot sesame bagels and *pita* from the bakery up the street, thick brown bean and tomato soup from the pot in the back kitchen, and a scattering of salads appeared on the table. Cohen dug in immediately, smiling at the first swallow of soup. She tentatively followed, starting with a piece of bread dunked in a sauce of smoked eggplant. Her expression echoed Cohen's appreciation of the food.

"And crazy," she added, digging in for a deeper scoop of the eggplant. She tapped at the green *s'hug*, red and green peppers mashed into a glittering brown of hot sauce.

"At first," Cohen suggested. Her eyes widened and she nodded vigorously, dramatizing the fact her mouth was full and she couldn't talk.

"It turned very bad," she finally admitted, after a deep gulp that made her throat seem even longer. Then suddenly she burped, as the hot sauce rebounded inside her empty stomach. "Great!" she chortled, drinking a long pull from one of the water bottles that Zevik's heir brought to the table.

But it still wasn't easy for Cohen to find out exactly what was the bad craziness, let alone the good, nor how she was there when Levi-Tsur disappeared, or where.

She continued telling her story, how the weeks went by from restaurants to parties, discotheques to nightclubs, card games and pool games. "And lots of fucking, of course," she emphasized. Before she used the word she explained to Cohen that she was definitely not referring to what she would rather call making love. "Though I must admit he was better than most in his age group," she added apologetically, then burped again. "Until it got bad."

"How bad?" Cohen asked.

"There's a difference between lots of sex and too much sex," she said, "when it's like machines." Then there was silence for a little while as she concentrated on the soup. When she finished, she started another spiral of story for him.

Her name wasn't really Vicki, of course. It was Bracha, old-fashioned and conservative and she had changed it legally as soon as she was sixteen, and moved to Tel Aviv. She was nineteen and was proud to say the motorcycle was hers, and her license was for real, not a fake like some she had seen. She earned it modeling. And there were the gifts, of course, she added. "From rich men. And whatever you want to say about Simon, when he was nice, he was very nice. He gave me this," she said, pointing to her watch. Cohen was no expert, but it looked expensive, especially against the background of the old Formica tabletop. She sighed. "It's just that he turned mean so easily." There was another pause, and then she looked up at Cohen with a smile of understanding. "Of course, that's true about most men."

Cohen liked her as much as he disliked Simon Levi-Tsur. He didn't push her story forward impatiently. He let her tell it at her own pace and in her own way. He didn't know whether he won her confidence by guessing her name outside the club or because Dromi had promised her millions. But it was as if once she made up her mind that she would be with Cohen, she was entirely with him, focused entirely on being herself for him. There was no other way to explain it, Cohen thought, as she drew closer to the point of her tale.

"It all started with the acid." She reached across the Formica table and patted his hand, which was resting on his packet of Noblesse. There were five cigarettes left. He was proud of himself. It was now two in the morning. He had bought the pack on his way out of Jerusalem at noon that afternoon. Fifteen cigarettes in a day was a third of his intake a month earlier. She patted at his hand. "It's so cool the way you aren't shocked by drugs. But I can see you care," she said. "I wish I had you as my father."

"I'm old enough to be your grandfather," he pointed out.

"My father was fifty-two when I was born. When I grew these," she added wryly, pointing at her breasts with her thumbs and smiling at Cohen who kept his eyes on her eyes, "he made a point of proving to me that even old men can do it."

He coughed. She laughed. He smiled, aware he had blushed.

"I'd do it with you, if you want," she said.

"Why?" Cohen asked patiently.

She studied his face. "I like your eyes." She batted hers at him. "I think you like mine. Sometimes that's reason enough."

Cohen didn't blink. "Tell me what happened," he asked her. "After you took the acid."

She sighed. He couldn't tell if it was because she was disappointed that he wasn't pursuing sex or because she preferred the flirtation and seduction to the recounting of an annoying tale from her past. "We were at the club, and he invited some people back to his place. "You know it?" she asked.

He nodded.

"Upstairs and everything?"

He nodded again.

"So, we were up there, you know. . . Some of us."

"Who?" Cohen asked.

"I don't know if I should say. I mean, they left when it got really *bizarre.*" She used the French word in the way the English mean strange, then pulled a napkin from the dispenser on the table and used it to blow her nose. Cohen couldn't tell if it was the spice or emotion that affected her sinuses. "I should have left with them," she added.

"But you didn't."

"I didn't know what to do. It started when we were on the porch. The acid was real good. We went out on the patio on the roof, to smoke a little, look at the stars, let the air dry off the sweat." She smiled at Cohen.

"And?"

"He started crying."

"Crying?"

She nodded vigorously. "Tears and sniffling, the whole thing. He looked at me and asked for my forgiveness. He got down on his knees. It was so weird."

"What did you do?"

"I felt sorry for him. I patted his head."

"And?"

"We stayed like that for a while, and then he got up and wiped his eyes and asked me if I would go to Jerusalem with him. Right then and there."

"Jerusalem?" Cohen asked, astonished.

"Exactly my thoughts," she said. "I didn't want to go at first. But he said we'd go for the sunrise. Up to the Mount of Olives and watch the sunrise on the city. 'It's gorgeous,' he promised me."

"You've never been?" Cohen asked.

She shook her head. "That's the thing. I hadn't been to Jerusalem since I left home, and believe me the last thing my parents would let me do when I was with them was go to the Mount of Olives at dawn. They used to make us all go visit my uncle's family for the holidays. I hated it. But Simon was saying that it's great when you're stoned, that the sunrise is absolutely beautiful, that it's a whole new way of seeing the city. It all seemed kind of, well, romantic." She looked away from Cohen, embarrassed by the word.

"Did you go?"

She nodded at the pile of bagels, not at him. Then she looked up, and there was an anger in her eyes that answered his question.

"How'd you get there?"

"He drove. Fast. Up the mountain, right through the city, past the old city right into *intifada* land. Up to the Mount of Olives. When we got there it was still dark, before dawn, and that made him change his mind immediately."

"Why?"

"I don't know, he was really crazy. He decided that we should go to the *kotel.*"

"The Wall?" Cohen checked.

"Yeah. Now, I wasn't really dressed for it, if you know what I mean. I mean, I was in a miniskirt. And it was winter in Jerusalem. End of February. And I've been to that place enough to last me a lifetime."

"So, you didn't go . . ."

She shook her head, but then plunged on with her story. "'You'll miss the secret,' he said. He was nuts, dancing around, saying he was going to tell me the real secret. Sure," she scoffed, "him telling me a secret about the *kotel.* I grew up in a house where we weren't allowed to watch TV because of graven imagery, and he was going to tell me about secrets at the *kotel.* Forget it."

"I understand," Cohen said. "What happened next?"

"When I said I wasn't going out to the *kotel* with him, he said I could wait in the car, but he was going to the Wall. Okay, I said. But I wasn't going to traipse around down there at the Wall in the middle of the freezing night dressed the way I was. Besides, I might not like the *dossim*, but I don't think I have to do things just to make them mad. You know what I mean? Live and let live."

"Yes, I know what you mean," Cohen sighed. "So, he went alone?"

"He didn't understand why I didn't want to get out of the car. 'The sun's going to come up right over the Wall,' he shouted at me. 'We can't miss it!' 'So, go to the fucking Wall,' I said. 'I'll be fine. I'll wait.' " Vicki shook her head at the memory. "I was so stupid," she complained, more to herself than to Cohen.

"Why?"

She sighed. "Because he didn't come back, did he?"

"Excuse me?" Cohen asked.

"Five minutes went by. Ten. Twenty. I closed my eyes. Maybe I fell asleep. Maybe it was the trip. I closed my eyes. An hour later the sun was in my eyes. And he wasn't there. I got out of the car, but just then some *dossim* walked by and thought I was a tourist and called me something nasty. I scared the shit out of them, when I snapped back in Yiddish." She laughed at the memory.

"Then what?"

"I waited another half hour. Then I went out to the guard gate and got one of the civil guard soldiers to look for Simon." She said it as if it was above and beyond the call of duty for her.

"Did he find him?"

"No."

"What did you do then?"

"I said fuck it and split."

"How?"

"I thought of taking the jeep. But decided that wouldn't be fair. Not that Simon was fair. But I didn't want the responsibility for it. So, when I saw a taxi drop off some tourists, I grabbed it and went to visit a friend of mine. Yossi Agassi? The artist?"

Cohen knew Agassi, an often drunk polio survivor whose virtuosity as a painter focused on the virtue of sex. Agassi had gone home one night from his favorite bar and discovered a dozen paintings stolen. Luckily there were photos of the paintings—all portraits of the same redheaded model. It took Cohen's office half a morning to track her down, and she explained to Cohen in his office that "after painting me, fucking me, and making me cook and clean for him, Agassi threw me out without a shekel. So I took the paintings."

Cohen used some gentle persuasion to make Agassi pay the woman, keeping it out of the court and papers. Cohen assumed Vicki also modeled for Agassi. But he surprised himself when he realized he was wondering if Vicki did more than model. Not that she'd be the type to clean any house, he decided. It made him think of another question. "Simon threw a party?"

"Purim. Costumes. Horrible. He ended up throwing everyone out."

"How long after the party did you go with him to Jerusalem?"

"Two weeks, no, three weeks, no wait a second, what's today's date? No, that won't help. Let me see, the Purim party, then I had to go to Milan for a show, and then I was back, and when we got together it was a week later, and then we played for a few days, and there was Ori's party, and that went on for two nights, no, what am I talking about? It was three nights, if you count the trip up to Tiberias where we ended up staying at Ditza's, and then . . . My guess," she finally decided, "three weeks after Purim."

"What do you know about these drugs?" he asked, reaching into his pocket for the prescription bottle.

"Let me see that," she said, reaching across the table. He handed it to her. "Where did you get this?" she asked, amazed.

"In his apartment."

"Simon was on this shit?" she asked.

"Apparently not anymore," Cohen murmured.

"Lithium," she said, admiring the drug. "If I knew he was on this shit, I never would have done the acid with him. But it sure does explain a lot. He sure was manic."

"What?"

"This is what manic depressives take. To come down from their euphoria. You know?"

"You are sure?" he asked her.

"Sure I'm sure. I've been around," she said, then changed the subject. "I was serious when I said I liked your eyes," she said to him. He smiled at her. "And I know you like mine," she added. He smiled again. "So?" she asked. "Where do you live? I could give you a ride."

"I have a car," he said, standing up and pulling out his wallet. He plucked a fifty shekel note out and dropped it on the table.

"We're going?" she asked.

"I am. Thank you."

"Wait for me," she said, grabbing her helmet and following him out the door.

They came out in the alley. Her bike was parked just as she had left it.

"I could meet you," she offered.

"I'm going to Jerusalem," he said, knowing it would cool her ardor for an adventure with him.

"You think you'll be able to find him?" she asked, waiting for the answer before she pulled on her helmet. Cohen shrugged. He really wasn't sure. Nor sure that if he found the boy, he'd want to go back to his grandfather. There were at least a dozen *yeshivot* that preyed on types like Levi-Tsur—drug-addled tourists at the Wall were easy to seduce with promises of finding out what God meant when he created the world.

"At least take my number," she said, her voice slightly muffled by the lower jaw of the helmet. She unzipped a pocket on her leather jacket and pulled out a postcard.

On one side was her photo, glamorous and sexy from a lingerie ad that Cohen had noticed in the papers a few months before. The other side listed her vital statistics from height to weight, the size of everything from shoes to bras, plus the address and phone number of her modeling agency. Cohen studied it for a second, and then realized it was the same agency that Yaffe pointed out in the hotel. He looked up at her and smiled.

She read something into his look, and drew a pen from the same pocket where she had plucked the card. "Here's my home number," she said, taking the card back and writing the number in a childish hand. "You can always leave a message for me on the machine if I'm not home."

"Thank you for your time and patience," he said, taking the card back. He added it carefully to the envelope of information he was carrying in his hip pocket.

"Now, what about yours?" she asked.

"My what?"

"Phone number," she said. "Aren't you going to give it to me?" The look in her eyes was clear, but then she added with a smile, "in case I learn something. About Simon. For your case." She handed him another one of her cards, and added the pen she pulled out of the zippered pocket. Cohen wrote down his number.

"Where's your car?" she asked, pocketing it after reading the numbers aloud to make sure she understood the handwriting. He told her. "Get on. I'll give you a ride," she said.

A few minutes later, his face flush and his eyes wet from the wind of her race down Allenby into Mograbi and then up Hayarkon, he stood beside his white Ford Sierra.

"A cop's car," she said, as he used a page of newspaper he plucked from the city trash can to dust off the yellow powder of the sand deposited by the *sharav*'s winds from the desert. "I'm used to millionaires in Mercedes," she added.

"I'm not used to being a millionaire," Cohen said.

"So I can see," she tossed back. "I think that's what makes you so charming."

"Thank you," Cohen admitted, once again embarrassed by her own charms. He threw away the paper in the trash can and came back wiping the dust off his hands.

"You'll call me?" she asked, sitting on her bike beside the car as he opened the driver's door.

"If I need you," he promised.

"I think you do," she said, flipping down her visor and, gunning the bike, she sped away, leaving Cohen standing beside the car wondering if she was right.

· 10 ·

The *sharav* intensified. It was even hotter on Jerusalem's mountain-top an hour later, than by the sea. He'd sleep a few hours, he decided, then resume the search with the *yeshivot*. Meanwhile, turn-ing off Emek Refa'im into his little street, he noticed Yitzhaki on the sidewalk outside his shop unloading the crates of produce from his wholesaler. Cohen felt a suddent urge for mango.

"Yusuf called," Yitzhaki told Cohen, who picked out the largest of the sunburned fruits from one of the crates on the sidewalk. "His sister is better. Now it's just the damn curfew keeping him from work," the greengrocer complained. Cohen reached into his pocket for a coin and asked Yitzhaki what his wife said about the Arab returning to work. "I told her that if the army thinks he's safe, there's no reason we shouldn't," he said proudly. "You know Yusuf. He's never been political. Never been arrested for nothing. They'll let him through," he pronounced confidently.

"And maybe there will be peace," Cohen added softly, almost under his breath. He waved away the grocer's offer to make change from the five shekel coin and walked back up Emek Refa'im's side-walk to his little street, thinking about how money can rot a person until they leave a trail of stench.

He pitied Simon Levi-Tsur but held no affection for the rich kid. He despised Levi-Tsur's grandfather for his belief in money, and he hated the minister the way he hated all politicians, for the pleasure they took from power. He was exhausted and confused, bitter and angry.

Cohen wasn't surprised by the ease with which he picked up Simon's trail but wasn't looking forward to the visits he'd make to the *yeshivot*, worried about someone as disturbed as Simon falling into the kind of *yeshiva* where they talk about blowing up the

Moslem mosques on the plateau above the *kotel* to make room for the Third Temple.

He was thinking about all this after taking a shower, standing naked in front of the fan in his bedroom, letting its artificial gale help the *sharav*'s heat dry him off, when the phone rang. He let it ring twice while he pulled on a pair of clean trousers and a shirt, then a third and fourth time while he padded barefoot to the kitchen and turned on the gas flame under the kettle. He finally answered the kitchen phone at the seventh ring. His answering machine would have picked up at the eighth.

"Commander Cohen?" It was Caroline Jones. There was something in her tone that made Cohen tighten his clench on the phone.

"Yes?" Cohen answered warily.

"I'm calling now instead of tonight because we didn't want you to waste any more of your time. The boy has been found." There was a pause that confirmed his apprehension. "He's dead, Mr. Cohen."

He sat down on the kitchen chair, stunned. For a long lonely moment he felt repentant for all the anger he felt toward the old man, the missing boy, and even the secretary. He blamed himself for not conducting a more thorough search of the apartment. He didn't know how it would have made a difference, but it would have been his own contribution to the effort to prevent just such an outcome to the mystery of what happened to Simon. He cut his emotions out of the equation and drilled "How? Where? When?" at her like commands, as if he were back at work and Nissim Levy had come in with the news.

"I really don't know very much. We were just informed. By your police minister. Mr. Levi-Tsur is taking it very hard, of course. But he made sure to prepare the bank order for your payment. As always," she added, slightly changing her attitude to one of a loyal employee suggesting admiration for her boss, "he's being very generous." Her voice went one step lower. "Twenty thousand dollars," she said, and then, in the silence with which Cohen responded, the secretary suddenly turned officious. "If you want, instead of a check I can have it sent bank to bank for you."

Cohen felt anger beating against his rib cage. He clenched the phone until his knuckles turned white. He listened to his breathing, forcing it to slow down.

"Mr. Cohen?" the banker's secretary asked, worried by the silence on the line.

"What did Nahmani tell you?" he asked, saying each word deliberately, lest his anger explode.

"Well, he actually spoke with Mr. Levi-Tsur. Simon was a 'victim of the peace process.' That's what Minister Nahmani told Mr. Levi-Tsur. Apparently some Arab killed him."

Cohen checked his watch. The half-hour newsbreak on the Army Radio station was four minutes away. "Hold on a second," he said, leaving her on the phone to go to the salon, where he turned on the sound system, pressing the buttons to make the speakers that Udi Hasson had installed in the kitchen carry the broadcast.

"Where?" he asked, when he got back to the phone. "Nahmani must have said where they found the body."

"Near Herodium. Herod the Great's summer castle . . ."

"I know it," he said. It was an archeological site off the road from Bethlehem to Hebron, a solitary hill overlooking a great slope heading east toward the Dead Sea. The slope was broken by dry riverbeds that could sometimes fill in winter to create flash floods that rolled down to the Jordan Rift valley, the lowest place on earth.

Simon was chasing another sunrise in the desert, Cohen thought. "What was he doing there?" Cohen asked.

"God knows. I never met the boy, but I heard he was entirely unpredictable. Of course you know that ownership of the area is under contention with the Palestinians. Or so Minister Nahmani informed us."

"Yes," Cohen admitted hesitantly. "How long was he dead?"

"Mr. Levi-Tsur asked me specifically to tell you that we do not regard you as responsible," Caroline Jones said in her most officious tone.

The five beeps of the news arrived on the transistor radio. Cohen adjusted the volume, to hear better. The broadcast began with a report on the expectations for the bourse's performance that day. An *intifada*-related murder would take precedence over the bourse.

"So, we really no longer need your services," Caroline Jones was saying.

"Who found the body?" Cohen asked.

"Really, Mr. Cohen, I don't think there's any need for any further inquiry. It is clear what happened. The boy was unstable. We all know that."

"You or Mr. Levi-Tsur could have mentioned drugs," he reprimanded her. "In particular, lithium carbonate. It is used to treat people with a mental illness. I would have wanted to speak with the boy's doctor."

She stayed cool. "Perhaps you're right," she said perfunctorily. "But that's all under the bridge now, isn't it? As I said, your services in this matter are no longer necessary."

"Where is the body now?"

"By now, I hope it is aboard the plane we hired to bring the boy home." Cohen snorted at the word home. She didn't notice or pretended not to notice. "The minister was gracious enough to let us have some time before the news is announced," she continued. "He promised us as much discretion as possible, but we know that the sensationalists will eventually find the story. The media are such vultures, no?" She didn't wait for his answer. "So, about your payment?"

"It won't be necessary."

"Then you'd prefer a check. To your home address?"

He tried not to explode. He was furious with Levi-Tsur, who had obviously totally misjudged him. Cohen hated when people misjudged him. "It won't be necessary," he repeated, and to make sure she understood added, "No payment."

"Oh dear," she said, totally surprised. "How extraordinary. Perhaps a favorite charity . . . I'm sure Mr. Levi-Tsur would be deeply touched. I'll have to check with him. I could get back to you . . ."

"Miss Jones?" Cohen stopped her.

"Yes?"

"Those papers Simon was supposed to sign?"

She hesitated. "Yes?"

"Were they very important? For the bank, I mean?"

"I don't think that's any of your concern, Mr. Cohen," she snapped back at him. "Now, I really must get back to Mr. Levi-Tsur. His doctor has arrived. His heart has been giving him trouble, and this news, as you can well imagine . . ."

"One last question, Miss Jones."

She let loose an exasperated sigh. "Yes, Mr. Cohen"

"Did you know that Simon was last seen at the *kotel*?"

"The *kotel?*" she asked.

"I thought you understood Hebrew."

"I'm afraid my Arabic is better. I took Semitic languages when I was planning on an archeology career."

"The *kotel* is what the Jews call the Western Wall, and what you perhaps refer to as the Wailing Wall." Silence. The line buzzed loudly. He tried again. "Miss Jones?"

She confirmed she was still on the phone with a quiet "yes."

"You will report to Mr. Levi-Tsur that I traced Simon to the *kotel,*" Cohen commanded. "I suspect he has spent the last few weeks at some *yeshiva*. You do know what a *yeshiva* is?"

A beat passed before she answered. "Yes, of course."

"Of course what?"

"I know what a *yeshiva* is, and yes, of course I will tell Mr. Levi-Tsur about your search."

"Good," he said, and then, to end the conversation, added *LeHitraot,*" the Hebrew for au revoir. She understood the Hebrew phrase—and what it implied. He could hear her voice from the ear-end speaker as he hung up, trying to impress upon him that his services were no longer needed by Mr. Levi-Tsur.

Only when he hung up did he turn off the capless kettle that had silently blown steam into the room throughout the conversation with Caroline Jones. He turned off the flame and dumped a heaping teaspoon of finely ground Turkish coffee and sugar into a tall Pyrex water glass, which he then filled halfway with the hot water. After stirring it vigorously, he left the spoon in the glass and set it aside to cool. Meanwhile, he sliced off the two sides of the mango, then crisscrossed slices into the orange meat of the fruit.

Bending back the slices, little cubes popped up, and he bit them off deliciously, all the while thinking about why Levi-Tsur was trying to pay him off, how it would affect Nahmani's decision regarding Nissim Levy's return from virtual exile, and why Nahmani himself had not called him with the news.

One thing was certain, he decided as he took the first sip of the coffee and lit a cigarette to go with it. He would find out what happened to Simon Levi-Tsur. He sipped slowly at the coffee.

When all that was left was the black mud at the bottom of the glass, and the cigarette was burned down to the filter, he reached for the phone.

He asked for Nahmani. The secretary asked who was calling. Cohen identified himself. The secretary passed the call to Yaffe. "Believe me, Avram," Yaffe said as soon as he picked up, "the minister only filled me in this morning."

"When was it found?" Cohen demanded. "And who found it?"

"We were lucky. An army patrol found it. Last night."

"After Nahmani briefed me," Cohen checked.

"Yes. He reads the incoming in the mornings. Bodies are always the top of the list. As soon as he saw the report, he brought me in and told me what it was about."

"I know, I know," Cohen said impatiently. "I want to see the report."

"Forget it, it's over," Yaffe insisted, looking for the easy way out like water running to the lowest place. "The family's already taken the body. It's out of our hands."

"Who identified the body?"

"There was a wallet. Full ID, including photos."

"Someone must identify him," Cohen insisted. "It's procedure."

"As soon as Nahmani saw the morning bulletin he called Levi-Tsur. All the old man wants is for his grandson's body to be returned to London. He hired a whole airplane for it," Yaffe said, with unveiled admiration, then added a question in a conspiratorial tone, "Tell me, Avram, what's he like? The old man?"

Cohen thought for a moment. Old, he decided, in the bad sense of the word. But he didn't say that to Yaffe. "Why did the minister tell the family it was an *intifada* killing?"

"It's obvious, no?"

"No," Cohen said softly.

"Hold on, hold on, let me find the report," Yaffe sighed. The phone clattered on the desk. There was a shuffling of papers and then Yaffe was back on the line, with another groan. "Pretty gruesome," said the politician's politician. That's Yaffe, Cohen thought. Always preferred the office to the field, cocktails to mud coffee.

"Read it to me," Cohen commanded.

"Urgent to minister's bureau, inspector general, Shabak, IDF Intelligence . . ."

"*Yalla*," Cohen snapped, knowing the distribution list for unidentified bodies. "Meshulam, get to the point."

"Let me see, let me see," Yaffe mumbled to himself. "About a mile southeast of Herodium."

"Not at the archeological park?" Cohen asked.

"No, I told you, southeast," Yaffe said, "heading down to the sea."

Strange, Cohen thought. It was at least ten miles as the bird flies downhill to the Dead Sea from Herodium. "There's nothing out there," Cohen said.

"Hiker's paths," Yaffe said. "The kid was out hiking. It's obvious."

"Who found him?"

"According to this," Yaffe said, "A squad of first-year paratroopers were on navigation exercises. They were coming up from the Dead Sea."

"They used a radio to contact a base?"

"From the time they found the body until Marciano got there barely an hour passed. Not much traffic that time of night. You know, he's deputy chief of investigations now, under Avi."

Avi Sasson was chosen to replace Cohen. Sasson was nearly twenty years younger than Cohen, Yoram Marciano almost thirty.

Both were good boys on the job, who knew how to read the scorecard. But Sasson was a womanizer and Marciano knew the sports pages better than the law. Cohen would have named others— if the fifth floor had deigned to listen to him. And he never had needed a deputy. Nissim Levy was an assistant, not a deputy.

"Yoram went down with the lab guys," Yaffe said, then went on. "I'm quoting now. 'Wounds: Blow to the head. Estimate of weapon: Ax.' End quote. Poor kid."

"Estimate of time of death?" Cohen asked.

Yaffe mumbled to himself as he scanned. "Here it is," he said. "At least forty-eight hours."

Cohen's heart sank. He wondered if he could have found the boy in time. Those three days between Caroline Jones's first call and Nahmani's extortion could have cost the boy his life.

"Avram?" Yaffe asked, filling the silence created by Cohen's guilt.

"Tell me, how was the body dressed?" Cohen tried.

"Enough, Avram. Enough. You aren't going to investigate this," Yaffe insisted. "It's obvious. The Hamas got him. Let the Shabak handle it."

"What was he wearing?" Cohen insisted.

"Av-ram," Yaffe whined, "leave it."

"What was he wearing?" Cohen shot back a third time.

Yaffe gave in. "All right, all right, hold on." He murmured aloud to himself as he read further down the report. "Trousers. Shirt. Shoes. That's all it says."

"Color?"

"Of what?"

"The clothes," Cohen hissed.

Yaffe mumbled to himself as he scanned the piece of paper in front of him. "Dark trousers. White shirt," he finally conceded.

"*Kippa? Tzitziyot?*"

"What?" Yaffe asked, astonished by the question.

"Was he religious?"

"Let me look, let me see." He mumbled to himself as he read down the report. "Doesn't say."

"Car in the vicinity?"

"Nope."

"And nobody reported him missing?"

"You already knew that."

"Find out if any rental companies have reported an unreturned jeep," Cohen demanded. "And make me an appointment with Nah-mani."

"He said you'd want that," Yaffe admitted, referring to Cohen's request for an appointment. "But you have to understand he has a busy schedule." Yaffe was doing his job. "He's on his way to a northern district convention of security services." But Yaffe wasn't very good at his job, Cohen knew, noticing Meshulam didn't ask why Cohen needed information about a missing jeep. Cohen repeated the request, explaining that Simon Levi-Tsur apparently abandoned the vehicle at the *kotel*. "I'll have to talk to the minister about that," Yaffe said.

"He must have a phone in the car," Cohen said, picking up a blue Pilot Tecpoint. He opened a drawer door and pulled out a little yellow carton-covered pad from a packet of ten that he always kept in his desk. He'd carry all his notes henceforth inside the pad, wearing it in his shirt pocket behind his packet of cigarettes. "What's the number?" he asked Yaffe.

"He's got a journalist in the car. Big weekend interview. I'm sure he won't want to discuss this with you over the phone."

"Tomorrow?"

"Knesset in the morning. And there's a special cabinet session scheduled to decide on the national health bill. You know how those things can go on . . ."

"I'll go to the Knesset," Cohen offered.

"Are you crazy?" Yaffe cried out, immediately lowering his voice to go on. "Just what he needs. Meeting you in the Knesset. Forget it. You know what people are going to say if he's seen meeting you. With the judicial inquiry underway? Are you kidding? Forget it. Maybe I can squeeze you in on Friday. In the morning. But in Tel Aviv."

Cohen was suddenly very tired. He sighed heavily. "Do what you can, Meshulam," he said. There was a softening in his tone that even Yaffe noticed.

"It's the Shabak's problem now, Avram. Let them handle it. And let me make a suggestion. Leave the family alone."

It was the wrong thing at the wrong time for Yaffe to say. "The Shabak takes care of terrorism," Cohen pointed out stiffly. "But terrorists don't kill people without telling the media. Nobody told the media the boy was missing. Nobody told anyone. Someone has to find out why." His burning anger stifled all of Yaffe's huffing and puffing, just like the old days. It made Cohen feel better. "And don't forget to check the rental companies for the missing jeep," he commanded before a curt shalom for good-bye. Like Caroline Jones, Yaffe only managed to splutter in the air while Cohen hung up.

· 11 ·

He was close to exhaustion. Another shower helped. In the kitchen he dug the makings for a sandwich out of the refrigerator. Some pâté with scallions on toasted black bread. A squeeze of lemon and some salt and pepper always helped Ahuva's chopped liver. He chewed slowly, thinking about what he knew. The boy was obviously a walking tragedy waiting to happen. But what did happen? he wondered.

He could call Marciano for details, but that would get to Sasson, who'd kick any request for help from Cohen so far upstairs that it would end up back on Nahmani's desk. He thought for a moment. Annie Pinkas was still working in transport. He dialed the number from memory.

"Annie," he said, recognizing her Moroccan-French "Hallo."

"Yes?" she answered.

"Shh, it's Avram Cohen. Please don't say my name out loud."

There was a creak of her wooden chair turning. He could imagine her at her desk, turning her back to the entrance to the office, facing the big wall map of Jerusalem. "Whatever you say," she whispered hoarsely. Her voice was like a saw through wood, from years of screaming at cops who mishandled her vehicles. "You know that."

"I need a favor. Last night, a body was found near Herodium. Can you tell me what vehicles went down?"

"Sure, no problem Avram. You back at work?"

"The vehicles, Annie, please," Cohen said, intuitively lowering his voice as if he also needed to hide the subject of his conversation from eavesdroppers.

"My eyes, you haven't changed," she exclaimed, still keeping her voice low. "Always want yesterday what you ask for today. Got something going, eh?"

112

"Between you and me, Annie, just you and me," he appealed to her.

"Like the old days, eh?" she answered. "Hold on." He closed his eyes and saw her leafing backward a page—or maybe two, if there was a lot of action during the night—in the big black book on her desk. But instead he heard the tick-tack of a computer keyboard. He regretted not being on the force for that change.

"Okay, here it is," she said. "Transporter van 896, Sammy Sameah logged out on it at zero zero forty-seven. Brought it back zero four twenty-five."

"Who went?"

"Yoram, of course, 'cause it was a body. And Yossi Blumberg."

"Blumberg? From forensics?"

"Yes. He's an inspector now."

That was lucky. It was Cohen who pushed Blumberg from patrol to forensics after the young patrolman proved himself a natural for finding evidence on the scene of a crime. Blumberg would talk to Cohen and would keep his secrets.

"Annie, you are a princess," Cohen said as sweetly as possible. She was addicted to humus in pita, and probably weighed two hundred pounds.

"From you, flattery always helped," she tried to twit. It came out as a squawk.

"You don't happen to know if Yossi is on shift?" he asked.

"Haven't seen him all day."

"One more favor," he asked.

"Anything, sweet."

"Don't tell anyone I called."

"Wouldn't think of it."

He thanked her again, and then dug up his little telephone directory, looking for Blumberg's number. It rang seven times. Cohen was about to hang up on the eighth when an angry voice finally answered.

"Who the hell is this?"

"Yossi, it's Cohen. I hope I didn't wake you."

"Yeah, you woke . . . Cohen? Avram Cohen?"

"Yes."

"God, how are you?" The anger was gone from his voice, but the

113

sleepiness remained. It was contagious to Cohen even over the telephone wire. He wondered how much longer he could go without sleep. No matter what Ahuva said, he felt old sometimes.

"Yossi, I need your help."

"Of course."

"Last night. The body you guys picked up. Any estimate of how long . . ."

"Thirty-six to seventy-two hours," said Blumberg. "It looked like an ax wound," Blumberg went on.

"Marciano's report said at least forty-eight," Cohen pointed out.

"So he made an average," Blumberg said.

"Sloppy. Like not making a visual identification by a next of kin."

"We found the wallet near the body. No cash or credit cards. But full of ID's. I made a preliminary ID, and Avram, I emphasize the word preliminary, from pictures on his driving licenses. And I mean licenses. He owned four. Israel, U.S., England, and France. I told the Shabak guys who picked up the case that there should be a formal identification. They said everything was taken care of."

Terrorists would have taken the documents. Cohen was more confused than ever.

"Was he religious?"

"What?"

"When you first saw the body, did he look like he might be religious? From the clothes, I mean."

"Now that you mention it . . . Black trousers. White shirt. It makes sense . . . I didn't find a *kippa*, but it was windy out there . . . Maybe."

"I suppose Sasson sent someone back today."

"Doubt it," said Blumberg. "The Shabak took over the whole thing. *Intifada*, you know."

"So, you didn't find any *kippa*? No *tzitziyot*? Nothing like that?"

"No. There was a plastic bottle. Mineral water. We took it for prints, but I handed it over to the Twins. They were waiting for us at the Russian Compound when we got back and took the entire package," Blumberg explained. The Twins were a pair of agents who did, indeed, look alike, and worked together so long that they were no longer referred to as anything other than the Twins. It was just as well, because in any case Rafi and Danny were no more their real names than the fact that they looked alike made them brothers. Cohen had never liked either of them. They tended to rely on their brawn as much as their brains.

"Yossi, you've been a great help," Cohen thanked the forensic lab technician.

"Sir," Yossi responded, just like in the old days. "Can I ask what it's all about?"

"I wish I knew," Cohen sighed. "I wish I knew," he repeated. "Thanks again. And this was between you and me? Okay?"

"Of course."

One last call and then he would definitely lie down, he decided. He dialed a familiar number. "Shmulik, please," he asked the switchboard operator.

"There's no Shmulik here," came the nasal answer from the woman at the other end of the line. For a second, Cohen couldn't remember Shmulik's last name. But then it came back to him. "Kagan."

"Ahh," said the woman. "He's in Tel Aviv now."

Cohen slapped at his forehead. Of course, he remembered. Shmulik had finally made it to Glilot, Shabak headquarters north of Tel Aviv. Cohen was forced out of the police before the new government was elected. Shmulik held on long enough to see the priorities change, as they always did when policy changed. He hung up, thinking.

Again the phone's ring surprised him. He checked his watch. It was close to nine in the morning. It was Ahuva. "So?" she asked, not even saying hello, eager to hear his news from the meeting with the minister. "What happened? Do they want you back?"

He went over the entire case as he understood it so far, providing the information as if he was standing in her courtroom giving testimony in a trial. But aside from a general recrimination of Levi-Tsur and Nahmani, he couldn't accuse anyone of anything—except perhaps himself, for not conducting a more thorough search of the apartment, certain he must have missed something that would have led him past Simon's mysterious disappearance at the *kotel*.

"You can't blame yourself for the boy's death," she said when he finally fell silent, with nothing left to say.

"I know. I know," he sighed. "But something is nagging at me and

115

I can't name it. But it doesn't make sense to me, it doesn't make sense. What was he doing down there? He didn't just disappear. If he was at a *yeshiva*, they would have reported him missing. And if he wasn't at a *yeshiva*, then where was he?"

"The boy was crazed. You said so. Those drugs. Who knows what goes through the mind of someone like that?"

"The boy didn't disappear down a crack in the wall."

"Of course not," she said. "You're probably absolutely right about him ending up in a *yeshiva*."

"So why didn't they report him missing?" he asked again, unable to hide the bitter feeling that information was being hidden by people who had asked for his help. "And I don't like the way they're telling me not to investigate," he added.

There was a long silence as both of them thought. "You don't need permission, do you?" she finally said, a gentle prod.

"No," he admitted.

"Go as far as you can go, and when you get to where you can't go any further, you'll know what to do." It was so typical of her, he thought. Pragmatic, optimistic, certain of his abilities. He was less sure. But it was always that way between them, and he knew she was right about one thing—even if she didn't spell it out for him. He needed to find out what had happened to the boy. If not for Simon Levi-Tsur's sake, then for his own.

· 12 ·

He picked up the empty bottle of drugs. Cohen looked toward his bookshelf. There was something else he might buy, he thought. A new encyclopedia. He sighed as he pushed himself up from the chair and went to the shelf. The 1963 *Britannica* told him how lithium was used in everything from air-conditioning to highway flares. In those years the chemically reactive metallic element was also used for antihistamines and synthetic vitamins. The encyclopedia, of course, was too old to know about lysergic acid—LSD.

He needed a psychiatrist to explain what would happen if someone taking lithium carbonate traded it in for lysergic acid. He smiled to himself, as he realized he knew just the person who'd have an answer.

Baruch "Buki" Bender was once a bane in Cohen's life. Bender was a teenager then, and one of the wildest. Cohen, too, was much younger. Cohen first encountered him when Bender was still called Buki, son of a Hebrew University professor of physics and the rebellious daughter of a Mea Shearim rabbi. Cohen and Buki began by running foot races, that when the kid grew older turned into car chases.

Bender was tall and fleet, Cohen shorter, but not someone who could be called sprightly. On those occasions when Cohen did manage to catch Bender and his gang, it would only rate a warning. Over the years, Bender's name came up in connection with hashish, joyriding, and breaking into his high-school building.

Bender's rebellion included being a proud spokesman for the benefits of drugs, though he never was caught as a dealer. His political involvement in causes sympathetic to the Palestinians, combined with his long hair, torn jeans, and posturing at peace demonstrations, made him a target for thugs from the right. Bender fought back with no little success.

When he turned eighteen and was drafted into the army, he surprised everyone by volunteering for an elite unit, and then surprised everyone twice by lasting all three years, turning down another year in officer's training to go abroad to school.

He was gone almost twelve years. When he came back he was a psychiatrist. And he wasn't called Buki anymore. It was Dr. Baruch Bender, Hebrew University professor, with an appointment at the Weizman Institute, specializing in psychopharmacology.

Cohen found the professor's home number in the phone book. "Buki," he said after the man answered the phone. There was a pause.

"Say that again, please," the man said.

"Buki," Cohen repeated.

"Cohen. The policeman," Bender laughed. "My God, Superintendent," he said, using the last rank Cohen filled when Buki was still getting into trouble. "I haven't thought of you in years. I hope you don't think I'm a suspect in something. And please don't tell me you're digging up an old case in which my name might have been mentioned. Like that kiosk raid." The very first time Cohen came across Buki it was when he and his gang made a fool of a kiosk owner, raiding his candy stock once a week by finding a loose board—or breaking one. Cohen caught six of the gang one night with their loot. Buki got away.

"I heard you were conducting research into the effects of LSD," Cohen said, ignoring Bender's natural haughtiness by getting right to the point. "I think I need your help."

"Having a bad trip, Superintendent?" Bender laughed again at Cohen, giving him the feeling Bender's comments were being made for the benefit of an audience.

"I have a few questions."

"I have all the appropriate licenses for my research," Bender said, unable to hide the apprehension in his voice. "Besides, I heard you were no longer on the force."

"I have a personal interest in the subject," Cohen said.

"I read somewhere that you were too vociferous about the syndrome," Bender said. "Would it be presumptuous for me to ask if your query is connected in any way to that phenomenon?"

Cohen paused before he answered. "I don't know," he decided to admit. "Perhaps you'll be able to tell me."

"Interesting," Bender admitted.

"It is somewhat urgent."

"You want to see me now?"

"I could come to your place, or if you preferred, we could meet . . ."

"I have a patient now," Bender said.

"What happens if someone stops taking lithium carbonate and takes LSD?" Cohen asked bluntly.

A woman's voice in the background at Bender's flat interrupted the long heavy silence that fell on the telephone connection. "I'll be right there," Bender said to the woman, then spoke to Cohen. "I've seen some case studies . . . There's a possibility of suspension."

"Suspension?" Cohen asked.

"Astral traveling," Bender explained.

"Astral?"

Behind Bender, the woman's voice spoke up again, this time closer to the phone. "Doc-tor," she whined. "Aren't you coming back to . . ." The sound from the phone disappeared. Bender must have covered the mouthpiece with his hand, Cohen thought. A moment passed, then half a minute, before Bender returned.

"Where were we?"

"Astral traveling?" Cohen asked. "What is this?"

"I have to know more," Bender said. "And surely even you understand that this is not how to diagnose such a case."

"Try."

Bender sighed. "Tell me about the subject."

"Twenty years old. An orphan raised by his grandfather. Extremely wealthy."

"Male or female," Bender asked.

"Male."

"Manic or depressive?" Bender asked.

"Excuse me?" Cohen said.

Bender sighed with exasperation at Cohen's ignorance. "Lithium carbonate is used to balance the presence of norepinephrine in the brain. Too much norepinephrine results in mania—euphoria, obsessive energy, sometimes obsessive sexual drive, overwhelming feelings of great power . . . there's a whole list of symptoms. Too little norepinephrine causes depression. Very serious depression. What about your subject? Euphoric or depressed? When he came off the lithium and took the acid?"

Cohen thought about Simon. "Would it make a difference?" he asked.

"Manic depression comes in cycles. Ups and downs. Like the bourse."

"Manic," Cohen decided.

Bender was quiet for a second. "He'd be looking for a significant event," the psychiatrist said. "The meta-human projections of an LSD experience would . . ."

"Meta-human?" Cohen asked. The terminology was confusing him.

"You've never taken the drug, have you?" Bender asked.

"No," Cohen admitted.

"You ought to try it. I could arrange it, if you would like."

"Another time," Cohen said. "Right now, I need to understand. What did you mean by suspension?"

"By suspension I mean that the subject might have out-of-body experiences. He or she would appear to be in a coma, or perhaps catatonic, but in fact be somewhere else entirely."

"Excuse me?"

"Astral projection. In the simplest terms, flight."

"I've seen what happens when people think they can fly on LSD," Cohen snapped back.

"No, no, no, I'm not talking about flying with their bodies. The body stays behind."

"Doctor . . .," Cohen prodded sarcastically.

"I am serious," Bender said. "In the simplest terms, our essential being is only carried inside our physical bodies. Indian yogis know how to do it with meditation. Lysergic acid, under the proper conditions, can generate the same kind of experience of meta-human identification with the godhead. A subject already experiencing the profound elevation of mood resulting from manic depression, under the added influence of LSD, could enter a condition of suspension, literally leaving the body behind. But I need to know more. Where did the experience take place?"

"The *kotel*," Cohen said softly.

The psychiatrist let loose a long slight whistle. "I tripped at the *kotel*," he finally said. The sudden use of slang was jarring after the professionally mystic jargon. "It was a long time ago," Bender

120

added, more to himself than to Cohen, and making it sound like something he'd never forget and would never talk about. "Was he alone?" the psychiatrist asked.

"He was with a girlfriend, but then went alone into the plaza. Just before dawn. She said she lost track of time waiting for him but he never came back."

A call-waiting mechanism kicked in, telling Cohen there was a caller trying to get through to him. He tried to ignore it, but each ring cut off the line to Bender. "Hold on a second," he said to the doctor, and clicked twice to take the other call. It was Meshulam. Cohen asked him to call back.

"You're the one who wanted to know about rental car companies missing a jeep," Yaffe scolded Cohen.

"What did you get?" Cohen asked.

"I can't believe I'm doing this, but here it is," Yaffe said. "You were right. Hertz asked the police to be on the lookout for a jeep. Land Rover. Rented to the boy."

"So Nahmani and Levi-Tsur strung me along. The police were already investigating."

Yaffe sighed. "You know how it is, Avram. Things get missed. It showed up today. The minister didn't know anything about it. I've got a printout in front of me, if you want."

"Hold on," Cohen asked. He went back to Bender. "Can you hold on for another minute or two," he asked the psychiatrist.

"I have a patient and she is being very generous with her time . . ."

"Please," Cohen asked.

"I never thought I'd hear you asking for my help this way."

"Please," Cohen asked again. There was neither whining nor pleading in his voice, of course. But inside, it hurt him to have to ask that way. Bender agreed.

Cohen clicked back to Yaffe and took down the information. The jeep was rented in Tel Aviv at the Hayarkon office, to Simon Levi-Tsur, just before Purim, with a month-long contract. After the month went by, Levi-Tsur called in, identified himself, and said he'd keep the car for another month, asking that the same credit card be charged. But when that month passed, and no call came from Levi-Tsur for an extension, the computer automatically kicked in the request to the police. "That was ten days ago," Yaffe said.

"Did they find the jeep?"

"Not yet," Yaffe admitted. "It's probably somewhere in Gaza, by now," Yaffe added. "Do you . . ."

"I'll get back to you," Cohen said, cutting off Yaffe without any explanation.

"You still there?" he asked Bender.

"Barely."

"Would the LSD effect, this suspension you talked about, would it have to be immediate?" The call waiting signal came on the line again. This time, Cohen ignored it.

"It depends how much was taken. And maybe it didn't happen. In any case, with a manic-depressive, the euphoria can last a long time. I've seen subjects go days without being able to sleep—and not wanting sleep, too busy with their obsessions."

"The subject was a gambler," Cohen said, "with strong feelings regarding religious people. From what I can tell, he seemed to hate rabbis."

"That could easily turn around. Especially because of the acid," Bender said. "He's very wealthy, you said?"

"Extremely," Cohen said. The caller waiting for him—Cohen was sure it was Yaffe—finally gave up.

"Earned or given to him?" Bender asked about the money.

"He didn't have to lift a finger."

"An orphan?"

"Since he was a baby. His grandfather took responsibility but gave the job to professionals. Tutors, schools." He paused and then added, "Psychiatrists."

Bender thought for a moment. "I'll tell you something," Bender said. "Something to think about. Nobody uses psychoanalysis anymore for manic depression. Lithium carbonate does the job. But in a lot of cases, there's something more than just chemicals behind the symptoms. A loveless childhood. An overwhelming sense of personal guilt for some secret hidden in the subject's past, usually at some level of the subconscious. I'm not saying that uncovering those secrets, for example, is going to change their fundamental condition. Even lithium doesn't do that. But this is where your syndrome comes in. Don't its victims all see themselves as serving some larger cause, a divine mission?"

"Yes," Cohen admitted hesitantly.

"They want to take some grand action that will resolve the confusion in which they live, and give purpose and meaning to their lives. If the acid sent him into suspension, he might have been experiencing something mythological in proportion, some absolute truth about his own condition in the world that would justify the symptoms of the euphoria. He'd have proof of his belief in his own powers." Behind Bender, the woman called out again.

"So," Cohen asked, "what does it all mean?"

"More than anything, he's someone who could be driven by the need to do something of real significance. Something that would validate his existence. Now, Superintendent," Bender said, changing tone from generosity to impatience. "I really have to get back my patient."

He hung up thinking about what Bender called suspension. Absurd, he thought again. Leaving the body behind. Absurd. Someone must have seen the boy at the *kotel*. He must have been somewhere between the last time Vicki saw him and his body's discovery. Blumberg was adamant. The body was not in the desert longer than a few days.

Cohen was confused. He sat staring out the window, into the heat of the *sharav*, trying to make a decision, trying to find a path through his confusion. The wind was still coming from the south, gusting occasionally, creating a flutter in the gray window curtains that Ahuva wanted him to change. He sat that way for a long hour, thinking, just as Bender suggested, about Simon Levi-Tsur's need to do something that would free himself from the restraints of his life.

When he realized his eyelids were heavier than the glass of cognac at his side, he got up slowly, went to his bedroom. A lot of work lay ahead of him. He knew where it would begin. As he fell into his dreams, he wondered where it would end.

· 13 ·

"From Laskoff," shouted the messenger behind the door, when Cohen finally woke to the incessant ringing of the doorbell, clutching a sheet around him against his nakedness. The messenger, still in his helmet, handed over a brown envelope marked only with Cohen's name and address, then pulled out a pad for Cohen to sign as proof of delivery. Cohen clutched the sheet and envelope with one hand while he used the other to sign. It was past four in the afternoon.

The messenger gone, Cohen dropped the envelope on his desk and went to the bathroom to wash his face, then the kitchen to make coffee. While the water boiled, he showered quickly. Then, taking his coffee to the desk, he sat down and opened the envelope.

The handwritten note attached to a thick envelope that came inside the brown envelope was simple. "I thought this material might be interesting to you," it said. Laskoff's signature swirled at the bottom of the page.

The envelope contained a collection of newspaper clippings going back to the sixties. In each one, the name Levi-Tsur was underlined. They were all photocopied pages from newspapers and magazines and the stack was as thick as Cohen's stubby thumb was long.

On some pages, the items were as short as two paragraphs. Every once in a while, Cohen found a longer story, but only six or seven paragraphs. Some of the stories were accompanied by photographs, but the xerography was too poor to make any distinction among the profiles showing Raphael Levi-Tsur or one of his two brothers—Gabriel and Emmanuel—in essentially the same pose: handing over a check to someone.

In some the recipients were university officials. In others, they were rabbis. One photo, accompanying a weekend magazine article, showed Raphael with his two brothers. It was taken when all three were much younger, and showed they all shared the same square jaws, hawk noses, and high brows of the family.

Already back then, Cohen learned from the article, Gabriel handled the eastern part of the globe and Emmanuel the western, while Raphael oversaw the entire enterprise. Or at least so it said in the story, a gushing account in which the reporter seemed to sympathize with Levi-Tsur's preference for charity rather than business in Israel.

He drained the coffee after the first round of reading, and made himself another cup. Again he heard a bell, a warning signal. Again, he couldn't identify the reason for the feeling. He reread the entire file, looking for the source of the feeling nagging at him.

All the while, he made notes, making lists, including one for all the institutions named in the newspaper clippings. Gradually a pattern began to emerge. They gave as much to science as they did to religion. Inside the scientific world, they gave to archeologists and mathematicians.

In religion they balanced their contributions between Hasidic courts, which emphasized a cultist devotion to either a living rabbi or his tradition, and were generally antinationalist, regarding the state's founding without the revelation of the messiah as an aberration to be tolerated, while the other kind of *yeshiva* on the list were those devoted to a militant mystic nationalism, believers in the political-spiritual trilogy of One People, One Torah, One Land.

Another pattern emerged as Cohen studied the list. He found himself making two lists—one for science and one for religion. Raphael seemed mentioned most in connection to religious institutions, Emmanuel was the archeologist, and Gabriel supported research into prime numbers.

There were nearly fifty names on the list by the time Cohen was done. He knew about half by name, and guessed another 25 percent. There were a dozen he had never heard of, including two *yeshivot*. He saw mentioned most of the Israeli universities, several key archeological digs, and a chair in cryptography.

Cohen was mostly an autodidactic, and as such, when focused became extremely methodical, making lists he'd study and follow like maps, drawing charts and tables of crisscrossed possibilities of connection among pieces of evidence. In his old office he did it on sheets of clear plastic hanging in layers over maps and the other cartographics of a case: photos of dead people or missing property, IDs, checks, and passport pages enlarged by copying machines, and thick black and primary color lines were drawn with water-based markers like roads connecting the evidence.

As CID chief more than two hundred people worked directly under him, ranging from the clerks and secretaries to undercover detectives in the criminal underworld and the most radical political and religious fringes, where freedom fighter or terrorist, they operated according to a higher law, whether they believed it was a god's or a cause's.

At home, with neither the luxury of staff nor supplies, he worked at the little round dining table in his living room, Suspect at his feet, Annabella Levi-Tsur-Cohen playing Brahms with her cello on the stereo, and, scattered across the surface of the table, the news clippings about the Levi-Tsurs, the Jerusalem phone book, and the few notes he had made after his conversations with Levi-Tsur, Nahmani, Camara the African, Dado the pool-hall owner, Vicki-Bracha, and Buki Bender.

His original instincts on his way back to Jerusalem from Tel Aviv that morning told him to canvas the *yeshivot*, searching for the boy. He was still most bothered by the question of what had happened between the time Vicki last saw Levi-Tsur at the *kotel*, and when Simon—or his body—reached the desert. The death didn't change Cohen's focus on a *yeshiva* as the probable stage Simon passed somewhere between the *kotel* and the desert. If, as he suspected, the boy was drawn into a *yeshiva*, surely they would have reported him missing, sought him out someplace.

And Bender's description of the susceptibility of Simon to a suddenly comatose condition made him wonder why no hospitals reported his arrival. And if he was comatose, why was an ax blow to the head necessary before his body was dumped in the desert?

He was also driven by larger questions: the secrecy and speed of the old banker's desires and demands. Questions for Laskoff— what kind of documents would need signing at the age of twenty-one. Questions for Nahmani—why did he permit the police to break all the rules of police procedure and let the body out of the hands of the authorities without a formal identification? And his own secret guilt created by his initial refusal to deal with the Levi-Tsur problem made Cohen ask questions of himself.

At one point during his long afternoon nap, Cohen dreamed about hovering above his body, with the distinct sensation of flight. It was so real that it woke him with the feeling that if he could write down how he did it, he'd be able to read the instructions whenever he wanted and be able to recapture the experience. Waking, of course, shattered the illusion. Not for the first time in his life, he cursed Bender under his breath, then snorted a laugh, punched his pillow, and went back to a more peaceful sleep until Laskoff's motorcycle messenger showed up, and Cohen discovered the *sharav* had broken. He always preferred night work, and set about his self-appointed job with the serenity of the new stillness in the air that replaced the southern wind.

He began with all the *yeshivot* that he originally considered as possible havens for a tourist looking for a spiritual adventure in Jerusalem, but added those *yeshivot* supported by the Levi-Tsur donations. He followed leads he won from male school secretaries to *rebbetzin* whose rabbi husbands were too important to bother with the details of where the newcomers were given places to sleep. With some he used his name. They knew Cohen from his old days on the force. Others had heard of him. He was known as fair and firm, someone to be feared if crossed with a lie, someone who could be trusted for his word. With some calls, to *yeshivot* where he knew his name would be known with less than sympathy, he pretended to be a distant relative of a young tourist searching for himself in *yeshiva* life.

He asked about all newcomers of that age and that look, all the way back to Purim, despite Vicki's attempt to place the date afterward. There were two new boys from Boston at one *yeshiva*. At another, a cartoonist from Colorado recently signed up for lessons.

At one *yeshiva*, the school secretary agreed to tell him the only foreigner to show up lately was a "very important personality from the French entertainment world" who was paying for private sessions from the *rebbe*. For a second, Cohen wondered if Simon could have taken on an entirely different personality, claiming to be someone he wasn't. His French was probably as fluent as his other languages. But the rock and roller was a woman, interested in her Moroccan-Jewish roots, the secretary explained.

There were eight new conversion cases, spread out through seven *yeshivot*, but Cohen's instincts—and they were all he had to work with—said he could drop them to unlikely.

By ten o'clock it was late at night for the world of *yeshivot*. By midnight, he set a course of action for the next day. First the *kotel*, then back to Tel Aviv. If he played it right, he might be able to get Shmulik for a quick meeting in the city, before going back to Simon's flat for a more thorough search. But as he stretched on the bed before settling into sleep, he realized that there was still something nagging at him, something deep in his memory, which he couldn't quite trace so couldn't yet name.

· 14 ·

There was a chill in the predawn air of the desert city. Fog no less deep than the cold smothered the streets. The coolness made Cohen roll down his shirtsleeves as he walked up the steep stairs from the parking lot below Dung Gate to the entrance to the plaza, where the fog diffused the yellow lights of the guard booths at the entrance.

A dog barked somewhere in the Arab neighborhood at the bottom of Siloan valley, below the hill where Solomon's temple once reigned as the centerpiece of an empire based on commerce with the rest of the known world.

Beyond the guard booth, fortified by a metal detection gate, two reservists sat in the guard booth. A green jeep from the Border Patrol was parked in the VIP and emergency vehicle lot just past the guard booth.

Through the open windows to the booth Cohen could see that one reservist was wearing a knitted *kippa*, reading hunched over a table. The other was standing and facing north into the yellow fog. He wore his hair in a ponytail. As Cohen approached he saw the religious reservist was studying the sports section from the previous day. The soldier with the ponytail blew a thick stream of smoke into the air and pulled at his Uzi's strap on his shoulder.

"Shalom," Cohen said quietly.

The reader glanced up and then back down at the newspaper, pointing with a finger to Cohen's left. "There are *kippot* over there," he said.

"Yes, I know," said Cohen, not moving.

"So, what do you want?" asked the standing soldier. The reader looked up, surprised Cohen was still there.

"Reserves?" Cohen asked, knowing they were, but needing the opening.

"Naw, we're *Sayeret Matkal*," the soldier with the ponytail said sarcastically, referring to the most elite army unit known to the public. The standing soldier was much younger than the sports fan with the *kippa*.

"This your regular spot?" Cohen asked.

"What's it to you?" the reader asked, suddenly suspicious.

Cohen reached into his pocket and pulled out the photo of Simon with his grandfather. "I'm looking for this kid," he said, passing the picture over the windowsill to the ponytailed soldier. "He was here a couple of weeks ago."

"Thousands of people come here every day," the soldier said, taking the picture, studying it, shaking his head, and then passing it to his partner.

"Not at . . .," Cohen checked his watch, "quarter to five in the morning. A sexy girl in a miniskirt, blonde, came through later, looking for him. You would have remembered her."

"I do," said the reader, looking up at Cohen, then turning to his partner. "After Yossi and Boris changed with us, I came back because I forgot my stuff. Boris was alone, I asked him where Yossi was, and he pointed to a prostitute, standing over there." The reader pointed to an outcrop of rocks at the edge of the archeological garden. "Boris explained that she asked them to go down to the *kotel* to look for a friend of hers. I gave Yossi hell when he came back. Abandoning his position like that, for, for," the reader stammered suddenly, unable to say what he was thinking.

Cohen rescued him. "But he didn't find the kid."

"No."

"And you don't remember him coming in?"

"How can I remember everyone who walks through? If they don't ask for something and the buzzer doesn't go off when they pass the gate, why should I remember. You, I'll remember. Such questions. Some young man on his way to prayer, I should remember?"

The standing soldier rolled his eyes behind the religious man's back. Cohen stared at him. "You don't remember the kid, either?"

The younger soldier shrugged. "People come, people go. The metal detector does the work. And if anything happens, we've got them," he said, nodding toward a pair of border patrolmen across the plaza, M-16s slung over their shoulders. By pointing them out, he made Cohen notice the soft thud of their boots' echo in the vast square.

"Do you remember exactly what day it was?" Cohen asked.

"It was the first week of reserves. Three weeks ago."

"Lot of regulars down there?" Cohen asked, pointing down past the guard booth, toward the Wall itself, which was hidden from view by the long path leading up to the green door to the Mograbi Gate's opening into the surface of the Temple Mount, where the Moslems had built Al Aksa mosque.

"As usual," the ponytailed reservist said. "A few *dossim, haredim,* some settlers, you know . . ."

Cohen did. He thanked them and headed toward the electronic security gate. "*Kippa!*" the religious reservist reminded him. Cohen paused, smiled guiltily, then took one of the brown cardboard *kippot* piled in the stand. He carried it in his hand through the gate, half expecting the alarm to go off because of the keys in his pocket. The alarm wasn't that sensitive.

The Wall and plaza were always lit, for there was always someone there; saints or scoundrels, it drew lonely people who wanted to be alone, and it drew lonely people who needed the company of God.

Cohen rarely went to it, and always felt uncomfortable among the believers, whether they pressed tear-streaked cheeks against the stone or rejoiced in dance in its shadow. He never tried to send a request to heaven by jamming a note into one of the cracks between the huge stones. He hated the way politics combined with religion to make the stones something to die for, and he loved how birds found perches in the wild scrub bush that sprouted from its upper reaches, beyond the hands of even the tallest believer.

At night, the plaza was ablaze with lights, giving a theatrical look that always perturbed Cohen. But at this hour, just a few minutes before the planet's turn would make sunlight change everything, the fog was so thick it seemed as if the *kotel* was a bride wearing a veil, her features softened, her eyes truly mysterious.

Only when he was much closer, just outside the corral-like fence dividing the men's side from the women's and the prayer area from the rest of the square, could he begin to pick out the people at the foot of the monument. There were four *haredim,* one beside the other, in black hats and coats, wearing telltale knee britches with white socks that said they were from the rabbinical courts of the most virulent anti-Zionist of all the ultra-orthodox of the Jews. They were standing directly in the middle of the men's section, and were shuckling back and forth with fervor. To their far right was a fifth, much less energetic *haredi*, sitting on a chair, one hand on the stone, the other holding a little prayer book. Cohen guessed him to be older than the four praying *haredim*.

The oldest, by far, was a white-bearded *haredi* man, shuffling across the bottom of the Wall from the far corner near the women's section, past the praying men, toward the entrance to a tunnel that led to further archeological digging into the base of the remains of the First and Second Temples of the Jewish commonwealths of ancient history.

Light-blue plastic chairs were scattered around the men's area. Cohen took one and angled it for a view of the entrance from the plaza to the men's area. He was patient. He wouldn't interrupt a praying man. He checked his watch and looked up at the sky.

Dawn was an important part of what Simon was seeking at the *kotel.* Cohen would wait for it as well, knowing it would come from the east, from the desert, the mountains, and the deep valley of the Afro-Syrian rift. It would climb those hills, over the place where Simon Lev-Tsur's body was found, over the army camps and the Bedouin encampments, over hundred-year-old Arab villages and twenty-five-year-old Jewish settlements, until it would hang above the Mount of Olives like a crown suddenly placed on the city. At the *kotel,* the change from night to day takes longer. The Wall is tall and for those at its feet, shade lasts until midday.

Four settlers arrived while it was still dark. They were all dressed for day, not night. One wore a T-shirt with the slogan "The Prime Minister's a Traitor" on his broad, overweight torso. Another wore a checkered shirt over old baggy jeans. The other two wore blue work trousers and faded white shirts. All four wore large, white, knitted *kippot,* and all were bearded and carried Uzis. Two carried pistols worn in holsters on their hips.

In the vast empty square, their chatter was loud, though the words were indistinguishable. The solitary *haredi* looked up from his prayers and scowled at them, shifting on the chair to turn his back to their raucous behavior. The four *haredim* were too immersed in their prayers to notice. The four settlers quieted, taking up positions at the far end of the area, nearest to the divider from the women's area, each opening a little prayer book and beginning their reading.

Cohen was watching them when a movement at the opening to the archeologically excavated tunnel at the northern corner of the *kotel* caught his attention. It was the old man wrestling a wooden podium toward the center of the men's area. Cohen walked over to the old man to help him carry the chair the last few steps.

The old man glanced at Cohen, who said softly, "Shouldn't you have an assistant?" as he followed the old man's lead for the placement of the podium.

"Blessed be his name," the old man answered, "I still have my health." He leaned against the heavy wooden stand, obviously resting from the exertion.

"And your memory?" Cohen asked with a friendly smile.

"You need a book?" the old man asked back. "Can't remember your psalms?" He grinned back with half a mouth of teeth.

"No, it's not that," Cohen admitted. "You work here?"

"Do I work here or am I paid for my work?" the old man asked back, again grinning at Cohen. "And you, are you here to pray or to work?"

"I need help," Cohen admitted.

"Who doesn't need help?" the man said.

There was a streak of yellow and brown in the old man's beard beneath the lower lip. "Can I offer you a cigarette?" Cohen suggested. He pointed out of the men's area, to the foot of a flight of stairs that led up into the Old City's market. "Perhaps we could move over there?" he added.

The old man looked up at the sky, as if for inspiration. "How long until dawn?" he asked.

Cohen lied. He looked at his watch and said another fifteen minutes.

The old man was dubious. He clucked his tongue. "I don't think so," he finally said. "Sooner. But we have enough time. A cigarette. Yes."

He walked faster than he shuffled at the foot of the Wall, but still so slowly that Cohen adjusted his own pace. It gave the old man time to say that yes, he was a volunteer. "Ever since the Six Days," he said, referring to the 1967 war. "My son died fighting for the *kotel*," he said, looking for Cohen's reaction. Cohen nodded slightly. "It is my duty, my honor, to come here every day to prepare for the *shaharith*," he said, about the morning prayers. "And I don't have much time. The *rav* will be here soon."

Cohen pulled out two cigarettes, offered the old man one and stuck the other in his mouth. The old man savored the cigarette first, holding it under his nose, and then looking at its watermark label on the paper. He frowned, recognizing the Noblesse label, then shook his head, and holding it in his mouth leaned forward to Cohen, waiting for a light. The old man inhaled deeply, enjoying it.

"I'm looking for someone," Cohen said, putting away his lighter and pulling out the Polaroid.

The old man took the picture, holding it close to his eyes to study the faces.

"The boy," Cohen said.

"A rich boy," the old man said. "He doesn't look like this is a place for him. Is he a Jew?"

Cohen nodded. "His name is Levi-Tsur. He was here. A few weeks ago. Very early in the morning. He was acting strange, perhaps. Talking to himself?"

The old man smiled again, letting the smoke out of his mouth so it billowed for a second in front of his face. "Many people come here and look like they talk to themselves."

"Still, maybe you remember this boy. He was on drugs. Maybe he was very loud or disrespectful. Maybe someone here calmed him down. Took him home?"

The old man's eyebrows went up, and he left the cigarette in his mouth to clutch the picture in two hands, as if to draw from it information through his fingers as well as his eyes. The cigarette hung from the lips, its burning tip hanging above the slight crevice burned out of the beard.

Cohen took a deep puff from his own cigarette, his second of the day. It made him cough deeply, until the phlegm rose into his throat. He scowled, unable to bring himself to expectorate in the plaza so he swallowed, keeping his eyes on the old man's face.

The old man's luxurious beard rose all the way on the face so that only the tops of his cheeks were hairless. His brow was curiously unlined for such an old man. But there were deep dark circles under his eyes.

He finally looked up, away from Cohen, first to the sky, and then across the plaza until his eyes settled on the four settlers for a long moment, his eyes narrowing to look at them.

Suddenly, he looked at the cigarette in his hand as if suddenly discovering it, threw it down, and crushed it out with his aged leather shoes. He picked up the butt and dropped it into his black jacket's pocket. "I must go. I still have to bring out the books."

"I could help you," Cohen said.

"No, no, no need," the old man said, "thanks for the cigarette." His walk back to the *kotel* tunnel was even faster than his shuffle after Cohen for the smoke. But he had given Cohen his clue.

· 15 ·

He waited nearly an hour, until the sun indeed crowned the city, though it was still too early to eliminate the Wall's shade. Finally, the four settlers came out of the men's area, which meanwhile filled with praying people for the morning *shahnarith* prayers. The four left in two pairs, heading toward Dung Gate. Cohen lagged behind.

The reservists changed shift, and were beefed up for the day. More police vehicles were present in the emergency lot for the day's security. He recognized Karmpinski, the head of patrol, dressing down six border patrolmen and their officer. Cohen made sure Karmpinski didn't see him, scuttling through the security gate as he followed the four men.

He was about fifty paces behind them, still on the stairs going down into the parking lot, when a tourist bus swung into the huge parking lot, then paused, as if the driver was getting instructions—or trying to decide—where to position the bus. The settlers passed in front of the bus, and then disappeared behind it. Cohen waited for the bus to move. But then the front door to the bus swung open, and passengers began pouring out, making Cohen nervous. He took the stairs two at a time, and strode across the lot, passing his own car, then the bus, to seek out the four settlers. There was no sign of them.

He turned, scanning in all directions across the lot. South was the steep drop into the bottom of Siloan, where the original source of water for the city used to once meander in the open gorge. Now covered, piped, and protected, the fresh water flowed into city pumps, while the valley was settled at the bottom by Arabs, and by Jews from the settlers movement who embarrassed the government by secretly buying properties in the neighborhood and then one night moved in, declaring their neighborhood to be the resurrected Jewish settlement of the original City of David.

Cohen couldn't believe he had lost the four settlers. It was as if they vanished. A car engine started. A van parked at the far southern end of the lot shot out of the parking lot, taking a left up the hill and then right, onto the road that traced the perimeter of the Old City walls, dropping into Gethsemane Valley. The driver had a gray beard.

Cohen trotted to his car, fumbling for his keys as he ran. A minute later he was on the road, following the van. The rear bumpers and windows were covered with all the stickers of the right-wing. From "Hebron Forever" to "With the Golan," from "The Prime Minister's a Traitor" to "The People Against Hostile Media."

The van moved along the roads quickly, taking the road up to the Mount of Olives cemetery, then turning left across the street from the old Southern District Police headquarters, up the road into the ancient cemetery. It pulled into the small parking lot overlooking the city from the east.

Cohen drove past slowly, and because of the curve in the road, he parked on the left-hand side of the road for a side-mirror view of the parking lot exit on one side. To his immediate left was the low wall of the cemetery.

He wished he had a radio in the car to contact headquarters to run the license plate through the computer. He wished he had an assistant to keep an eye on the settlers while he went to a phone to contact his forces. But he didn't wish he was doing something else.

Two more cars pulled into the lot in the next few minutes. One was red, a flashy BMW sedan with a rental agency's license plate. The other was an old Fiat 127, a tiny yellow box with two seats in front and a backseat that could carry three children or two adults. The BMW carried two passengers. The Fiat was more crowded, and they weren't children in the backseat.

Cohen opened the glove compartment and pulled out a gray canvas-and-cloth work hat. In his last years on the force, long blue-billed caps like those worn by American baseball players, and branded with the police force's symbol—though not rank—had become the standard hat for work under the sun. Cohen preferred his old *kova tembel,* a graying sailors' cap with the brim turned down. The cloth cap was large enough for him to shade more than half his face, whether against the sun or recognition.

He looked around, getting out of the car. It was too early for the

Bedouin and his camel, which the tourists rode for their scrapbook picture of them on the beast and the holy city below. No children were playing in the street, waiting for cars wearing yellow Israeli license plates, prey for their stones.

He used his car's rear bumper to help him up and over the stone wall to the cemetery, careful to drop into the narrow space at the head of the graves of Moshe Ben-Avraham Levi, and his wife, Rachel. They were buried side by side, face up, so that when the messiah arrived, and the dead were resurrected, Jerusalem would be the first thing Moshe and Rachel would see.

He walked slowly around the treeless ridge, trying to stay in the slight shadow of the cemetery's eastern wall, but soon he was directly under the southern sun of a spring morning. The marble graves were all white and the sheer reflection of the sun in a cloudless sky on a windless day made the cemetery's hot surface into a furnace.

He was sweating by the time he reached the southern edge of the slope, seeing a couple, whom he guessed were from the BMW, six or seven rows of graves below him. The man was holding a bouquet of flowers. Their leisure clothes seemed interchangeable. He couldn't tell how old they were, but guessed them to be Americans. The woman was lighting the *yahrzeit* candle in a little copper-and-glass lantern built into the standing stone above the grave they were visiting.

He didn't pause, moving on to the stairs, climbing up to the parking lot above him. He went up the stairs like an early morning mourner returning from a relative's grave, pausing at the eight-faucet water fountain at the top of the stairs to wash his face.

The van and the Fiat were parked side by side. There were now seven men, the four settlers plus three others. But instead of the large, knitted white *kippot*, checkered shirts, and T-shirts and jeans of the settlers, the three additional men were dressed in the casual wear of *haredi yeshiva* students: white shirt, black trousers, black *kippa*.

It was a strange combination, Cohen thought. The settlers wanted more than anything to be considered the ultimate vanguard of Zionism. *Haredi*-ism regarded Zionism a heresy that at best should be exploited for temporal needs of the ultra-orthodox community.

He spent a few minutes at the water fountain, washing his face, drinking water, taking in the view of the desert all the way to a tiny blue corner of the Dead Sea far below, pretending to ignore the seven men, deep in discussion on the other side of the parking lot. The Old City, the Mount in its east, seemed within reach of Cohen's hand. The king of Jordan recently had paid for the regilding of the dome of the Rock, and it caught the sunlight like a dagger. The silver of al-Aksa mosque was a duller, almost pewterlike gray.

He wet his hat and wrung it out, drank some more, and then cocked the floppy brim hat over his forehead down to his eyebrows and pulled out his little notebook, changing his persona from mourner to researcher. Ready, he started walking across the sun-drenched lot, carrying his little yellow pad in one hand and an open pen in the other, making notes on his way. As if deep in thought, he paused twice, looked up as if to calculate in his head, and then jotted another note. But each time, he gathered more information about the seven men.

The three *haredim* were Sephardim. All were black-bearded, covering their faces up from below the throat up the cheek, and with black *kippot* on their heads. The tallest stood hip-cocked, one leg shorter than the other, and his thick black beard was scarred by a white fan of hair covering his chin.

The settlers he already knew, but now in the parking lot he found identifying characteristics that he etched into his memory: one had a hawked nose, another wore a bronze beard. There was the off-tan coloring of a large deep scar in front of the right temple of the man in the "The Prime Minister's a Traitor" T-shirt. Their apparent leader was the driver. His beard was gray and wispy but made up for what it lacked in fullness with a wild length that in the breeze on the hill gave it a life of its own.

Their conversation came to an immediate, obvious halt, when one of the *haredim* interrupted the dialogue between the two leaders, pointing out Cohen's approach. Each in his own way pretended not to notice him, but each in their own way eyed him silently as he crossed their path, studiously making notes of their identifying characteristics.

He noted their postures as they turned slowly to watch him pass, and he estimated their heights and weights. It was all routine for him, a habit made from suspicion and the sheer pleasure of observation. He was certain the settlers he followed from the *kotel* had not noticed him at the Wall. He did not recognize any of them, except for the vague resemblance to the description of the mad mourner in the city. Nor did he recognize any of the three *haredim*, though there was something familiar about the hip-cocked stance of the tallest *haredi*.

It all sped through his mind as fast as an experienced driver knowing the route of his race, yet as Cohen left the lot, aware that the seven men remained frozen and silent until he was out of earshot, he had the uneasy feeling he had missed a turn in the course.

· 16 ·

He was nauseous. The cigarette was nasty in his mouth and he threw it away, out the window, still waiting in his car for the van and the Fiat to depart. He waited more than twenty minutes in his car, slouched in the passenger seat with his head below seat level, roasting in the heat of the cabin, keeping an eye on the parking lot exit.

The windows were only open on the wall side of the car—he didn't want the settlers or the *haredim* to know he was waiting for them, so he didn't turn on the engine for the air-conditioning, lest the exhaust tell its tale. Nor could he lower the window on the passenger side, visible to the road and any car coming out of the parking lot. He listened to the radio. There was still no mention of an *intifada*-related murder near Herodium. Just after the nine A.M. news, the aged Fiat's tailpipe scraped the asphalt of the parking lot incline, and Cohen began to follow, thinking about the narrowing of ideologies—settlers and *haredim*—to a peculiar intersection of belief twisted into self-contradiction and therefore allied for more conflict, not less.

For Cohen, the use of force was to stop others—it didn't matter who—using force. But that's when he was on the force, and he knew that there were many more walls in the city than the Western Wall of the ancient Temples, more domes than all the gold on the Haram al Sharif, and more skeletons than all the priests' bones hidden in the cellars of the city's monasteries.

In a city of faiths, each wore a uniform, for whatever reason they chose. Simon went black, Cohen thought, using in his mind the local terminology—the color of the clothes, the bent of the politics. He didn't regard belief alone as dangerous, but he didn't trust true believers. Their higher laws were easier for them to follow than the more ambiguous laws made by people. In a city holy to more than one religion, that's a prescription for danger.

141

Now, chasing Simon Levi-Tsur's sunrise, he found himself following something as threadbare as the *tallit* worn by the old man at the Wall, whose forehead changed suddenly from innocent smoothness to worried wrinkles as he looked across the white-lit plaza toward the four armed settlers with all the right prayer books.

With a shift of gears, the old little Fiat stormed out of the parking lot and blasted a puff of burned oil, accelerating down the southern crest of the Mount of Olives. Cohen started his engine, and turned the wheel, ready to make the U-turn.

Right after the Fiat, the van came gingerly out of the parking lot, turned left, and headed down the hill. Cohen let out the clutch, and was quickly on their tail, opening all the windows in the car to let the wind, instead of air-conditioning, keep him cool in the hot morning air.

Both cars wove southwest, taking the right turn that ran down into Gethsemane, then avoiding Damascus Gate's intersection with East Jerusalem's Salah a-Din, retracing the same route the settlers took to the parking lot beneath the entrance to the Western Wall's plaza, only this time the Fiat led, turning off at the parking lot above Siloan in the City of David.

Cohen followed the settler's van over Mount Zion to the Valley of the Scapegoats, into the Sultan's pool and up past the Cinematheque. It was as if they were on their way to Cohen's German Colony apartment until he found himself following them past Yitzhaki's on Emek Refa'im, past the Persian's stand a few blocks before the railroad tracks, and then skirting the industrial zone, onto the road heading south to Hebron.

The van reached Bethlehem quickly, and just as quickly braked in the gravel on the side of the road just beyond Rachel's Tomb. Cohen sped past, then slowed down to watch in his rearview mirror. A man carrying a plastic bag in one hand and wearing an Uzi over his shoulder, and a woman carrying a baby, were climbing into the van. A half dozen soldiers were in the area that Cohen could see. He was sure if he got out to look around he would find at least twice that many in the area.

Ever since the massacre, the holy sites had become security zones. Fear of retribution from the Moslems was as rife as the fear of another Goldstein, the doctor who had sprayed bullets into the backs of praying Moslems in the hall beside the stone sarcophagi marking the graves of the Bible's patriarchs.

Cohen knew another man named Goldstein who would have loved to be strong enough psychologically to massacre praying Moslems as a way of claiming Jewish rights to the Holy Land, believing he'd be doing God's will, ready to die for his belief. But Cohen's Goldstein had also been killed, under far more prosaic circumstances. On this very road, Cohen thought, disappointed as the settler van bore to the right instead of the left at the southern intersection leaving Bethlehem. Left would have taken them toward Herodium. Instead they took the right. It also led south toward Hebron.

On this very road, Cohen resumed thinking about the Goldstein he had known. It was a head-on accident—a taxi loaded with seven Palestinian workers plus a driver, and Goldstein driving his own closed-cabin pickup with a lieutenant in the passenger seat beside him and the back filled with five more followers of the assassinated American preacher-rabbi who had promised Jewish salvation through the expulsion of the Arabs from Israel. Goldstein and three Arabs were killed on the spot. All the others ended up crippled in various ways, from lost arms or legs to head injuries that would probably never heal. Friends of the dead from both sides blamed the other driver for deliberately causing the accident.

Cohen followed the settler van on the same road, all the while careful to keep at least two cars between them, and sometimes as many as six. The traffic was a mix of Arab-owned cars from the Occupied Territories, Israeli cars driven by settlers, usually accompanied by some sort of security vehicles, green jeeps and gray jeeps, some with the white-on-black of army license plates, others with the white-on-red of the police.

There were a few straightaways, but mostly the road was long curves around the slopes of the ancient hills. That didn't stop both Israeli and Palestinian drivers from trying to pass each other. In south Lebanon, Cohen thought, making his white Sierra fit easily into the traffic, the Israeli army regarded as suspicious any vehicle trying to pass an army car or truck. That was Lebanon. Here, much closer to home, accidents, not suicide bombers, were the daily occurrence. They were approaching Hebron.

Cohen made his car slip in and out of the rearview mirror of his prey. Just before the intersection at the northern end of the town, a wave of siren-singing vehicles rushed past both Cohen and the van. Coming to the intersection that broke away from the main road and turned up a hill to Kiryat Arba, Cohen saw that the emergency vehicles—police cars, army trucks, and a big army jeep with a dozen antennas whipping the air, signifying it was the command-and-control field headquarters for a general—were all heading to the hilltop settlement, the first of all the Jewish settlements in the West Bank after the Six Day War.

In the distance, over the settlement that looked down with a combination of patronization and suspicion on the Arab town below, he saw a pair of helicopters landing somewhere behind the apartment blocks at the top of the hill. The van took a left onto the road to Kiryat Arba. So did Cohen. He saw the van speed past a pair of soldiers on guard duty at the electromechanical gate guarding the broad avenue leading up to the settlement. But Cohen's care at being discreetly behind the van failed him at that most crucial moment. A truckload of soldiers was coming from the south on the road and pulled into the broad avenue's entrance in front of Cohen, stopping in front of the gate. A platoon of soldiers jumped down from the truck and began taking positions around the road and the intersection.

Cohen pulled in slowly amid the bustle. The officer in charge, a young lieutenant, approached Cohen's car. The officer peered through the windshield at Cohen and then came around to the driver's door, his lips pursed. His face appeared in the frame of Cohen's open window.

"Yes?"

"I'm going up there," Cohen said, nodding toward the settlement's apartment blocks, four-story buildings with small windows and balconies overlooking the road.

"Who are you?" the officer asked.

"A visitor," Cohen said.

"No visitors now," the officer said.

Cohen scowled. "Don't be ridiculous," he said.

The officer shook his head. "The media hasn't reported it yet?" he asked.

Cohen turned up the radio. He had been listening to the Voice of

Music, playing Tchaikovsky for the forty-minute drive. It took the outbreak of a war to disrupt a concert for breaking news on that channel.

He hit the volume button by mistake trying to go to another station, making the car speakers blast strings, then quickly lowered the sound and found Army Radio, where they guaranteed actuality around the clock. It was playing rock and roll. Cohen looked at the reservist, the question in his eyes.

"I guess not," the officer admitted. He adjusted the strap of the Kalashnikov hanging in front of his waist from his right shoulder. "Kiryat Arba's a closed military zone," he added perfunctorily. Just then, movement in the rearview mirror caught Cohen's eye. A large blue Volvo pulled into the intersection behind him. A moment later, a brown Mercedes, and then a Land Rover pulled up behind the Volvo.

"Why'd you let them up?" Cohen asked, nodding toward the van at the top of the hill.

The young man looked up at the hill with a forlorn expression on his face. For the first time Cohen saw the soldier was wearing a *kippa*. "They got past us, but now it's closed."

"Why?" Cohen asked.

"There's been an incident." It was euphemism for a terror attack of some kind.

"When?" Cohen asked.

"Half an hour ago," the officer said. "Now, unless you live up there," he said, "or you're with the police," backing away from the car to look at it for a second before adding "or the Shabak—and have a document to prove it—then you might as well turn around and let us do our work."

One of the cars behind Cohen honked. The officer looked toward them, a scowl on his face, waved at them to wait, and then turned back to Cohen.

"At least tell me what happened," Cohen asked.

The young officer looked into the distance for a moment. "They got Eli Bookspan," he finally said.

No wonder security was so tight. Bookspan was among the most fiery of all the firebrands of the Jewish settlement movement. A selfless father of twelve, his supporters called him. A Jerusalem District Court convicted him of murdering two Arabs, but a political lobby in the Knesset finally persuaded the president to grant clemency three years into the sentence. He was welcomed home to Kiryat Arba as a hero. Since getting out of jail, Bookspan had confined himself to dealing with government agencies responsible for providing public utilities and services to the Jewish settlements. But after every terrorist incident, when meetings were held between settler leaders and the generals and colonels who tried to explain that there was no way to provide absolute security in the territories, Bookspan sat in the back row of the hall, a silent presence reminding all concerned that there was a way to fight back. After the famous handshake on the White House lawn, when overnight the terrorist enemy became a partner in a peace of the brave, Bookspan's name started coming up in the news in the front ranks of increasingly violent demonstrations against the peace process. Bookspan had said nothing in the media about the massacre in the mosque. Cohen decided that Bookspan probably would have been against Goldstein if only because of its apparently suicidal nature. And he knew that during the years of *intifada,* Bookspan was involved on more than one occasion when settlers defended themselves against stone-throwing Arabs. Bookspan carried an Uzi, and usually wore a pistol. "How did it happen?" Cohen asked the soldier at the roadblock.

The officer shouted at one of the soldiers to "go take care of the media," and then turned back to Cohen. The car behind Cohen honked again.

"I knew who he was," the officer said. "I didn't always agree with him but I knew who he was." He didn't have an answer to Cohen's question but wanted to reassure himself that he wasn't to blame for Bookspan's death—or his ideologies. "There are a lot of angry people up there," he said, nodding toward the first of the apartment complexes built on the hilltop, nearest the road. "And there are going to be plenty more here in a few minutes. So, if you don't have anything to do here, out." He jerked a thumb over his shoulder, pointing away from the settlement.

"Listen," Cohen tried. "I have a friend up there. He's expecting me. He was probably a friend of . . ."

"Nobody goes in," the officer insisted. "Especially press," he added, watching one of his soldiers talking to the lead driver in the convoy of TV crews lined up behind Cohen's car.

"I'm not press," Cohen tried.

"Doesn't matter. You can call your friend, there's a phone over there." He pointed back down the hill behind Cohen, toward a bus bench sheltered by a concrete frame, and a phone booth beside it.

A pair of police cars swerved around Cohen's car and raced up the hill without stopping. Another press car joined the line behind him, and all four began honking together. The soldiers around the cars were getting nervous.

Cohen sighed, twisted the wheel, and turned his car around in the entrance to the broad empty avenue, pulling over to the side of the road to think. The soldiers blocked the entrance to the journalists. Like Cohen, they made U-turns, but instead of leaving, like him they took up positions along the side of the road, then piled out of their cars.

All four carried television cameras in their trunks. Cohen watched them through the side mirror. He recognized two of the camera-and-sound men—Na'im and Kobi. They had been working the streets of Jerusalem for years for an American television network. To Cohen's dismay, Na'im recognized him and came over to his car, camera on his shoulder. Kobi carried the recorder and microphone boom, and the umbilical cable to the camera.

"I thought you retired," Na'im said. He wore a thick neatly trimmed black mustache against the mocha color of his skin. A bald spot in the middle of his curly hair on the top of his head gave him the look of a depraved monk.

"I did," Cohen said.

"That explains it," Na'im said.

"What?"

"Why you're down here, and not up there," said Na'im, plucking a pack of cigarettes out of his shirt pocket.

"What happened?" Cohen asked.

"That's what we're here to find out. A tipster called us." Na'im offered Cohen a cigarette, which to the cameraman's surprise Cohen turned down. "So, if you're not here for the incident, then what's up?"

A pair of police vehicles turned into the avenue and headed past the clots of camera crews and soldiers. One was the mobile forensic lab from Jerusalem, a gray jeep with two technicians Cohen recognized. Raoul, the Argentinean-born medical coroner, was in the backseat of the other car, a white Ford Sierra just like Cohen's.

Two of the cameramen panned their cameras after the passing police. Na'im was more curious about Cohen's presence at Kiryat Arba's entrance that morning. Cohen turned his face to hide it from the driver of the white Sierra. Behind the wheel was Sasson, his replacement in Jerusalem CID. Sasson would be sure to let the fifth floor know that Cohen was spotted at Kiryat Arba that morning. The car passed. "Nothing," Cohen finally answered Na'im. "I just happened to be driving by when I heard the news."

He started his engine, and then turned it off again. A convoy of several cars arrived at the entrance to the avenue and pulled up in front of the soldiers. Na'im finally got his action. The vehicles—a closed-cabin pickup, two relatively new Japanese vans, and three beat-up cars from the late seventies—disgorged settlers of all ages. The officer called his troops into a formation to guard the gate—waving frantically at the two soldiers in the guard booth to close the gate, which was still wide open.

As soon as it became clear that the soldiers weren't going to let them in, the settlers lined up opposite the soldiers with posters and placards declaring the prime minister was a traitor making deals with terrorists who should be killed.

As the cameras panned them, some of the teenagers in the crowd started shouting "Death to the Arabs!" Just then, the army radio station, playing quietly in the background in Cohen's car, broke through the rock and roll with its first newsbreak on the story.

Bookspan was killed early that morning, on his way down by foot to the center of Hebron. His body was found just before eight by three *yeshiva* students taking the same path, which came out of the industrial zone and cut through an untilled field of rocks and boulders, passing a cluster of Arab houses on each side of the open land. He wasn't one to be there before dawn, like Goldstein. But he was there daily, and the entire town, Jew and Arab, knew his path. Nobody ever dared to touch him. "Until this morning," the talk show host summed up, taking over the newsbreak and reporting that a curfew was imposed in Hebron on both Jew and Arab. Kiryat Arba was declared a closed military area. Roadblocks sealed off the area.

Cohen stared ahead. The roadblocks didn't manage to stop the convoy approaching, twice as many cars as appeared in the first. The dozen cars pulled to the sides of the road and emptied their passengers. At least three people were carrying cellular phones and were busy using them as the bulk of the crowd began challenging the young officer's authority to deny them entry to the settlement.

A tiny woman under a huge yellow straw hat was raising her finger at him like an angry teacher. "Since when does the Israeli army, the Jewish army, the army of our people, use its force against us, Jews who have the people on their side?" she scolded him shrilly.

He was trying to stay calm. Cohen could see the anxiety in the young officer's eyes as he signaled for his radioman. Some teenage girls in long denim dresses that almost swept the street, wearing simple strap sandals and carrying posters, pushed together in a formation toward the gate. The soldiers tried to prevent their weapons from striking the girls and tried to push back without using force.

"A saint among us has been cut down, and instead of finding the killer the army fights the Jews!" someone shouted.

The officer grabbed the microphone his communications officer handed him. Just then a car wove its way into the intersection, and as the demonstrators recognized the driver and his passengers, they began to accompany the vehicle up the hill until it was directly in front of the gate.

Cohen got out of his car to watch as the two members of Knesset from the opposition got out of the Japanese family car and faced the red-faced young officer. One was religious, the other secular. Both had also been ministers in the past, in governments that gave grants and easy credit for housing purchases in the territories.

The shouting became more enthusiastic and rhythmic. "Death to the Arabs," shouted a teenager wearing a T-shirt emblazoned with a clenched fist holding a rifle against the map of the Greater Land of Israel, which included Israel and Jordan, as well as the West Bank in between. An older demonstrator hushed him, but the teenager pranced at the edges of the crowd, wielding a stick.

The politicians were immediately swarmed by the demonstrators, beseeching them to use their authority to make the soldiers let them through the gates up to the hilltop settlement.

"They need us," the people closest to the politicians cried out.

"The army has no right to stop us," someone shouted. "Don't be puppets for a leftist government," he added, aiming it at the soldiers. "Worse than Nazis!" he screamed at the soldiers.

The secular politician was appalled, and began lecturing the settler on the neutrality of the army. "Keep the army out of this," the politician ordered. "And keep the Holocaust out of it," shouted someone else.

The settler scowled in disgust and turned his back on the secular politician, and looking out over the crowd, shouted, "They have no right to stop us!" The crowd pushed forward again at the infantrymen trained for combat, not for riot control against Jewish mothers and children.

In the chaos, Cohen could see the religious politician punching in some numbers on a cellular phone, then listening for the ring. He had seen enough. He wasn't investigating Bookspan's death, he decided. He was looking for Simon Levi-Tsur.

He had the license-plate numbers from both cars. As he restarted his car he wondered if it was time to ask Nissim Levy for help. Meanwhile, he wanted to go back to the Levi-Tsur apartment. There must have been something there that he had missed, he realized. Something among the books, perhaps. As he left, the soldier was holding the religious politician's telephone to one ear, and using his radioman's handset for a second conversation with his commanding officer.

· 17 ·

He left Kiryat Arba just before eleven and spent a fruitless hour at Herodium. The two guards on duty knew nothing about any body found nearby. Nor did the ticket salesman and ticket taker at the archeological gardens. Not even the two pairs of soldiers patrolling the grounds knew anything about a body found about a mile east. But looking out over the plain falling down to the Dead Sea, Cohen decided he'd need better coordinates than a mile east if he hoped to find the scene.

He got back in his car and drove to Jerusalem, which was as clogged as ever, with the settlers' tent demonstration on the edges of the government complex. "And a helluva lot of suspicious objects today," said a traffic cop who recognized Cohen at the jammed intersection near the Foreign Ministry at the western end of the Valley of the Cross. "Thanks God, no bombs, though," he said as a farewell to Cohen, when the light changed.

So it was nearly two o'clock before he was on the highway to Tel Aviv. Two hours to get through roadblocks and traffic. He remembered when the ride from Hebron into Jerusalem took half the time.

The highway west to Tel Aviv went quickly. But outside the city, construction work slowed him down. It was going on everywhere. No more money for settlements. It was time to invest inside the Green Line. The mysticism was taken out of the political rhetoric at the highest levels. Cohen applauded that, but it only raised his anxiety about civil war, something at the constant edge of consciousness in a country that twice before, when run by the Jews, eventually descended into the whirlpool of self-destruction.

He tried to find a parking place near Simon's flat but ended up in a public lot near the American embassy on Hayarkon Street. There was a pool hall directly in front of the large brick building, so he pulled out the Polaroid, dog-eared in the envelope in his pocket and showed it to the three people there at midday. One was the guy behind the counter, who remembered Simon as a player for higher stakes than most, and with a nasty temper when he lost, which he did more often than not.

The other two were no help at all. They had just finished the army together and had been across the street getting their visas for the trip to America. All three looked at Cohen as if he were the strange one, when he asked if they had ever seen a settler-rabbi reciting passages from Job and looking for just men in Sodom.

Something was wrong. Something had changed. With the sun directly over the apartment, the light falling through the blinds created elaborate shadows in the corners of the room different from those Cohen had created at sunset and last saw in the dark.

The piles of clothes had disappeared. The ashtrays, glasses, and plates were washed, piled cleanly and neatly on the kitchen counter. The balls were gone from the pool table, and it took Cohen a second to realize they were racked. He remembered coming across three pool cues, but now he saw there were six standing properly in their wooden case. The papers that had revealed nothing to Cohen the last time he sat at the desk end of the table were now clipped into two piles beside the computer, which was covered properly with a clear, antistatic nylon cover.

He went to the kitchen sink, past the table for twelve, and realized the stone floors had been washed. He took one of the clean glasses. There were nine altogether, each one different, except for two very heavy large beer mugs. In the sink someone had started the copper pots on a soak. He touched the water. It was still soapy, even though the bubbles were gone. He filled a water glass from the faucet, and then turned to face the room, downed the drink, and then refilled the glass for more.

Little touches in the cleaning job convinced Cohen that someone who knew Simon, someone who wanted to help Simon put his life in order, had arrived too late.

He walked across the room to the wide seating area around the sound-and-television system. Three sets of magazines were on the table, European and American fashions in clothing, sports, and current affairs.

They all wore subscription stickers, but when Cohen looked closely, he saw they were from an address in London, the last address where Simon had lived under his grandfather's roof, even if his grandfather was only there once every few weeks or months. He looked at the date on the magazine he was holding. It was a year old. The bookcases below the windows running around half the room were also put in order from the last time Cohen had seen them. He went to the corner where the shelves met. There was a logic to their placement—history here, fiction there. He followed the three-shelf bookcase all the way to the half-open door to the narrow terrace outside. Plants had been watered.

He went back inside, directly across the room to the round stair-well that began beside the entrance to the first floor, and climbed up to the smaller second floor with the much larger patio.

The mattresses scattered about the floor had been turned into three sofas, with pillows waiting for their covers piled at the end of each one. The rancid towels and dank sheets were gone. Outside, the hot tub was drained. Here, too, plants had been watered.

He went back into the bedroom, past the open shower, opened the door to the toilet, and closed it. Everything had been cleaned. At the polished concrete sink and counter, a selection of aftershaves and pimple creams stood like soliders in their ranks.

The door slammed on the floor below. He listened for sounds. First there were two thuds, and a sigh of relief. He couldn't tell if it was a man or a woman's sigh. There was silence, and then the sound of running water. Cohen remembered he had put down his glass of water on the coffee table next to the magazines. He drew the Beretta hidden under his shirttails tucked into the small of his back in the waistband.

On sneakered feet he started down the stairwell, slabs of concrete on metal shelves down a tight 360 degree turn around a central pole, crouching low for an early view of the floor below his feet. Two large plastic bags, so stuffed that they couldn't be closed at the top to protect the folded laundry, sat under the circular stairwell beside the front door. When he was halfway down, able to see all the way across the room, the rest of the mystery was solved. He put away the gun.

Barefoot, she stood at the open sliding glass doors to the south looking down to Jaffa curving out into the sea at the end of the beach. She was wearing tight black bicycle rider's pants stretched over buttocks no wider than her shoulders, and was wearing a T-shirt tied into a halter to expose her stomach.

"Shalom Vicki-Bracha," he said. She spun, shocked, but the surprise turned into a smile, and then into even a greater joy.

"It's cosmic," she beamed. "You showing up like this. I was practicing what I was going to say when I called you. Oh God," she said, wiping her brow, suddenly confused. "Right," she added to herself, concentrating. "Right," she said again, lifting her eyes to his and beginning a speech, suddenly much more wooden than her usual animation.

"I wanted to tell you that our conversation, I mean your questions, made me do some very serious thinking about my life. And what I was doing with it." She stopped for a second, looking into his eyes for understanding. He was kicking himself for not asking her if she owned a key to Simon's flat. "And I confess that it also reminded me that I left behind a few things of mine," she summed up.

There had been bras and panties among the underwear Cohen had found during his first visit to the upstairs room. Valuables, too, which Cohen had collected and put into a kitchen drawer. A couple of watches, some rings, a few pendants on gold and silver chains. Nothing overtly feminine. Nothing necessarily masculine, except the watches, except perhaps for one of them, Cohen remembered, a thin band of solid gold with a clock face mounted at the widest point of the band, opposite the wrist opening. She could have stolen it all, Cohen thought. Instead she cleaned up. She obviously was affected by something.

"If you've taken any drugs, it looks like they have an opposite effect on you than they did on Simon," he said, referring to the housecleaning.

"No!" she stated emphatically. "No drugs," and then let out a chestful of air, sighing. "I knew this wasn't going to be easy," she said, as much to herself as to him. "I mean, yes, I had a kind of revelation. You could say that. I mean, I was the last person I know to have seen him, and I did, you know, was with him for awhile. We did have a connection."

"And you hope the family will appreciate it?" he asked.

"No," she repeated, even more emphatically. "Simon. When you find him," she added confidently. "With my help. If you want. If you need. Anything. You see, I figured that was the problem with Simon. Wasn't it? He thought he needed to buy his friends, love, everything. It was all about money for him, not feelings. And nobody showed him any real feelings. I mean, I know I didn't. I mean, well . . . I just wanted to let him know that people have feelings and that means that I know he has feelings, too. You see what I mean? I mean, I was going to call you to tell you all this, because I thought you could understand, and that I could help."

She still charmed him. He didn't want to tell her that Simon might be dead. He was still outraged at the way the boy's body was released before it was properly identified and wasn't going to believe it for sure until he heard from Raphael himself. But meanwhile he had no choice but to operate on the assumption that the boy could either be alive or dead.

He wondered how he would break it to her and how she would take it. Three days ago, he thought, she would have said she wasn't surprised. Now she was pinning too much of her own redemption on Simon's. He postponed the decision. "How was the room when you found it?" he asked.

"I know, I know," she said, raising her hands in a gesture of surrender. "You're not supposed to touch things at the crime scene. But it wasn't the crime scene, was it? I mean, I don't even know really what the crime is, but going off to some *yeshiva* isn't a crime. Maybe for some people it's okay. I'm not sure it's okay for Simon, if you understand what I mean. It would be such a waste for him to go back to the Middle Ages. And believe me, I know, it's the Middle Ages."

"Well, as a woman, you certainly filled your part," Cohen said softly. It was a bad joke, he realized as he said it, but she shrugged it off.

"I didn't come here thinking that I was going to clean up the place," she said. "But as soon as I began looking for my stuff, I realized it was the right thing to do. And then I . . ." She suddenly halted, thinking of what she did next, realizing she was caught in a lie.

She decided to tell the truth. "Okay, I smoked a joint while I cleaned up. Helped me make the time go faster. But I'm not stoned now."

"Fine, fine, I believe you," Cohen said. "When did you start?"

"Last night. This morning I took the laundry, came back and finished, and now I'm back from picking up the laundry, and here you are, and what do you want me to do?"

"What did you find when you arrived last night?"

They were still standing at the edge of the terrace facing south, and she pointed north, over his shoulder into the room, leading him inside. "There were some piles of clothes over there," she said, waving a hand in the direction of the sofa area, "and there," she added, pointing near the pool table. "Upstairs, all the laundry was piled in the middle of the floor. Other than that, it was just the way it was when we left that night—except for his goodies. You know. The watches, gold and stuff, into a drawer in the kitchen. Weird, huh? Kitchen drawer?"

"Are you hungry?" he asked.

"What's with you? Always eating?" she said, then touched his stomach, testing it for flab. There wasn't much. He did have the slightly flimsy wrapping of his muscular structure in looser skin than someone twenty years younger, but that was a condition of age.

"I'm very hungry," he said. "I haven't eaten since yesterday."

"I could eat," she admitted, licking her lips. They were standing close together at the head of the dining table. He surprised her by giving up the sweet scent of her sweat and went to the kitchen counter, his hand above the drawer where he had put the valuables.

There was a look of expectancy on her face, and then she read in his eyes what he was thinking, realizing that he had been the last one in the apartment. Finally, her eyes dropped in disappointment. "You think I took something," she said sorrowfully.

"Habit," he admitted, pulling open the drawer, and then shutting it quickly. "I have to ask you to show me what you've taken," he said.

"Just some personal stuff," she said. "Alright, some panties. And a couple of books he gave me. And some pictures."

"Pictures?" he asked.

"Yes, pictures," she said resentfully, begrudgingly.

"Show me."

She stared at him, then her face broke into a grin, almost lascivious, but wanting to provoke him. "Sure, why not," she said, crossing the room and getting her bag from the sofa, coming back to him with an expression that carefully balanced pride with defiance in the gesture as she handed them over.

The first half dozen weren't in order, but they were taken at the same time, as she undressed deliberately for Simon, holding out pieces of clothing and offering parts of her body to the camera.

The next three showed that she went topless to the beach. In one, she was in the water holding a wet string proving she took off the bottom, two other girls behind her doing the same, and Simon displaying his groin above the water line, like the girls proudly holding up his dripping bathing suit.

Vicki filled half the next picture, making a model's pose in her red jumpsuit against a Roman pillar at sunset.

He held it up to her, the question in his eye.

"Herodium," she said.

He wasn't surprised.

"Just the two of you?" he asked.

"Yes."

"Why?" he wanted to know.

"Why what?"

"Why there?"

"We were on a bike ride. That's one of the reasons I liked him. He never felt afraid on the back of my bike. Neither did you," she added, in a softer voice.

"But why there?"

"Where? Herodium? We were riding and he saw the sign and patted my tummy—that was our signal when we were going too fast to talk—and I slowed down and he said he wanted to stop."

"Why?" Cohen asked.

"What?!" she complained, not understanding what he wanted from her.

"Did he say why he wanted to stop? At Herodium? Did he say to you, 'Let's go to Herodium,' or was it just a place to stop and play? Was he looking for something there? Or just taking a piss? Why did you stop at Herodium?" He was asking the questions with the kind of intensity he had reserved in the past for recalcitrant suspects in an interrogation, when he really needed the answer and there was very little time.

It frightened her into a stammer. "He wanted to see it. We were out for a ride. That's all. Sometimes we went to Galilee. Sometimes we went to the Dead Sea. Sometimes we went . . ."

"To the territories? To the *intifada?* To the settlements?"

"Nobody ever threw anything at me on my bike," she huffed. "We were out for a ride. On the motorcycle. That's all. I remember, it was nice. The road, I mean, empty. I could really pour it on," she said, trying to concentrate, to reconstruct the experience, seeking the answer in her memory to satisfy Cohen's demand. "The park was officially closed," she finally added. "But we rode around a little off-track."

"He must have said something to you, about why he wanted to go," Cohen tried. "Was he interested in archeology?"

"I guess you think the fact that he was never there and felt like a tourist isn't a good enough answer," she cried.

It made him pause, annoyed with himself for losing his cool, feeling sorry for her. "I'm not angry at you," he said softly.

"What's so important about Herodium?" she sniffled, and tested his waters with a smile before wiping away a little sweat from her brow.

"I remember some bottles," Cohen said, looking around the room. "Cognac?"

She wordlessly went to a kitchen cabinet and pulled out two brown bottles. "And there's vodka in the freezer," she said, turning to him and offering him a choice. She checked the labels, nodded at the second, and put them down on the counter before picking two glasses—a balloon for him and a shallow martini glass for her.

He waved a finger no at her. While he crossed the room to retrieve the water glass he had left on the coffee table, she pulled a bottle of soda water from the refrigerator. He came back to the kitchen, and she poured until the golden brown was halfway up the glass at his forefinger signaling her to stop.

"Listen," she said, going to the freezer door and pulling out an ice tray that she dropped on the counter. "I've been thinking. You're hungry, I'm hungry, why don't you stick around here, and I mean, I guess you came back 'cause you didn't do a very good job the first time, so you want to look around, and I could help, I mean, I've been working for two days here. I know where to find everything."

It was extortion as well as the truth, and it worked on Cohen. They were standing close to each other under the clear light of the kitchen's northern exposure. He looked around at the room trying not to focus on how much she resembled a younger Ahuva he never knew—and Annabella Levi-Tsur-Cohen. "You did a very professional job," he said about the housecleaning.

"Hey, don't get me wrong. I'm not going back to what my mother, may her memory be blessed, went through. You don't think I'm gonna do this for a living?" She waved her hand at the expanse of the room.

"I didn't think so," Cohen admitted.

"So, are you going to tell me about Herodium or not?" she demanded with a hopeful smile.

"First," he said, "food? A restaurant, perhaps?"

"I brought groceries," she said, remembering. "I was sure that you'd find him and I just wanted everything to be ready for him when he came home."

He looked at her silently. He wasn't flattered by her confidence in him. It was another burden. But it only added to the increasing pace of his heartbeat. He took a deep breath, taking in all the smells, from the salt of the sea and city beyond the open windows all the way to the faint fragrance of her sweat, which was strangely sweet.

"I must stink," she said, misunderstanding, and her own embarrassment broke the tension. She put down her empty glass and ducked out of the kitchen, making an abashed face smelling her armpit, and then continuing to embarrass herself by almost falling over the chair at the head of the long glass table. "I've got some stuff in that laundry bag, I mean, they packed it all for me, and I should have told them to put my stuff at the top, but, well."

"No problem," he said, waving good-bye, relieved he was being left alone with his thoughts.

As soon as she went upstairs, carrying one of the laundry bags, he sat down at the phone and punched a number. "You know who this is?" he asked, when the switchboard patched him through to Nissim Levy.

"Yes," said Nissim.

"I need ID on two car registrations. Ready?"

"Yes."

Cohen read off the numbers.

"I have to go to a terminal," Levy said.

"I'll wait." He could hear the shower begin to rain upstairs, and

159

then through the phone, the sound of a dot matrix printer zipping out its lines, before Nissim came back.

The Fiat was fifteen years old, and when Nissim read out the name of the owner, Cohen slapped his forehead, realizing what he had missed in the parking lot at the Mount of Olives.

Avner "Avi" Bitusi. Cohen knew Bitusi as a cat burglar. Cohen sent him to jail once, and probably would have done it again except for a miscalculated jump that dropped the burglar four stories into a rocky garden. He hadn't seen Bitusi in at least a decade, and always assumed the religious turn in his life took hold. He vaguely remembered there was a wife, who "returned to the answer," as the born-again repentance movement is called in Hebrew, taking her injured husband with her. He couldn't be absolutely sure it was the same Bitusi—the last time Cohen heard about him, Bitusi was a rabbinical student and still using crutches, a year after the failed burglary. But the address in Mekor Baruch, a dense quarter of *haredim* across Jaffa Road from the *shuk,* made sense.

Jeremiah Ben-Alon, who owned the van, was a resident of Kiryat Arba.

"Ever hear of him?" Cohen asked Levy.

"No," Levy admitted.

"Okay. That's all. And not a word," he said, seeing Vicki-Bracha come down the stairs. She had changed her clothes. Her long bare legs were interrupted by a short skirt wrapped around her hips. Her stomach was exposed with a man's shirt tied into a knot to clutch her breasts and reveal all the cleavage. He wondered if she was doing it on purpose for him. She touched him lightly on the head as she passed him, heading to the kitchen.

"You were right about me," he said, hanging up.

"When?" she asked, disappearing behind the refrigerator door.

"When you said I try to learn from my mistakes," said Cohen, following her into the kitchen.

Her head popped back up and she let the fridge door close. She was holding two large onions, a wrapped packet of fresh mushrooms, and a plastic bag. "I said that?" she wondered, then settled on an understanding of his meaning. "Because I said you came back for a second look? Correct?"

"Correct," he said.

"Good," she said, bending to get something from a kitchen cabinet below the counter, and then reappearing with a bottle of olive oil. She went to the sink and began dealing with the pots.

There was a garlic rope hanging over the sink. Cohen opened a drawer where he remembered knives. He reached up over her head, and cut off a bulb of garlic.

She turned, facing him.

"Can you handle this?" he asked her, offering the garlic. There was something in his tone of voice that made her understand he meant more than whether she liked garlic in a meal.

"Sure," she said, her eyes on his, reaching for the bulb.

He put it on her open palm. "A body was found. Near Herodium. Simon's wallet was also there."

The garlic dropped from her hand. Her eyes began to blink quickly. "He's dead?" Three days ago her reaction would have been completely different. She said she was trying to redeem herself. He wondered if she made it a habit, and then wondered how many habits a person so young could have.

"Maybe," he finally said. "Probably. I don't know." He checked his watch. "The body should have arrived in London by now." He changed to a more businesslike tone, asking, "Did Simon ever talk about Kiryat Arba?" he asked. "Politics? Settlements? Palestinians? Peace? Any of it?"

She shook her head no to all his offers.

"Did he talk while you were there?" Cohen tried. "At Herodium?"

"He was always talking," she said, looking into his eyes. "Who knew when you could believe him? Except, of course, he had the money. So just when you were doubting something, he'd make it come true. Usually with money." She was talking to herself as much as to him, thinking about herself as much as Simon. " 'It all started here,' he kept saying. I asked him what he meant, but he wouldn't tell me. Called it 'a big bloody secret.' " She shook her head at the memory, trying to make sense of it. 'And it all started here,' he said."

"What started there?"

"Well, I don't know," she admitted angrily, a burst of emotion that she tried to keep under cover. "It was his fucking secret, isn't it," she added bitterly.

The mix of tenses of past and present was an expression of her confusion, and realizing that she had mixed the tenses about him, she finally bawled, "and we'll never know," and reached into Cohen's comforting embrace.

They stood that way for a long time, his one hand on her bare flesh exposed between the shirt and the skirt, the other holding the back of her head as her tears dampened his shirt collar, her breasts pressed against his chest. His body embarrassed him by flirting with its own willpower at her thigh.

Gradually, the sobbing stopped and the dampness at his neck where she buried her head turned into something hotter than tears, as her arms around him first loosened their clench and then her hands tightened, pressing him forward, toward her. He could hear her breathing even faster than his and felt guilt rising as stiffly into his mind as the strain against his trousers. At first her mouth moved like a cat stretching, as it slid from shoulder to neck to just below his ear, and then it was like a bird, flitting across his face and pecking at his cheek, seeking a better place to perch, at his own dry mouth suddenly filled with the sweet juice of her own taste.

His hand slid down from her back, the other slid down the side of her face until his palm was on her breast, thumb on the hardening nipple, fingers spread to the ridge of her uppermost ribs, pressing with the same growing intensity with which she was seeking between his legs with her strong thigh.

As they sunk to the kitchen floor, pulled down by her intentions and his weakness, he felt the departure of guilt from his mind like a soul leaving a body at death, leaving behind the past as he gave in to her young body's demands, and his own desire for the freedom that exists only in the present.

They passed out at the same time, but she woke first, delicately disentangling her legs from his, while he pretended to be asleep and watched her from a crazy angle, lying on the floor. She padded nude to the circular stairwell and up it to the second floor, leaving him alone in the large room.

The air was dusty from the *sharav*. The floor became suddenly uncomfortable. He felt dirty, and angry at himself for giving in. He checked his watch, the only thing he was wearing. When she was finally gone he sat up, slightly dizzy from the sudden move.

He found a towel in the laundry bag she left on the first floor, and went back to the phone. His answering machine sent a message back to him that someone had called. He pressed again. There was a beep. "Caroline Jones here, from the House of Levi-Tsur, confirming the body's arrival. Yes. It was indeed the boy. Thank you Mr. Cohen. Good-bye." Beep.

He had hoped that the broken rules of proper police procedure for the sake of the House of Levi-Tsur would reveal their fault with the surprise that it wasn't Simon's body found in the desert near the archeological park. Even after hearing from Caroline Jones, he still wanted to hear it from Raphael Levi-Tsur. He'd call back.

Vicki was coming back down as he hung up. "Your turn," she said cheerfully. He didn't turn to face her. "I can call you Avram?" she continued. "Right?" She came into view, now wearing only one of Simon's long tailed shirts. But when he didn't answer, she came around to face him. "Are you all right?" she asked.

He nodded silently, but still didn't look at her.

"You're awfully quiet," she said. "You're not going to turn heavy over this. I mean emotionally or anything." She sounded like she was protesting too much. "Well, it's not a good idea," she went on. "Shit," she suddenly said, smacking herself on her forehead and by doing so making Cohen's mouth twitch with a grin, because he sometimes did the same thing when he realized he had forgotten something.

"Condom," she said. "That's it. We didn't use a condom. You're worried about AIDS." She looked at him for a reaction, but he was stone-faced, still thinking about Simon Levi-Tsur and why he went to Jerusalem and Herodium. Most of all, Cohen wondered why he was so sloppy. "Well, I was tested last week," she was saying. "It's a regular checkup for me. How about you?"

"You are the first person I have been with in more than ten years," he finally said. It made her face change into an expression of amazement, and he realized that he hadn't phrased himself clearly. "I mean, it's the first time in ten years that I've betrayed my . . ." he looked for the word to describe his relationship with Ahuva, whose name meant beloved.

"Your wife?" she tried. There was something angry in her tone

163

that was aimed at herself, not him, as if she should have known better from the start and shouldn't have been surprised.

"No. No. My friend," he finally decided.

"Oh," she said, surprised. Then she grinned victoriously. "Is she nice? As nice as me? I mean, I could be your friend . . ." She must have seen his expression change, because suddenly her tone did another one of those twists and turns like a diver changing direction halfway through the jump. "Master of the Universe," she called out for help, using the expletive from the streets of Bnei Brak, not Tel Aviv. "I don't know how you do it," she added to Cohen, "I'm never saying the right thing with you."

He stood up from the chair beside the computer. The towel fell away from him, and she couldn't stop the smirk. Still, his expression didn't change. He picked up the towel from the chair and tied it around him.

"Oh God," she cried again, and again misunderstanding his expression. "It's not that important. Really."

"I believe you," he said. "I heard from London."

It took a moment for it to sink in. "He really is dead," she said. He nodded. She looked around at the room, sighed, then shrugged, as if she should have known better than to expect better from fate.

"But I don't understand why," he said to himself as much as her. "Or how," he added.

"You said an Arab did it."

"I said that's what the family was told."

"And you don't believe it?"

He shook his head. "I don't understand it, and I try not to believe things I don't understand." He felt suddenly ridiculous, an old man wearing only a towel. He checked his watch.

"I got steaks," she tried. "Simon liked steaks."

But his mind was elsewhere. He wanted to speak with Shmulik, about the Twins. But before anything, he wanted to wash. The dust from the *sharav* gave a yellow tinge to the bright white light of the sun beginning the afternoon just above the beach, beginning its descent to the horizon. The grit on his skin was annoying. He mumbled, "Fine, fine," shooting her a grin that said everything was going to work out, and then, after collecting his clothes, he started up the circular stairs.

Cohen hated himself at that moment. He was on a forced pension, worthless to the system, which from what he saw outside Kiryat Arba obviously needed some help. And he was rich overnight, he thought, angry at his confusion about the money. The kid was rich and look where it got him, he added to his list. Richer, he scorned to himself. He looked around at the room. No doubt there was an extravagance at work. But there was also something anonymous. The boy owned things. But nothing personal. Not even the pool table. No paintings or photos. No rugs. No warmth. Money didn't seem to confuse the kid. Love did.

He kicked himself all the way up the stairs, wondering what he would tell Ahuva—or if he should tell her about Vicki-Bracha—trying to figure out what he had forgotten in his first too easy search of Simon Levi-Tsur's apartment.

The laundry bag made him realize what he had missed. The closets. They were white, with recessed handles and smooth folding doors that covered the eastern wall of the room. He had missed them entirely, and to soothe his guilty conscience he decided it was because he picked up the kid's laundry, and it had been years since he carried a checklist into a crime scene—or needed to do all the cataloging himself. It was lame, he knew, and he would have bawled out any junior who offered such an excuse. "Stupid," he muttered under his breath. "Stupid, stupid, stupid." By the fourth stupid, he was past self-recrimination, opening the closet door,

It opened like a fan. A row of hanging clothes, in no particular order, was revealed. The clothes rack was broken by a set of chest drawers above which there were open shelves for folded items. Banker suits hung amid flowered shirts; boxer-style bathing suits were clipped in pairs to the crossbeams of hangers. Cohen patted pockets, but knew he was looking for something more than a stray matchbook.

He yanked opened the bottom drawer. An electric blanket. He opened the middle. Three socks, a dozen ties rolled and piled in a separate compartment, and a limp slip of underwear with a torn elastic. The top drawer held even fewer items. Cohen figured most of the kid's everyday clothes were in the plastic laundry bags.

But he wasn't looking for clothes. He dragged a canvas and wooden director's chair from the patio into the room, and used it as a ladder, carefully placing his feet on the wooden frame instead of the cloth, reaching up into the highest shelf.

He felt something solid—a suitcase, he realized, as he pulled it halfway out the shelf. It didn't feel empty. Indeed, it was heavy enough to start toppling his balance as he yanked at it to pull it off the shelf. Finally, he gave a jerk that made the bag slide all the way out, heavy enough to make him let go. In the momentary desperation that he was losing his balance, he became aware that the top of the bag flew open on its way down. He heard two thumps behind him after the bag flew past. But at least he didn't fall.

"Hey, what's going on up there?" Vicki shouted from below. "You aren't doing it alone, are you?"

Cohen winced, but didn't answer, concentrating on getting off the chair without making another thump.

There had been a brown leather attaché case inside the suitcase, which had burst open when it hit the floor. A large brown leather accordion folder was inside the attaché case. He shook his head at the kid, and picked up the accordion folder. It was as heavy as the briefcase, with the scratched and faded golden embossing of a crescent on its side. It seemed empty at first glance into the first pocket. But the third pocket revealed a file of photocopied newspaper clips.

As he leafed through the clips, he began to think it was actually a dream, that somehow the heat and the cooking, the sweat and the flesh had driven him mad.

The clips came from a variety of newspapers. Several were from New York, a few from other cities in the U.S. He knew, because if the clip itself, photocopied from microfiche, didn't name the newspaper, then a fine, sloping handwriting that Cohen could only then guess was a woman's, listed the date and the newspaper's name.

Two items by the United Press summed up the whole file: One was headlined BIBLICAL CROWNS STOLEN IN ISRAELI MUSEUM BURGLARY, and was datelined Tel Aviv. It had appeared in the *Chicago Sun,* and the delicate hand wrote that it appeared as a "filler on page thirty-seven." The second UPI item, as picked up by the *New York Times,* reported HEROD'S CROWNS SAID STOLEN FROM ISRAELI MUSEUM. He didn't have to look at the date on any of the clips. He knew the date all too well.

· 18 ·

There were late rains that year, which made Pessah seem early, even though it was late. As a bachelor without family, then Inspector Cohen was assigned to the seder shift as duty officer for the *mador*, the flying squad. He didn't mind. It was usually quiet on the holidays.

He was due to start an interrogator's course the following month. The course would put him on track for a deputy superintendent's rank. And he had handed in a transfer request to Jerusalem.

He told Tzippi, a patrolwoman with whom he was having an on-again, off-again relationship at the time, that he was hoping to get assigned to Jerusalem. "Why there?" she asked, amazed anyone would want to work in the backwater town at the end of the twisting road up the mountains.

"It's smaller," he admitted bluntly. "Maybe I can make a difference."

Tzippi scoffed at his innocent belief that police work could make any difference at all. But she also admitted that it was what she loved about him. Nonetheless, she tried to talk him out of the transfer.

"I've made up my mind," he said. "I'm leaving Tel Aviv."

The holiday at the end of the week turned into a very long weekend. And a late-in-the-season, noisy rainstorm of drumming rain, thunder, and lightning made sure the long weekend was very quiet.

The Sunday morning sun began beating away the clouds and cold, but he'd sleep through the morning, he thought, leaving the station, walking the mile and a half home for the exercise. By nine he had eaten breakfast, showered, and washed, and was fast asleep. The nightmare began almost immediately, with loud pounding that jerked him awake at the last minute before descending totally into sleep.

"Avram," shouted a familiar voice in between three bangs on the door.

167

Cohen wrapped the blanket around his naked body, cursed at the chilly floor, and then opened the door into the brightness, recognizing Mizrahi.

"You better get dressed," the aged policeman said grimly.

"What's happened?"

"The new museum."

"What about it?" Cohen asked.

"It was burgled. During your shift."

Cohen had only been to the museum once, just before the official opening, when a half dozen investigators from the *mador* were invited for a demonstration of its security system. A dedicated phone line was set up for the alarm system, with a bell and flashing light on a board at the station on Dizengoff, barely two miles away. The museum was new, the alarm system was new. Progress was coming, the bureaucratic deputy commander said proudly as he announced the day's schedule.

The cops at the demonstration joked bitterly that it was easier for the museum to get a phone line than for Victor, the *mador*'s tough Bulgarian-born commander, who had been waiting months for a telephone to be installed in his apartment. The museum director, a stout academic with a German accent much stronger than Cohen's, shook his head at the comparison. He suggested the demonstration begin.

A small bespectacled man, introduced as the chief scientist for the project, called for volunteers to try to unlock either one of the doors to the main hall, or one of the glass cabinets. Victor used his Motorola to tell Sima back at the office to keep an eye on the red alarm, and to quiet everyone down to hear the bell.

Cohen managed to open a locked door using a pair of sticks from the little burglar's tool kit he carried in his pocket. Victor's walkie-talkie remained silent. The deputy commander turned red. The chief scientist said there was still fine-tuning to be done. "And only when completed, will the collections be installed," the museum director promised, as they followed him into the main hall.

"Touch a case," the scientist asked the deputy commander. He did. Nothing happened. The scientist took a breath, and then suggested, "Try applying pressure as if to move it, or force it."

Yossi Shoham smacked the case beside him. It made an echoing slap in the large hall, making the German museum director jump and Victor's walkie-talkie squawk with Sima's voice back at the *mador*. "It works," she said. "I've got a red light flashing and listen, an alarm." Over the walkie-talkie, the alarm sounded like a lot of static.

The museum director shook hands with the expert from the security systems company, proud of their accomplishment.

"You mean there are no guards overnight in the museum?" Victor asked, speaking what was on the mind of all the cops, except the deputy commander for the Tel Aviv District, who reprimanded Victor for his conservative distrust of the new technology, while the museum director clucked his tongue at the paranoia of the primitive policemen, who didn't understand what great advances were being made in electronics.

Cohen still wasn't sure he wasn't dreaming. His mouth felt dry. He wet his lips and realized he wasn't dreaming. "What happened?" he had asked Mizrahi. "I don't know exactly," the elderly officer admitted. "I know there was a robbery. They sent me to get you. I think you should get dressed."

"The alarm didn't ring," Cohen protested, stumbling back into the room, nearly tripping on the sheet around his waist, heading for his clothes. Mizrahi followed him into the room, looking around at the spartan quarters. A few books were on a shelf above Cohen's bed. A large radio sat on a table that doubled as a desk. There were no pictures on the walls.

"The museum will need a scapegoat. And so will the force," Mizrahi warned Cohen as he tied his sneakers.

"The alarm didn't ring," Cohen protested again, raising his voice.

"What alarm?" It was Vicki-Bracha. She came up the stairs and was standing behind him. "Are you all right?" she asked.

He only nodded, still grasping the newspaper clips, trying to decipher something written with green ink, in an extremely sloped, cursive handwriting, on the second page. "Hope this is what you were looking for," the handwriting said. It was signed only with a large *A* made from curlicues at the legs, and the mathematical symbol for infinity as the crossbar of the capital letter.

"What alarm?" Vicki-Bracha repeated as she flopped to the floor beside him. He handed her the two pieces of paper absent-mindedly, looking into his memory back to that spring morning.

The rains over the weekend had cleaned the sky and the city, giving everything a crisp, focused look. But in Cohen's mind, remembering those first minutes, everything was out of focus. Mizrahi gave Cohen a ride to the museum, where the formerly haughty director was now red-eyed from tears. Victor, of course, was furious, and Cohen could only tell the district commander that no alarm rang in *mador* headquarters during the long weekend. The burglars were professional—there was no doubt about it—even if the security was sloppy. No fence, gate, or guards had prevented them from parking behind the building, out of view from the road.

They had used an acetylene torch to get through the bars covering a short, high window that opened directly into the Coins of the Biblical Era pavilion, chosen to house the collection because of the artistry of the metalworks. As if deliberately mocking the police, the burglars had left behind some uneaten sandwiches and empty bottles of orange juice, suggesting that they had spent more than a few hours in the building without being caught.

They had stripped the museum of the centerpiece of its collection—twelve royal crowns, dating to the Roman era. Each crown had sat in its own glass case. Each case had been opened with a circle carefully cut into the glass, large enough to reach in and pull out the precious objects.

They were all solid gold. Several were inlaid with precious stones, but it was the largest that most intrigued the historians. Shaped like a pomegranate, it was engraved with the images of three symbols of good fortune among the religions of the region—fish, calves, and cats. The engravings were a clear violation of the Jewish law against graven images. According to the weepy museum director, there was an academic dispute whether the large crown indeed belonged in the collection.

Cohen was trying to remember more, but Vicki-Bracha interrupted his thoughts.

"Why would Simon be interested in some old robbery?" she asked Cohen. It was what Cohen was asking himself. He was not on the special investigating team. Three weeks after the robbery, he was in a course up in the north. All he knew of the case was the gossip, and the painful memory of being the one who didn't answer the alarm that never went off.

Already that first day, two schools of thought developed among the detectives on the case. One school said the robbers stole the crowns to melt them down for the gold and jewels. The other school of thought said that a collector had decided to steal the crowns and hired professionals from overseas for the job. An obsessive collector might not care if the stolen collection never again saw the light of day.

Every known fence in the country was hit by the cops looking for the crowns. Most had heard about the robbery, but none wanted to touch any of the items, even if it came their way. "Too expensive." "Too hot." "Too much for me to handle," said the fences.

Jewelers known to use their smelting labs for occasional questionable acquisitions were questioned. So were burglars known to be adept with acetylene torches and glass cutting. But everywhere they went, the detectives ran into dead ends, while the effort to identify collectors overseas was stymied by the natural difficulties of international communications.

Mizrahi's warning about a scapegoat was timely. The deputy district commander began referring to Cohen as "the one who didn't answer the alarm that didn't ring." Cohen was even less amused by the fact that he was not put on the special investigating team established for the inquiry, even if he could only serve for those three weeks before he went to the interrogator's course.

Cohen came out at the top of his class at the end of the three months. He wouldn't be a scapegoat again until the very last case of his career. Within the year, he was in the suddenly reunited Jerusalem after the Six Day War, starting undercover, on the street.

The crowns were never recovered. Nobody was ever charged with the crime. Cohen never forgot, but he had not thought about it for years. The last time was four years earlier, when he heard that Victor was in a home for the aged outside Jerusalem. Cohen had planned to pay a visit, but events overtook the plans. He wondered now if Victor was still alive.

"Weird? Huh?" said Vicki-Bracha.

But Cohen continued staring into space, thinking. Nothing in the clips Laskoff sent him suggested that the Levi-Tsurs were the donors of the crowns. He rose slowly to his feet, reaching for the clips in the young woman's hand.

She jumped up. "I'm making steaks," she said. "Can you smell the sauce?" The aroma of onions and garlic, marjoram and thyme frying in olive oil floated up the stairs to him.

"I have to make a phone call," he mumbled, and went down the stairs to the near end of the dining table where the phone waited. Vicki-Bracha followed silently, going to the kitchen while he went to the phone.

A woman's voice answered with only a "Yes?" and he asked for Shmulik Kagan. "One moment please," she said.

The phone rang four times, and then Shmulik answered.

"Shmulik," Cohen began, "it's me. You recognize my voice?"

"Say something else."

"Syndrome."

"I recognize the voice," Shmulik said.

"I need a meeting," Cohen said. "Today," he added.

There was a brief silence. "Where are you?" Shmulik finally answered.

"Near the beach in the city."

"Well, that's a surprise," Shmulik said, breaking security.

"We can talk at the meet," Cohen interrupted, a slight reprimand in his tone. "Where and when?"

"Okay," Shmulik said. "Meet me at Leah's."

"Leah's?" Cohen asked. "The café?"

"Yes."

"It's still there? She's still there?"

"Yes."

"So maybe the world isn't changing so fast," Cohen said.

"No," Shmulik said, wiser than Cohen on the point. "Leah hasn't changed. Let's say five o'clock."

Cohen checked his watch. It gave him three hours.

"Fine," said Cohen, hanging up, and then dialed another number. Mrs. Bornstein, Laskoff's secretary, wasn't surprised to hear from Cohen, her boss's favorite client. "He said you might call," she told Cohen. "He's out for the rest of the day, but said you could find him at Aharoni's tonight, at eight. Or after midnight at home."

Vicki-Bracha was stirring the onion and garlic sauce, studiously ignoring him. He looked at his notepad, and then the phone. He called Information. There was no number registered to Avner Bitusi,

172

according to the address from the car registration that Cohen gave the operator.

"All right, give me a number in Kiryat Arba," he said.

"Kiryat Arba?" she asked.

"Yes, near Hebron," he sighed.

"It's a mess there today, no?" the operator said.

"Yes," he sighed again. "Please, the number."

"Please wait," she said.

A moment later, a computer was reciting the number. Cohen wrote it down and then immediately tried it. It rang eight times before someone answered, a child.

"Is daddy home?" he asked.

"No," said the child.

Cohen hung up. But the operator's mention of Kiryat Arba's troubles made him realize that he hadn't heard any more details from the Bookspan slaying. He got up from the dining table, and went to the stereo system.

"Music?" Vicki-Bracha called out from the kitchen.

"The news," he said.

"Oh," she said, crestfallen. But then she realized that Cohen was lost amid the buttons and slide bars of the system. "Which station you want?" she asked.

"Army Radio?"

"Good choice," she said, coming over to the stereo, wiping her hands on a towel before touching the machine.

She might have rebelled against her family and its traditions and her father's abuse, but at that moment instead of a promiscuous golddigger he saw a young woman who had proved to herself that she knew how to make a home from an apartment, even if it was too late, and even if this particular apartment never would be hers.

A love song came on the radio. He looked at his watch. They were ten minutes away from the half-hour news bulletin. He looked for the volume button. She found it for him, lowering the music.

"I don't think we should stay here much longer," he said softly.

She nodded, looked around the flat sadly, and then back at him with a slight welling of tears in her eyes. "Tell me something," she said, trying to sound cheerful, her voice caught in her emotions. "Do you think that maybe if I had, you know, done this . . . ," she waved at the room she had preened so carefully for the sake of a kid who probably didn't deserve it.

"He wouldn't have gotten into trouble?" Cohen filled in the end of the sentence for her.

"Stupid of me, huh?" she admitted.

"I don't know," Cohen said. "Maybe it would have had an effect on him. Maybe. It should have," he added, for her sake.

"The sauce!" she exclaimed, breaking the silence that suddenly fell on them in the room. She skipped back to the kitchen, yanking the pan off the flame, grabbing a spoon to stir it, and then taste. She frowned. "It's ruined," she said glumly, as if she should have expected it, and dropped the pan back onto the stove, turning off the flame.

"Let me see," Cohen said. He could smell the burning of the onions but knew a trick to repair the damage. The radio news gave him some more details about Bookspan's death, while he doctored the sauce with a pinch of sugar, a few drops of lemon, and quarter teaspoon of mustard.

The demonstrations inside Kiryat Arba had forced the police and army to arrest dozens of settlers who wanted to demonstrate at the crime scene, the reporter announced breathlessly, describing it as the middle of the empty field between the fence around the settlement's industrial zone and the first houses of Arab Hebron less than a hundred yards away. Bookspan, the reporter continued, was apparently struck with an ax to the back of the head.

At the word ax, Cohen paused in mid breath while blowing at some cooling sauce to taste on the spoon.

The assailant had disappeared into Hebron, the reporter said, and the Arabs and the Jews of Hebron were still under orders to stay inside for a curfew. Deep inside him, he heard a voice say "They'll think you're crazy."

"Those Arabs," said Vicki-Bracha, reading into his frozen posture of concentration her own disgust. "An ax!" she added with a shiver, and then adopted a tone Cohen heard far too many times in his life. "How can we make peace with people like that?"

With those politics, she wouldn't take kindly to what was going through his mind. Yossi Blumberg had said that it could have been an ax that caused the wound in the back of Simon's head. Now,

Bookspan with the same thing. Vicki-Bracha would say it was the same Arab. Or, that's what was to be expected from Arabs.

Maybe. Maybe not, Cohen thought. But as he resumed taking care of the sauce, he thought of the little voice warning him that he'd be considered crazy if he asked the question prematurely, and more than anything, with all his heart, he hoped his unspoken fear about the syndrome was wrong, and wondered why Simon Levi-Tsur was interested in a robbery that almost everyone had forgotten—except Cohen.

· 19 ·

Shmulik was wrong. Things had changed at the café. Plastic chairs had replaced the folding wooden chairs of thirty years ago.

But Leah was the same. She was standing in the doorway, like a captain on a ship watching sailors hoist the sails. Instead of sailors she was watching two workmen wrestle the remains of an old refrigerator out of her café.

Her hair was still purple—widowed too young, her hair had promptly turned white. She still wore too-tight frocks, and she still wore a chunk of costume jewelry mounted on her bosom like the figurehead on a flagship's prow.

She caught Cohen's eye, but if she was staring back she concealed it with naturally hooded eyes that he could remember widening suddenly with a large laugh, or narrowing even further when listening to someone with a problem and considering whether she could help or how.

The workmen dropped the machine on the sidewalk. One started walking away. "Where's he going?" she demanded suspiciously of the other, who sat on one of the city's low concrete domes that prevented cars from climbing the sidewalk.

"To get the truck," the worker answered.

"Shavit," she called out behind her to a waitress, "bring him some water." But she stayed in place watching suspiciously as Cohen cut into the open aisle between the three rows of tables on one side and the two on the other making his way into her place.

In the late afternoon, with the sun already pouring up the street from the beach to the west, the canvas canopy was useless. There were no customers outside, except for a white-haired man on an aisle seat. He was wearing a pair of Bermuda shorts, plastic sandals, and a faded flower-print shirt, drawing what Cohen couldn't help noticing was a cartoon of a pair of trees speaking in English.

"Avram Cohen," she finally exclaimed, grabbing Cohen's arm. No, Leah hadn't changed, Cohen thought. For a moment, he regretted agreeing to meet Shmulik at Leah's. He should have realized that if she recognized him she'd make a ruckus about it. "By my life, it's Avram Cohen," she repeated in her booming voice as she pulled him inside. "Where are you?" she shouted at him with affection, her smile changing her entire face, from hooded eyes to wide open, from small dour mouth to wide and full of teeth, even though most were false.

She looked him up and down, as if he was a child from the neighborhood now come home all grown up. "What happened to you? Where have you been? Jerusalem?" she declared, answering her own question but always the collector, wanting some detail, a tidbit of information that she could call all her own.

"I'm retired now," he said softly.

She put on her glasses, which hung around her neck on a string of gold, another piece of costume jewelry, leaned back, and studied him up and down.

"You don't look retired," she pronounced. "Avram Cohen," she summed up, as if the mere mention of his name carried all the reason for amazement at his reappearance in her café. But before she let him go, she wrapped a weighty arm around his shoulders, and pointed to the two shiny industrial air conditioners hanging like spacecraft over the cash register at one end of the long counter and the espresso machine at the other. "Look, you've arrived just in time," she chortled. "I finally decided it was time to get air-conditioning."

"Congratulations," he said softly, giving her a grin, looking beyond her, relieved to see that the only people who had heard her effusive welcome was the brown-haired waitress Shavit, back from giving a glass of water to the workman, and a young couple talking quietly in the corner to his immediate right.

"No, you haven't changed," she said to him. "Still have that worried look of the whole world on your shoulders." She punched him on the arm, a true sign of affection in her vocabulary of emotions.

He looked around. There were still caricatures and drawings, snapshots and paintings on the wall behind the counter, but not everything was in its same place, and there were pictures missing as well as new pictures he had never seen. The furniture seemed the same, however. Square Formica tables. Most were gray. A few newer ones were an almost hospital green and they were rectangular.

He tried to shrug a confession, but she was too strong to let a mere shift of his shoulders change her grip. "Go, go," she finally said, "Go to your friend," she added, surprising him as she pointed out Shmulik.

He was sitting behind one of the two tree trunks that Leah captured when she expanded the café onto the sidewalk, until City Hall had put an end to her occupation of the eastern sidewalk, zoning the street residential, and leaving her the southern sidewalk for her outdoor tables—and the two tree trunks inside her café.

The tree trunks were still being used for notices. In the distant past it was for work being offered in construction or *kibbutzim* searching for volunteers to help with a harvest. Down the street was *Davar*, the newspaper owned by the Labor Party, and in the old days of ideology and sacrifice for the common good, ministers and politicians would stop off at Leah's to read the galleys of their opinion pieces that would appear later that week.

Nowadays, he noticed as he sat down opposite Shmulik, the tree trunks were stapled with announcements for ambiance parties and yoga lessons, rock and roll and science fiction. Computers and rental flats were advertised up for grabs on the leaflets. Beside Cohen's head a used refrigerator was being advertised next to a postcard that showed a leaking condom, with the slogan "Cheap is Expensive."

It made him think of Vicki-Bracha. To help him think after finding the news clips, he took over the cooking of the steaks, flash frying them with some cognac, then smothering them with onion and garlic sauce. She tried asking more questions while they ate, but he had no answers for her.

When she asked him if he regretted the sex, he only looked up at her from his plate. It made her make a decision. She put down her fork and knife, pushed herself away from the table, and went up the circular stairs. A minute later she came down, a stack of clothes in her hand.

"This is my stuff," she said. "I'll be going now."

He sat still while she deliberated whether to say any more, and then she surprised him by planting a daughterly kiss on his cheek, said good-bye, and went out the door. It made him feel even worse.

After she was gone, while he put the dishes in the sink and gathered up his notes, folding the photocopied news clips into his notebook, he realized that yes, he did regret the sex. But no, he didn't regret meeting Vicki-Bracha. He wondered if their paths would cross again on the track to the answers he was seeking.

All this went through his mind as he settled into the chair opposite Shmulik. "You see, it's the same as it was back then," said the officer from the Shabak.

"She certainly hasn't changed," said Cohen about Leah.

"She still keeps cognac behind the counter," Shmulik suggested, as Shavit, the silent waitress, appeared at the table side.

Cohen nodded for the cognac to the waitress. "And a glass of soda with ice," he asked, catching her before she walked away.

"So, how are you? What have you been doing? What's going on?" Shmulik began, seemingly the one eager for the meeting. Cohen was certain Shmulik knew the answers to the first two questions. The third was the real reason they were meeting.

Cohen reached into his shirt pocket. Shmulik offered him a cigarette. Cohen pulled out the little yellow notebook. He flicked it open a few pages deep, looked up at Shmulik, and said, "Jeremiah Ben-Alon, of Kiryat Arba." He read off the vehicle registration number from inside the notebook, then looked up.

"Why?" asked the secret service man, a frown of apprehension, not ignorance, crossing his face.

"You want a why?" Cohen snapped back. "Why did the Twins pick up a body at the Russian Compound before it ever saw the inside of a forensics lab, and take it to Lod in the middle of the night to put on a plane to England?"

Shmulik's answer was a frown that turned into an apologetic grin, as if to say it wasn't his idea, but that's the way things turned out sometimes. But then he realized the significance of the question. "What do you care? Why are you in it?"

"The kid was murdered," Cohen said.

"Right," Shumlik confirmed. "An Arab. It happens. Especially to Jews wandering alone far from any settlement, without any protection, in the territories. And doubly especially to *yeshiva* students."

"He wasn't a *yeshiva* student."

"I know, I know," Shmulik sighed. "He was a rich kid. A super-rich kid. So what?"

Cohen took a deep breath, anticipating Shmulik's next reaction, so plowing on. "He caught the syndrome."

"What kind of fucking talk is that?" Shmulik snapped. "Caught the syndrome? Caught the syndrome?" He repeated it as if to prove his incredulity. "It's psychological. You of all people should know that. A manic-depressive, using lithium to balance his brain, rich as Solomon was at his age, and maybe too smart for his own good or maybe not smart enough, but believe me, not a genius, this kid stops taking the lithium and then starts in on LSD." Shmulik was leaning forward, trying to drive home his point. "Look, I'm not a chemist and not a biologist and not a psychologist or a psychiatrist, but I know what I saw." He paused, waiting for Cohen's answer, but before the old detective could respond, Shmulik's expression changed to a broad grin.

He pointed over Cohen's shoulder. Shavit had appeared at the table, a metal tray in her hand. She laid out cognac in a tall water glass, soda water in a can, and half a glass mug of ice. She was gone as suddenly as she arrived.

"You knew the kid?" Shmulik asked, his tone changing once again. But before Cohen could reply, Shmulik answered his own question. "Obviously. You're rich now. You got rich and ended up with rich friends."

Cohen glared.

"Sorry, sorry. I heard you were touchy about it," Shmulik apologized in a tone that made a slight mockery of Cohen's sensitivity.

"Jeremiah Ben-Alon," Cohen asked again about the owner of the van he had followed from the *kotel* to Kiryat Arba. He still had not decided whether to mention Nahmani, and certainly not the museum robbery. Not that. Not yet.

"And I have to ask, why do you want to know?" They were at a standstill. Again Shmulik displayed a weakness by giving something away in answer to his own question. "I mean, we knew you started asking questions. But everyone said that when you heard the body had made it to London, you'd drop it."

"How long have you known I was interested?"

"Since yesterday," Shmulik admitted.

"Was it him? The body?" Cohen asked. "Was it him?"

"You're more paranoid than ever."

"Was it him?" Cohen pressed again.

"Of course it was."

"Why didn't you check the kid's apartment?"

"What? Are you kidding? We were a transport team, that's all. Get some warm bodies out there, pick up a body, take to airport. Contact. Done. To tell you the truth, if I had handled it from the start, I never would have sent the Twins. I would have used it as an exercise for trainees."

"So you don't have anything on the kid? Friends, associates, acquaintances?"

"I'm telling you, a phone call came, in the middle of the night, to The Head. He called operations, they handled it. I only got called in afterward. Actually, when your name came up. So, how did you get involved? For that matter, why? A rich kid gets killed. Okay, a mixed-up rich kid. Drugs, you say. But why is it your problem?"

"First tell me about Jeremiah Ben-Alon."

"Fringe. That's all. Fringe."

"What kind of fringe? How involved?"

"What do you mean?"

"What kind of activity?" Cohen asked. "Does he hand out leaflets? Does he give speeches? Does he shoot up Arab houses? Does he teach at that camp of theirs? The one where they're teaching kids how to use guns and to hate Arabs?" He was speaking barely above a whisper, but he spat each question with a growing fury. "Does he take them to Goldstein's grave to say Kaddish?" Kiryat Arba and the Goldstein family and friends had turned the dead doctor's grave into a monument venerated by the most radical of right-wing Jews of the West Bank.

Shmulik waited coolly for Cohen's rage to subside. "Have a drink, Avram," he said, doing nothing to hide the patronization in his voice. "It used to help you keep things in proportion."

Keeping silent about the museum robbery was behind Cohen's fury, along with his experience with Vicki-Bracha. But most of all, it was his past, his anger at the impotence of the system to handle the extremists, who hid behind political backers and rabbis, behind claims that all they did was done in the name of the people. Shmulik was right. He did want the drink. And a cigarette. He took one from Shmulik's packet on the table, but didn't light it.

First he drained half the tall glass of cognac, and while he waited for the burning to subside, opened the soda can and poured some over the ice. The drink foamed, almost spilling over the glass. Cohen considered the cigarette in his hand. He took Shmulik's offered light.

"You're the nervous one," Shmulik whispered, picking up the clear plastic lighter, flicking it, and looking at the flame instead of Cohen.

"The syndrome, Shmulik," Cohen said softly. "The syndrome. The situation's ripe for it. Goldstein. The massacre. Because of the peace deals. The old man's making things happen, giving back the territories he won in sixty-seven. You said it yourself. The world's changing. It's making people crazy. You know it and I know it. Now think about it, the syndrome. He was ripe for the promise that his life could have meaning. And I have reason to believe Ben-Alon—or one of his friends—got to the kid."

Shmulik raised an eyebrow with more interest. "Do you think he could have given them money?"

"Not as far as I know." But Cohen admitted to himself that he only had the grandfather's word about the movement of money inside the kid's account. "Maybe," he added.

"How do you know?" Shmulik asked. "How did you get into this?"

"Nahmani," Cohen admitted. "He got me into this."

Shmulik was impressed, but after a second's thought, was worried. "You think he got to The Head?" Shmulik asked, worried. The Head was the chief of the Shabak.

Cohen considered the possibility. The prime minister ran the Shabak, not the police minister. There were dirty politics involved somewhere in the background. He started again, slowly and quietly. "You used to be able to tell me the difference between Wadi Haddad's nihilism and Ahmed Jibril's Marxism. Tell me about Ben-Alon. What's the difference between him, and, let's say, Bookspan?"

Shmulik shook his head. "Now you're going to tell me you see a connection between the two?"

"I don't know, do I?" Cohen said angrily. "Come on, Shmulik. I'm not saying it. But none of us were surprised, were we, by Goldstein?"

Shmulik sighed. "You're asking the wrong person," he said, changing his tone. "I'm with embassies. There are lots of them now," he said. "And they all want to find out the secrets of the Jews," he added cynically. "They won't say so up front. But that's what they want." He shook his head sadly. "Everything's changing. It's crazy now. We're working with people we were trying to capture a year ago. Everything's upside down. What did Golda used to say?" he went on. " 'The situation's never been better?' That's what I'm supposed to be feeling, right? Peace is breaking out all over," he added bitterly, and must have seen something in Cohen's eyes, for he quickly explained himself. "I'm all in favor, don't get me wrong. But you know what? It makes it pretty hard to look back with pride on my past."

Cohen was about to say something, but Shmulik seemed to have enough. "So," summed up the secret intelligence service officer, "if you're all hot and bothered because some rich kid took some drugs and thought he saw God and ended up spending some time in Kiryat Arba, and then went out to the desert looking for God, and got himself killed by some Arab wanting revenge for something, believe me, there's nothing new in it. Leave it, Avram. That's my advice. Forget it."

But Cohen couldn't forget it. Neither the career of his protégé Nissim Levy, nor his guilt over his failure to find Simon Levi-Tsur, was now propelling him forward. The truth was all he sought.

With access to the archives, he'd look in two directions—the museum and the underground currents of the extreme right-wing. But meanwhile he could only rely on memory. And just as throughout the whole case, he had a feeling. He was running out of time.

Leah wanted to talk after Shmulik had gone, so by the time Cohen left the café, dusk was beginning to change the colors of the city. He told her that Jerusalem had changed so much that he didn't like what he saw. She told him that everything always changes, like the air conditioner. And everything else new in the neighborhood, which she listed in detail for him. Cohen smiled back at her, glad to see that she at least had not changed.

It was a four-block walk to the restaurant where he would meet Laskoff. It took him though the residential neighborhood where he had lived in that one-room apartment on a rooftop before the Six

Day War. The trees were much bigger. Houses he remembered as new were in various states of repair and disrepair. Buildings he remembered as old were gone. An art school had opened across the street from the secretarial school that Cohen remembered. A pair of restaurants cornered a block across the street from a building already old in Cohen's years in the city but now restored to look new.

He had turned his back on Tel Aviv thirty years before. But now he saw it with different eyes. Like Leah, the city had changed and remained the same, more of itself than ever, the opposite of Jerusalem, which had jumped from town to metropolis without a city in between. For Cohen, Jerusalem was best as a village, but as he walked up a residential street of three- and four-story apartment houses in Tel Aviv, he realized that Jerusalem had turned into a fortress for many, and a prison for him.

Part of it was politics, he knew. The new government had reversed a policy going back to the Six Day War, and was finally negotiating directly with the Palestinians. The rest of the Arabs were lining up to join in. The race was on to make claims for Jerusalem, and while the government was trying to remove God from the debate, religious tensions were only growing.

For Cohen, possession of the city was irrelevant. The only thing that counted was its peace, and for all those years that he had had the authority, he tried to use it to seek the day-to-day banal truths that guaranteed its peace. Now, retired, indeed banned from the system, he could only watch with trepidation as those who claimed to understand a divine message demanded immediate implementation of their religious visions.

It didn't matter to Cohen: Jew, Christian, or Moslem, he saw them all fall, religious or not. He hated seeing religion used as an excuse for crime, and it was his final refusal to accept it in Jerusalem that finally had forced him out of the police.

Politics wasn't the only thing that had changed Cohen's view of Jerusalem and himself in the city. The money had changed him, as well. It made him confuse laziness with luxury. Made him lapse rather than rise. Made him lazy, instead of hungry. Tracking the truth behind the slaying of Simon Levi-Tsur had put him on a search for a truth about himself as much as it was about the facts of the kid's death.

Laskoff was coming up the street. Usually he wore slightly out-dated but tailor-made suits, so Cohen was surprised by the light blue, three-button tricot-cotton jersey tucked into dark blue trousers. But, as always, Laskoff wore loafers, with a slight skip in their hard leather tapping. When Laskoff was directly across the street from him, Cohen stepped out of the darkness calling out "Ephraim," in a short sharp rasp of loud whisper.

Laskoff almost jumped as he turned, looking for the voice.

"Over here," Cohen said from the edge of the sidewalk, between a parked car's hood and a pickup truck's rear.

A broad smile crossed Laskoff's face, which turned into a grim-mer look as he crossed the street into the edge of darkness where Cohen was waiting. "What's the matter? Why are you out here?" Laskoff asked.

"I've got to get back to Jerusalem," Cohen said, aware of the muddy yellow dust of sweat and *sharav* air that stained his shirt. He was taking care not to be noticed, and he had no idea who might be in the restaurant. In the daytime the clientele ranged from a few tourists, whether for pleasure or business, to politicians and bankers, corporate executives and their brokers, to generals and newspaper publishers with their sources of information and money.

Looking into Laskoff's eyes, Cohen realized he couldn't go into the restaurant, for just as Shmulik implied, it was Cohen who appeared mad, like an old man grabbing strangers' arms on the street to begin raving a tragic tale. Laskoff rescued him. "I asked Udi Hason to come in. Check the phones. He showed me some-thing that he found."

Cohen nodded sadly. Shmulik implied that they'd first look in the direction of his money for his connection to the missing boy. But he didn't tell that to Laskoff. "There's something more impor-tant," Cohen said. "What kind of papers would a twenty-one-year old have to sign that would be important for the House?"

"Of Levi-Tsur?"

"Yes."

"It could be many things," Laskoff thought aloud.

"Like what?"

"A transfer of possession," Laskoff tried.

"Of what?"

"Stocks, shares, accounts, property. Voting rights on boards. Twenty-one makes a difference in the United States, and most of Europe. Here, it's different. Eighteen to the army, eighteen for everything. Transfer of possession," Laskoff said. "Why are you asking?"

Cohen thought for a moment. "Who would want to prevent such a transfer?"

Laskoff shook his head. "There's no way of knowing unless we know what's being transferred—and in which direction. But a signature is a commitment, the assumption of legal responsibility for something."

"Taking that responsibility away from someone else?"

"Maybe," Laskoff said. He was about to say something else, but Cohen moved back further into the shadows as a taxi pulled up directly opposite them, at the front entrance to the restaurant.

"You're making me paranoid," Laskoff whispered with a nervous grin. "Why?"

A middle-aged couple got out of the car. Cohen took another step backward.

"Why?" Laskoff repeated as the couple went into the restaurant without even looking in Cohen and Laskoff's direction.

"What?" Cohen asked.

"You called me to ask about the House of Levi-Tsur. Now we're standing in the shadows and you're asking about the legal age. Does this have anything to do with the rumors?"

"What rumors?"

"That the House of Levi-Tsur is interested in one of the banks. Maybe even Leumi." It was the largest of the banks the government was trying to privatize.

"I thought they don't do business here," Cohen said.

"Haven't you noticed? Things are changing," Laskoff said. He was shorter than Cohen, and the light falling across his face gave Laskoff's deep-set dark eyes a masklike quality. "Peace is coming."

"So the last thing in the world Levi-Tsur would want is to help right-wing settlers," Cohen said.

Laskoff raised an eyebrow. "I thought you understood. He's stayed out of business here because it has been better business to work with the Arabs," Laskoff explained patiently. "Now the Arabs are doing business with us, so he's ready. Besides, remember Armand Hammer, Robert Maxwell. Rich Jews get old, they start feeling guilty, especially if they haven't done anything for us until they get old."

"Maxwell committed suicide," Cohen said. "And Hammer was in his nineties when he showed up. Besides, a bank costs more than a sentiment can afford."

"Don't tell me that you haven't looked around at the world and looked at your life and wondered what's God going to ask you when the time finally comes," Laskoff said. "And with peace coming," he added, grinning, "the whole world's going to be doing business with us."

Cohen rubbed at the stickiness of sweat on the back of his neck. He wanted only to be able to say without lying that he did his best. But now he was concentrated on a connection between Simon's disappearance—and death, he reminded himself—and the documents that needed to be signed. He grimaced.

Laskoff thought it was a grin. "Why do you want to know about legal age?"

"Raphael Levi-Tsur's youngest grandson, Simon," Cohen began, but car lights flared down the hill at him, and he stepped out of them quickly, deeper into the shadow of the sidewalk. The car drove past.

"What about him?"

"He was found dead earlier this week. Near Herodium."

"My God. Shocking. For such a family. How could such a thing happen?"

"The family's been told he was a victim of peace," Cohen said, unable to withhold the bitterness from his statement of fact. "An Arab. An ax."

"You sound like you don't believe it."

A young couple, obviously lovers, were coming down the sidewalk. Cohen sighed, envious of their energy. "It's a long story," he finally said as the couple went up to the restaurant door.

"Maybe you can give me the short version?" Laskoff asked.

"Do you remember the theft of a collection of crowns from the Land of Israel museum. When it was new?"

"When?"

Cohen told him.

"I was in Geneva that year."

"Simon was curious about the theft," Cohen said.

"Simon?"

"The missing kid. The dead kid. The grandson," Cohen explained again. "The youngest of his generation in the family," Cohen said, quoting the grandfather.

"What was stolen?"

"Gold crowns. Roman era. They were either stolen for their gold—about nineteen pounds—or their historic value."

"Maybe he's interested in archeology."

"His uncle's interested in archeology," Cohen pointed out. "You sent me the clips."

"Remind me," Laskoff said. "Which one?"

Cohen plucked his notebook from his shirt pocket, and leafed through it, needing to step into the light to see what he had written. "Emmanuel, " he said.

"The New Yorker, right?" Laskoff checked.

Cohen nodded grimly. "They were never recovered. As far as I know, nobody was ever arrested." He thought of something. "Do you have a telephone number to call him? Emmanuel?"

Laskoff chuckled. "Avram, I know you think I work wonders. But the Levi-Tsurs home numbers?? I ate once in the same restaurant as Emmanuel in New York. Maybe he knows of my work. Maybe not. I doubt it. And the truth is, I hope he doesn't." He came to an abrupt halt as headlights swept over them. But as soon as the lights were gone, Laskoff continued. "I wouldn't want to be swallowed up by them."

If Cohen called and left a message, Caroline Jones would call back and say the boy had an interest in archeology. There were three books on the subject in the kid's bookshelf. He had checked after Vicki left, looking for any titles that indicated the contents related to Herodium—or to Roman-era crowns. He looked in the index of several books. But none gave him a clue. The boy didn't care about archeology. Of that Cohen was certain. Car lights coming down the street flared hypnotically into Cohen's eyes as he thought.

"Avram?" Laskoff said. "Are you all right?" Cohen blinked. Laskoff added, "You suddenly turned pale. I could see it even in this light."

It was true. Cohen suddenly felt the fear. An intuition as much as a conclusion, fear was an emotion he had learned to conquer when he was eleven, in Berlin, and forever since he beat it back. It existed inside him and for that he was grateful, for it made him careful. Now, he pushed it away, though still wondering if he should have watched out in case Shmulik put a trainee on his trail when he left the café.

He tried to remember the people he had seen on the sidewalk, retracing his walk from the café to the restaurant. But it was foolish of him, he realized. He could remember perhaps half the faces. He wasn't sure that he hadn't been followed.

Car lights blinked twice. Laskoff's expression changed as he turned to look at the sudden darkness. A car swung into an illegal parking spot. Laskoff waved.

"My friends," the banker apologized to Cohen. He stepped forward, close enough to put a hand on Cohen's shoulder. But he didn't. "I hope you're not thinking that Emmanuel was involved in the robbery," he whispered.

"Go," said Cohen, backing away as the first of the car doors slammed closed and people began getting out of the car. "If they ask, tell them I was a beggar asking for change." His sneakers padded on the sidewalk as he strode down the street away from Laskoff, heading toward Allenby a couple of blocks away. From there he could grab a cab down to his car.

· 20 ·

Cohen had never volunteered for the police. He was recruited, indeed, practically speaking, he was transferred, by the same people who had noticed his activities in Europe after the war and made sure he was taken care of when he arrived in the country on the eve of the war of independence.

He had survived a Nazi camp young enough to be strong enough to become an assassin, one of the *nokmim,* the brotherhood of avengers who had searched through the rubble of Germany taking revenge on the Nazis they knew and found. The friend who left his millions to Cohen nearly fifty years later was the leader of that cell of the *nokmim.*

But after a year of hunting, Cohen chose life over death, boarding an illegal immigrant ship in Naples to run the British blockade against Jews trying to reach the Land. The boat beached in the dark halfway between Haifa and Tel Aviv. The British police tried to catch the immigrants—and the Jews on the beach who helped them—but Cohen got through.

The people who had noticed him in the *nokmim,* and then on the ship, took care of him when he arrived. They sent him to a kibbutz to learn fluent Hebrew, a language he learned for the bar mitzvah he never had had because of the Nazis. Everyone on the kibbutz would refuse to speak German, and none of the teenagers would know anything more about him than that he had survived a camp.

His Hebrew improved rapidly, and with a few kibbutzniks he also practiced his English, the language his Budapest-born mother had chosen for him as a mother tongue. She was the Zionist in the family, in retrospect more practical in the 1930s in Germany than Cohen's father, who preferred German literature and psycho-

190

analysis and looked forward to one day running the publishing house on his own, without Cohen's grandfather breathing down his neck.

From the kibbutz, Cohen went to the army, to intelligence, and from there, eventually, to the police and the city. In the state's service his entire life, learning to break everything down into routines based on the essence of the purpose, the habits of a lonely man. Even the relationship with Ahuva was a sharing of two solitudes, and it too was a routine, though couched in a secrecy originally dictated at least in part by their respective jobs—him, head of CID in Jerusalem, her, first a magistrate judge and, now, a district court justice. Though the secret was out, they both refrained from making the final commitment that meant giving up their essential independence, even for the comfort of love.

It was after ten when he got home. He showered, pulled on his tricot-cotton bathrobe, and poured himself a drink, before taking his messages off the machine.

"I have something on that subject we discussed earlier," Nissim Levy's confident voice said on the phone. "I'll try again later."

The electronic squeal rang. "I don't know if you've heard," the next message began. "The Levi-Tsur kid. The family identified the body in London. I knew you'd want to know." There was a pause. "So, what are your plans now? Give me a call." Another pause, and then, "Oh, this was Meshulam," before the hang up.

Ahuva was eager to hear about his progress—if he wanted to talk about it. "I'll understand if you don't. But if you do, let me know," she said.

He called Nissim back first. Hagit answered. She didn't sound happy to hear from Cohen. "He went to Jerusalem," she said. "He left this morning and isn't back," she complained, making it sound as if it was Cohen's fault. He apologized, asking her to tell Nissim to call him as soon as he got in.

Ahuva was next. He didn't tell her about Vicki-Bracha. Not yet, he decided. He asked if she remembered the museum robbery. "Vaguely," she admitted. "I was very young. At the cinema. The movies. That's right. I remember it from the Carmel news clips. Before television, when they gave news before the movies."

She added a jurist's angle to the question of Simon's signature at the age of twenty-one. "I'd want at least a year to transpire before I'd accept the boy was missing. And an unnatural death so close to the signing would make me wonder."

Wonder about what? Cohen thought as he lay back in bed considering his next moves. As he began falling into the dark of sleep, he thought of Victor, his former chief in the Tel Aviv detective squad. He must be closer to ninety than eighty, if he's still alive, Cohen was thinking as he crept into sleep, dreaming of a heavy rain beating down on golden crowns.

His dreams were always difficult. That night, he stood on the slope between upper Herodium, where the king had built the fortress at the top of the hill, and lower Herodium, where archeological digs revealed the estates of the royal family.

It was just past dawn in the dream, and the rising sun in the east was blinding. Cohen looked away from the sun, west up the hill. The top of the hill glimmered with the sunlight until it was gold, and the glimmering turned into a vibration that he felt beneath his feet. He looked down and realized he was naked. The rumbling grew stronger, like an earthquake, but, suddenly, the gold glimmering at the top of the hill turned into the shape of huge crowns falling like an avalanche in Cohen's direction, huge bouncing boulders racing down the hill at him. Just as one blocked the sun completely and was heading down to crush him under its weight, Cohen woke.

The neighborhood was quiet. He checked his watch. It was one-thirty in the morning. He concentrated. A car shifted gears on Emek Refa'im, half a block away. He listened harder, and a siren on the far side of town seemed to drift into the room.

A much closer sound struck. It was the creak of the gate outside, an almost sweet whistle of rusty iron that Cohen knew as well as the sound of his own voice. The squeaking stopped. He sat up straight in bed and then swung his legs off and strode quickly to the living room, where the Beretta sat on its shelf in the bookcase. It was a close-range weapon that endangered only those who got in its way.

He looked down from the living room window to the garden. A man was at the bottom of the stairs, about to take the first step up to Cohen's front door. Cohen pulled back on the barrel, cocking the gun quietly. Leaning through the open window, he looked down the barrel at the man. "Halt," he said.

"Avram," the man whispered, looking up. The moonlight caught his face. "It's me," said Nissim Levy.

Cohen took a deep breath, loosening his grip on the gun. "Come up," he said. He went to the bedroom for his robe before opening the door to his former assistant. "Hagit said you were in Jerusalem," he said, as he opened the door.

"She called you?" Levy asked, worried. There was a slur in his voice. Cohen could smell alcohol as Levy stumbled past into the room. He shook his head.

"You've been drinking," Cohen pointed out.

Levy lurched to the sofa, running a hand through prematurely gray curly hair as he fell into the seat. "I never should have married," he said. "Big mistake. Big big mistake."

Cohen sat down in his armchair. But he remained silent, looking at Levy through hooded eyes. "She doesn't understand the job. She wants me home every night, on the dot. And that town . . ."

"She didn't call me," Cohen said. "I was returning your call."

"And she said I was in Jerusalem," Levy said.

"Right."

Levy smirked at Cohen, and then pointed his forefinger at Cohen as if it were a gun. "I thought you might need help."

"On what?"

Levy looked at his forefinger and then put it to his temple, as if it were still a gun and now he was going to blow his head off. "I know, I know," he apologized. "I shouldn't have done anything. Not without knowing what it was all about."

Cohen nodded.

"But the name. Jeremiah Ben-Alon. Your van driver. I started looking."

"That's why you're in Jerusalem?"

"A funeral, actually," Levy said, with an absurd grin on his face that fell into a frown. "My uncle. But you're not interested in that. You want to know about Ben-Alon. I can tell you. A hundred percent." He nodded to himself, then burped.

On rare occasions, Levy had raised a glass with Cohen, but usually didn't even finish the single shot that Cohen would pour for him. He had never seen Levy like this. "I'm not worried about Ben-Alon right now. What happened to you. Why? Why this?"

"I'm drunk?"

"Yes," Cohen pointed out to his young friend.

"Stupid of me, right?"

"Probably."

"You drink."

"Tell me about Hagit," said Cohen, ignoring the comment. "What happened?"

"She hates Yeroham. She hates me. I hate me. What am I doing there? Chasing a few junkies? Kids vandalizing the school? Russian drunks beating up their wives? What am I doing there?" He was in civilian clothes and was looking at his bare toes in his sandals. "There are things going on. Important things. I'm missing them." He looked at Cohen, as if for the first time. "You're missing them. At least that's what I thought."

Cohen didn't interrupt, nor correct. He decided to let Nissim talk some more.

"I didn't ask any questions. You called. The first time in weeks. It fell out of the sky on me, but I say nothing. Then, the next day you call again. Fully operational. On the job. Do I ask you what for? Do I ask you why?"

Cohen stayed silent, letting Nissim continue.

"I'm thinking, he was right when he said the commission wouldn't invite him in. I'm thinking, why didn't he just go and volunteer? And maybe he did, I thought then. Maybe he did. An address in Kiryat Arba. Maybe I didn't understand. So I started looking deeper."

He paled, suddenly turning white as a sheet. Cohen stood up to grab one of the weekend papers Ahuva left behind. But Levy didn't throw up. He threw himself into a prone position across the sofa, ending up leaning on an elbow, his head propped on his fist, his knuckles under his cheekbone. "And you know what I found out?" Nissim asked, pleased with himself.

Cohen was wondering how much Nissim had drunk. No more than three glasses, he decided. On a full stomach. One full glass on an empty. "What did you find out?" Cohen asked.

"It's not his name," Levy chortled. Then he lowered his voice as if to impart a secret. "I went all the way to Jerusalem to find it out." He hiccupped. "You know why?"

Cohen shook his head.

"Those," Nissim said, pointing across the room at Cohen's PC on its trolley, and smiled mysteriously at Cohen.

"Go on," Cohen prompted.

"You see, in Yeroham I could get only so far. There was nothing in criminal records from the national database on Jeremiah Ben-Alon, until this year. When the settlers set up their tents across from the prime minister's office, and those first few nights they tried getting to the gates? That first night of arrests. It killed me, watching it on TV, instead of being there . . ."

"So did I," Cohen said softly.

"I'm driving Hagit crazy, you know. Complaining all the time."

"She didn't tell me anything," Cohen said. It wasn't exactly a lie. "Why did you have to go to Jerusalem?"

"That's the best part," Nissim said, sitting up just as suddenly as he had fallen across the length of the sofa. He pulled up to the edge of the foam-rubber mattress that made the seat of the wooden-framed sofa, and leaned forward to tell Cohen a secret. Cohen held the weekend's business section ready in case Levy's digestive system declared war.

Levy laughed again, this time more cynically. "My password in Yeroham doesn't get me out of the LAN, and my old password from Jerusalem doesn't get me into the LAN. And I wanted to get into the Interior Ministry's database. My uncle dying was a great excuse," he said bitterly.

"Did you go to the Russian Compound?" Cohen asked. It was the Jerusalem District Police headquarters, an ivy-covered former hostel built by a czar at the end of the last century for Russian Orthodox pilgrims to the holy land.

Levy shook his head, remorseful. "Sheikh Jarrah," he confessed. The five-story building in East Jerusalem was an incomplete Jordanian hospital when the city was reunited in the Six Day War. The Israelis finished it, making the building the national police headquarters.

"But don't worry," Nissim added. "Nobody knows I was doing something for you. I had a good excuse for being there—my uncle's funeral. I visited with a friend. Nomi Hazani. She's head of the bureau for Commander Hasdai. She's nice. Very nice. Too nice. Oh, God, why did I get married?" He clenched his head in his hands and shook it by clenching his curly hair. It only made him dizzy. He looked about to swoon.

"I'm going to make you some coffee," Cohen suggested. He wanted to get Nissim back on track about the man whose name wasn't Ben-Alon.

Nissim thought about the offer of coffee, a hand on his stomach. "Not a good idea," he decided. "I'll be okay. Shit," he muttered to himself. "I'm really drunk," he realized, letting out a breath of air in a deep sigh. "She did it to me," he suddenly accused.

"Hasdai's secretary or Hagit?" Cohen asked.

Levy thought for a moment. "A bit of both." He thought some more. "It's worse. I used Nomi," he added. "To get to a terminal."

"And to get to Beno," Cohen suggested.

"For Hagit's sake," Nissim protested in self-defense.

"Your sake," Cohen threw back. "Who is Jeremiah Ben-Alon?"

"You ready?" Levy asked, fumbling in his pocket and pulling out a piece of paper. He unfolded it and looked up and down at it as he went on. "His real name is Jerry Oakland. That's to say, his original name is Jerry Oakland. American. Forty-six years old. Birthplace, Baltimore. A convert. Married. Eight kids. At the end of last year, he applied for an Israeli passport for the first time, and made his Hebrew name official. And why did he need the passport?" Levy asked, looking up triumphantly from his notes.

Cohen shook his head.

"To go to America. He didn't use his American passport. He used his Israeli one."

"Why?"

"To raise money," Nissim grinned. "For *Yeshivat Ohalei Levi'im*," he finally said. "You remember. The breastplates? The Temple?"

Cohen remembered. But studying Levy's face another concern rose in his mind. "Tell me what happened with Hagit," he asked.

Yeshivat Ohalei Levi'im began in a living room in the Jewish Quarter, the result of two missions in the life of Rabbi Menachem Levine: bringing wayward souls back into the fold of Judaism, and preparing the instruments and clothing, the ritual objects and the architectural plans for the resurrection of the Temple on Mount Moriah.

Trouble was, the Moslems had long since built two monuments to *their* faith on the plateau. The Dome of the Rock was built over the rock the Jews said was the site of Isaac's near-sacrifice by his father Abraham, and the Moslems said was the place from which their Prophet Mohammed rose to heaven. The silver-domed Aksa mosque was built atop what the Jews believed to be the royal portico of Solomon's Temple, rebuilt by Ezra and Nehemia, and rebuilt again by Herod the Great.

As long as the mosques were on the Temple Mount, Rabbi Levine taught the Boy Scout slogan, "Be Prepared." Architectural drawings were made on the basis of instructions in the scriptures and the Talmud. Robes were woven, musical instruments re-created, wine goblets and incense carriers were made from precious metals.

The pride of the *yeshiva* was a high priest's breastplate. It was incomplete, due to a dispute over the interpretations of the biblical names for all twelve Grace Stones representing the twelve tribes. Each stone had a place on the breastplate worn by the high priest for his ceremonies in the Holy of Holies, the resting place for the Ark of the Covenant.

Cohen's attention had been drawn to Levine's *yeshiva* in its earliest years, when it still was in the rabbi's apartment, mostly because of Levine's tendency to bring ex-convicts into the fold. But it was the breastplate that put the *yeshiva* on top of the pile of files on Cohen's desk.

A wave of jewelry shop robberies led to an ex-con, who led to the *yeshiva*, which by then fully occupied the rabbi's apartment. The rabbi's family—his wife and six children—never complained as they were put up by the rabbi's followers in temporary housing as the *yeshiva* and its crafts shops grew.

The ex-con, Yosef Abuhatzeira, was one of those brought to religion by the rabbi. Abuhatzeira used the skills he learned before he put his mind to Torah and, seeking favor with the rabbi, cut corners to get uncut stones for the breastplate.

Levine claimed innocence, of course, and finding no evidence to prove the contrary, Cohen believed him. There was a naïveté in the rabbi's devotion to his cause—and his insistence that nothing should be done to harm the mosques, while everything should be done to get ready for the Temple. As far as the rabbi was concerned, it would be up to the messiah to deal with that problem. But others took more activist approaches that sought to hasten the messiah's arrival by taking care of the mosques for him.

It was Cohen's constant nightmare as CID chief in Jerusalem, especially after the national consensus broke down and the public split over the question of whether to partition the Land of Israel and allow the Palestinians their own state. If the government was going to hand over to the *goyim* any part of the Land of Israel, especially any part of Jerusalem, it was, to some people, tantamount to treason. The chief rabbinical council issued statements saying that in any peace deal, the only legitimate sovereignty over the Temple Mount would be Jewish. The Moslems could maintain their mosques. But the Mount belonged to the Jews. The Moslems, of course, said it belonged to them.

And the rabbinical council's statements were considered far too moderate by some who argued that if the government was ready to cave in to international pressure, and wasn't proud enough, strong enough, indeed worthy enough to rid the Temple Mount of the abominations—the mosques—on the plateau, then Jews with stronger spines would act.

Cohen had three conversations with Rabbi Levine, as a result of the jewelry thefts. The first two took place in the apartment, which was bustling with the work of the artisans. A loom filled the former master bedroom. A children's room turned into a carpentry workshop. Those working with Jerusalem limestone searched for ways to break and cut it without using any metal, the basic material of weapons and forbidden as an implement of construction for the Temple.

In the first meeting, the rabbi told Cohen that yes, Abuhatzeira had brought him the jewels.

In the second, Cohen told the rabbi that the jewels had been returned to their rightful owners.

The third meeting was in front of the Jerusalem Magistrate's Court, as Abuhatzeira was led shackled and handcuffed across the Russian Compound parking lot from the police station holding cell to the old courthouse. The rabbi, most of his family, and many of his followers had gathered to give succor to the wayward member of their flock before the sentencing. Levine was being interviewed by a gaggle of journalists as Cohen headed into the building for another case.

Cohen paused to listen to the rabbi's answers to the reporters' questions. Shocked by his student's action, he was more saddened than outraged. He never truly condemned the theft, but instead tried to explain it. The *yeshiva* was poor. Government subsidies were not enough. And if the government were living up to its responsibilities, it would be actively seeking the establishment of the Third Temple, not the incarceration of a misguided believer.

The *yeshiva*'s pro bono lawyer got Abuhatzeira's probation violation reduced from five years to three years, two for good behavior. The thief's lapse was considered just that, a lapse. Cohen had not heard of Abuhatzeira, since.

But all that was in the past, nearly a decade old. Now, the *yeshiva* was housed in a proper building, in Siloan, the original site of the city built by the biblical King David after he beat the Jebusites and established his rule from Jerusalem. Though outside the walls of the Old City, the *yeshiva* was now much closer to the original realm of the City of David.

The building was acquired secretly in a purchase from an Arab who took the money and left for America with his wife and children. Several other properties on the ancient slope were bought the same way. Then, one long wintry night, the settlers came in, occupying nearly a dozen houses in a coordinated operation.

It was the winter before the Hebron massacre, and Cohen was already out of the police. There was fear of bloodshed. City Hall couldn't say no to the settlers, and the government was a secret partner in the deals, with its offices handling the transfer of ownership. Lawsuits filed by some of the Arab families, claiming that the sellers had no right to conduct the transaction, forced the evacuation of several of the buildings. But a few remained—under heavy security—including *Yeshivat Ohalei Levi'im*.

· 21 ·

Cohen left Nissim Levy asleep on the sofa that morning, and by nine was parked in the same lot where he had left his car going to the *kotel* in his search for Simon's sunrise. But instead of climbing the stairs to the Western Wall plaza on the other side of Dung Gate, he started walking down into Siloan.

It was a long walk down and a longer one back up. But while he knew he'd draw attention if he walked, he'd draw much more if he drove all the way down to the bottom, where the map said he'd find the *yeshiva,* according to the address Levy had pulled out of the Interior Ministry database.

A pair of Palestinian boys were playing hoops with an old bicycle wheel and a stick. One caught the tireless wheel and held it, to stare at Cohen while he passed on the long hill down the street. An obese Arab woman in a gold-and-red embroidered robe, her head covered with a white shawl, walked heavily uphill. She averted her eyes from Cohen's. A Subaru came up the steep hill behind her. Two Arabs were in the front seat. They eyed Cohen suspiciously but passed.

A few seconds later a car horn honked behind him. Cohen turned. A van—not Ben-Alon's—was heading down into the valley. A Jew wearing a large, white, knitted *kippa* stuck his head out of the passenger window as the van reached Cohen. It slowed down with no less suspicion than the Arab. The Jew looked Cohen up and down, then pulled his head inside, and the van continued its descent down the road, parking behind a Border Patrol jeep facing uphill on the right hand side of the road far below.

The jeep didn't make Cohen happy, especially as he approached closer and saw that he recognized the master sergeant who was leaning against the hood smoking a cigarette. Farez would recognize him. The last time they met was right after the elections. The right-wing was angry at their loss after a fifteen-year rule, throwing tantrums in demonstrations outside the prime minister's house. Cohen had gone out for a late-night walk, taking a hike from the German Colony up the hill to the Talbieh-Rehavia border to see the demonstrations.

Farez was a good man to have on the scene that night. Like all border patrolmen, he was trained to be a spring wound tight and ready to use force. A Druze, Farez possessed a rare quality most useful to a policeman. He exuded an awareness that force was a last resort, with an easygoing grin that could win over the most intransigent of angry demonstrators.

Not only Arabs fight with the police in Jerusalem, but especially when the demonstrations were about the issues that divided Arabs and Jews, Farez always seemed able to stay fair. Cohen appreciated that quality in the man, whom he guessed was now in his forties and still looked thirty.

"*Ahlan Usahalan,*" Farez said, welcoming Cohen in Arabic, then snapping to easy informal attention, itself rare in Israeli uniformed service, except Farez believed in honor, using the respect he gave to earn more for himself.

So, enjoying life and liking Cohen, his first reaction on seeing him there was the pleasure of the moment. His second, as Cohen saw in the policeman's eyes, was curiosity. "But there are no bodies for you to inspect here," he said, more joking than serious, nonetheless wanting an explanation for Cohen's presence.

Cohen smiled at Farez, and looked to his right, up the hill. Stone steps were cut into the wall of the mountain's slope, up a path to five olive trees on a terrace above them. He could only see the top of the first building off the stone steps cut into the mountain. So, he backed away from the jeep, and went out to the middle of the street for a better view. The three-story building rose up behind the row of trees on the terrace. A large, white, wooden sign hung from the roof and was painted in black Hebrew and English lettering, announcing the site as *Yeshivat Ohalei Levi'im.* A black-on-yellow sticker that said, "Prepare for the Coming of the Messiah" was pasted to the top of the sign.

"There been any trouble lately?" Cohen asked softly.

Farez frowned. "Not for a while," he said. Then he grinned suddenly. "Of course, now that you're here there probably will be."

Cohen smiled back, walked to the side of the van, then looked back to the house before brushing off some dust and peering inside the van. A piece of cloth covered a large object. Cohen tried to look deeper into the shadows of the closed cabin, but even after clearing a bit of dust with a knuckle he couldn't make out the object the cloth covered.

"A harp," Farez said behind him. Cohen turned. Farez strummed an imaginary harp. "They make all sorts of things inside there."

Cohen nodded, brushing the dirt from his knuckle. He looked around for Ben-Alon's van. Farez interpreted it to mean something else.

"And they make all kinds of things over there," Farez added, pointing further down the hill, toward a cluster of Arab houses. "And I'm right in the middle." His nose had been broken twice. A scar appeared to make a third eyebrow over his right eye. Cohen knew it had been made when Farez, off duty, wrestled a knife from the hands of a terrorist who thought he would get to meet Allah if he stabbed as many Jews as possible in the *shuk*. Then, for the four minutes it had taken for the nearest patroling squad to get through the crowd to the scene, Farez defended the young Arab—who had wounded five people—from an angry lynch mob. But Farez always kept his smile, a white-toothed grin that found ironic humor wherever possible.

"How long have you been posted here?" Cohen asked, taking a deep puff on a cigarette, after honoring Farez with one.

"A couple of days," Farez said.

"The roster down?" Cohen asked, wondering if the choice of the Druze Farez for the daytime position outside the *yeshiva* was an indication of rising tensions between the handful of Jews vastly outnumbered in the neighborhood by the Arabs.

"No," said Farez. "I've got a platoon in training."

Cohen looked around. None of Farez soldiers were immediately in view.

"They're here," Farez said confidently. "And what brings you here?" he asked Cohen.

"*Tiul*," said Cohen, using the Hebrew word that could mean anything from a walk around the block to get some air on a hot summer night to a round-the-world tour. "So?" he asked. "It's quiet."

"The Palestinians are quiet. The Jews are quiet. Everyone is quiet. Too quiet, sometimes," Farez said. "Now everyone waits to see what happens when Arafat comes to Jerusalem."

"It will pass," Cohen said.

There were voices from the slope above them, and then two young men, in black trousers and white shirts, wearing brim hats cocked on the backs of their heads and their sports jackets hung from the inside collar across their shoulders, the empty sleeves waving in the air, strode quickly past the border policeman and Cohen, heading up the hill. "It's funny about these types," Farez said. "They talk about pride, but they seem very afraid."

"They're a minority," Cohen pointed out.

"Like me," Farez laughed.

"No. They think they speak for the majority."

"I just follow orders," Farez said.

"A policeman, no?" Cohen grinned.

Farez laughed. "You're well?" he asked Cohen. "Your health?"

Cohen smiled, nodding perfunctorily. The truth was his and his alone.

"That's all that really counts," Farez tried.

"Yes," Cohen conceded. "Is the rabbi in?" he asked.

Four soldiers from the training platoon came down the stairs. They were dressed for a war zone. One carried a walkie-talkie on his back, and the antenna whipped at the leaves of some wild vines that overhung the steps just before the bottom. Both carried M-16s. They wore helmets in case of rocks, and flameproof flak jackets in case of Molotov cocktails. A dog barked somewhere below. Farez waved, sending the patrol down the hill.

"They're good boys," he said, watching the patrolmen pause for water from a large plastic vat in the back of the jeep. "Yes. He came in about an hour ago." He looked at Cohen with curiosity. "You're taking Bible lessons?"

Cohen stubbed out the cigarette. "Just a *tiul*, Farez, just a little *tiul*," he repeated. "Take care of the kids," he added, nodding to the four young troopers as he left Farez and headed for the stone stairs leading up to the *yeshiva*.

The path up the stairs was narrow, up an alley of vines and brush covering the stone walls supporting the terrace built out from the mountain's side. The wall on his left was old, made of stones that probably came out of the ground during the building of the terrace. The wall to his left was topped with barbed wire. To his right was the low end of a second terrace. Just before the entrance to the *yeshiva* at the first door to his left in the alley, a new cinder-block wall was going up, built, Cohen decided, by the Arabs from a house made of three terraces going up the hill opposite the *yeshiva*.

A new Multi-Lock steel door was installed inside the ancient arched entrance through the wall surrounding the property. A laminated sign announcing the *yeshiva*'s presence was pasted to the door. Above it, a weather-protected video camera spied on all those approaching the gate. He looked up at it.

A buzzer responded to his ringing. But in that moment he glanced toward the *yeshiva*'s neighbor, behind the new cinder-block wall. On the second terrace of the house, a boy watched him. The boy wore a T-shirt with the logo of an American sneaker company. Just as the buzzer rang, a woman dressed in the head-to-toe black of a devout Moslem came onto the terrace and pulled the boy away from his vantage point over the *yeshiva*.

At the end of the little garden at the northern entrance to the *yeshiva* property an open door led to the first floor of the old building.

The ground floor was made of the oldest, largest stones irregularly cut to make the cement holding them together look like random rivulets across the face of the lower part of the building. The second and third floors were built after industrialization took over the stone-cutting job, giving the stone a uniform, clean-cut look.

"Welcome," said a young woman wearing a white shirt under a long blue dress that reached her sandals, and a floppy knit hat that covered her hair, indicating she was married. She appeared at the door, beckoning to him. He guessed she couldn't have been more than twenty. "Are you interested in getting ready for the Temple?"

He smiled as he walked past her into a small lobbylike entrance, where glass cases and shelves, built into the walls, created a gallery-like environment for the arts and crafts of the *yeshiva*, mostly gold and silver objects ranging from chalices and goblets to incense holders and tongs.

"Tourist?" she tried in English.

Cohen smiled again at her, but didn't say anything.

"I can explain the objects to you," she tried again in Hebrew. "For example, that's a priest's robe," she said about the exhibit Cohen was studying. The robe filled an entire recess, and was hanging from fishing line so at first glance it appeared to be hovering mysteriously without any support, the wide sleeves spread out to show their size. Cohen leaned closer. Tiny hairs of soft wool protruding from the weave made the robe look like it would be very itchy. Turquoise-blue stripes were dyed into the material.

"We have brochures," she tried again in English, and then her expression brightened with a new idea. "*Russi?*" she tried, picking up some colored leaflets from the desk and holding them out to him.

"Is Rabbi Levine here?" he asked, looking away from the exhibit to the young woman.

"You do speak Hebrew," she said, surprised. "I thought you were a tourist. So, you want to see the rabbi?" she asked.

When he nodded, she smiled broadly, deciding that Cohen was seeking religious instruction. Suddenly her face dropped. "You don't have a *kippa*," she pointed out. She picked up a basket from a small stand blocking the thick-walled exit from the room into the rest of the building.

The basket was full of knitted skullcaps. Some were large and white, made from a yarn. Others were crocheted from a thinner thread, with designs woven into the circle of cloth.

"Fifteen shekel for the big white ones," she said cheerfully, "twelve for the little ones. I know it's a little expensive," she added apologetically, "but the money goes to the *yeshiva*, to help the work." She beamed, waiting for him to pick one.

"It's not that kind of meeting," Cohen said.

"Is he expecting you?" the girl asked.

"He knows me," he said. "Tell him it's Avram Cohen."

"Lots of Cohens come in here to see what we're about," she smiled. "People with open minds, looking for meaning in their lives."

He snorted a little laugh, making her frown slightly. "If the rabbi asks, you can ask him where he got the first set of stones for his first breastplate." He repeated his name for her. "Tell him it's me," said Cohen.

"Good idea," she said. She picked up a large drawstring bag lying on the floor beside her, and began to search for something. Just as he was about to ask for the rabbi a third time she pulled her head out of the bag. "The keys," she apologized. "I'm not supposed to leave the desk unlocked if I'm not in the lobby."

"Maybe you can tell me where to find him," Cohen tried.

"No, no, this is the way it's supposed to be done. It's okay."

"I'm impressed that as a married lady, you're allowed to work in such a job. Being alone in a room with a man?" Cohen asked.

"People don't understand that my father's really very far advanced," the girl said proudly, as she locked the top drawer, gave it a slight pull to make sure it was closed, and left Cohen alone in the little gallery.

In less than thirty seconds, Menachem Levine came into the room. His married daughter lurked behind in the dark thick-walled corridor that led into the rest of the building.

Levine was younger than Cohen by ten years, and much smaller, a slight, ascetic-looking man wearing faded black trousers, a patched white shirt, and a large white *kippa* over thinning black hair streaked white throughout his beard. It gave him a prophet's look, not a saint's.

"You haven't changed," said Levine, reaching out to shake Cohen's hand. There was a natural grimness in the little man's expression, matched by a grip unexpectedly strong for such a small hand. "Rivka says you didn't want to buy a *kippa*," he said, releasing Cohen's hand. He smiled with a twitch. "Abuhatzeira's been out for years, you know. Managing fine. Never been in trouble again."

"I'm not here about Abuhatzeira."

"Well, I can't invite you in for a tour unless you cover your head," Levine said. "We have Torah scrolls inside."

"No need. Just a few questions."

Levine squinted at Cohen for a second. "I thought you were retired."

"Helping a friend," Cohen lied. "Have you ever seen this boy?" he asked, pulling out the photograph.

Curiosity filled Levine's intelligent face. He took the picture, and held it slightly away from him, mumbling apologetically, "I'm not wearing my glasses," and then held it closer, bringing it into focus. His eyes narrowed, making Cohen's heart speed up. But then

Levine shook his head, and by saying, "not the boy," he first shattered Cohen's theory, then bolstered it in an unexpected way. "But I know the banker. Levi-Tsur."

Cohen tried not to show his anticipation. "You approached him for money?" he asked.

"Years ago. You were partly responsible, I suppose. After the business with Abuhatzeira, I realized that even if he was wrong in his methods, his intentions were good and he pointed to the real problem—we needed money. I began fund-raising."

"But you don't recognize the boy?"

"He looks more grown up than a boy," Levine said.

"Pictures can be deceiving," Cohen said. "Tell me about your meeting with Levi-Tsur."

"I didn't really know where to start. So I started with rich Levites," he said. "I asked everyone I knew for names. He was in the country, I saw in the newspapers. Making a donation to a *yeshiva*. He was gone by the time the picture came out, but I knew the rabbi at the *yeshiva*. He gave me the address. There was a correspondence, and we met the next time he was here. Maybe two or three years later. But nothing came out of it."

"Why not?" Cohen asked.

"He thought we needed a more archeological approach," Levine said, scornful of the science, "and less religious. He didn't understand what we are trying to do."

The mention of archeology shocked Cohen. He suddenly realized something else. He pointed to the photo again. "What's his name?" he asked, pointing at the elderly banker.

"Emmanuel," the rabbi stated. "Emmanuel Levi-Tsur," the rabbi said.

Cohen shook his head slowly, not so much to correct the rabbi as an involuntary reaction to the confusion.

"It's not Emmanuel?" the rabbi asked, incredulous. "He looks like him."

"They're brothers," Cohen said.

"Let me see the picture again," the rabbi asked. He looked carefully. "You're right. This one's older. But they have the same face."

Cohen nodded. He tried something else. "Jeremiah Ben-Alon," he said, hoping the name would bring a response.

"The *Gare Tzedek*," Levine said, using the religious term for a righteous convert to Judaism.

"You know him," Cohen stated.

"He has tried to raise money for us," the rabbi said.

"Tried?"

"It's not easy. It hasn't worked out as well as we both hoped."

"Did you convert him?"

"I am a rabbi," Levine said simply. "He studied with me."

Cohen noticed the use of the past tense. But before he could ask his next question, Levine had one of his own. "Why all these questions?" the rabbi asked.

"Call me a friend of the court," Cohen said.

"I don't have much faith in the courts nowadays," Levine said haughtily. "And I would think you are appalled by the use of administrative detention against citizens of the state. In a *democratzia*." He was as scornful of the Greek political concept as he was of the need for an solid archeological foundation to his work.

"I never heard you were appalled when it was the Arabs held without trial," Cohen said.

"I have never denied my people are more important to me than anything else," Levine declared. "The welfare of other nations is not my concern."

The argument would go nowhere, and Cohen still didn't have all the information he wanted from Levine. He tried a different tactic. "Have you ever heard anything about a collection of Roman-era crowns stolen from a . . ."

Levine's face broke into a sudden grin, interrupting Cohen in mid sentence. "For that," the rabbi said, "you'll need a *kippa*," beckoning Cohen to follow him into the bowels of the building.

Levine had never seen the crowns. "Too young, of course." he mourned. "I only heard about them a few years ago. But ever since I learned about them, I've thought about them on Tisha B'Av." It was the ninth day of the eleventh month of the Jewish calendar, a fast day to lament the destruction of the Temple.

Levine led Cohen out of the little gallery lobby into a large workshop that the rabbi said used to be a stable and barn for the previous owner's animals. Now it was a carpentry and metal shop with a

tracked crane for moving heavier objects out to a long neglected ter-
raced garden facing the west. A small tractor was parked in the garden. The driver was sitting in the shade of a rear wheel, eating a
sandwich, a bottle of water beside him. Levine waved to him, as he
explained to Cohen that work was being done to bring the road up
to the rear of the building, "so we can transport things more easily."

He pointed to doors on the other side of the room. "Toilets. All
new plumbing. Electricity," he pointed to the industrial-quality
lighting hanging from the high ceiling. "All new wiring."

In every reference to them on his tour of the building, Levine
used the phrase "previous owners," instead of Arabs, to describe the
people who sold the house to the *yeshiva*. As they made their way
across the floor of the workshop, where nobody worked at any of
the carpentry and metalwork positions, Levine handed Cohen a
white *kippa* from the basket in the lobby and made sure it was firmly
pinned to Cohen's head before they went up the stairs to the second
floor.

Like the first floor's workshops, the second floor was dominated
by a large single room, with a door leading to a tiny southern terrace
Cohen had not seen as he went into the building from the northeast. The ark for the Torah scrolls was at the northern end of the
large room, so the congregation in prayer would face the Temple's
place in the world. The tables were paired, as in every *yeshiva*, so the
paired study groups, known as *hevruta*, which learned together by
explaining the Talmud's passage to each other, could face each other
while studying.

Across the large room Cohen recognized two faces from the van
with the harp in the rear. They were sitting across from each other
with a third young man, whom Cohen assumed was the driver, listening to the argument over the text.

"Have a seat," Levine said. "Now, if you want to hear about
crowns, first you have to know something about the times when
Jerusalem was the House of the Kingdom."

Cohen tried to interrupt. "I know the history of the Temple," he
said.

Levine's expression made clear he doubted it. "You asked me
about crowns," the rabbi pointed out. "You want to hear me on the
crowns?" he continued. "Then you have to listen from the start."

Cohen looked at his watch. The director of the old age home where Victor was coming to his end said that Cohen could come visit before two or after five. It gave Cohen time to listen. He let Levine talk, hoping it would lead to something he didn't know.

"Solomon's Temple was the most fabulous building in the known world in its day," Levine declared, beginning a practiced speech. As he listened, Cohen looked through a large arched window to the northeast, and the glistening sun-backed cemetery on the Mount of Olives. "When Solomon died, his heirs started mucking it up, but the Temple lasted four hundred years," Levine went on. "That's when the Babylonians showed up and tore the whole thing down. But," Levine said, lowering his tone to a dramatic whisper, "within fifty years, Jews were coming home to the Land, rebuilding the Temple."

"Get to the point," Cohen interrupted.

"I'm getting there," the rabbi said. "A whole city grows up around it. People are coming from everywhere. Alexander the Great comes to see the splendor. He's so impressed he starts cultural exchanges between Jerusalem and Athens," Levine said. "And you know Jews. They'll do anything for a little culture. So the Jews got a lot of culture and the Greeks denied ever getting anything from the Jews," he said bitterly.

"I thought this was about the Roman era," Cohen tried again.

Levine gave him a twitchy smile. "Patience," he said. "Now, the Greeks would eventually get their due," Levine explained, "but only because the Jews deserved what they got for taking up Hellenistic ways. A king from one of the local Greek-supported regimes in the region, a Syrian ass named Antiochus, raided south with an army and hit Jerusalem. He made a mess in the Temple. Our sacred temple was violated," Levine mourned, but then his tone changed again, to pride and glory. "It doesn't take long, and the Jews throw him out."

"The Maccabees," Cohen said, hoping it would hasten Levine's history lesson to its conclusion.

Levine grinned again at him, pleased by his student. "And *they* botched it up, too. Their heirs. It only took a few generations and they were fighting each other. Within about a hundred years. By which time, the Romans are knocking out the Greeks everywhere, and have come to Judea. And we get to the point." He paused.

"Which is?" Cohen asked.

"The Romans liked Herod. And so did we."

"We?"

"The Jews," Levine said. "For what he did to the Temple."

"What did he do?" Cohen asked.

"He turned the Temple into what it's supposed to be."

"What's that?"

"A place of awe," Levine said simply, sitting back with arms crossed.

Cohen thought. "Where did the crowns come from?" he finally asked. The history lesson led him nowhere except into Levine's mind.

"You still haven't explained your interest," Levine pointed out. "Who is the boy? Obviously a Levi-Tsur. But which one?"

"The boy's grandfather is Emmanuel's older brother, Raphael."

"You think the boy came here?"

Cohen thought about where to begin, how to explain his suspicions without sounding as mad as Levine sounded to him. "I'm checking in with *yeshivot.* The boy was last seen at the *kotel,* and I thought he might have decided to become religious."

"A tourist?" Levine asked.

"Not exactly. He lived in Tel Aviv."

"Why the interest in the crowns?" Levine asked.

"I found some material about the museum theft. In the boy's possessions."

Levine nodded. "Let me see the picture again," he asked. "Maybe the light here is better."

Cohen stood up to get to the picture in its envelope in his rear pocket. It was dog-eared by now. He handed it to Levine.

The rabbi used a finger to cover the boy's clean shaven chin and cheeks, putting a hand over the face so that he could only see the eyes and forehead. "A boy grows a beard and becomes a man," he mumbled to himself. "A different person. Bar mitzvah, if he is a good Jew."

He handed the photo back to Cohen with an uncertain expression on his face. "Many people come here," he said.

Cohen looked around the large room, empty except for them and the three students in the corner.

"Today," Levine apologized, "it happens to be quiet. The tent settlement outside the prime minister's office," he explained. "But ordinarily, this room is full of students. Some come regularly. Others come once, twice, and if they stay, and have commitment, we let them join a *hevruta*. Like them." He pointed to the study group across the room. "I'm afraid I don't get to meet all the newcomers immediately. And I'm afraid I can't help you with the boy. Maybe you're right. Maybe Jeremiah can help. He has brought newcomers. He is very devoted to the cause," the rabbi summed up.

"Like Abuhatzeira was?" Cohen asked, with no little irony in his tone, standing up to pocket the picture. But he didn't sit down again. "Where can I find him? Will he be here today?"

"The truth is I haven't seen him for several days," Levine admitted. "But you want to hear more about the crowns, no?"

Cohen nodded.

"Wait here," Levine said. He went up the third flight of stairs at the back of the prayer and study hall. Cohen gazed across the room at the arguing *yeshiva* students. They were discussing a measurement used to determine the size of the blocks of the Temple. Levine came back down the stairs, clutching a file.

There were three documents. One was a folded poster announcing the exhibition, a large black-and-white print of a photo of the pomegranate crown. The second was a sixteen-page catalogue. There was a black-and-white photo for each item and an essay that was dense and academic in a very small typeface that began with styles of Hellenic and Roman jewelry and ended with metal smelting techniques and stone polishing in the ancient world. The third document was a six-page, single-spaced letter from a New York company made up of two names and an ampersand.

While the rabbi sat with the three students, plus four more who joined them, Cohen plowed through the catalogue essay. The article dismissed the legends attached to the crowns. It rose above the controversy over the question of whether they were true archeological finds by citing them as "sublime interpretations," adding, "sadly, by an artist who remains anonymous."

It called "hasty, and in retrospect, unfortunate," the Royal Geographic Society's decision to expel the member archeologist who came back from his journeys to the Holy Land with the collection and a silent Bedouin companion, declaring the crowns to be the original Herodian crowns.

"The shortsightedness of the London scientists was tragic, for the crowns certainly came out of the East," the article explained. "No European goldsmith ever created such designs. If not genuine artifacts of an ancient civilization, they are nonetheless genuine pieces of art, created by a master of his craft."

The article summed up that all the classicists of the time agreed that the works were magnificent examples of the blending of the Roman and Mesopotamian influences of the Eastern Mediterranean. The lines drawn in nineteenth-century academic circles over the archeological origins of the crowns gradually faded, but the treasure remained. "The artisans—and artists—of our young state," said the essay writer, "struggling with the creation of a new cultural identity made from the ingathering of the exiles, have much to learn from the artistry of these crowns about the aesthetic roots of this part of the world." It was written by the same pompous museum director whom Cohen remembered from the demonstration of the alarm system.

It was tiresome reading in Hebrew. Now he faced six pages of single-spaced typing in English, a six-page letter written by the head of antiquities for a New York auction house called Childes & Childes, in response to a letter from Rabbi Levine asking about the known history of the collection.

The English archeologist was actually a Scot named MacDonald, expelled from the Royal Geographic Society at the height of the controversy about his claim the crowns were Herodian, found in a cave overlooking the Jordan Rift Valley. The archeologist took the crowns—and the Bedouin whom he had brought back to London from the desert—to the Paris World Fair.

There, a Frenchman who ran the buggy-whip cartel in Paris was happy to put up the money for a chance to own Herod's crowns, especially when scientists using the latest techniques declared the items to be "at least several hundred years old." The Scot took the money, which he said he would use for an even greater expedition, and disappeared to the east with his silent Bedouin in tow.

The success of the automobile wiped out the Frenchman's buggy-whip fortune, so he sold the crowns to a German baron, who in turn gave up the collection to finance the rebuilding of his family holdings after Germany lost World War I. Then they went back to London—but not with a Briton. An American expatriate, a friend to the Prince of Wales, paid a princely sum—one million dollars American—for the crowns. But he, too, would also eventually lose the crowns, when Wall Street crashed in 1929. He sold them to a German-Jewish banker known to have a keen interest in archeology. Within six years, the Jew disappeared in the Holocaust, the crowns with him.

But a few months after V-E day the crowns resurfaced—through the auction house from which the letter was written. "An anonymous owner, variously rumored in the press to be either an American soldier who recovered them from the Nazi who stole them from the German Jew, or a Nazi seeking to finance his escape, put them up for sale," said the letter, which said nothing to confirm either rumor, nor anything else to clarify the identity of the seller.

The bidding reached two and a half million dollars when a long-distance phone call from the Continent came into the New York auction house. The caller was doubling whatever bid was on the floor at that moment. "I have only heard about it and read about it," the auction house writer told Levine in the letter, "but I am sure you can appreciate the drama of the moment. Nobody was ready to match the offer."

The next day, a man arrived with a cashier's check drawn from a Wall Street investment bank and made arrangements for the collection's delivery to that bank's address. They'd handle the shipping the rest of the way. That was the last the auction house had heard of the collection, until it was donated to the museum in Tel Aviv nearly fifteen years later—and stolen within weeks of its installation.

"I'm afraid the identity of the purchaser passed away with the death of Mr. Childes," wrote the head of the antiquities department, before signing off by saying that he had enjoyed looking into the old records, from long before his time with the house. The letter ended with regrets that the Israeli police never succeeded in solving the crime, and wished Rabbi Levine good luck in his research.

Cohen put down the letter. Levine left his students and approached Cohen.

"What made you write to the auction house?" Cohen asked.

"There's a donor," Levine admitted. "A Texan. A Righteous Gentile, always ready to help our efforts," he said. "He told me about the crowns. He asked if I knew anything about them. He gave me the name of the auction house. By the time I wrote to them, I had the museum catalogue."

"What's his name?" Cohen asked, doubting Levine would provide it.

Levine shook his head. "But I can tell you this. If those crowns were to come up for sale nowadays, he'd be first in line to make a bid. And he'd be ready to spend more than five million dollars. As far as we are concerned," Levine said, "if the crowns still exist, their value goes far beyond the gold or the artistry. For if they are real, and they could be brought back to Jerusalem, their recovery would be a great symbol of progress toward fulfillment of our efforts, our goal."

"Which is?" Cohen asked.

Levine looked at him like a parent patiently explaining a simple truth to a slow but beloved child. "The rebuilding of the Temple, and the reestablishment of the monarchy."

· 22 ·

An Arab male nurse took Cohen through the lobby of the Home for the Parents, as the Hebrew called the old-age home. It was a relatively new building on the old road between Jerusalem and Beit Shemesh.

"He has days when he's just mean. And days when he thinks it's forty years ago. He doesn't get many visitors. His daughter comes once a month. Brings her kids. We take it day by day with him." The attendant led Cohen to a large northern porch with a view down to the coastal plain.

About twenty of the residents of the home were on the porch. Many were in wheelchairs, and most were sitting around the five round tables on the patio, playing cards, talking, or sipping occasionally from glasses of juice. A few sat alone.

Cohen recognized the shape of Victor's darkly tanned skull, and the inevitable aviator-style sunglasses that Victor always wore against the bright light of the Middle East sun. Cohen remembered Victor as bald, burly, and eternally skeptical, with thick hands that made hard fists. Victor was still bald, but the burliness became a hollow-chested cough. The hands trembled. And instead of a natural irony in his gaze, the old man was almost completely blind, able only to differentiate between dark and light.

They were not friends when Cohen was in the *mador* and Victor its commander. Cohen was much younger than Victor, and that also contributed to the distance between them. But years pass, and age becomes less a matter of the gap between self and ambition and more a matter of the distance to death.

"He rarely has visitors," the director had told Cohen on the phone, and the attendant confirmed Victor's essential loneliness, expressing too cheerfully the surprise of "your friend's visit," mak-

216

ing the old man look up with more anger at being disturbed than pleasure of surprise from the visit.

"It's me," Cohen said, looking down at his former boss. "Avram Cohen."

"He can't really see you," the attendant reminded Cohen.

"From the *mador*," Cohen added. "Tel Aviv."

"I remember you," Victor suddenly said. "The one who didn't answer the alarm that didn't ring," he added, grinning with pleasure. His attitude suddenly changed to suspicion. "What are you doing here?" he asked.

"He's come to visit and you're asking questions?" the attendant asked Victor, in a teacher's tone. "And where's your hat? It's too sunny for you to be without your hat."

Cohen interrupted. "Please," he asked the attendant, "leave us alone."

"It's up to him. But it's going to be two o'clock soon," the attendant said.

With a skinny finger, Victor beckoned the attendant to lean closer. "I'll decide if I want to nap," he said loudly, "or to wear a hat," he added even louder. It made Cohen stifle a grin, and the group of old people at the nearest table a few strides away look up with horror at the eccentric old cop. "Get out of here," Victor said to the attendant, who shook his head sadly at both Victor and Cohen, and departed on sneakered feet.

"Is he gone?" Victor asked Cohen.

"Yes."

"All right, what do you want?" the old man asked, with a tone that rang familiar to Cohen. It was as if it was thirty years ago, and they were back in the office, a cluttered room of wooden desks, chairs, and piles of files stacked wherever there was spare space, and as usual, Victor would manage through interruption.

"I have some questions," Cohen said.

"About what?"

"The museum robbery. The crowns."

Victor let out a long breath of air and lifted a trembling hand to his skull, to rub away a sheen of sweat. It was as familiar a gesture as the tone in Victor's voice when he asked what Cohen wanted. It meant that Victor was thinking.

Cohen spotted the hat, a baseball-style cap lying on the tile floor beside the wheelchair. He bent over to pick it up and dropped the hat on Victor's lap. But the old man ignored it, still rubbing at his skull, still thinking.

Cohen turned to the view from the terrace. Although there was a haze over the metropolis around Tel Aviv, the sea could be clearly distinguished as a break of the landscape. But the sky and sea merged at the horizon.

Victor was still thinking. It made Cohen nervous. Some skin flaked off as he scratched slowly at his forearm. He noticed he was doing it and stopped, losing his patience. "What happened?" he demanded. "You spent another five years at the *mador*. But I never heard of an arrest, never heard of any suspects."

"Why?" Victor finally said. "Why do you care?"

"It's turned up," Cohen said. "In another case. A missing person."

Victor always scowled when curiosity struck and he was formulating a plan. "Do you have a cigarette?" he asked.

"You're allowed to smoke?" Cohen wondered.

"I'm outside. It's not smelling up the place."

"Your health?"

"Fuck it," Victor said. "You think this is life? Light a cigarette."

Cohen pulled out his cigarettes. He had smoked two on his way from Levine's *yeshiva* to the old age home. He lit one, took a puff, and handed it to Victor, who took a deep drag and coughed deeply, a hollow screech that made Cohen wince, feeling guilty about the danger of the bribe for his informant. He always felt that way when the payment only made the *shtinker* more dependent upon him.

Victor felt around to his left, lifting a towel on the chair beside him to reveal a stainless steel cup. He tapped with his trembling fingers, moving the cloth and then taking the cup, held it up close to his mouth, and spat a wad of dark phlegm into it.

One of the elderly women at the nearby table frowned at Cohen, who took the spittoon from Victor when he finished coughing and then held it in his own lap, covered by the towel, before setting it down in its place on the chair beside his former commander.

"What happened?" Cohen tried again, in a softer, more relaxed tone.

"Did they send you?" Victor asked.

"Who?" asked Cohen, surprised.

"I've been waiting for them. For years."

"Who?" Cohen asked.

"It's crazy of me," Victor said suddenly. "I know. They're all dead by now. They should be. Like me. You know," he added, lowering his voice, "they won't let a person die in peace."

"What happened to the investigation?" Cohen asked.

Victor shook his head—not to deny Cohen any information, but at the incredulity he still felt regarding what had happened to the case. "It was all wrong. It never should have happened the way it did."

"What?" Cohen wanted to know. "Who would send me to you?"

"You see, you're trying to trick me."

"Victor," Cohen tried patiently. "Did you have any suspects?"

"Poor Cohen," Victor said, squinting into the sky. "Didn't answer the alarm that didn't ring." He grinned. "Of course it didn't ring."

"Why not?"

"Well, it wasn't because of the rain," said Victor. "Was it?" It was triumphant but rhetorical, a reference to one of the possibilities Cohen suggested at the time might have gone wrong—the rain dampened the wires between the museum and police headquarters.

"What was it?"

"Why did they send you?" Victor suddenly demanded, his paranoiac tone giving Cohen an idea.

"They said it was time for it all to come out," he said. "To lance the wound," he tried.

"It's too late for me," admitted the old man. But he seemed to relax, suddenly, as if pleased that whoever it was who sent Cohen finally had decided to allow it all to come out.

"That's right, that's what they said," Cohen continued. "They said 'Victor can finally talk. Tell his side of the story.' "

"You know they threw me out," said Victor. "They made me leave. But not because I was some kind of goody-goody, like you. That's right. I heard what happened to you." He smiled at the sky. "Not me. They caught me with my hand where it shouldn't have been." He shook his head, more at getting caught than at regrets for the bribery. "I couldn't complain. At least they didn't put me on trial."

"Was it connected to the museum robbery," Cohen tried. "The crowns?"

"No!" Victor exclaimed, a grim, thin-lipped expression on his face. But then it suddenly softened. "You're always so serious," he scoffed, almost lighthearted, but at the same time shaking his head to indicate Cohen still didn't understand. "When are you going to realize that there's more to life than work," he asked, again reminding Cohen of life in the *mador* under Victor. "Have some fun," the old man ordered, suddenly thirty years younger and once again at the head of the hottest police unit in Tel Aviv, the only city in the country at the time, appreciating Cohen's lonely single-mindedness, distrusting his quiet stoicism.

"Where's the paper?" asked Cohen. "Victor? The paperwork. Tell me where to find the paperwork and I'll leave you alone. Won't ask any more questions," Cohen suggested.

Victor shook his head. "There was a lot of it. A helluva lot. I covered every airport and seaport departure for the week before, during, and after that weekend. I went through lists of gold experts and lists of burglars and we put everyone on it." His expression changed. "You left. For what?" he tried to remember. "Jerusalem, right? You wanted the transfer. Wanted to make a difference." He laughed scornfully.

"First I had the interrogator's course," Cohen said.

"And now you're interrogating me," said the old cop.

"Trying to find out what happened."

"Why?" demanded the old man.

Cohen had no answer, except the truth. "It's personal," he said.

Victor laughed, which made him cough. Cohen handed over the stainless steel cup and Victor went through his routine with the spittoon. But when he was finished, he was ready. His expression changed. "There was a reward," he said softly. "A few cranks called in. But there was one nibble. Serious. From Jerusalem. Someone who knew things that we kept out of the papers. Lord of the Universe," he suddenly exclaimed, "we were close. Real close. The state attorney was ready to make a deal. State witness. Plus the reward. We were close."

"And?"

Victor scowled. "We set up a meeting, of course."

"When was this?" Cohen needed to know, for his own sake, more than anyone else's.

"About a month after the incident," the old man said.

It relieved Cohen of a burden, making him prod Victor on. "You set it up?" he asked. Victor nodded, biting at his lower lip.

"His name, Victor, did he have a name?" Cohen wanted it. He wanted the name of the informant as much as he wanted the itching on his forearm to stop.

The old cop rubbed a hand over his head again. Cohen held his breath.

Victor wanted to get it right, but the name was eluding him. He tilted his head, as if he was trying to capture the name from a point in the air that only he knew. "Sarusi? Tabori?" Victor tried.

"Bitusi?" Cohen asked.

"Maybe," Victor admitted. "I can't be sure." But then he surprised Cohen by grabbing his forearm as if he could see it, and with a grasp matched in intensity by the rough whisper, Victor pulled Cohen toward him and said, "All I know is that he wanted to talk with me. Only with me. I let him pick the spot. The third curve of the Seven Sisters. That's what he wanted."

The Seven Sisters were seven switchback curves on the old road from Jerusalem, through the mountains down to the coastal plain. Cohen had driven up the seven curves when he turned off the highway to the old Motza road, a shortcut to reach the old-age home.

"It was in the merhav," Cohen realized, using the term for Jerusalem police headquarters before it split off from Southern Command and became a district command of its own as it approached the half-million population mark. For a moment, Cohen felt a terrifying remorse, the loss of the little city he knew as his home, an internal echo that he could only explain by recognizing that Victor, too, lived with the shame of knowing he had done his best, and failing, lost something much more valuable than gold crowns.

"Of course I brought in Jerusalem," the broad-faced man said bitterly. "What did I know about Jerusalem? I was from Jaffa. What did I know about the mountains. Now look at me," he added, almost enjoying the irony. "Still dying out here. Right by the Seven Sisters." He coughed. Cohen handed him the cup.

"He's not supposed to talk so much," a blue-haired lady screeched politely from the table nearby.

Victor waved a lazy, uncaring hand at her. "You want to know how I can afford to be in this place?" he asked Cohen.

"Well, it wasn't what I made from the police or being . . . ," he searched for the word. "Connected," he decided. "I volunteered," Victor said proudly. "For an experimental treatment," he added. "They take this," he said about the stainless steel cup containing his phlegm, "and run forensics on me. Before I'm dead. Can you believe it?"

"I believe it," Cohen said.

"I sleep with oxygen, you know," Victor tossed out. "I'd rather be dead."

"Nonsense," Cohen pointed out. "What happened at the Seven Sisters? You missed the source. But did he show up and you lost him or did you ever get to meet him?"

Victor raised a trembling hand to his head, clasping his skull as if it was going to fly off. "We don't know," he finally admitted. "We were in place. I was sitting at the bus stop at the third curve, just like he wanted. We spread people out from the top to the bottom of the mountain. I waited. And waited. He didn't show up on the first bus, so I waited for the second. And third. He didn't show up. I died out there. Let me tell you I died out there."

"Did he reestablish contact?"

Victor shook his head with dismay, and then crooked a finger for Cohen to listen closer. "We lost the end of the thread. But I don't think we were ever meant to find it."

· 23 ·

Cohen could feel the noose tightening. But he still couldn't tell if he was tying the knot or was about to find the rope around his own neck. He had no certainty about the direction the questions were leading. He wanted the paperwork. The case never closed, the files couldn't have been shredded, no matter how old they were. But he doubted Nahmani would authorize it and wondered how he'd get into the archive on his own.

Meanwhile, he'd find Bitusi. When he turned on the radio in his car, pulling out of the parking lot at the old-age home, the radio was reporting that the entrance to Jerusalem on the highway from the west was badly blocked all the way to the Motza curve. The radio blamed a demonstration by farmers from the Golan, arriving by tractor after a four-day drive south, to remind the prime minister he had promised not to give away the Heights in exchange for peace. "Naive of them," Cohen mumbled to himself, taking the back road to Jerusalem. "Believing a politician."

A report from Hebron said Palestinians were claiming that, after Eli Bookspan's funeral that morning, some settlers had rampaged through town and soldiers just stood by watching. Two Palestinians were dead and several hospitalized. The army spokesman's office issued a statement saying they would conduct an internal inquiry. The news reader said a group identifying with Hamas, the Islamic fundamentalist group, faxed a statement to the Reuter offices, taking credit for the slaying of the famous settler.

Cohen slammed the steering wheel at the red light in Beit Hakerem, still a quarter of the city away from the *shuk* and Mekor Baruch, the aged religious neighborhood just north of the open market. Traffic was horrible, but that wasn't his frustration right then.

There was no way the secret of Simon Levi-Tsur's death would have been kept so long if done by an Arab believing it would make him a hero if he succeeded, a *shahid,* a martyr for Allah. Success would gain the Arab entry to a terrorist cell. Failure, to heaven. More than ever, Cohen realized, he was right and the initial conclusions by the police and Shabak that it was an *intifada* killing, were wrong.

It took another half hour of stop-and-go traffic for him to find a parking space within walking distance of the little alley in Mekor Baruch where the car registration said he'd find Avner Bitusi. It was a street parallel to Jaffa Road, opposite the *shuk,* and named for one of the wealthy Sephardi families who were among the first builders of new Jerusalem as the city began growing in the twentieth century after centuries of neglect in the far corner of the Ottoman empire. The first row of houses were commercial on the Jaffa Road side, facing the bustle of the *shuk.*

But the alleys behind those shops led to a different world. Old houses built over cisterns and made from huge stone blocks on the first floor, turned into a jumble of additions of floors and porches as the neighborhood grew without becoming richer, expanding without leaving the natural border of Jaffa Road in the south and Kings of Israel Street in the north, heading to Mea Shearim, just to the east of Mekor Baruch.

The Bitusi address was across the street from a pita bakery in the middle of the row of five houses connected at their east and west, leaving only a northern exposure for the windows of the buildings.

Only one street number was on the building, but there was an open door at ground level, actually a few steps down from the street, into a cellar storeroom of canned and bottled goods guarded by a middle-aged worker.

To the right of the cellar door were the first steps of a flight of stairs going up to an apartment that opened to a narrow terrace stretched out in front of the apartment's blue door and three square windows. From the terrace, the stone stairs turned into a wrought-iron staircase leading to a balcony and a little boxy house with a red-tiled roof overlooking the neighborhood. There were two mailboxes. One said Bitusi. The other said Caruso. Both mailboxes were empty.

Cohen climbed the stairs to the terrace, finding a ceramic sign announcing it was the Caruso residence. He climbed the stairs to the balcony outside the little boxy house built on top of the old building. He rang the bell. He could hear the chime. But nobody came to the door. He tried knocking at the door, but nobody answered. He turned to look out on the neighborhood from the little balcony, considering what to do. He could jimmy the lock. But below, in the alley, a woman was standing on the street, staring up at him, holding some bags of *shuk* shopping in one hand and, in the other, she held the hand of a little long-haired child standing beside her.

"Bitusi?" Cohen called down. "Mrs. Bitusi?" he realized. She nodded stiffly, and he went back down the stairs to meet her.

Cohen knew there was a wife. They were married soon after Bitusi's release from Ramle the second time. He even heard that she truly didn't know anything about Avner's return to his old ways, when the police went knocking on her door with the bad news about her husband taking the big fall. He also remembered, during the few days of coma, and then weeks of Bitusi's recuperation, that the wife stuck by him, first in the hospital, then at home, and "yes," it was said one day in a session around Cohen's T-shaped desk on the second floor of the Russian Compound, "she's been getting Avi back onto the straight and narrow."

He realized that she recognized him. He doubted she knew he was now retired. "Let me help you take those bags up the stairs," Cohen said. The woman looked at him with astonishment, surprised by the congeniality of a man she knew to be all-powerful when it came to the case of her husband.

It was impossible to guess her age. Bitusi was at least fifteen years younger than Cohen, and she must have been even younger than that. But she wore a mousy brown wig, and her sharp, almost Hellenic features were dulled by a doughiness derived from an apparently sunless existence.

They let the child set the pace of the climb up the stairs. Cohen wondered, looking at the little square-headed creature with the never cut hair who already at that age had the natural grace of the gymnast, just like his father, whether many more children belonged to the Bitusi household.

The mountain sunset was coming early to that place on the ridge top of the mountain range that makes Jerusalem. The rough-cut of the white limestone was turning the colors of the sky. "Yoav," she called to the child, who paused on the steps. "I'm tired," she added, "please." By calling him Yoav, she identified the long-haired child as a boy. At two, he would get his first haircut.

The little boy sighed slightly, and got up from where he had sat down on the step, clutching the railing with both hands, looking out at his corner of the city and how it reflected the sunset's dimming light over the mountain town.

"You're here about the gold, aren't you?" she finally said, as they reached the balcony. He raised an eyebrow. "I don't know where to find Avner," she added bluntly, almost blankly, resigned to her situation without ever asking for it, but now that she was there, all she could do was tell her side of the story. Her side ranged from the hope she gave Bitusi when it looked like he was dying, all the way to the kid pulling at her hand as she tried to put the keys into the lock.

"What about the gold?" Cohen tried.

"I don't believe it exists," she said, just as bluntly as before. But then her face changed, for a second seeming to be ten years younger as she looked into his eyes with a question. "You're the one who decided not to hand over the case to the state attorney's office, aren't you?" she said. "When he fell," she added, as if to be sure he remembered.

He pursed his lips. "What happened to him?" he asked, ignoring her question about his past.

She frowned. "He never mentioned the gold to me, never said a word about it. Until . . ." she asked herself. "Today's Thursday, right?" she asked him.

"Yes."

They were still on the balcony, her arms folded so the keys were out of reach of the child. He waited while she calculated in her head for a second. "Yesterday it was three weeks," she decided. "Exactly."

"What happened then?"

"He told me about the gold, the first time," she said, as if Cohen was a child. "And began going mad from it," she added softly, to herself more than Cohen.

The sunset was expanding across the city. Windows caught the sun with flashes of golden light, while the ragged cut of the

Jerusalem limestone captured all the yellow and orange and red, and even the blue of the changing sky. "Maybe we could go inside," he suggested. "And you can start from the beginning."

Her name was Miri, from Miriam, and she had to cook for her children—the other five, led by the oldest sister, would be back soon. He listened, prodding her with questions but letting her own desire to see the issue resolved propel her sad tale forward.

The children kept her faith, not her husband—and not because he didn't try to keep his. In a way, Avner tried too hard. "There was always something *obsessivi* about him," she admitted, using a modernist slang that seemed at first out of character for a religious woman. "He's always been a difficult man."

But as her story unfolded to him, all became clear. "Now, this business, about the gold, it's been too much for me." She wanted to discuss it before the kids came home. "I don't want them to hear about it," she told Cohen. It was bad enough that Avner talked about it in front of them, "looking," she said, "like some madman at the *kotel.*"

She didn't want to dignify her husband's talk "about a fortune that would finally be ours because it was our rightful due," she said. "What we deserve," she repeated, twice, each time slightly more cynically.

In response to his question she said, "Avner went straight. Really. He stayed religious. He believed in the *rebbe,*" she said, nodding toward a photo of the Lubavitcher hanging on the wall slightly higher than the other pictures and photos of rabbis, Ashkenazi and Sephardi, hanging in cheap plastic frames in a large cluster on one wall like an exhibit of all the strains of orthodoxy. It was as if they searched for one who would satisfy their needs. "We all want to believe the *rebbe's* going to rise up," she explained to Cohen. "Like all the righteous, to bring the kingdom of heaven down to earth."

He noticed she didn't mention crowns. Only gold. It bothered him, but he decided to wait before asking, looking for the right moment when even her ignorance would have some meaning that she didn't intend and that Cohen would need.

She talked the same way she prepared food, haphazardly but well-meaning. She started cutting potatoes and then realized she should wash them, but a kind of passionate inertia took over, so she found herself washing onions before peeling them. She sliced the potatoes and onions with angry chopping that made him worry she'd lose a finger. He watched her pour cooking oil into a frying pan and if he hadn't stopped her, she would have dumped the sliced potatoes and onions into the oil without turning on the flame. She sighed, tapped at her wig as if to put it in place, and smiled abashedly at him as she lit the flame with a wooden match.

The apartment was much larger inside than it appeared from the outside, though it was still too small for Cohen to feel comfortable when the other five children—three of them boys under the age of ten—returned. There was no television—at least none was evident in the family room, which had a large dining room table and three children's mattresses stacked behind the faded brown sofa. Cohen realized that at night the room turned into a bedroom for the three oldest boys. A pair of soccer balls sat in the corner, one very old, another pretty new, beside a set of bookshelves for school books, which were all religious, Cohen noticed, except for an arithmetic primer that he guessed didn't go past the four basic functions.

Cohen sat at the head of the dining table nearest the kitchen area, at the far end of the apartment. It would have overlooked Jaffa Road—if the windows facing out to the street and the *shuk* were open. But they were closed years ago, against the noise and soot of Jaffa Road, the oldest commercial drive in West Jerusalem. A vague light penetrated the soot-covered windows at the southern end of the apartment, creating a cloistered, almost claustrophobic ambiance in the room for Cohen.

As the kids poured into the house, shocked to see a strange man sitting in their home—and a secular one at that—the two older daughters instinctively knew that it was a matter for their mother and scolded the four little boys into silence as they took over naturally from Miri in the kitchen.

Cohen smiled as gently as he knew how at the little boys looking up at him with trepidation and went out to the porch in silence, realizing how surprised he was that the woman even allowed him into the house. A religious woman, indeed a married religious woman, alone with a strange man, was absolutely forbidden.

Finally, she joined him. "I wasn't always religious, you know," she said, as if reading his mind. "But that's not why I let you into the house. Avner's a good man. Really. He needs help. When he started talking about the gold, I was afraid it would come to this. The police. Again. In my house." She sighed, not looking directly at him, but also not giving Cohen any room to interrupt. They were standing close enough for Cohen to smell her dried sweat. She looked out over the neighborhood. He looked at her.

"I came here," she said, a plea for understanding in her voice. "I kept Avner here, so that I could live the rest of my life without ever seeing a policeman again in my house. In the home of my children," she added wistfully, looking through the open door to the kids. The boys were trooping in from the bathroom, where they had been sent to wash their hands, and now all six were taking seats, each murmuring the appropriate prayers as they dug into the bread, fried onions, and potatoes in a cream sauce the teenage girl had made, and a compote that appeared from the aged refrigerator. "And because it was you," she finally said. "They told us that you were the one who recommended no prosecution."

"Tell me about the gold," he asked softly.

"Do you have a cigarette?" she asked. He fished one out of his shirt-pocket packet and realized as he did so, taking one out for himself, that it was only his tenth of the day. It made him feel good for a moment, and then foolish.

She tapped the cigarette filter on her thumbnail, and held it to her lips waiting for a light. "I don't care if anyone sees," she suddenly said, exhaling a cloud of smoke and surprising him as he lit his own cigarette. "I asked to meet with the rabbi, for his help. I told him that Avner was crazed, talking about how we'd have gold, but not telling me anything to explain why it was his father's and now ours, and why, if it was ours, we were living the way we do." She paused, as she realized something else. "And he didn't tell me why he needed to disappear in order to get the gold."

"What did the rabbi say?" Cohen asked.

"Not much," she sighed. "The Lubavitcher Rebbe just died. Those who could, were going to New York," she said bitterly, making it sound as if no matter how much she believed in the Lubavitcher, she would have found better use in her household for money than to fly halfway around the world.

"How did he know about the gold?" Cohen asked.

The woman shook her head. Her wig was slightly awry. He felt sorry for her. The children were quarreling about something, but it hadn't become violent, just raised voices in combat, testing some limit somewhere. She took a deep drag on the cigarette, leaning on the railing looking out at the northern neighborhood and shook her head. "I don't know. But that Wednesday he came back from the kotel, excited, and talking about the gold and how all our prayers had been answered." She paused, remembering, reflecting on what she had just said, then added, "They weren't my prayers, that's for sure." She stubbed out the cigarette, then looking down at it on her balcony floor she mumbled something to herself and bent to pick it up. Looking to see nobody was in the alley, she tossed the butt into the street.

"You said he came home from the *kotel*," Cohen pointed out.

"Yes?" she wondered.

"Was it morning? Afternoon?"

"Morning. He went every Wednesday, to a special minyan, and then to study."

"A special minyan?" Cohen asked. It was a quorum of ten men for prayers.

She nodded. "The dawn minyan."

"Dawn," he repeated.

She nodded again.

"What did he say about his father?" Cohen asked.

She shook her head. "I don't know. I don't understand. His father died when Avner was a child. I doubt Avner remembers much of him. That's one of the reasons the whole business is so crazy."

"His mother?"

"She passed away the week after we were married, may her memory be blessed. Right after he got out of jail." A siren blared on Jaffa Road, almost drowning out the last of her words.

Cohen realized that he had never spent much time on the cat burglar, whose acrobatic skills getting up drainpipes and over porch roofs had always been more impressive than any loot he managed to grab. For him, Avner Bitusi was just another underworld figure, slightly more independent, reportedly somewhat eccentric, but nonetheless just another hood on the make in a city like all other cities, even if for some it was holy.

Cohen's decision not to prosecute Bitusi, when he was found nearly dead on the boulder below the flat that he never managed to rob, was made for the efficiency of the force. When Yoram Marciano came in saying that he was beginning to believe that Bitusi really was turning religious, Cohen made his decision. If Avi Bitusi stayed religious—and out of trouble—Cohen and his cops would have no problem with him when he was released from hospital.

"But if he strays . . . ," Cohen warned, and Marciano said he'd make sure Bitusi and his lawyer understood the message. From then on, Bitusi had kept clean. Until now.

So, looking at her, wondering where he would find Bitusi, and how Bitusi's father was connected to the missing gold, he felt a tremendous sadness for himself and her, and at the same time a satisfaction that he had made the right decision then, four children ago, when the decision was his to make. For as far as Cohen was concerned, all the crimes of the city could never be totally eliminated, only postponed until a later date. Meanwhile, reason should prevail.

"Something must have happened at the *kotel*," Cohen tried. "Did he say what?" She shook her head. "Was it something he learned?" She shook her head again, slower. "Someone he met?" Cohen tried, adding, "did he ever mention someone named Simon. A young man. Levi-Tsur? Simon Levi-Tsur?"

She pursed her lips, and a third time, she shook her head, making him feel like beating his own head against the wall.

"Jeremiah Ben-Alon?" he tried. "An American?"

She shook her head. "He came home that morning and said he'd have to go away for a few days. But when he came back he'd have the money."

"You said gold," Cohen noticed.

"Gold, money? What difference does it make. He's not here. But you are here. The police are here. I think that proves my point, no?"

The little kids' quarreling was getting out of hand, and when one of the little boys shouted, "There is gold. I know it. Abba wouldn't lie," Cohen realized it was time for him to go.

"Where could he be?" he tried once more.

She shook her head. "I don't know. He hasn't been home since."

"Three weeks?" Cohen asked.

"Yes."

"Enough!" one of the girls screamed, trying to quiet the boys.

"How are you managing?" Cohen wanted to know.

"I have to go," she pleaded. "Please," she asked going to the door. "Find him. Before it's too late."

"Too late for what?" Cohen wanted to know.

It made her pause at the open door and turn to face him, looking directly into his eyes for the first time. "Too late for all of us," she said, closing the door behind her, before he could at least tell her to tell the children he was someone who remembered her when she was a child, long before she knew their father. But her sudden shout of pain and fury that he heard through the closing door was followed by the silence of children utterly protected in the knowledge of their mother's love, convincing him his help would not be needed inside.

· 24 ·

He was starved. And being followed. He cut across Jaffa Road coming out of Mekor Baruch, thinking about food, vaguely aware of a slender young man in a white shirt and black trousers, with unpolished shoes and an Uzi slung over his shoulder, crossing the street with him.

Traffic in the other direction was completely stalled. No traffic cops were in sight. A taxi driver stalled in the west-east lane of Jaffa Road told Cohen there was a suspicious object down near Zion Square and the bomb squad was taking care of it. That's when the young man who crossed with him caught Cohen's attention a second time. A car braked with a squeal of tires and a blast of the horn as the young man dashed across the traffic jam, just as an impatient driver inched forward.

Cohen crossed the street to the Jaffa Road opening into the *shuk*. Lights were on, but it was an uneven light of shops still open and of the faded colors of corrugated iron shutters already pulled down and empty vendor stalls folded shut and locked.

But he wasn't going into the mouth of the closing *shuk*'s main street. He was heading to Agrippas Street thinking about a *meurav*, a mixed grill. It would hit the right spot in his long-empty stomach.

However, as often happened to him lately, he had second thoughts, pausing in midstride to reconsider. The spicy meats in the pita would keep him awake all night and he wanted to be back at the *kotel* early in the morning tomorrow. On the other hand, he could find Ben-Alon at the tent protests, and a twenty-minute walk down the Valley of the Cross and then up to Givat Ram would help him digest the jumble of meats and spices in sauce-soaked bread. There was no fat in the food, unless one counted the cows' nipples, and the grill was clean where he usually went. But without the *ambah* and *s'hug,* and a few extra dashes of the restaurant's own dried spices, the *meurav* wouldn't be any fun.

He shook his head sadly and turned in a different direction, still not sure where he was going. By doing so, he noticed for the third time the young ultra-orthodox Jew with the Uzi—by itself a relatively rare sight—fumbling with a newspaper he had picked up but didn't want to buy, dropping it into the hands of the street salesman instead of paying.

But it was the yellow *kippa* pinned to the back of the young man's head, where unusually long hair for a *haredi* hung as unruly as the *payot* blending with the kid's sprouting beard, which nailed Cohen's attention. The African cleaning man in the apartment beneath Simon Levi-Tsur's had mentioned a yellow *kippa.*

Cohen was not amused by the clumsiness of the tail. He began walking, a slow stroll up and down and in and around the vendors' stalls along the two main alleys of *shuk* between Jaffa and Agrippas.

For the next half hour, he played hide and seek in the *shuk* with an opponent who didn't know it was a two-way game. Cohen strolled from stall to stall, saying hellos to vendors he knew, buying a cucumber from one, and rinsing it at the sink inside the little warehouse behind the stall, watching through the mirror decorated with pornographic decals, as the young man stood embarrassed beside a bin of female underwear, trying to keep an eye on Cohen inside the storeroom.

From there, they stopped in at a fishmonger's where Cohen bought marinated herrings. He chatted for a few minutes with the owner, keeping his eye on the mirror behind the counter, able to see the young man outside, pretending to be interested in a bin of tomatoes.

Cohen said good-bye to the fat man in the stained white shirt and cut down the street into a butcher shop he knew, with two exits across a corner, and into a short alley with its own tributaries of pathways that crisscrossed the side streets off the lower alley of the *shuk.* As Cohen stepped behind a rusted corrugated metal wall of a shed, the young man rushed into the alley and immediately realized he had lost Cohen.

For a moment, Cohen considered making his own move, but the young man surprised him, pulling a cellular phone out of the waist pouch he was wearing. Cohen was close enough, and the bustle of the main avenue of *shuk* was far enough away to create a quiet that made it possible for him to hear the young man's side of the conversation.

"Let me have Jeremiah," he began, tapping his foot as he waited. "Finally," he said. "Where have you been? Listen, you were right," he said excitedly. "I couldn't believe it. You were right. He showed up. At the Bitusi house." There was a pause. The young man shifted foot to foot with an impatience born of dismay at his own ignorance until finally he burst out, "I don't know what they talked about!" There was another pause, and the confidence dwindled even further. "I did follow him," he protested. "but . . . ," he said, and then, seeing someone coming down the alley, he turned his back to Cohen.

By doing so, his voice was suddenly lost to Cohen's ear, still behind the corrugated wall. And at that moment, a very large *haredi* man with a gray beard filled Cohen's truncated view of the narrow alley. He was carrying plastic bags stuffed with early shopping for Shabbat and was followed by two other, younger *haredim*. Cohen guessed they were the *haredi*'s sons, in those brief seconds when they blocked his view of his prey, and he thought he was going to lose it.

But when the three *haredi* men passed, the young man was still there, hitting the phone's end button and flipping it closed, to deposit in the waistband pouch, which like the weapon and the cellular phone was a strange accessory for a religious man to be wearing.

Now it was Cohen's turn. He stepped into the alley and tapped his prey on the shoulder. The young man turned.

"What did he say?" Cohen asked, almost whispering, standing barely a half stride from the young man.

The young man's surprise turned to shock and he took a step backward up against the wall, instead of a feint and dash. His eyes shifted each way, looking for a way out. To his right was the last bustle of the *shuk*. In the other direction was a short steep hill with steps at the bottom.

"Too late," said Cohen, feinting to his right and then left, catching the kid off balance, then grinning as he asked, patiently, "Where is he?"

"Leave me alone!" the young man said..

"Kiryat Arba? The tents' demonstration? The *yeshiva*?" Cohen continued.

"I know who you are," said the kid, his eyes narrowing with a blind hatred.

"I don't think you want me to get angry," Cohen said even softer.

"Arab lover," spat the young man.

Cohen's move was simple—his forearm rose fast and true, well-practiced, between windpipe and chest, knocking the kid off balance and pushing him backward against the stone wall of the narrow alley.

So far, nobody had used the alley since the big *haredi* man and his sons went through. But there wasn't much time for this kind of behavior, Cohen realized. "When I let you go," he said softly. "I'll be taking your weapon." His hand clasped the strap.

The young man's eyes bulged. Cohen smelled the sour sweat of fear and it made him push again for the kid's surrender. Still pressing with his forearm, Cohen carefully lifted the Uzi strap off the young man's shoulder. When he was sure he had cleared it from the young man's body, he stepped fully back, not exactly training the Uzi on the kid but with a small gesture that made the barrel slightly rise and fall, making it clear he was ready to use the weapon. He wasn't. Not really. Not in the *shuk* and not without cause. But the young man with the yellow *kippa* didn't know that. Cohen's grin twitched, making the kid shiver in the early evening heat.

An elderly woman wheeling a wire mesh shopping cart came into the alley, looking curiously at the young religious man rubbing his chest, and at Cohen standing aside for her, a rare gentleman in the Middle East, bowing his head slightly as she shuffled by, but keeping his eye on the sullen youth. The beard was too thin for him to be much more than twenty, Cohen guessed. The kid's complexion was sunburned and oily. Once the woman was gone with her shopping, Cohen asked for his name.

"Why should I tell you?" the young man asked.

"How old are you?"

"None of your business," said the young man.

"You said you know who I am," Cohen said. "I'm surprised you're not being more cooperative."

"Why should I? You're not a cop anymore."

"I have friends," Cohen said.

"Not what I heard."

Cohen made the Uzi nod up and down. "I don't think you want to hear this one," he said, adding, "what's your name?"

"Baruch," the kid admitted, after a pause. "You wouldn't use that," he added, but not very convinced.

"You're right," said Cohen. He slung the Uzi over his right shoulder, aimed generally in the kid's direction, and with a finger on the trigger guard. Now he used his left hand to draw his own weapon, the Beretta he kept hidden in the waistband in the small of his back under his shirt. He gave the kid a glance, reslung the Uzi so it hung barrel down, and then asked for the cellular phone.

"It's not . . ."

"What?" Cohen asked. "It's not yours? I didn't think so. Give it to me," he ordered.

The kid unzipped his pouch and reached in. "It better be a phone that comes out of there," Cohen said.

The kid nodded sheepishly. "It is," he said, handing it over.

"Open it," Cohen ordered.

Baruch did.

"Give it to me," Cohen asked, holding out his free right hand.

Baruch held it out but didn't put it in Cohen's right hand.

Cohen drew the Beretta with his left. "This doesn't make very much noise," he said. "And it really isn't very good for long distances. But this close?" He shook his head. "Give me the phone."

Baruch dropped it instead, and ran. He headed for the steps several strides to his right, where a beggar was coming up the steps at the end of the alley. Baruch knocked the beggar aside and in that fleeting moment, when Cohen had no clear shot to wound the kid in the leg, Baruch was gone.

There was no way Cohen would try to outrace a frightened kid. He bent over to pick up the phone. As he did, the beggar's frightened eyes caught his. Cohen smiled at him, and said, "Don't worry, it's only a dream. The *shuk* is back that way." He pointed over his shoulder and walked past the filthy creature in the same direction Baruch had run. He didn't have to worry about Baruch, he realized, holstering the Beretta back into its hiding place under his shirt.

The phone's little green light told him he could dial. He didn't. He pressed redial. The computer chip remembered the last call.

"Committee," the woman's voice answered. "Hallo? You have to speak up, it's very noisy here right now."

"How's the demonstration?" Cohen asked, raising his voice and speaking clearly.

"Huge, fantastic. Thirty buses are already here. But the Bolshevik police won't let us anywhere near the prime minister's office. Who is this?"

"Is the American there?" Cohen asked.

"Jeremiah? Yes, of course. Somewhere. But I can't see him right now. Who is this?"

"Leave him a message for me," Cohen said.

"Who is this?" the woman asked again, suspicion finally in her voice.

"Tell him that Baruch wasn't so blessed," Cohen said, making a pun on the kid's name as he turned off the phone.

A traffic cop he knew, working on Jaffa Road, let him make an illegal U-turn out of the parking lot onto the main street and then cut across to Agrippas Street, which would lead down to the Valley of the Cross.

But as soon as he reached the intersection at the bottom of the hill, he knew it had been a mistake to take the car. He blamed the incident with Baruch for the folly as soon as he recognized it, stuck in the traffic within view of Givat Ram, the ridge west of the Valley of the Cross, where the Knesset sits on the highest hill, flanked by the government's ministries and the Supreme Court.

He'd get there faster on foot in the gridlock of family cars and trucks and taxis and tourist buses and the demonstrators in their flag- and poster-bedecked cars, looking for their way to the protest, intent on shutting down the government's special cabinet session.

But just as he was about to twist the wheel onto the edge of the pedestrian triangle, the light changed and he flowed down with the traffic into the valley.

He punched on the radio. The state-run radio was carrying a special broadcast from the demonstration, while Army Radio was carrying Israel TV's evening news broadcast, which opened with the news of the demonstration.

He caught the TV anchorman saying that the Committee for the

Land of Israel was calling the rally "a spontaneous response" to a press conference statement by the prime minister, who said that Israel's policy had always been and would always be free access for believers to the holy sites of all the religions. "That means Arafat can come to Jerusalem," the broadcaster explained. "Now," he continued, "let's go live to the demonstration."

The next thing Cohen heard was the wail of loudspeaker feedback and then the radio suddenly blared "creeping division of the country and the city," followed by an orator's pause for the loudspeaker's echo, "is a treason that shall be punished." It was a familiar voice, made difficult to discern because of the distortion—and the muted rough-voiced rhythm of the crowd's chaos of shouting and chanting and the whistle-blowing Cohen already noticed among the demonstrators around him, hiking from the center of the city to the government complex.

Demonstrators coming out of the center of town, down the eastern slopes of the Valley of the Cross, were joining the cars in the street. There were no traffic cops in the long avenue, which is bounded on the west by a park. The news combined with the car's closed windows for the air-conditioning—which became necessary in the windless heat of the traffic jam—was making Cohen feel claustrophobic.

He pressed the button making all the windows descend, letting in a din that ranged from distant sirens to the car horns of frustrated drivers blaring much closer. But there was more than the ordinary sound of the city at evening rush hour.

People on their way to the rally were blowing whistles. Some carried Purim noisemakers. Cohen saw two yellow-and-black T-shirted teens walking with a rock in each hand, knocking them together.

Cohen opened the door and stood with one foot inside the car and the other out, trying to see how badly jammed the traffic was through the valley and up to the Givat Ram ridge. At the first set of lights below him, at the bottom of Bezalel Street, a crowd was gathered around a car at the light, where a driver probably had started arguing with the hikers on their way to the rally. But beyond, the traffic jam continued for as far as Cohen could see, a band of red brake lights winding like a piece of jewelry along the western edge of the park below in the valley.

Almost all the protesters marching on the government complex were religious. Most were teenagers, ranging from kids in jeans and T-shirts to more orthodox Jews in black pants and white shirts. The knitted *kippot* of the settler movement outnumbered the black and white garb of the *haredim*, two to one. But the religious outnumbered the bareheaded, secular protesters by nearly ten to one.

Many of the people on their way to the rally moved in small gangs of mostly the same sex. But there were also couples, and families, including, saw Cohen to his dismay, babies in strollers and papooses. From what he was hearing on the radio, people were probably getting hurt on the hill. It was no place to bring a baby.

"We are here to stop the leftist, treacherous government from dividing the country, from stabbing a knife of terror into the heart of Jerusalem and the People of Israel," the radio blared at him from Israel TV's live report from the demonstration.

To his right, in the park, groups of demonstrators were carrying flags, banners, and posters and hiking across the lawns, heading for the road that would take them up to the ridge of Givat Ram.

Some were trying to climb into the forest on the eastern slopes of the Knesset's hill. Cohen shook his head at their ignorance. The Knesset Guard never let a demonstration past the gates to the building's plaza. The rest of the building was surrounded by electronic fences and a round-the-clock staff of guards, answerable to the Speaker of the Knesset. On a night like this one, Cohen thought, there would be squads of the Border Patrol on the Knesset perimeter as well.

"From stabbing a knife into the back of the people," continued the orator at the rally. Now Cohen recognized the voice. It was the scarecrow rabbi, the leader of the Jewish settlement inside Hebron. There was a sudden pause in the Army Radio broadcast, a long silence broken by a different voice.

"Our apologies for the technical difficulty," said the news anchor. "That was our reporter with the demonstrators in Jerusalem. Now we'll go to our police reporter, with Jerusalem District Commander Haim Reshef."

Cars moved down the street and Cohen rolled with them, listening to the broadcast, catching up to the same couple with the baby who had passed him two minutes before.

He knew Reshef well. A soft-spoken patrolman who rose as a

brilliant administrator through the ranks until he got the job Cohen had never wanted—commander of the police in Jerusalem. For Cohen, the job would have been a disaster. For Reshef, a natural diplomat, it was perfect. Cohen turned up the radio.

"Thousands of demonstrators are trying to get to the government offices," the reporter began. "They're trying to get to the prime minister's office where the government is in session. The police are having a difficult time, with reports of wounded demonstrators. Three policemen have already been injured," the reporter went on. "More than twenty protesters have already been arrested, including several of the organizers, say the police. But meanwhile, the organizing committee says the police are using excessive violence against children, women. With me is Commander Haim Reshef," the reporter finally said. "Commander, what is your response to these allegations?"

The chain of brake lights in front of him slid forward. Cohen let his foot off the brake, and the car glided forward another few yards. The light at the bottom of the hill was still two hundred more away.

"The police, in fulfillment of its function as protector of law and order, will not allow any demonstration, no matter what the cause, to disrupt the functioning of this city," Reshef was saying, "or the government."

"Ya'akov," another reporter suddenly broke in, calling for the anchorman's attention. "The education minister's car just left the parking lot outside the prime minister's office, and police are using horses to force the crowd back away from the car. The education minister was the first to try to leave the session. Yes, now I can see it, the minister's car is backing up, returning to the parking lot, back behind the fence around the government compound."

"What's all that noise in the background?" Ya'akov the anchorman asked his reporter.

"The organizers said they would use no violence but would do whatever they could to prevent the government from being heard," the reporter said. "As you can see, the demonstrators are using whistles, noisemakers, anything to make it impossible for the ministers to conduct their work." Cohen couldn't see, but already here, a mile from the rally, the protesters, on their way in small and large groups, were using the noisemakers.

"Ya'akov," the TV reporter went on, "I can tell you—and Commander Reshef—that from where I am standing, I can see the police are not able to stop the crowd from taking over the entire entrance to the government and are having difficulty preventing them from advancing up the road to the prime minister's office. And Ya'akov, while the vast majority of demonstrators are limiting their protest to the whistles, a fringe minority are trying to break through police lines to reach the prime minister's office. The police are taking the organizer's slogan—'shut down the treasonous government'—very seriously. Back to you Ya'akov."

Cohen scowled. Ya'acov the anchorman said, "The stock market is also not happy with the pace of the peace process. But the market seems to want it to move faster. We go now to our correspondent on Ahad Ha'Am Street at the Tel Aviv Exchange."

Cohen swore, and punched at the radio buttons, looking for more news. But the Voice of Israel state-run radio's newscast was over and an hour-long program about an AIDS conference in Japan began.

Cohen's distress finally broke. He inched forward, pulling up onto the sidewalk with a bounce of the car over the curb, braking hard to avoid lurching into a pair of demonstrators sitting on the stone wall. They were a boy and a girl, in their teens, both religious, and when they turned to look into Cohen's headlights they were clearly embarrassed by being caught in a romantic interlude rather than on their way up to the rally. The girl stood up huffily, and walked away down the sidewalk, followed sheepishly by the boy.

He fully expected the car to be towed, but would worry about it later. Meanwhile, just in case, he left a note with Baruch's Uzi in the trunk in case the police, finding the car abandoned, decided it deserved investigation as a possible bomb. He signed the note with his name, and put in parentheses: DC Chief CID ret.

He smiled to himself when he found himself deliberating whether to cross out "retired" and put in "reserves." But Haim Reshef—to whom the note was addressed as a point of reference for the sapper who'd open the trunk and find the weapon—didn't have much of a sense of humor.

He moved along the edges of the stream of people who were driven by the purpose of passion that brought them out of their homes at the end of a work and school day to demonstrate against the government. Many of the adult men carried weapons, signifying they were settlers and therefore allowed to use the guns for self-defense against Arab stone-throwers. Most of the teens moved in packs, singing various anthems for their cause, many chanting, "The prime minister's a traitor, the prime minister's a terrorist."

Sweating, and slightly breathless, he climbed southwest across the valley park until he reached the road again where it bisected Givat Ram's ridge. There he joined a crowd that swelled across the avenue.

The first police line prevented a right-hand turn into the southeastern corner of the government and Knesset complex on the hilltop. Nobody was challenging the police line, for the tent settlement demonstration was on the southwestern side of the hill.

Around him he could feel the power of a tide sweeping the marching demonstrators forward. By the time he reached the museum entrance on the left, the crowd was moving fast and thick. Still he pressed ahead, looking for the point of contact with the police.

The noise level rose. The blue lights of police vans, the red lights of ambulances, and the cold white lights of the television cameras were as hard on the eyes as was the noise around him as the crowd advanced on the police line of the green-uniformed Border Patrol. A few—officers, Cohen could see as he approached and the metal ranks on their epaulettes caught the lights—carried batons. Two horsemen from the Jerusalem police cavalry flanked the line at each side of the avenue, posted to halt the marchers' advance on the intersection ahead by funneling the demonstration into the field across the avenue from the government complex, into the licensed demonstration area marked by the tents. These ranged in size from big army-style canvas to even larger booths wrapped with the netting farmers use to protect sensitive crops from the direct sun of the desert. There were thousands of people milling about, in front of an improvised stage for speakers.

Cohen's hope to find Ben-Alon at the demonstration was based on a description that Levine had confirmed for him—the tall, balding man with the long wispy beard whom Cohen saw at the Mount of Olives cemetery. He assumed Ben-Alon, as one of the organizers, would be either near the speakers' platform or among the tents.

He worked his way toward the speaker's platform, a semitrailer for shipping containers deposited by a sympathizer who owned a trucking company. The speaker was a woman, a former member of Knesset whose speeches were always a heady mixture of fire and tears. He recognized her voice before he could see her.

"They call us irrational," she was saying. "They call us fanatics, they call us obstacles to peace. But who, if not we will preserve the Land? Who will save it from the traitors? Us!"

A loud blast of sirens interrupted her speech. It came from above the crowd, behind the semi-trailer. He made his way through the crowd toward the stage. There were about a dozen other speakers on the trailer: politicians and rabbis, a writer and a professor of nuclear physics. They were all listening to the raven-haired woman with her heaving bosom, waving her finger in the air as she spoke.

But there was nobody on the stage—or even near it—with a long, gray, wispy beard. Cohen moved around the trailer, coming into view of the most advanced lines of the demonstrators facing off against the police trying to prevent the rally from climbing onto the avenue.

At the very front line there was pushing and shoving. A long row of policemen both in blue uniforms and in the green uniforms of the Border Patrol, and stretched to their limits, were holding hands to keep the crowd back.

Cohen worked his way behind that front line, looking for Ben-Alon and a familiar face among the policemen who would let him through the line so that he could stand on the police side and see the faces of those trying to break across the avenue.

The woman concluded her speech with a lamentation, and was followed by the professor, who started by saying that ordinarily he would have to disagree with his predecessor's remarks concerning the uniformed security services' responsibilities, and how it was unwise for any politician to encourage a break in the discipline of the police or army or Shabak. There was a dramatic halt to his speech that seemed momentarily to calm the crowd. Even Cohen paused to listen. "But these are not ordinary times!" the professor shouted.

The crowd roared, and suddenly there was a rush forward that propelled all in its way. Cohen, too, was carried forward by the crowd pushing behind him, and found himself breaking past a pair of sweating, grim-faced Border Patrolmen who had lost their grip in the human chain trying to hold back the protesters.

A gunshot blast shook the air. But it was only tear gas flying down from the police lines on the other side of the avenue, where hundreds of teenage demonstrators were taking over the street. Cohen walked slowly as around him demonstrators ran across the asphalt, chased by policemen. The tear gas wafted in his direction. He strode toward its acrid stink, blinking away the tears streaming from his eyes.

"What are we? Arabs?" shouted the professor's voice from the loudspeakers. "They're using gas on Jews! Gas!" he cried. The chaos was increasing, as teenagers ran forward into the fray while older, and less adventurous protesters began escaping the stinging gas.

But the gas didn't deter those in the midst of the brawl, nor did it deter Cohen from continuing forward, certain he'd find Ben-Alon closest to the fighting. He was standing in the middle of the avenue, on the grassy median strip, scanning the crowd, when he heard someone behind him calling, "Cohen! Avram Cohen!"

He turned. Yoram Marciano, the young deputy chief of CID, was approaching him, followed by two policemen. "What are you doing here?" he asked. He shouted to make himself heard in the uproar around them.

"Ben-Alon, Jeremiah Ben-Alon," Cohen said. "An American. From Kiryat Arba." He pantomimed a long beard. "Bald," he added. "You know him?"

Marciano nodded, as if he wasn't at all surprised by the question.

"You seen him here?" Cohen shouted to be heard.

"Why?" Marciano asked, naturally suspicious.

"I need to speak with him," Cohen said. The business with Baruch had changed all the rules. He didn't care if Reshef heard about him asking questions. He didn't care if the inspector general would be embarrassed or Nahmani would be angry. He didn't care any longer. The rules had changed when Ben-Alon sent young Baruch to Avner Bitusi's house to watch out for Cohen.

"What about?"

"I think he was involved in the Simon Levi-Tsur business," Cohen said bluntly, "with Avner Bitusi."

Marciano's expression changed from suspicion to a narrower look. Bitusi was his case.

"I'm not saying it's your fault," Cohen said. "It was probably mine, years ago. You wouldn't have any way of knowing."

"What was the connection?"

"Later. First, where did you see him?"

Marciano looked around at the scene, thinking. Cohen watched three border patrolmen wrestling a squirming black-bearded demonstrator into a police van parked across the street with its doors open. "By now," Marciano finally said, "he should be at the Russian Compound. He was in the first round of arrests."

"What did he do?"

Marciano grinned. "He threw a punch at Haim Reshef. Now tell me, what does he have to do with that kid?"

Marciano's Motorola squawked on and off with reports from the field. About five hundred demonstrators had made it to the gates of the prime minister's office parking lot. Reshef's calm voice came on the air, sending reinforcements.

"Is Reshef up on the roof?" Cohen asked, nodding vaguely toward the building that housed the prime minister's office. There was a police control-and-command position up there.

"You can't get up there," Marciano said.

"I don't want to go up there," Cohen said, making a decision. He climbed down from the median strip onto the avenue and stepped aside for a border patrolman hustling a crying teenager across the street before walking away from the rally, back toward the Valley of the Cross, to his car—if it was still there—and to his new destination.

"Where are you going?" Marciano called out to him, but Cohen ignored the question. "You didn't tell me what Ben-Alon has to do with that kid? Avram? Cohen?" Marciano tried again. But his voice was drowned out by a siren starting up as one of the police vans, loaded with arrested protesters, announced its intentions to begin to move.

And twenty minutes later, Cohen was back at his car, getting there just in time to prevent the city tow truck from taking it away. It took all his self-discipline not to rub at his eyes, still itching from the tear gas. But he didn't mind. With a little luck, he felt, he'd soon know what happened to Simon Levi-Tsur. Meanwhile, he decided, he could eat and get some sleep.

· 25 ·

Before he showered, before he ate, before he listened to the messages on his answering machine, he made a call to Meshulam Yaffe to make arrangements for the morning. Waiting for Yaffe to answer, he read the note Nissim had left behind: "Sorry for being an idiot. Spoke to Hagit. It will work out. Left at noon. Your hangover remedy worked."

The conversation with Yaffe started off with some difficulty. But even Yaffe understood that a search for one missing object—even when it's a person—can lead to the discovery of another. Cohen was careful to leave out any mention of the syndrome while at the same time making it clear that he was holding a thread from Victor to Bitusi, through Baruch's Uzi to missing gold, if not to a crime for god, and that the weave, while ragged, at least deserved a chance to be seen in full.

Baruch's Uzi was the clincher, of course. Cohen suggested a messenger be sent over to pick it up so forensics could get going on it. Yaffe said nothing would be done until the morning.

"Then have them deal with it in the morning," Cohen ordered, and for a moment it was just like the old days, and when Yaffe said he'd see what he could do about looking up the museum robbery files, Cohen jumped in with his real request.

Yaffe was primed to agree, but it took a final bribe from Cohen. They were Levi-Tsur's twenty thousand dollars, not his. "A donation to the police charity," Cohen promised, "on one condition."

Thus Yaffe promised Cohen he could get Ben-Alon in an interrogation room at the Russian Compound. He laughed to himself at Yaffe's spluttering when Cohen added a final string to the donation by saying he'd pick the charity. But they hung up with an agreement to meet in the morning at the Russian Compound.

After the shower, came the food—a fresh Greek salad and half a chicken, spiced from his garden and broiled with thin slices of oranges he slid under the skin of the breasts and thighs. Only after he ate and had washed the dishes did he play the messages on the machine.

Ahuva had called in. "I can see the demonstration," she said. "It is not a pleasant spectacle." He had seen the lights on at her tenth-floor apartment overlooking Givat Ram from the eastern slopes of the Valley of the Cross but deliberately chose not to go to her flat. It would have been making a spectacle of himself, something he was careful never to do with Ahuva.

The second message was from Caroline Jones. Her voice was softer than usual. "I'm sorry to report that Mr. Levi-Tsur passed away last night," she said. "His heart. The tragedy of the boy. It was in his sleep, thank goodness. I, I, I felt you should know. I, I, don't know if you will be hearing from me again. The board will be meeting after the seven days of mourning."

Shmulik was next. "I thought you might want to know that the person you were asking about today is under arrest at the Russian Compound, from the demonstration."

There was the click and the sound of the tape rewinding. He sat back at the desk, looking at the spread of notes, slowly rubbing at the small flaky patch on his forearm until he stopped himself, leaned forward, and reached for the phone.

First he called the Levi-Tsur voice-mail box and left condolences for the family, asking Caroline Jones to call him back at eight A.M. on Friday morning, Israel time. That was ten hours away. If she wasn't able to make the call then, she should try from noon on, every hour.

Then he dialed Laskoff's home number and left a message on the machine asking the same thing he planned to ask Caroline Jones. "That man you saw in the restaurant in New York," Cohen said to Laskoff. "It turns out I do need his telephone number. Please see what you can do."

He made a note. Yaffe had sounded genuinely surprised when Cohen told him that Jeremiah Ben-Alon had been arrested. How did Shmulik know so quickly? Cohen wondered.

He sat for hours making notes like that and others, drawing dotted lines and question marks, letting his mind follow the speculation like a hiker discovering a bend in a wadi. Just after midnight, a motorcyclist showed up at his front gate. Cohen carried down the Uzi, after wrapping it in a plastic garbage bag. The motorcyclist asked Cohen to sign a form, which for a second made Cohen remember all that he hated about the police.

He kept trying to put himself in Simon's shoes. A rich kid, with a secret, desperate need for meaning in his life, Buki Bender said. Could the secret become the lever for a new identity? And what was the secret? Were the Levi-Tsurs the donors who gave the museum the crowns? Bitusi's father plagued Cohen. He wished Victor had remembered the name.

By two, the Glen Miller disk had played *Chattanooga Choo Choo* for the third time, and Cohen realized much would depend on what he could understand from Ben-Alon.

As he closed his eyes in his bedroom, wondering when he would have the courage to speak with Ahuva, he remembered something Vicki had told him about her trip into Herodium with Simon. It was a "big bloody secret," she said, angry that she had never been trusted to share it. For the first time Cohen wondered if Simon, too, might not have been trusted with the secret.

He fell asleep thinking of secrets. In the dream, faces appeared in each flicker of light. Most came at him out of his past, and none would go away from his eyes until he could remember their name, their testimony, and their innocence—or guilt. It sometimes didn't matter to him, as he tried to find some truth about what he knew, what he felt, what he could prove. After awhile, a few of the faces came to him from his present, from the search for Simon Levi-Tsur and the meaning of the missing museum pieces. Most of these were vague, like artist sketches that caught an essence but never could be recognized as the perpetrator until they were caught for an entirely different reason. Thus, his dreams revolved around memories both recent and past, catching him in little whirlpools of self-doubt caught just before drowning by a branch overhead to which he could reach a hand and pull himself to safety. Like he wished he could do with cigarettes, he learned to control the dreams. It had been a long time since he woke sweating, convinced he was about to die.

He woke a minute before the alarm, grateful for the first full night in bed, aware that he still had a long way to go but certain he was heading now in the right direction. As it was Friday, he had a schedule to keep. It was a schedule that began with Yitzhaki, and included Mikey Ha'Yivani, the Greek who sold papers and, from the back room, Cohen knew, occasionally headier stuff, but never anything made in a lab or properly delivered by a medical physician. Mikey was a source of sorts, a chubby little Greek Orthodox Christian whose personal devotion to Jerusalem was more familial than spiritual, but who somehow found something funny to say about every headline in the national newspapers.

From Mikey's, where Cohen would hear an analysis of the day's daily events that Cohen knew to be no more or less sophisticated than what prime ministers heard over the years from their experts, Cohen would go to Michelle's.

She was originally Belgian, married too young to a Turkish importer who had lost a small fortune trying to compete with the local rug manufacturing monopoly given to a *haredi* Jew who guaranteed the coalition half a dozen votes in the Knesset whenever necessary. The Belgian woman had turned the apartment she won in the divorce into a second-floor café with a porch overlooking Emek Refa'im. Cohen was a regular there on Friday mornings.

Yitzhaki's was closed, confusing Cohen. He hiked three blocks down the street to Mikey's, but the Greek newsstand owner and the Iraqi grocer hadn't spoken since Yitzhaki's daughter said no to Mikey's son. Mikey knew nothing about why Yitzhaki's was closed.

Cohen picked up his papers but spent no time on the headlines with Mikey, though even Cohen had to admit they were exciting: the government announced that the prime minister would be flying to Washington for another breakthrough in the peace process—a public meeting with King Hussein of Jordan. Cohen wasn't surprised. But he was glad. Nonetheless, he was due in the center of town in an hour, and Yitzhaki's was closed. He wanted to know where he'd get food for that evening's dinner with Ahuva. He crossed the street to Michelle's.

"What are you doing here at an hour like this?" she asked from behind the bar, as Cohen came up the stairs. Closer, she read reason for his early arrival on his face.

"Yitzhaki?" she asked.

"What happened?" he wanted to know.

"His Arab," she said, "what was his name?"

"Yusuf," Cohen said softly.

"Was shot dead," she said. "Yesterday morning. There was some rioting. After Eli Bookspan's funeral?"

Cohen nodded, stunned. Poor Yusuf, he thought. Poor Yitzhaki.

"Yitzhaki's blaming himself," said the woman. "At least that's what I hear."

Cohen could only shake his head and rub at his fresh shave. He was running out of time. "Tell Yitzhaki I'll be over to see him," he said.

For a moment he considered leaving his newspapers at Michelle's, where he usually leafed through them but rarely read any piece from beginning to end, distrusting the newspapers more than he distrusted many of the criminals he had known. But then he remembered Caroline Jones. He wanted to be home by noon. Latest one o'clock. And he didn't know how long he'd be at the Russian Compound.

· 26 ·

Already at the guard booth Cohen was noticed. In the driveway he was accosted by old friends. By the time he reached the little lobby with its elegant, curving, marble staircase made to specifications approved by the czar's chief architect, people were coming out of offices, looking out their windows, asking if it was true that Cohen was in the building.

Transport branch's Annie Pinkas actually caused almost as much a stir as he did when, hearing he was in the driveway, she heaved herself out of her chair and crossed the parking lot, chasing him to the lobby, where she was rarely seen, because she was never known to climb the broad stairs. "Good luck, whatever it is," she called out to him, just as he reached the top step, about to face his former office. He smiled down at her, and at all the other faces who had come out of the first-floor warren of offices to see him back in the building.

The door to his old office used to be greener, was his first thought, as he looked across the wide nicked-wall hall. He tried not to stare. One of the old-timers from the burglary squad followed him up the stairs, one hand on Cohen's shoulder and the other pumping his hand while the aging detective told his old commander how much he was missed.

It wasn't the CID commander's office anymore, he knew. Avi Sasson had won a bigger space, especially after it became apparent he needed a deputy, not an assistant, and that it would be years before either Sasson or Marciano alone could fill Cohen's shoes. The sign on the door said it was the spokesman's office. Press was more important than investigations, it seemed, judging from the hierarchy of offices. He swallowed his disgust and turned to his left. The huge aerial photo of Jerusalem, with the Temple Mount in the center, signed by a Phantom squad dedicating it to the Jerusalem

252

police, was still in place. Cohen smiled at the nervous patrolman clutching his cap in both hands and leaning elbows on knees, staring at the floor, probably worried about what Reshef would rule in his case.

"Avram," Yaffe said, coming out of the door to Reshef's bureau and pulling him inside, away from the clutches of the old timer from burglary and a pair of young desk sergeants who had come out of their office around the bend in the corridor to get a look at the famous Avram Cohen.

"He's not a movie star," Yaffe snapped at the two women, sending them scurrying. "It's great, it's great," he told Cohen. "Forensics is already at work on the Uzi." He was wearing one of his tailored uniforms, something that always made Cohen apprehensive. "Ruti," Yaffe said, "look who's here!"

She was already blushing as Cohen came into the little office that sat between the chief's and his deputy's. She had been Cohen's secretary, getting pregnant after he left the force. When her maternity leave was up, Reshef offered her the job as his bureau secretary. She consulted with Cohen, asking him if he thought she could handle it. "With your hand behind your back," he promised her.

"Shalom," he said smiling at her as he came into the room.

She beamed, standing up and coming around the desk to take both his hands, which he extended with a paternal gesture, taking her pecks on each cheek and then backing up to let her admire him. He noticed that the baby had thickened her waist, but her wide smile remained the same. "You haven't changed. I heard so much. But you're the same," she said.

"Avram?" called a dry hoarse voice from the next room. It was Reshef.

Cohen shrugged. She grinned. "You haven't changed, either," Cohen told her, before entering Reshef's office.

Cohen had seen nearly a dozen commanders come and go in the Jerusalem police station, going back to the days when it was barely that, a station. Now it was a district command, but it still had the same look: the wall-size map of Jerusalem and its environs, the plaques and banners and medallions and flags framed and hung on the wall, the glass cabinet full of officious books about criminology and coffee-table photo albums brought as gifts from international visitors.

Behind the desk, a low bureau of two-drawer filing cabinets and drawers held the chief's paper work. His desk sat at the head of the long leg of a "T" made by a conference table surrounded by a dozen chairs. The only thing new for Cohen was the computer terminal on the desk, and he understood how much that changed everything beyond his current reach. But at least it didn't make him nervous.

Yaffe took a chair in the armpit of the T-shaped desk. Cohen took the nearest chair at the end of the table.

"I've got to tell you the truth, Avram," Reshef began, lighting one of the three pipes that sat on a rack on his desk. "I don't like this."

Yaffe tried to interrupt, but the district commander's rank was still more powerful than Yaffe's administrative position. He held up his palm to silence Yaffe. "No offense," said Reshef. "It's not personal, Avram, but it's not the way things should be done. You're retired. I can't let every retired policeman in the force dance in with a personal vendetta."

"It's not personal," Cohen said softly.

"Haim, it's all been explained to you," Yaffe said, exasperated. He had done his best and now the two key players looked like they were about to claw each other to pieces. Cohen glanced at Yaffe, feeling a creeping chill that gave him shivers and began to ride up the back of his neck to his skull.

Reshef picked a piece of paper off his desk. "It's not often I get a memo directly from the police minister. I mean one addressed to me and sent with a drop copy to the inspector general. Usually, it's the other way around." He dropped the piece of paper on the table, and leaned forward looking at Cohen. "I want to know what this is all about. Before I sign off on it."

"I told you," Yaffe whined. "It started as an old, unsolved case. The museum robbery. It was before your time and mine. But Avram here came across some information and it's turned bigger than expected. So, you don't have to worry. As you can see, the minister is behind this."

Cohen found himself locked in a stare with the district commander. The Motorola on the counter behind him played a nonstop stream of voices speaking local police code. They both ignored the report of a suspicious object in the central bus station. Reshef was studying Cohen's face, looking for a clue to Cohen's intentions.

"I'm not coming back to the force, Haim," Cohen rumbled. "I'm not here to step on your toes."

Reshef sighed. He pulled out a fountain pen from the pocket in his badly ironed shirt pocket and scrawled his signature across the bottom of a piece of paper attached to the memo from Nahmani. Then he slid the paper across the table to Cohen. He didn't look at the document, just folded it up and slipped it into his little notebook, which he put back in its place in his shirt pocket.

Reshef called on the intercom for Ruti to ask Yoram Marciano to come in. Marciano would be his representative in the interrogation.

Yaffe breathed a sigh of relief. He had things to handle, people to meet, places to go. He'd be heading over to national headquarters, where the Uzi was in forensics. Files that went back long before the computer needed to be pulled from archives. Everyone could only hope they still existed. Besides, Yaffe didn't want to actually attend the interrogation. A consummate politician, he wanted to make sure that if something went wrong, none of it stained his tailored uniform.

Marciano, dressed in Cohen's mold, but instead of twill trousers, wearing jeans, and instead of a white shirt, a T-shirt, joined Cohen for the walk down the stairs to the first floor. Their sneakers padded the same rhythm as they went down the winding corridor that twisted and turned through the warren of offices built into the much grander nineteenth-century rooms and hallways of the czar's contribution to his church.

It was all so familiar to Cohen, and yet he felt removed. He smiled at familiar faces smiling at him, and felt like he was in a dream where he was supposed to uncover a hidden meaning in the most ordinary events. Yet something was gnawing at the back of his head, an aching sensation that told him the dream wouldn't last. He didn't know how to define it better than that, so he pushed it aside, pretending it didn't exist.

Marciano stopped in front of the closed door of one of the interrogation rooms. Cohen's deal with Marciano was simple. Yoram could run the tape recorder. He could take notes. But he'd remain silent unless Cohen asked him a question. If Ben-Alon addressed Marciano, Cohen would answer. It was his show, not Marciano's, and Cohen knew the stage well.

The tiny interrogation room had space for a single desk without drawers and five chairs, which stood packed around the table in the room. High above, an air-conditioning duct hanging from the ceiling blew cold air into the room, which had a thick-walled recessed window protected by a thick steel mesh net and looked out onto the courtyard deep inside the compound.

As the junior detective guarding Ben-Alon closed the door and left Cohen and Marciano alone with the suspect, the familiar noise of the busy station faded to a dull background rhythm and Cohen's concentration focused entirely on Jeremiah Ben-Alon; Jerry Oakland, the American convert who brought lost souls to *Yeshivat Ohalei Levi'im;* the Righteous Convert, whose very being was proof of the essence of what Levine, at any rate, saw as the true Judaism. Ben-Alon's back was to the door, his white *kippa* covering almost his entire bald skull. He was neither handcuffed nor shackled.

Cohen picked out a chair and pulled it up to the other side of the desk from Ben-Alon, who had studiously ignored Cohen and Marciano's entry, instead reading to himself from a tiny psalm book, stroking his beard, and murmuring the words loud enough for only him to hear.

Marciano put the little tape recorder on the surface, and nodded to Cohen that the tape was running. Ben-Alon's eyes, behind half-rim reading spectacles, shifted to the little black machine and then back to his psalms.

Cohen leaned forward, folding his forearms on the desk. "For the tape—I am deputy commander Avram Cohen . . ."

Ben-Alon looked up, surprise on his face.

Cohen paused, then continued. "On temporary assignment for the police, interviewing Jeremiah Ben-Alon, also known as Jerry Oakland."

Ben-Alon looked back at the little book.

Cohen went on. "In the presence of Yoram Marciano, deputy to chief of the Criminal Investigations Department, Jerusalem district." He pulled his little notebook out of his shirt pocket, where it was stored behind a new packet of cigarettes he had bought that morning at Mikey's and still hadn't opened. But he didn't open the notebook. Not yet. "You have regards from Baruch," he began.

Ben-Alon shifted in his chair but didn't lift his eyes from the book.

"I didn't get much time with him," Cohen went on, "but appreciated all his help."

"I don't have to talk to you," Ben-Alon suddenly said. "I have apologized to Mr. Reshef," he added suddenly to Marciano. "At this point, I do not see why I have to be held. It is almost Shabbat. Jail is no place for a Jew on Shabbat."

"Depends what they've done," Cohen said, impressed with the clarity if not the accent of the man's Hebrew. He certainly had studied. Vietnam two years, Levy had said, Green Berets. "And you do have to talk with me," Cohen added as he opened the notebook and flipped it to the back page. There, folded up into a little rectangle to fit behind the pages of the little pad, was the piece of paper signed by Reshef, an authorization for the temporary appointment, giving Cohen his previous rank—though not his title—and without any pension rights but with an expense stipend worth about ten dollars a day for those days when he was occupied by the temporary work he was doing for the police.

It was a standard letter, though rarely used, and it was the blue stamp of the district commander's office at the bottom of the type-written letter that gave the form its authority. Cohen slid it across the table at Ben-Alon, and waited for him to pick it up.

Ben-Alon's curiosity got the better of him. He picked up the document, carefully unfolded it and slowly read, pulling at his beard with a worrying gesture as the words sank in. Finally he put it down, continuing to stroke his thin beard thoughtfully, and looked at Cohen with suspicion. "All right. You are a policeman again," he said, challenging Cohen to the duel.

"I gave a lot of thought to the questions I wanted to ask you," Cohen began. Ben-Alon tilted his head, taking the measure of Cohen's next words. "I thought I'd start with the question of why young Baruch was keeping an eye on Bitusi's house. And especially on the lookout for me . . . ," Cohen went on, testing the waters. It was a level check of a sort, and it worked. The American interrupted him.

"You sound paranoid, Mr. Cohen. Maybe you ought to try some of this." He held up the psalm book. "It calms the spirit," he said, adding softly. "Blessed be his Name."

Cohen went on. "But it all really did begin with the boy, didn't it?" he said, finishing his sentence. "So, let's start with the boy,"

Cohen suggested. "He came to the *kotel*, he took a trip. You know about trips, don't you? Is that how you came to Judaism? Through trips?" It was a guess, based on nothing more than intuition. Yaffe was setting the wheels in motion for the Americans to provide any information they had on one Jerry Oakland, originally of Baltimore, now of Kiryat Arba. Cohen had hopes, but not much faith, that the Americans would turn something up. But it was worth the try. Meanwhile, watching Ben-Alon's face, he saw he was right.

"LSD?" Ben-Alon asked, pretending to be astonished by the question. "I haven't done acid in years," he added, grinning at Cohen with a silent snarl. He was missing a tooth on his upper jaw in the right-hand corner of his mouth. Then the grin was gone, just as suddenly.

"You could see he was high," Cohen said even softer. Marciano leaned forward and used a slender forefinger to adjust a button on the little machine. Cohen's lungs suddenly revolted against something. He coughed.

In the corner behind his chair he noticed that there was a wastebasket. Ben-Alon remained silent. Marciano looked away, embarrassed. Cohen leaned back in his chair and reached for the wastebasket. Holding it close enough, and turning his head away from the others he coughed and spat a wad of phlegm into some dumped newspapers, the remains of ashtrays, and leftovers of some policeman's morning snack—broken eggshells and a banana peel. "Primed, is my guess," Cohen finally said, putting down the basket and facing Ben-Alon again. "Ripe. Ready for a missionary."

"So?" Ben-Alon said. "It's the Jews who taught the world that a person who saves a single life saves an entire world."

"Yes," Cohen said, adding a grin. "Probably," he even admitted. "But nothing would have come of your rescue mission, nothing more than another student for your favorite *yeshiva*. Except for one thing," he added, again using a short smile as a form of ammunition. "You didn't quite understand Bitusi, either. I imagine that business about his father must have been very confusing to you. You dreamed of crowns. He was thinking of gold. Of course, Simon had his own problems, too, when it came to family traditions. It really must have been very confusing for you, no? You were seeking one thing, and Bitusi another."

Ben-Alon tried to interrupt. But Cohen didn't let him. Sometimes it was best to add frustration to the cocktail the prey was
forced to drink, in order to make the truth come pouring out. So,
Cohen went on. "What I'd like to know is who first realized that
young Simon wasn't going to provide them with either the crowns
or the gold? Did you figure it out first? Or Bitusi? My guess is you."
He paused to watch his opponent's face. It was creased with sun and
wind and a premature aging. The white *kippa* gave Ben-Alon's head
a hint of a halo, but the gray wispy beard was that of a visionary, not
an angel.

A door down the hall slammed, and there was a short scream of a
youngster shouting, *"Abba."* Its painful sadness flew through
Cohen's mind like an owl at night in the forest. He had felt the sorrow the moment he came into the building, and it, far more than the
promise Reshef wanted to hear from Cohen before signing the temporary appointment, is what made Cohen realize he was done with
the force, done with the past. He'd not be coming back here again,
he decided, if he could avoid it.

The realization in that moment of understanding made him smile
to himself. And the smile, so out of place at the end of the question
he had just asked, made Ben-Alon's eyes narrow suspiciously. Marciano's chair creaked. A vague voice echoed in the maze behind the
ivy-covered walls. Hard leather steps strode down the stone corridor.

Ben-Alon's smile grew to a wide grin. But it was forced. "And
what makes you so sure you know what you are seeking?" he finally
said. It wasn't a confession but it wasn't a denial, and in the very
question was also an admission that he had made a mistake. It was
an opening. "What makes you so sure you know what happened,"
Ben-Alon tried a second challenge, thinking it was a decisive retort.

But Cohen felt relaxed, easygoing. "I know there must have been
a moment," he said, like a patient teacher pointing out the obvious
to a student from whom he had higher expectations, "when Simon's
dreams and your dreams and Bitusi's dreams all turned out to have
different meanings, different endings, different reasons for being. It
must have been quite a shock. For all of you, each in your own way."

Yaffe opened the door. Cohen kept his eyes on Ben-Alon, watching for a reaction. "Think about it," Cohen scoffed slightly, then
shot a smile as he stood up suddenly, making Ben-Alon shift

uneasily. "I'll give you a minute or two," Cohen said. "But between you and me," he added so quietly that Marciano worried it wouldn't be heard on the tape, "I think you're going to blame it all on Bitusi," before tossing Ben-Alon another one of his deadly grins.

He walked around the table to the door, pointing to the tape recorder. Marciano checked his watch, stated the time, added his identity and the fact that Cohen had left the room to confer with Commander Yaffe, before turning off the machine.

Sunlight was pouring through a tall window deeply recessed in the thick stone walls. Like the window in the interrogation room, the glass was covered with a strong wire mesh, which made criss-crossed patterns of shadow across Yaffe's face.

"Listen, we've got to stop," said the politician's politician as soon as Cohen closed the door on Ben-Alon staring back at him, and on Marciano, looking forlorn.

"Right," Cohen said sarcastically, not believing it, his hand still on the doorknob about to go back in.

"I'm serious," Yaffe said.

"He made a mistake," Cohen went on, ignoring Yaffe's remark. "That Baruch didn't turn out to be . . ."

Yaffe interrupted him. "No, no, you don't understand," said the politician. "You're right about that Baruch. We found him through the serial number on the barrel of his Uzi. It matches a shooting in Hebron yesterday morning. During the rioting after the Bookspan funeral."

Cohen's eyes went to the stack of files and computer printouts under Yaffe's arm. He reached for the files. Yaffe held them back.

"There's more," Yaffe said. "Much more," said the politician's politician. "Enlarged photocopies from microfiche of the museum case. And," he added, delighted with himself, "that Ruti of yours . . ."

"You mean Haim's Ruti," Cohen pointed out.

"Yes, right. Ruti. A wizardess. She found the Bitusi file."

"What about the father?"

"You were right. He was a climber. A real acrobat. Bitusi just fol-lowed in his path. And Marciano was right. The father was killed when Bitusi was a kid. Hit and run. The same year as the museum robbery."

"Same year?" Cohen asked, disappointed.

"About a month later," Yaffe said, smiling.

"What about Victor's files?" Cohen asked. "We have to check the dates," he said urgently. "Compare the dates of the accident and the aborted meeting with his source at the Seven Sisters."

"Give us some time," Yaffe snapped, then repeated it softer, "give us time," he said, adding a "please."

"So if everything is so wonderful?" Cohen asked, noticing the use of the word us, already understanding what was about to happen, rolling with the gathered speed of inquiry he had set into motion. "Why do I have to stop?"

"Because it's much bigger than you think," Yaffe said. "Much bigger. The Shabak's getting involved. Your Baruch has turned into a gold mine. When the cop showed up, to tell him his Uzi was found, young Baruch answered the door with another one already on his shoulder. Well, young Baruch was not expecting a visit from the police. You, yes. The police no. He broke down."

Cohen could see the politician's mind at work as Yaffe went on, explaining that in higher circles they didn't want to make the same mistake twice. "Nobody wants a repeat of the underground," said Yaffe. "This time," said Yaffe, "there's going to be preventive action. Administrative detention was fine right after the massacre. For a few hotheads. But here, we're talking about something much bigger." He lowered his voice. "Bookspan was part of it," he whispered. "Bookspan was the *kodkod*," said Yaffe, referring to the very tip of the top of the chain of command. "When he was killed, your friend in there formed a breakaway group." He pointed angrily at the door of the interrogation room.

Cohen wasn't surprised by the connections, but was perturbed by the ease with which the information suddenly was flowing. He asked Yaffe how it all came out so fast, wondering what the Shabak already knew before he began asking his questions about Simon Levi-Tsur.

Yaffe's cooperation, he suddenly realized, was above and beyond. For the second time, Cohen felt the pain, the ache that crept with chills and shivers up his neck to the back of his skull. It was as psychosomatic as the psoriasis on his forearm, but suspicion, not guilt, was the emotion that drove that particular sensation.

"It's your doing, Avram," Yaffe was saying. "Congratulations.

That Baruch," he laughed. "You really scared the shit out of him!" He laughed, patting Cohen's arm in appreciation.

Cohen backed up a step. Yaffe didn't mind. "Guess who Baruch's father is? Icky Fein, the singer who turned religious?" said Yaffe, turning nostalgic for a second. "I always loved Icky's music. Thank God he isn't involved. But talk about screwed-up kids. Baruch spent his first ten years in Tel Aviv bohemia and his last ten years with the *haredim*."

"Get to the point," Cohen tried, interrupting Yaffe, beginning to realize that his efforts were water flowing through his fingers, instead of a solid object that he could grasp with certainty.

"Poor Baruch. Seems he always tried on boots too big for him," Yaffe said. "You brought him back down to earth. I don't know what you did, or what you said to him, but I've already heard from the interrogators that he'd rather betray his friends than face you again. And everyone wants an earful of young Baruch," Yaffe said, lowering his voice, a sure sign he was impressed by something. "Even a certain white-haired man from the prime minister's office," which meant Mossad.

"Poor kid," Yaffe said. "Completely confused. He wanted to be involved in something important. Be taken seriously. Well, he sure got involved in something serious," Yaffe said. "And he's getting lots of people to listen to him now—because of you."

"Involved in what?" Cohen demanded.

"The mosques," Yaffe whispered. "They were after the mosques on the Temple Mount."

Cohen had forged a path in the wilderness, and now it was being trampled by people who thought they could reach the end without knowing where it began. "What about Simon Levi-Tsur?" Cohen asked.

"Avram," Yaffe whispered urgently. "We're talking about a conspiracy to hit the Temple Mount at Friday prayers next week. With a dozen antitank missiles stolen from the army. And you're still worried about that *intifada* killing? Okay, it created a connection. But that's not the point is it? They wanted to blow up the mosques, the peace process, everything."

Seek a rapist and you'll find more than one broken heart before the handcuffs go on. Look for a stolen crown and you'll turn up gold long before you're close to a monarch's heart. It was the truth of any investigation, and Cohen had learned it long ago. So he wasn't surprised that the framework, the entire security apparatus of the country, from the police to the Shabak, from the army to the Mossad, was much more interested in the conspiracy to hit the mosques of the Temple Mount with a barrage of antitank missiles stolen from the army and found in Bookspan's hidden arms cache as revealed by young Baruch than in the mystery of Simon Levi-Tsur's death.

"It wasn't an *intifada* killing," Cohen said, more convinced than ever. "It didn't begin with Baruch or even Ben-Alon."

"Read my lips," Yaffe said stiffly. "If Bookspan wasn't killed, maybe none of it would have come out," Yaffe explained. "But when he was killed, your American friend inside there," he said, pointing to the closed door to the interrogation room, "decided to take things into his own hands. So, thanks," Yaffe said, sticking out a hand. "Thanks for everything."

"It didn't begin with Bookspan," Cohen said softly.

"Of course not," Yaffe agreed. "It began with Goldstein in Hebron. And we're lucky this time. Really lucky. Thanks to you. Of course, you've always had the knack. I've always envied that about you, Avram." He checked his watch. "Beno should be here soon, to take over."

Cohen felt used. But he didn't know by whom. Nahmani? Raphael Levi-Tsur? Simon?

Yaffe went on. "And the army wants to know all about the missiles, of course. They're sending over someone from intelligence. And the Shabak's sending over someone to handle . . ."

But Cohen wasn't listening. He was already thinking about what he still didn't know, what he still didn't understand, and what he still needed to do.

He felt sick. Ahuva didn't understand what he was talking about when he tried to explain it that night. Instead of cooking, he had ordered takeout from a new Chinese restaurant in the city. The food wasn't as good as he had hoped, and they ate across from the television news, which began with a report on the arrests made that afternoon.

Half a dozen conspirators had been picked up by sundown. The TV reporter said that the arrests came after "intense investigations by the police and Shabak" and that "further arrests were not being ruled out." Beno Hasdai, tipped as the police minister's choice as the next inspector general, was "personally handling the investigation," said the reporter, announcing it as a scoop. Ahuva tapped her chopsticks together in light applause as he was seen on the screen coming out of the Russian Compound, a grim look on his face, ignoring the reporter's questions. But the TV news, while accidentally showing Cohen's face in a pan of the police station, said nothing about his involvement—Cohen was glad for that—nor did it make any mention of Simon Lev-Tsur.

Too much didn't fit together for Cohen to take any satisfaction. The police bulletin for Avner Bitusi's car had failed to turn up anything. Despite all Cohen's efforts, he was not much closer to understanding what had happened to the boy. But just in case Cohen didn't understand, Shmulik had called him at home late that afternoon.

"It's a lot more delicate than you might think. It goes back a long way up the chain," said the Shabak officer. But it was when Shmulik thanked him for the Bookspan tip—"the perspective you brought to the situation was most original," he quoted The Head—that Cohen's suspicions began to hurt again physically, a dull pain at the back of his head that only began to go away after he and Ahuva finished their first bottle of wine and he began a second.

He sat glumly in the chair of his living room, thinking, while Ahuva reclined on the sofa, sated by the food and delighted by Cohen's announcement that he had finally realized he was out of the police for good.

"There's something I have to tell you," he said to Ahuva.

"Yes, my darling," she said, slightly tipsy, holding out her empty wine glass for him to pour some more.

He was about to tell her about Vicki-Bracha, about the slide down to the floor of the kitchen in the penthouse in Tel Aviv, when it had felt like the chemicals took over and his mind ceased to function while his body surrendered to someone else. But she was looking at him with such trust, such pleasure at her own knowledge of him, with what he dared to admit to himself might even be called love, seeing his own for her reflected in her eyes, that all he could say was "it's not over yet."

"I'm just so glad you've got it out of your system," she said, as if not having heard what he just said.

He repeated it. "It's not over yet."

"Tell it to me again," she tried. "If you tell it to me again, maybe I can make some sense of it." It was an offer to play. Cohen joined the game. He had nothing to lose.

"Simon goes down to the *kotel*," he began. "He recognizes Ben-Alon, the same crazed rabbi he had seen in the pool hall. He apologizes—remember, this is a Simon Levi-Tsur who is testing out a whole new identity, seeing himself in a whole new way. He's not in control of his emotions—nor his mind. He is ready for anything. Because he was so hateful, now he will be full of love. Ben-Alon takes one look at this kid and sees two things: someone under the influence of LSD and someone rich. He's looking for ways to raise money for Levine, and he's always ready to help someone find the true path."

"So he picked up the boy?" she asked.

"Yes. I don't know who brings up the subject of the crowns first. From what Levine said, it was a subject on Ben-Alon's mind. I even asked Yaffe to see if anything turns up connecting Jerry Oakland to rich Texans known to be backers of the Christian movements in America. I have to admit it's pretty far-fetched to look for that kind of needle in the American haystack. But I do know one thing for certain. Avner Bitusi heard something as a child from his father about gold stolen from the museum. And I'm convinced that Simon was talking about it. Maybe he called it his secret. Maybe it was time for him to give up his secret. But he was talking about it, that's for sure."

"I still don't understand what the secret could be," Ahuva said. "You said he was a mixed up boy . . . And who killed him?" she suddenly demanded.

"I'm not sure. If the police find Avner Bitusi alive, it was probably him. But if he shows up dead, it's Ben-Alon." He considered that logic a little longer, and suddenly realized what it really meant. "I'll only be sure next week," he announced.

"Next week?" she asked.

"I still have a few questions I want answered."

She sat up, shocked, for the first time realizing that last case or not, it wasn't over for him yet. "What are you talking about? You just were telling me that you're done with hoping about going back to the force. And now you're talking about questions you want answered."

"I want to know why the boy wanted to know about the crowns." It was suddenly all so clear to him. "I want to see Emmanuel Levi-Tsur."

"He's in New York, you said," Ahuva pointed out, "and you hate traveling," she added.

But she wasn't entirely displeased by the fact that Cohen, who indeed hated anything that took him out of whatever routine he developed for whichever season he was in, was talking about taking a trip. By the end of the night, she convinced him that if, indeed, this was his last, final, case, and that he was ready to travel for it, she saw no reason why they couldn't travel together, and maybe it was time for Florence again. In short, still in love though never saying so outright, they played through the night with the possibilities, speculating about Emmanuel Levi-Tsur, and planning trips to places as far away as Hawaii.

He woke near dawn with a terrible thirst from a dream of a beach that might have been in the Caribbean, and quietly left the bed so as not to wake Ahuva. He sat with a glass of cold white wine for a little while in the dark, looking out at the dagger of the moon in the sky, until he reached for the phone and dialed a number.

The voice-mail box was disconnected. It explained why Caroline Jones had never called him back. It didn't surprise him as much as it saddened him.

Suspect jumped onto his lap. The cat yawned, gave a quick wash to his chest, and then reclined on Cohen's lap, confident of his master. Cohen was not so certain. He closed his eyes to the soft cool breeze, but after awhile lifted the sleeping cat carefully and laid it down on the sofa before going back to the bedroom to lie down quietly beside his sleeping lover on the broad double bed.

· 27 ·

His plane landed in a thick storm of rain and cloud and wind. Cohen gripped the armrests with fear. The wheels touched ground and the rumble turned into a roar as the engines reversed and the plane slid down the runway. It was Wednesday morning.

A car and driver would be waiting for Cohen at Kennedy Airport. The hotel was one of the city's finest—and smallest, "for a more personal touch," Laskoff had said, picking it for Cohen.

Indeed, Laskoff's office had made all the arrangements except for the most important one—how to reach Emmanuel Levi-Tsur at home. But Laskoff did manage to come up with a phone number for the House of Levi-Tsur's New York office, as well as a new rumor from Ahad Ha'am Street, the financial district in Tel Aviv. It wasn't Bank Leumi that Raphael Levi-Tsur was seeking in Jerusalem. It was the biggest prize of all, said Laskoff. "The peace process. The House is involved. The rumor says it's behind the financing of the first stage of an inland port north of Eilat and Aqaba."

Cohen tried calling Emmanuel Levi-Tsur from Israel on Monday evening. The six-hour time difference made it just before lunch in New York. But Mr. Emmanuel Levi-Tsur was unavailable.

"Yes," the secretary said when he managed to get past a receptionist, "he's aware of your activities on behalf of the family in Israel. But he really is very busy now, as a result of Mr. Raphael's death."

"Tell him it concerns the crowns of Herod," Cohen grumbled over the phone. "Tell him I will call back," he added.

"The crowns of who?" the secretary asked.

"Herod," Cohen repeated.

"Can you spell that for me, please?" the secretary asked. He did.

Now, settled into the back seat of a limousine driven by a silent, tall, mustachioed man who had been holding a handwritten sign saying "A. Cohen" at the exit from Customs and passport control, asking no questions as he took Cohen's bag, it was time to call back the House of Levi-Tsur.

He used the phone in the backseat of the limousine, which felt more like a boat than a car as it rolled along the rain-swept highway toward the huge city hidden by the fog. But the air was warm outside, a strange sensation for Cohen, a Jerusalemite who knew rain only in winter, and had only the faintest memories of childhood sensations.

The secretary said, " Mr. Levi-Tsur has never heard of the crowns of Herod."

Cohen didn't protest, didn't argue, didn't say anything. He hung up the phone and leaned back in the seat, satisfied, indeed pleased. He had been right. Now it was time to find out how right.

The letter A, signed to the photocopied newspaper clips, had early on bothered Cohen, who didn't want to believe Annabella could be involved. But when he took the clips on Sunday to his friend Shimshon Oliphant, a handwriting expert who had worked for the police and quit for the private market, the mystery was at least partially solved.

"Ninety percent it's a woman," said Shimshon. "Creative personality. See the way the legs have curlicues? And the crossbar, it's decisive, too. Conscious. This is a practiced signature, invented by its user to provide both anonymity and a sense of intimacy."

Getting through to Annabella Levi-Tsur-Cohen was easier than getting through to Emmanuel Levi-Tsur. Benjamin Aarons, the world-famous Israeli pianist, long ago gave Cohen his personal number, when Cohen's detectives solved the theft of a pair of Picassos stolen from Aarons's apartment in Jerusalem. The pianist knew Cohen loved the cellist's work. No questions asked, Aarons gave him Annabella's number in New York. He punched it into the phone.

A man—a butler, Cohen guessed from the tone of voice—asked who was calling. Cohen said it was a friend of Benjamin Aarons.

A minute later, Annabella Levi-Tsur-Cohen's bell-like voice, with a two-syllable "Ye-es," was on the phone.

"My name is Avram Cohen," he began. "I am investigating Simon's death."

"Poor Simon," she said.

"I would like to meet with you, if possible," he asked. "Today."

It surprised her. "You're not in Israel?" she asked. "That's where it happened. Not here." She was not suspicious, but he could hear she was perturbed that the inquiry had reached so far, landing on her doorstep as if she was involved.

"I am in New York. I can come to see you, if it is convenient."

There was a pause. "Why me?" she asked.

"Please," he asked quietly.

"I haven't been in touch with Simon for almost a year."

The car was crossing a bridge in thick rain, through a thick cloud that obscured the view in all directions.

"Since when, exactly?" he asked, to make sure he heard correctly.

"The Jewish New Year's holidays," she said. "At Uncle Emmanuel's." There was a touch of the child, perhaps, in her honesty, in the way she answered his questions with nothing to hide, nothing to fear, nothing that could bring down her house.

"Last fall," he checked, "before Simon went to Israel."

"Yes."

"But you mailed him something," he tried.

"Mail?" she wondered.

"Photocopies of newspaper articles. About a museum robbery," he tried.

There was another long pause. Traffic on the bridge slowed down the car's momentum. "I'm afraid we'll be stuck for awhile," the driver said to Cohen, just as Annabella spoke. The two voices confused Cohen, who was using the fog's swirls to help him concentrate on the thread. He held up a hand to the driver's eyes in the rearview mirror and then turned away, asking Annabella to repeat what she had said.

"He did call me," she admitted, "to ask me to look up the newspaper stories. That's what I found. I sent them to him."

"Why was he interested in the museum?" Cohen asked, wishing he could see her expression when she answered. A lie is much more difficult to tell in person than over a phone. But he truly hoped she wasn't lying.

"He said he was getting interested in archeology, and the particulars of that collection were of interest to him."

"It's very strange," he said. "There was no other material on the subject in his apartment. And the photocopies were very carefully kept in a hiding place."

"Simon was always strange," she admitted. "Always running off at the drop of a hat, looking for excitement. He was a handful for his poor grandfather. A handful," she mourned.

"Yes," he said. "That's probably very true."

There was a pregnant pause that gave him some hope. He waited, not really knowing how he could twist her arm into seeing him, but hoping. But she had fallen silent, so he tried, "Simon was turning religious in his last few weeks."

"Really?" she asked, surprised. "Nobody told us, really. All we heard was that it was one of those dreadful terror things. Islamic fundamentalists. The same people who blew up the World Trade Center."

"Maybe," he said.

"Jews don't do such things," she declared.

The wind felt like it was trying to break into the car. The windshield wipers were only able to keep the glass clear for a second at a time. The rain drummed on the car's roof. He rubbed at his eyes, wondering when the jet lag would strike, as it had the last time he traveled. He had learned the lesson of jet lag in Los Angeles. His willpower could be stronger than his body. He wouldn't tempt fate, but he'd get his answers. "Miss Annabella," he said. That's what Benjamin Aarons called her. "I really think it would be best if we could meet."

"I really don't know how I can help you," she said.

"We'll only know if we try," Cohen said.

"Well, I would like to know that every effort is being made to find Simon's killer. But I would think you should be looking in Gaza or some such place, no?"

"Yes, that is also being covered," he said.

She sighed. "And you say you need my help nonetheless?" she asked.

"Yes," said Cohen softly.

She thought for a long moment that made Cohen grip the phone tighter.

"All right," she said. "You may come."

• • •

All he really wanted from her was a way to Emmanuel—and an autograph, perhaps, he thought, as the limousine pulled up in front of a wide, porticoed address facing a large park that Cohen guessed was the one they called Central. The driver would wait, double-parked in front of the building. "It's what they pay me for," he said.

The butler raised an eyebrow when Cohen identified himself, then silently led the Jerusalemite into the first room on the left, leaving Cohen alone.

The walls were lined with books except for the broad window and three small originals by Impressionist masters. But it was a photograph on a shelf that struck his attention. It showed Simon with Annabella and a man Cohen intuitively knew to be Emmanuel Levi-Tsur, all raising their glasses in a toast. Simon couldn't have been more than fifteen years old when the picture was taken. Behind them, Cohen could see the treetops of the park in front of the house. He thought they were standing on the roof, perhaps.

Annabella Levi-Tsur-Cohen was pregnant in the photograph. She had stopped performing with her first child. After her second child was born, she disappeared entirely from public view. There was something wrong with the baby, Cohen remembered from the press. Simon's free hand—the other was holding a glass toasting his great-uncle Emmanuel—was on the shelf of her belly, a casual touch that set the entire picture out of balance somehow, for she was holding her glass toward Emmanuel, but her expression was more concerned about Simon's test of their intimacy.

To a casual observer it was a familial scene. To the photographer's eye, Cohen realized, it was a moment to capture. It surprised him that nobody in Annabella's family—her husband, at least—had noticed that Simon's hand, in Annabella's eyes, was invading her privacy.

"Uncle Emmanuel loves that picture," the melodic voice said behind him. "It was taken five years ago."

He turned, pressing the tie he had added to his usual uniform of windbreaker over a white shirt, twill trousers over sneakers. But then he realized it made him feel only clumsy, which tied his tongue into a knot as he tried to cope with seeing her face-to-face.

It helped that she was a mother now, no longer an ingenue genius at the cello. Her face was still angelic. She was dressed in black, almost from head to toe: tights, a skirt, and a leotard top. A single row of pearls strung over her breast indicated she did not come from a dance lesson or workout to trim her broadened figure. Theoretically, he remembered, she was in mourning.

"My condolences," he said.

A question crossed her face, and then she said softly, "Poor Uncle Raphael."

"And Simon," of course.

"Yes," she sighed, giving it two syllables. He remembered she was Australian originally. So far all he heard was an American accent with a slight tinge of other former British colonies. "Poor Simon." She didn't sound shaken by either death, as if they both had been expected.

"So this must be Emmanuel?" he asked about the man in the picture.

She nodded.

He looked at the picture again before putting it away. There was something of the proprietor in Emmanuel's hand on Simon's shoulder and his arm around Annabella's waist, especially since they were toasting him.

"How old is he?" Cohen asked.

"In his sixties," she said, then rushed on with "Benjamin says you are very trustworthy."

Cohen nodded.

"And that you are not with the police," she added, demanding an explanation.

"Perhaps we could sit down?" he asked.

She pointed to the nearest set of armchairs, two wing-backed leather chairs facing each other over a chessboard. She took the white side, making Cohen sit with his back to the door. He hated that.

"Raphael came to me ten days ago and asked me to find Simon," Cohen explained. "I said no."

She started to say something, anger in her eyes. But he held up his hand, asking for patience.

"I finally accepted," he said. "But within a few hours, Simon was found dead."

"So you are to blame?" she demanded of him.

And he surprised her with his candor. "I don't know," he admitted. "There was no autopsy. I don't know, not for for certain, how long he was dead. Where he was killed. Those three days I considered your uncle's request might have made the difference. I might have been able to find him. I think I could have. Perhaps if I had reached Simon, he wouldn't have gone to the desert alone. If he went alone."

"You don't know?"

"What do you know about the crowns?" he asked.

"From the museum?"

"Yes."

"Simon said he was interested, and he knew I was spending time at the library last year. I was a doyenne."

He wasn't sure of the word and she could read it on his face. "Helping out," she said, then added, "and researching the origins of the instrument."

His stomach was feeling queasy and he desperately wanted a cigarette, because he had two very different questions that he wanted answered immediately. The first was whether she was planning on a return to the stage—or at least the recording studio. He took a deep breath and forced himself to ask the other. "You were close to Simon?" He could hear the croak in his throat, and in the silence that followed, he found himself waiting for her either to answer his question or at least offer him something to drink.

She sat back in the chair. "That's difficult to answer. He was never close to anyone, really." Cohen forgot how thirsty he had become. "He spent a few summers here at Uncle Emmanuel's, of course," she explained. "When we were all younger. But he always was a little estranged from everyone. It wasn't only his fault. I think the older generation made too much out of the fact that he was an orphan. And children can be so insensitive. A cousin from abroad who doesn't fit in, without any parent nearby to protect him. It wasn't easy for him. And he was always somehow both very immature about some things and very grown up about others. I remember how hard it was for me. Coming from Australia." For the first time he could hear the full Australian accent. "But at least I had the cello."

"That was his problem, really. He never had any real interests. Girls. Money. Sure. But nothing interested him, really. If at least he used all that energy for something creative, someting intellectual, something with his hands, anything. But he was without any focus. No focus," she repeated. "Nothing grabbed him," she suddenly exclaimed, holding up a fist in the air and then seemed to freeze, looking at the hand clutching the air, surprised it suddenly had appeared in front of her. She put her hand back in her lap demurely, making Cohen think of a bird who came to rest and folded its wings.

"You look friendly in the photo," Cohen commented.

"You think so?" she asked, slightly doubtful. "It's true, that summer we made friends. I thought. But sometimes I look at the picture, and realize that even before he left, I had realized he wasn't a true friend."

"Oh?" Cohen asked.

"He never sustained anything, you see. He could have been a brilliant scholar. But he used his memory for card tricks. And as soon as he traveled, he'd forget us. Never wrote a letter. He'd call sometimes. When he needed something," she added, slightly embarrassed at her own bitterness.

"Like the newspaper clips?"

"Yes."

"Why did he need the lithium carbonate?" he asked.

The question took her aback. "The what?" she asked.

"The lithium carbonate," he repeated. "It's used by some doctors to treat manic depressives."

"I know what it is," she said. "I just didn't know he was taking it."

Her words came out of her either as soft and solitary or in a rush of explanation trying to cover something. "You really ought to speak with Uncle Emmanuel."

He didn't know why it surprised him, but it gave him the opening he wanted. "I would like to meet with your uncle," he said softly.

She smiled sweetly and looked at her watch. "I called him, too. He should be here soon."

He smiled back, grateful on the surface, in turmoil beneath. He realized that she was neither naive nor innocent, except in the single matter of the truth that should have been closest to her, her family. She was a genius at the cello, and maybe a marvelous mother. But in the matters of the House of Levi-Tsur, he realized, she was ignorant of certain truths. He didn't know yet what they were, but he was going to get his chance.

"Why?" he asked her, just to make sure.

"Because it really has to do with the House, no?" she answered in her matter-of-fact tone. "Simon was about to turn twenty-one. Certain responsibilities were to devolve upon him, of course." It was an axiom, but he couldn't tell if she believed it or simply didn't care.

"How did he feel about that?" Cohen asked.

She raised her eyebrows and nodded, as if admitting that it had been a problem, but at the same time searching for the right word. "Ambivalent," she finally sighed.

"How?"

"He wanted the money. He didn't want the work."

"What kind of work?"

"The bank," she said. "Maybe that's why he felt comfortable with me. I didn't have anything to do with the bank."

"I know," he said softly. "I have all your recordings."

"Benjamin said as much," she said, smiling weakly.

"But there are other members of your family, I understand, who are also not in the banking business."

She sighed again. "My grandfather Abraham was old-fashioned," she said, leaning forward and whispering as if imparting a secret. "Very strict, they say. Patriarchal. And he structured the bank in his own image. Raphael held it together in the same way: 'No women!' he used to say. Personally, I admit I didn't care. I had my career. The bank never interested me. But my cousin Marianne, she's furious about it. I think she went into law precisely so she could challenge it. She fought Uncle Raphael for years about it. Poor girl, she won without winning. Now she'll get her chance and never know if it was because she convinced someone or because Uncle Raphael died. And the boys who didn't go to the bank? They fought for their professions. Believe me, if you are a Levi-Tsur and don't want to be a banker—or a banker's wife—your life is not as easy as it appears. But who knows, maybe things will change now," she said, trying to cheer herself up.

"Why do you think so?" Cohen asked.

"Because," said a voice behind Cohen that made him stand up quickly. "I am a much more modern man than my brother Raphael." Like his deceased older brother, Emmanuel had a hawkish nose and high brow. But while Raphael was frail and almost hunched, as if weighed down by the burden of his position, Emmanuel's vitality seemed to radiate light in the room.

His dark skin was tanned a deeper mocha than Raphael's. He was dressed for his work—a three-piece dark gray suit, and a bordeaux tie held by a gold pin. "So, you are the Mr. Cohen my brother spoke of," he said. "Anna?" he said, holding out his hand.

She rose without a word, accepting his pecks on her cheeks, and then turned to Cohen. "I hope you find what you are seeking, Mr. Cohen," she said rather formally.

Before he could offer his handshake, let alone ask for an autograph, she was gone. But his spine truly chilled when, turning to see Emmanuel taking her seat across the chess table from him, he realized that Levi-Tsur had commanded her departure and she had obeyed without question. He knew, therefore, he could not lose the attack. "It must have been a shock when Annabella called you and said I was coming."

"You really are a very persistent man," said Levi-Tsur. "And I'm afraid you have come a long way for nothing, if you think I have something to do with the death of my grandnephew."

"I never said that," Cohen grumbled.

They sat in silence for a long minute. Emmanuel broke it. "Like Annabella, I made a phone call to ask about you," he said.

"So, you probably know why I am here," Cohen said.

"Yes."

Cohen remained silent.

"Trustworthy," said Levi-Tsur. "Someone people talk to. Someone discreet. And, as I've learned, somewhat of a bulldog." He smiled, a practiced grin that promised far more warmth than his eyes. "Won't let go."

Just as suddenly as Emmanuel Levi-Tsur had appeared, the butler came in carrying a tray with a decanter of a golden liquid and a bottle of soda.

"Whiskey?" Levi-Tsur offered. Cohen took a glass. The butler poured until Cohen raised a finger halfway up the glass but turned down a splash of soda. Levi-Tsur took the same, and the butler left the tray on a side table at a sofa a few steps away.

"I asked them what it would take to make you go away," Emmanuel admitted when the butler was gone. "They told me it was impossible," he said, raising his glass as if to toast Cohen.

Cohen smiled and took his first sip. It was a single malt, with a slightly smoky aroma.

"So I asked why they didn't do something to stop you," Levi-Tsur added, ignoring Cohen's question with a sip of the whisky.

That chilled Cohen. The air-conditioning, reaching him through ducts from mechanisms hidden deep inside the building, made him feel slightly claustrophobic. The windows were closed. Behind the curtains, the rain beat away at the city outside.

"Who are you talking about?" Cohen asked quietly, putting the glass down on the chess table, not caring if he disturbed the pieces. He wanted a cigarette. His forearm itched. "Who do you mean, they?"

"The trouble with spies," Emmanuel went on, somewhat philo-sophically, "is that sometimes they get so used to living in the shad-ows, that they're afraid of their own. Shadows, that is. They said they tried. Or their colleagues tried. But that they couldn't do anything, as long as you were in Israel. Here? That's something different."

"The Mossad?" Cohen asked, not understanding. "What does the Mossad have to do with this?" The Mossad was responsible for all Israel's intelligence gathering and covert operations outside the borders of the country.

"We have come to a bit of a crossroads, I must admit," Levi-Tsur continued, still speaking to his own agenda, ignoring Cohen's reac-tions. "They don't seem to understand what's going on. I mean, they do realize that peace is much more profitable than war nowa-days. But they still believe in the old ways, too. Spies." He hissed the word. "They do mean well, I suppose. Like you mean well. Yes, I'm sure you do. For example, what if you knew a secret, which, if it came out, would not only ruin someone . . ."

"Like yourself?" Cohen interrupted.

"I was going to say 'who deserved to be ruined'—in your eyes, of course. But yes, if you insist, yes, for example, someone like myself," Levi-Tsur conceded. "But it could also ruin your country," he added with a grin. "Now this is a much more difficult question than whether you would betray a friend or your country. No?" asked the banker, enjoying his philosophizing. "Would you take the risk?"

It wasn't the first time Cohen had been asked that question. His answer was always the same. "The truth," he said to Levi-Tsur. "That's all I seek, the truth."

"You make it sound like it's for your soul," the banker said, taunting him.

"And you make it sound as if you would like to tell me," Cohen said, "for the sake of your soul."

Levi-Tsur's smile this time was a concession, but not yet a surrender. "Well, let me clear your mind of one thought immediately," he said. "What I told Levine was absolutely true. The House of Levi-Tsur had no theological interest in the crowns."

"So the House of Levi-Tsur did contribute the crowns," Cohen said.

It broke through Emmanuel's veneer like a Japanese X-Acto knife on a cardboard box. "Loaned," he snapped. "Not contributed. And not by the House. By the head of the house. Not the House."

"Your father," Cohen said,.

"Yes, yes," Emmanuel admitted, as if it was less important than what would come next. He looked Cohen straight in the eye. "But it was not a contribution," he said. "It was a loan."

"A loan," Cohen repeated, tasting the word to search for the hidden significance in Emmanuel's insistence on the distinction.

Levi-Tsur reached into his vest pocket and pulled out a cigar, then stood up, realizing he needed an ashtray. "Annabella hates these," he apologized, coming back from the next seating arrangement in the room, where he found an ashtray beside the tray the butler had left behind. "Would you like one?" he asked Cohen.

But Cohen already had pulled a cigarette out of his shirt pocket packet. Levi-Tsur shook his head sadly at the cigarette, but finally nodded a yes to Cohen's questioning eyes. "A loan," he repeated, sitting down heavily in the chair opposite Cohen and blowing a stream of smoke over the lined-up chess pieces. "Not a contribution."

The rain behind the curtains and glass windows facing the street drummed as loudly as it had in Tel Aviv that weekend when Cohen sat alone in the communications center for the *mador,* amid the phones and radios, keeping tabs on alarms and operations going on throughout the city.

There were call-ins by informants and a check-in from a new officer brought to town to go undercover in the Yemenite Quarter. It was just like the rain outside, Cohen thought, sitting in New York. But in Tel Aviv that weekend, only the mad, the lonely, and the desperate were out in the streets—except for the most loyal of families and tribes gathered for the Pessah holiday.

He had left the command-and-control room unmanned only for a visit to the toilet and once to meet a patrol car that brought him a sandwich from Arab Jaffa, where shops were open on the Jewish holidays. Maybe the alarm rang during those few minutes, he long worried. Even a hint of a flicker of the red light above the little bell box would have been enough for him to have sent a car.

The American newspaper reports at the time called the collection priceless, but insured for seven million dollars. It was a lot of money in the early sixties.

"You were supposed to get the insurance money," Cohen said. "They cheated you out of it."

Emmanuel's eyes narrowed with skepticism. "I thought you were smarter than that," he said with disappointment. "You really don't understand yet, do you?"

Cohen immediately tried a different tack. "Why Simon? Why did he get interested in the robbery?"

Emmanuel frowned, saddened by the thought of his grand-nephew. "He wasn't supposed to know. Not yet. Not until next week, to be precise. His birthday. And only if he pulled himself together," Emmanuel added, with indignation at the thought that Simon wasn't able to discipline himself to fit into the family's mold. But the hint of anger faded quickly. "He was a tragedy. A real tragedy. Searching for his meaning," he said, "when it was right here." He held out his hands as if to take in the entire building.

"Tell me about him," Cohen said.

"Raphael said it best. 'He's a gambler, not a banker.'" said Emmanuel, shaking his head sadly.

It wasn't a lament, but it carried a sorrow that Cohen could never be sure he'd quite understand. He was an only child even before he was orphaned. The brotherhood to which he belonged had nothing to do with siblings, nothing to do with brothers who looked alike but were so different. There was disappointment as well as love in the way the younger brother quoted his elder.

"He never mentioned you," Cohen said. "He never told me that

Simon spent time here. He never mentioned anything about Simon needing psychiatric care. All he wanted was for Simon to sign some papers."

"He probably didn't mention his son, either," Emmanuel said.

"Simon's parents died," Cohen said.

"Yes, yes, of course. But my nephew, David, Raphael's only son, father of Simon," Levi-Tsur said, with a bitterness that surprised Cohen with its sudden vehemence. "Was the apple of my father's eye. And my father ran the family the way he ran the House. Stick and carrot. Like the donkeys he knew as a child. Raphael? Our mother picked his name. But he was the first-born son, and his first-born son was to be the standard-bearer."

"So when David died . . ." Cohen tried to fill in the pieces.

"It was Simon's fate. And it was stupid, stupid, stupid," Levi-Tsur raged, not by shouting but by clenching his teeth tighter for each repetition of the word. At that moment, Cohen realized that Emmanuel was raging at his own fate as well, to live with the guilt of the witness able to see the tragedy before it occurs, unable to do anything to prevent it.

"Quite a burden. For an orphan. In such a family," Cohen said. "Raphael continued your father's traditions, I understand."

"I told you," Levi-Tsur insisted, demanding respect from Cohen. "I am a much more modern man."

It gave Cohen another opening. "Modern enough to take back the crowns or modern enough to arrange a murder?" he asked, trying to drive Emmanuel toward his abyss.

Emmanuel scoffed at the effort. "Far more modern," he said. "Protected. By your very own people. Our people. For contributions to the state. And I'm not talking about philanthropy."

"Why did your father make the . . ."

"Loan," Emmanuel said, taking preemptive action.

"Anonymously?" Cohen asked. "You and your brothers have been donating money to charities in Israel for years."

"In fact, since my father died."

"Why?"

"He was old-fashioned. Gave for giving's sake. But for him, the crowns especially required anonymity. He knew there would be people like Levine and that convert . . ."

"So, you did know Ben-Alon," Cohen broke in, immediately understanding the implication, he added, "so you knew Simon had fallen in with them."

Emmanuel stared back at Cohen for a long minute. Cohen could have counted his heartbeats. Finally, the new chairman of the House of Levi-Tsur stood up. "There's only one way for you to understand," he said. "Come," he added. "I will show you what you want to see."

· 28 ·

He thought he was in Annabella's house. But it was merely one of the addresses of the connected homes that made up the House of Emmanuel Levi-Tsur. They didn't have to go out into the rain, but they walked almost half a block, through hallways lined with paintings, past drawing rooms and dining rooms.

There were no people to be seen in the house, but occasionally, moving down the corridors, Cohen would hear the sounds of life from upstairs—a door closing, a vague snip of conversation floating down one of the three broad flights of stairs leading up to second and third floors that they passed before entering a narrow wood-lined corridor almost tunnel-like in its feeling. Small faux gaslights illuminated the way, until they came out into a small lobby through one of four doors, including an exit to the street, which faced onto an octagonal room.

A receptionist was sitting at a small table with a computer terminal and a telephone console, facing the broad doors to the street. A security guard in a crisp uniform sat by the front door, keeping his eye on a video monitor watching the approach from the sidewalk. Neither looked up from their job as Emmanuel led Cohen through without saying a word to either person, punching a code into a pad set into the wall beside one of the doors facing the small lobby.

The door led deeper into the maze of the building, past small elegant offices where mostly men sat behind desks, talking on phones or facing computer terminals.

"It's not much further," the banker apologized as they went down yet another corridor. There was a bounce in Emmanuel's stride, as if he was heading to an important, pleasurable rendezvous.

"Why are you showing this to me?" Cohen asked.

"What can you do with the information?" Emmanuel wondered,

almost gleefully. "What can you prove? That a car accident nearly thirty years ago was not an accident? Who would anyone believe? Me, or you? Besides, I don't know if you are a lover of great art, but I think you deserve a look. You've tried so hard to find out what happened."

"Did Ben-Alon murder Simon?" Cohen wanted to know.

It made Emmanuel stop in his tracks and spin on Cohen. "Don't you understand? If my brother Raphael had told me what was going on, Simon would still be alive. But neither of us knew that Simon had found out the secret. Neither of us knew. Until last week. When he was found. So, please, do not dare accuse me of arranging my grandnephew's death."

It was as much a plea as a threat, as much a warning as an excuse. It was Emmanuel's battle line. He had no problem with the murder of Avner Bitusi's father, who for a few euphoric days was able to brag to his family, just like his son would thirty years later, that soon they would be rich from gold. But Emmanuel drew the line at his responsibility for the deaths in his own family.

"What was the secret?" Cohen asked in his gravel voice.

"That we took back our loan, of course," Emmanuel said. "As soon as Father died. He didn't ask us. The crowns were ours. Not his to give away. Ours. So I got them back."

"It cost Itzik Bitusi his life," Cohen said.

"You really believe I was going to let some cretin take them away from the House?" Emmanuel asked, amazed at the temerity of the question. "As soon as he realized we weren't going to melt them down for the gold he went crazy. He wanted the gold, you see. The jewels. He didn't appreciate the art."

"How did you find him?" Cohen asked.

"I didn't, of course. I hired an Englishman. From Liverpool. A real professional. He was paid well and kept his mouth shut about it until his dying day. And no, he didn't die in prison," Emmanuel said, guessing what Cohen was going to ask.

"Were Raphael and Gabriel involved?"

"It was a fait accompli to which they could not object," Emmanuel said proudly.

"But you were caught," Cohen protested, finally understanding what had happened. Victor had said it. The police were never meant to solve the case. Many more Secret Services of the state were involved. "And you made a deal. You were allowed to keep the crowns, maybe even the insurance, but in exchange, you helped . . ."

" 'Help' is not the appropriate word," Levi-Tsur said proudly. "Think about it. The service we were able to provide. They gave us medals. In secret, of course."

"They were blackmailing you," Cohen pointed out.

"The arrangement suited everyone involved," said Emmanuel, but he cooled his temper, which seemed to derive from a strange disappointment that Cohen's questions didn't show an understanding of the ways of the world. Emmanuel walked another few strides to the final door in the corridor. Cheerfully, he announced they had arrived.

A key from his vest pocket opened a pair of wooden doors revealing a steel vault door with two combination dials. He twisted and turned at both—hiding them from Cohen's view lest he learn the numbers—then turned the round handle in the middle of the oval door.

Cohen expected the glitter of gold, but there was only darkness until Levi-Tsur reached to his right and flicked a single switch. Spotlights flared, illuminating a dozen pedestals, one for each of the gold crowns. Eleven stood in a semicircle. The largest, the bulbous pomegranate, with its own crown at the top, stood in the center. Cohen was entranced, taking the three steps into the vault behind Levi-Tsur, who went to stand behind the most distant pedestals, holding the three tiaras belonging to the princesses.

For a moment, Cohen was reminded of the story of Abraham, when the youth, sent to guard the idols breaks them all except the largest, which, he tells his father, had destroyed all the others. His father says, Impossible, the idols are only clay statues, and Abraham had his proof that the idols were not gods.

Emmanuel was opposite him, holding one of the tiaras made for a princess.

"Do you believe they were Herod's?" Cohen asked.

"Here," Levi-Tsur said, as if by holding one of the crowns, Cohen would have the answer to his question. The banker extended the tiara in his hand. Cohen didn't want to touch it. Levi-Tsur insisted.

It was heavy, and he could see the artist's hammer marks in the beaten metal. A ring of fish swallowing each other's tails went around the bottom of the round crown. Above them, olive branches echoed the pattern. The etchings in the gold were done by a graceful hand with an easy line that seemed almost alive in his hands. The delicate patterns of scales in the fish and the intricacy of the olive leaves were all worked into the shining metal.

"Look at the eyes of the fish," Levi-Tsur commanded. "You see how they once held inset jewels?"

Cohen returned the crown to the pedestal. His stomach was beginning to revolt against the hunger, the jet lag, the cigarettes, the whiskey, but most of all from the gleaming eyes of the man preening in the reflection of one of the polished crowns.

"You don't want to try one on?" Levi-Tsur taunted him. "Watch," he ordered, going to the largest, the one in the center of the semicircle. His face strained as he lifted the heavy object onto his head. "It takes balance, of course," Levi-Tsur smiled, holding his head tall as he modeled the crown for Cohen, saying, "The original owner had a head a little smaller than mine."

The nausea grew in Cohen's stomach like the cloud rising in the sky after a powerful bomb's explosion. There was a chair in the corner. He was thankful it was a simple armchair and not a throne to go with the crowns. The air-conditioning was powerful but that only made Cohen's nausea grow. "Air," he said, a croaking sound that he was sure wasn't heard by Levi-Tsur. "Please," he tried again. His body trembled. And then he vomited.

Levi-Tsur screamed, but in the realm of the vault, the high pitch came out a dull choking sound. The crown fell from his head and he screamed again. "Philistine!" he shouted, catching his breath. For a moment Levi-Tsur didn't know what to do next: pick up the crown or hit Cohen, who was looking down between his feet at the pool of vomit made mostly from the undigested drink. But the contraction that had emptied his stomach was so powerful that the sense of nausea passed almost at once. He rose, slightly light-headed but steadier on his feet.

Levi-Tsur was putting the crown back on the pedestal, weeping. "You have violated this sanctuary," he moaned. His complexion turned sallow, losing all its vitality, and his shoulders slumped, losing all the royal bearing he tried so hard to display.

"Come," Cohen said, putting his hand on Levi-Tsur's shoulder.

"Don't touch me," Levi-Tsur groaned.

"Please," Cohen said. "Show me the way out. I have seen enough."

Levi-Tsur held onto the crown a moment longer, and then his hands dropped almost in surrender. But Cohen could see an added tension as the banker flexed his hands before lunging at Cohen, who sidestepped the blow. That made the banker lose his balance and fall against the pedestal, which teetered for a second before crashing to the floor.

The pomegranate crown bounced with two melodic rings before rolling on its oblong curve back to where it began, not far from Cohen's feet.

Levi-Tsur also fell to the floor, clutching the fallen crown, moaning. "Poor Simon, poor Raphael, poor Simon, poor Raphael," he wept over and over again. "I'm so sorry, so sorry."

Cohen bent to help him up. "Come," he said. "It's over. Please," he repeated. "Show me the way out. I have seen enough."

This time, Emmanuel Levi-Tsur complied.

Cohen was never allowed to force a prosecution, of course. The prime minister called him at home and explained it very simply: Cohen was right to demand justice for Emmanuel Levi-Tsur's actions. But the House of Levi-Tsur was too valuable to the state to destroy with such a scandal—especially in the era of peace, when every international banking contact was important to finance the new future.

But a few weeks after that second historic handshake on the White House lawn, when the king of Jordan and the prime minister of Israel announced they were making peace, Laskoff called Cohen with the news. Gabriel Levi-Tsur was named chairman of the board of the House of Levi-Tsur. The item said he was replacing Emmanuel, who had chosen retirement rather than filling his late brother Raphael's seat.

At the airport in New York, looking up at the flashing destinations, Cohen thought about going further, all the way west to Asia, to ask Gabriel if the secret went deeper.

Compounding Ahuva's anger about Cohen going to New York without her, was a question about Vicki-Bracha. "Not only do I hope to surprise you with some travel brochures—not knowing you already went—but some girl called. She said she is a model," Ahuva complained, "and that you two have a special relationship, but that you are an extraordinary man and she hoped it wouldn't harm our relationship."

He laughed and reached out to hug her, telling her the girl was a witness in the case. But under her cross-examination he admitted with a chuckle that if he were twenty years younger, he might have felt differently. Besides, he explained to the judge, Vicki-Bracha was only after his money. Her honesty about it was what he liked best about her.

Indeed, Vicki did show up a few days later, on her motorcycle, bringing a packet of more photographs she had found in an old roll of film that turned up in one of her bags. She was contrite, admitting she should have remembered the visit to the museum. "But they changed the name and everything. I didn't realize it was even the same museum," she said. Maybe it was the drugs, she admitted as well, that had clouded her view. He thanked her, but told her she was too late for the case and that he was too late for her. He even kissed her, before sending her on her way. But it was fatherly, on her forehead, and it made both of them feel better.

Cohen did want to bring the charges to light. He wanted to see Emmanuel stand trial for the murder of Avner Bitusi's father.

Unless Bitusi and his Fiat showed up, there was no way to prove Bitusi had killed the kid after Simon managed to drive both Ben-Alon and Bitusi crazy with his stories of gold crowns of the Temple in a safe to which he could get a key but had decided not to, seeking God instead of gold.

But Bitusi disappeared, along with his Fiat, and the most Ben-Alon would say about Simon Levi-Tsur was that Bookspan was right, Simon's stories about Herod's crowns were the fantasies of a drug-addled teenager. When he heard that the golden crowns really did exist, Ben-Alon turned rueful then, referring to Bitusi as a *misken*, a sad case, who wanted his gold and was ready to give up his religion for it.

As the days passed, and Bitusi didn't show up, Ben-Alon started suggesting the ex-con who turned to religion as a way to salvation might have actually been the most treacherous of all. "He reverted to his Arabian roots," Ben-Alon would say to the interrogators who asked, "disappearing in Gaza."

It was hard to tell if he was mad or not. No politician, not even from the furthest corner of the right wing, could condone the plot. But two refused to condemn it. And several of the rabbis in the small, ideological settlements applauded it. Ben-Alon's friendship with the doctor who had set it all in motion in Hebron's Tomb of the Patriarchs was dug up, of course, as was his connection to the Texas Christian. But Levine's *yeshiva* kept operating, indeed as a result of the controversy, was able to raise even more money.

So the system kept the death of Simon Levi-Tsur a secret, just as Gabriel Levi-Tsur kept secret the existence of the crowns, leaving Cohen to decide on his own way of redressing the wrongs; something smaller perhaps than jail, yet in its own way a better retribution than any other he could think of to solve his own part in the puzzle. He asked Ahuva to marry him.

She wasn't making any promises, she said, until after they went on vacation. "Away from here. And not for work."

So, before they did just that, he arranged, through Laskoff, for Avner Bitusi's family to receive a monthly allowance for each of the six children through all their schooling. It would remain his secret, an anonymous donation that deep inside he knew was a small price to pay for his failures.